THE 52ND

Dela

ISBN 13: 978-1-940014-38-8

Library of Congress Catalog Number: 2014950581

Printed in the United States of America First Printing: 2014
19 18 17 16 15 5 4 3 2 1

Cover and interior design by James Monroe Design, LLC.

Wise Ink, Inc. 222 N. 2nd Street, Suite 220,
Minneapolis, Minnesota 55401

www.wiseinkpub.com

To order, visit www.itascabooks.com
or call 1-800-901-3480.
Reseller discounts available.

For Titina, for showing me the beauty in dream-chasing.

Contents

the 52nd

Lucas

PREFACE

December 24, 2012

Fear gets you killed. It waxes over your instincts and paralyzes your decision-making abilities, making you inefficient and useless, leaving you for dead. In my earthly eternity, I never feared anything, never needed to—except for now.

I didn't know how I could love my only fear, and I resented her for it. But over time, something inside me changed, and I came to the humble acceptance that my death was finally going to be for one stubborn woman. From the day we met, this sweet gem stole my heart and played with it—unknowingly, torturously, and without a flinch. It was a constant stream of electric pulses. Sounds lovely, I know. She was the best mistake I ever made.

I was a Watcher. We watched dead creatures abduct humans so they could be sacrificed in the Underworld by their god, no questions asked. My sister, her husband, my parents, and my good friend Tita were Watchers too. We were once a legend, a ghost story told to children at night by mothers of the Promised Land. But life moved on, and our unwritten stories were forgotten—*we* were forgotten. I hated this never-ending job, until it led me to Zara.

Zara was perfect in so many ways. There was fire in her—and me too, when I was near her. She saw the good in my arrogant, royal, still-beating heart. She made me want to be better. I hadn't felt such passion since the sixteenth century, but it scared me, and fear gets you killed.

I didn't think too much about that when I decided to save her. I was such an idiot.

Now I live with my consequences. And she's just across the way, lying in my spare room, really upset with me. *She* is upset with *me*.

Again, I was an idiot.

Tonight I will stop being an idiot and go comfort her. After all, that's what she wants. She only wants me. I'm ready to try now. Ready for fear to control me in new ways. And if I die, so be it.

I slip my shirt off and throw it on my bedroom floor, picturing how I've wanted her entirely the past few months, to devour her tiny, perfect body. I can practically taste her. I slide my sneakers off, chuck them by the bed, and walk to the French doors leading to the balcony. Her almond scent drifts in the night's salty breeze. I breathe in desirously, anxiously, ready.

I step outside into the humidity and hop over the gap between balconies. My heart pounds. Yes, immortals feel impulses. I stop between the swaying curtain sheers and look at her nervously through the midnight blackness.

Then, as her heartbeat plummets, I crack a hungry smile and advance.

CHAPTER ONE

January 1, 2012
The Council

It was 12:01 a.m., one minute into the new year, when I walked through the dark jungle in silence with my family. As the world celebrated, I imagined the rowdiness of kissing strangers. It made me smile briefly, before the thoughts of death returned.

Soon we were crouched behind the last layer of thick brush, staring ahead through the clearing. Ocean air dewed our faces as we waited for security to pass. The stone dwellings settled on this flat patch of land were once my home. Now they were surrounded by rope, each fragile building "preserved" as it slowly crumbled piece by piece. It bothered me, but my attention was on the vast structure on the cliff above, my head filled with more pressing matters.

The castle, with the small temple at its peak, was our greatest monument. Fog loomed around it tonight, dimming its brightness beneath the rising moon. It wasn't normal for Tulum to get fog at this hour, but it rolled in during every Council like clockwork.

After the short security man cleared our view, weaving in and out of the unusual mist, we resumed our trek across the moonlit clearing to the castle. We hopped over the rope barrier and started up the rotting stone steps. I had climbed them many times as a youth—it was tiring then, but my legs moved effortlessly now.

The 52nd

When they reached the top, my father, Ajaw Ecatzin, and my mother, whose name long ago was X'Vaal, turned to watch below. My sister, Cizin, or "Gabriella" as she was called in this modern world, walked alongside her husband, Hunahpu, or "Dylan." She sat against a wall and hiked her knees up, and Dylan stood beside her with his arms crossed. I walked past them to the center of the room.

Tonight marked the beginning of the fifty-second year, the last of the Mayan calendar round. I recalled it as the year of bloodshed long ago for kings and priests—I would never forget the blackened blood poured over their cloaks or the way it dried in their hair, making birds' nests of crusted strands. The year of blood, lots of blood. I would never forget because today, it still was. Only I was a part of it now, with the dead. I let out a huff of air—still just as pissed as I was on day one of my immortality—and leaned my back against the wall.

The way the world used to work, there was separation between the three realms: the heavens, where the Celestial gods lived; the humans on Earth; and the Underworld, where the dead and Xibalban gods lived. The Celestials monitored each other as well as those on Earth. They provided the rain for crops, and they were very generous to the humans for thousands of years. The gods of Xibalba cared only about themselves, and at one point in time, they confused the humans into sacrificing their own people to them. The Celestials did nothing because this deception did no harm to any realm, and so killing other humans to honor the gods became tradition.

When I was twenty-three, a human, Hernan Cortez, overthrew our land and all that went with it, including the bloody tradition. While under attack from the Spaniards, the natives also came under attack from the Underworld. The Xibalbans were upset that their payments of pulsing hearts had stopped, so they sent deceased kings back to Earth to retrieve human sacrifices. The humans couldn't withstand the onslaught from two realms at once, so the Celestials intervened. An agreement was formed: the Underworld would only be allowed to receive sacrifices every fifty-two years, and then only fifty-two victims.

Tonight would be the ninth Council I'd endured since my transformation 485 years ago. It was the only time the selected group of Celestial gods would gather to discuss the arrangement that kept the human race safe. As Watchers, this was our only chance to see whom the Underworld would choose for sacrifice. It was our job to move to each sacrifice's hometown and witness the abduction, then move on to the next victim's location.

"Mulac, the light," Father asked, calling me by my given name.

Father had lived a short mortal life; he was only thirty-nine when he turned immortal. He was nearly six feet tall and had a head of black hair that marked him as descended from generations of royal Aztecs. His blue eyes, however, were a fluke. No one in our gene pool carried frosty eyes. When he was younger, his prince-brothers each fought tirelessly to be the favored son. But no matter how hard they tried, my father's strange handsomeness made him the natural favorite, and his parents adorned his headdresses with precious metals and jewels.

The fog thickened, forming a cloud around the base of the stairs, as Father examined the ground below. The Council would be here soon. Obediently, I rolled up the sleeves of my flannel shirt, lit the pillar candle I had carried with me on our journey, and set it on the damp floor in the far corner.

The orange flame provided a soft light for our small space, creating a dim flicker on Gabriella's petrified face, a look I had gotten used to on these nights. She slouched against the stone wall as she noticed my gaze and then looked away to the leather bracelets on my wrist, some braided, some wrapped multiple times. I had Father's blue eyes, and they didn't express the sort of worry that sprawled across my sister's face—not with the unnerving anticipation that fueled me.

"Gabriella, calm down," I said.

Her bronze hands played with the hem of her shirt as dark hair cascaded down her shoulders. Thick eyebrows furrowed over her brown eyes; she was doubtful yet again of her competence at the burdensome task of watching. It was simple, really. We get in, we watch, we disappear. That was it, but the task always proved more difficult than originally planned.

Our immortality was a gift from the Celestials, and there were rules to it. She would never let them suspect she felt fear or sadness, but Gabriella couldn't control her emotions well, and I worried for her. Most Celestials saw emotion as weakness; I saw it as humanity. I liked to think my sister and I were somewhat human, even though we had never been such a thing. Father was the only one of my family who could truly claim he was once. This year was another round of sacrifices *we* had to endure. *We* had to watch the executioners abduct the year's chosen—young or old, women or men, even children, whatever they preferred—while the Celestials simply showed up for the Council and left promptly once the sacrifices' names were revealed.

As much as I despised them and this awful arrangement, a part of me felt the Celestials were partially right about emotions. Gabriella's mourning fermented so sourly in her soul that it weakened her. It always shadowed her personality for the five years following a round. I hated it.

"Honestly, Lucas, I don't know if I can do this any longer," Gabriella said, anxiously pulling at her loose cashmere sweater as she watched Dylan pacing back and forth.

I didn't answer her. At this point, I didn't know what more I could say to comfort her. I left Gabriella to join my parents at the entrance.

"*Mi amor,*" Mother said, stretching her arm out to me. She was short and beautiful, with black, shoulder-length hair. Its shiny sleekness was pinned up, leaving short strays to fall straight down alongside her cocoa eyes.

Mother was a Mayan goddess, raised on Earth by her father, Chac, for a human term of twenty years. He was a god too, of course. Other gods feared him because he was one of those who had created Earth—and, I imagined, because with his brow constantly furrowed, he always looked hard on the outside. But Mother promised he was irrefutably the most softhearted god she knew. Mother told me stories about how kind he was to her and to the humans she played with as a girl. I believed her because they had the same beautiful smile. I saw it every time they smiled at each other in our Councils. She hugged me briefly, her smile a soft echo of its usual blaze, then wrapped her arms around herself, hands tucked under the sleeves of her jade sweater.

"*Estoy bien, Mama,*" I answered, moving underneath the arched entrance. She nodded.

I leaned a shoulder against the deteriorating stone and stared up at the stars toward Ahau, my deceased godfather. He once was the shaman priest to my father and mother, the king and queen. I remembered him as I gazed into the galaxy, rolling my small *citla* between my fingers. It was a gift from Ahau, a tiny star carved from the wood of a ceiba tree, and the only small token left from my past. There was an Aztec tradition of giving your newborn child a token of the trade they would perform as adults. I was a prince and supposed to grow up to be a warrior; I never knew what gift I could possess that would have anything to do with a star. Besides, giving a citla to a *royal* was unheard of and frowned upon. All I knew was that it had deeper meaning, so Ahau had said. Ahau had known things I didn't, but even he did not know why he had been led to give me a citla. He called it a "prompting."

Ahau began teaching me astrology when I was young. We studied the meaning of the heavenly bodies' movement and the future it foretold. All that time, I wondered about the citla. When I turned twenty-three, my last mortal year, we knew. It wasn't the citla itself, it was what the star symbolized: perfection.

It didn't mean that I was perfect—no, I was mischievous in my mortal life, far from perfect. The citla meant that I was connected to something grander, perhaps something without flaw. It aroused questions that were not answered before Ahau passed on. But I never stopped searching.

At the dawn of the eighteenth century, it began to make sense. My friend Tita, a witch and fellow Watcher, prophesied about a girl in the unknown future, chosen as the fifty-second sacrifice. She went on about stars aligning, times changing, and loves being born, a vision of a beautiful time—a perfect time. The citla instantly meant more to me than my dreadful calling as a Watcher. I felt in my bones I was to know this girl.

After Tita, a member of the Council, Tez, came to me during the dry years—the years without sacrifices—claiming he'd had a vision of a sacrificial girl who would change the world. I'd shared the secret prophecy with no one, of course, especially not with any members of the Council. But I had no way to lie to Tez.

At first I worried Tez would give this information to the Council, but he did not. He wanted out of the Council, like I wanted out of being a Watcher. The other Celestials came together only once, on that fifty-second year, to hear the names. Then they disappeared until the next. And though Tez would leave with them, and I wouldn't see him for more than half a century, I trusted him to keep it secret because his foreseeing power showed him everything in this world.

At each Council, Tez got a short glimpse into the lives of the chosen moments before their abductions, like a rapid fanning of pictures: where they lived, their friends, their schools, their loved ones. It gave him guilt. Then he saw the kidnappings—always a chase, never a fight: the executioners were too quick and too clean to make a scene. But it wasn't the chases that crushed Tez; it was the victims' horrified faces when they saw *what* was taking them. He didn't want to see them any longer.

I thought Tez was lucky because his vision was veiled in the Underworld; he couldn't see the tortures its gods performed on their victims. We both saw this agreement for the bloody mess it was, from beginning to end. And we both wanted out. The job was absurd, babysitting the sacrifices to the Underworld; it should have stopped five hundred years ago, when Cortez ended everything else.

Tez had promised to let me know when things began to unfold. Since then, I'd showed up to each Council anxious. It would be here that he would forewarn me of the girl, for I had no idea who she was or when she would come. But because this fifty-second year also meant the end of the Long Count, I believed this would be the year the tale would come to pass, a time I'd secretly awaited for over five hundred years.

Gabriella watched me with glazed eyes. I knew she envied my faith that things could get better. She hated being a Watcher as much as I did. None of us liked seeing innocent people abducted, knowing what gruesome fate lay before them. Tita was the only other Watcher who had faith that this prophecy could change the entire game, but she wasn't here now. The Celestials wouldn't allow it. *Witches are untrustworthy*, they said.

Gabriella turned to her husband, who paced feverishly near the wall. He was a Hero Twin of Mayan legend, *Hero* because he and his brother were the only two gods ever to have gone to the Underworld and returned alive. He looked about twenty-five in human years, just two years older than I, but it was always hard to tell the age of a god. He was handsome, a tall brute with emerald eyes that drew humans toward him easily, and quite adept at deceit. His quick paces and whispering lips matched the psychotic tangle of his golden hair, snarled into angled chunks. Once the number of people offered for sacrifice reached the hundreds, he'd stopped bothering to comb his hair for the Council. On these nights, deaths from the past consumed him entirely.

"Honey, stop pacing like a madman, and settle down next to me," Gabriella pleaded.

Dylan didn't answer. His fingers twitched, and he rapidly mumbled numbers under his breath as if solving a mathematical equation. Gabriella sighed, unsurprised by his rejection. We all knew Dylan wasn't trying to solve a math problem; he was counting sacrifices from the past, and that was what bothered Gabriella most. Just as I had given up on her, she had given up trying to change the mad-scientist act Dylan put on before the Celestials arrived.

As Gabriella moved to join us, a bright spark from the crumbling back wall illuminated the tiny room. She stepped back toward us, watching as the floating light burst into rays and was gone more quickly than it came. In its place stood the Mayan goddess of sin, X'Tabay.

The fresh ocean air evaporated as X'Tabay's scent overtook our small space. No matter how many years had passed, the implications of her filthy incense had not been forgotten. Father's nostrils flared; we still could smell the stench of her last victim's blood.

"What are you doing here? Leave right now!" Father ordered, confronting her in the middle of the square room.

X'Tabay stepped closer. She was one of the few Celestial goddesses born evil. The last time I'd seen her was during World War II, luring a gentleman through the midnight woods of France to meet his deadly fate. Her face reminded me of a feline predator, lean and acute. Her figure hadn't changed since then, nor had her straight black hair, which hung to the lowest curve of her back.

"Tsk, tsk, tsk. You were much more fun when you were human. I've always liked you, Ecatzin, but never as an immortal," X'Tabay teased. She smiled like a would-be mistress, trying hard to seduce us.

"That is enough. Leave at once, X'Tabay!" Mother warned.

X'Tabay laughed, twisting a strand of hair around her finger as she walked toward my mother. Mother, calm as always, didn't move a muscle. If she needed to, she could wipe out X'Tabay with a swift movement of her hand. But that would destroy our meeting place and raise questions with the Council; we weren't allowed to hurt one another. As X'Tabay neared her, Mother squared her shoulders.

X'Tabay stopped within reach and glared with a taut smile. "Make me."

"Don't do it, Valentina!" Dylan shouted, his voice striking the decaying walls with almost physical force. He stood motionless in the far corner near the candle. His body coiled; he was ready to pounce if needed. Valentina was the closest thing to a mother he had ever had. They shared a powerful bond, and he felt an innate duty to protect her. As his words soothed her rage, a disgusted scowl replaced Mother's predatory expression.

"You make me sick," Mother said, her lips curling downward.

X'Tabay's smirk widened.

Father angled himself on the other side of X'Tabay. "Why are you here?"

"Thank you for asking . . . what was it? Andrés? I never understood why you took on modern names. The humans don't care." She snickered.

"Answer him!" I yelled, my arms stiff and shaking at my sides.

X'Tabay turned, pressing her lips into a line as she studied me. "Relax, sugar." She glanced at Dylan with a flirting grin. "Hunahpu, you would understand, right, sweetie? I always did like you better than your brother."

A low growl left Gabriella as Dylan's jaw hardened. His crazed glare seemed capable of piercing her.

"Whose side are you on?" he snarled through clenched teeth.

Delighting in his reaction, X'Tabay began to stroll. "I'm curious," she said in a malevolent voice. We wanted her dead, but we remained still, following her every move.

"About what?" Andrés spoke first.

"About the fifty-second, of course." She flicked her eyes to me and then turned to Father. "Aren't you?"

Her glance left me petrified, a stiffness that burned cold and drained the blood from my head. X'Tabay knew things I wished she didn't. She knew the sort of things the Council mustn't know. If they knew about the fifty-second sacrifice, it would sabotage the prophecy. They wouldn't allow a sacrifice to be saved. Ever.

I nervously reached for the citla in my pocket and spun it hard between my fingers. How would X'Tabay know anything about the prophecy? My family and I were the only ones to hear it. Tita had promised.

Before I moved to silence her, Father closed in on X'Tabay and pinned her against the back wall in a chokehold. The stone behind her crumbled to the floor.

"The sacrifices are none of your concern and never will be. Leave at once. I warn you . . ." Father cautioned.

"Or what? You'll kill me?" Her voice scratched as Father tightened his fingers around her neck.

Suddenly I found myself in X'Tabay's face.

"What do you know? Who told you?" I demanded.

With his fingers fastened around X'Tabay's throat, Father looked at me disconcertedly. He hadn't caught on. I nodded with narrowed eyes. When it jolted his memory, he loosened his grip around her pathetic neck and glared at her, expecting an answer. But the light of the candle expanded into a large glow, and fine lights sparkled all over the room as the members of the Council appeared. Their eyes drifted to X'Tabay against the wall, then to Father and me, full of questions that would never get answered—not if I had my way.

Dela

There were seven members in the Council, Aztec and Maya both, all once glorious, fine breeds. Now they were diluted. Their aura had faded over years of inhabiting Earth, and they were unhappy, though none of them would ever admit it. They valued humans and thus would live another five hundred unhappy years on Earth, all to protect their charges from the executioners. I never understood them. Still, they were set in their ways. The power they held in the Celestial realm—leading, judging, protecting, sacrificing in all manners other than blood—remained, unchanging, in this realm. I was stupid for what I was considering.

I looked away from them and glared at X'Tabay, backing away with Father as Huitzilihuitl, the Council's leader, stepped forward. He had a large nose and dark eyes that were set far apart. His black hair was pulled back into a knotted ponytail that hung past his broad shoulders, and his soiled work clothes were smeared with grease and stunk like oil.

"What are you doing here, X'Tabay? I will spare you if you tell me who sent you and why you are here. If you do not, I can make no such promise," said Huitzilihuitl.

He ran his fingernails, packed with black crescent moons of grease, along X'Tabay's shoulders. She wasn't accustomed to being touched. She would normally kill anyone who did, but because it was Huitzilihuitl, she gulped and stayed still.

"Child, if you do not speak now, you will surely perish," said Chac, Mother's father. He looked like a Mayan carving with his wide nose and square jaw, so still and calm. Mother had his sleek black hair.

My lips curled. I wanted to rip X'Tabay to shreds.

"She is not here of her own accord. She's a messenger," Xquic spoke up, her emerald eyes on X'Tabay. Xquic was Dylan's mother, a refugee goddess from the Underworld with skin the color of vanilla liqueur and a long, messy black braid. Most Xibalban gods didn't know all the Celestials, but Xquic knew precisely who the interloper was. Xquic was one of the more important gods of the Council. Using the ornate mirror hidden in a locket around her neck, Xquic had the power to see those chosen by the Underworld gods for sacrifice, a list she would soon deliver to us. "Aren't you?" she accused X'Tabay.

X'Tabay erupted into a mocking laugh.

"Speak!" Tez bellowed from the far right corner. His shout, so powerful his gelled hair loosened, rippled through X'Tabay and struck her silent. Tez shook in his gray designer suit. Wall Street was doing him good. He harnessed his shudders and stepped closer, a calm, political smile parting his face. He spread both hands out with palms up and raised his eyebrows. "Last chance," he warned.

Tez and I had worked hard to keep the prophecy a secret. But if X'Tabay got in our way, stopped us from saving this foreseen sacrifice, it could dissolve our plans of a peaceful society. Tez warned me with the slightest glint in his eyes to watch myself. I swallowed and looked away, trying to disguise my flaring emotions. Tez wouldn't have a problem getting rid of X'Tabay in front of Huitzilihuitl, even though killing another Celestial was forbidden.

"What's it to you?" X'Tabay spat.

"You don't ask the questions," Tez said, stepping back to deflect the Celestials' curiosity in his sudden interest.

Tez looked at me again, differently than he ever had during the previous five Councils. Tonight, strain showed in his subtle nod and around his eyes. As I stared back, making sure I had seen him clearly, I couldn't prevent my own eyes from growing wide with shock. My heart now pounded uncontrollably. *Is this it?*

X'Tabay surveyed the Celestials. Their eyes were like marbles, hard and shiny. They didn't blink as they gazed on her. X'Tabay straightened up uncomfortably.

"I wasn't sent by anyone. I came on my own," she finally

admitted.

"What for?" Huitzilihuitl asked.

"Let's just say it's about an old legend."

"Speak!" Huitzilihuitl ordered.

X'Tabay's glare snapped to mine, and she took a few slow steps toward me. "Years ago, I heard there would be a change at the end of the Long Count. The type of change that would mean a new monarchy, new ownership, and that it would come in the form of a pitiful sacrifice."

"You're lying," Huitzilihuitl said, throwing me a suspicious glance.

She looked at him. "Am I? Why would I risk coming if it was only a fable?"

"Which sacrifice?" Huitzilihuitl asked.

"I suspect it will be the fifty-second. I came because I wanted to see whom was chosen. I'm curious."

"Preposterous!" I shouted. "The treaty was signed because there was no other alternative, and now you think a nobody sacrifice is going to change all this? You've lost your mind!"

Chills flooded through me, even though I hadn't physically felt a fluctuation in temperature for nearly five centuries. From the corner of my eye, I noticed Father watching me closely. *Have I said too much? Did I give anything away?* Father and the rest of my family knew of the prophecy, but they didn't care about it like I had all these years. For some reason, I always felt cautious about it, the idea of saving a sacrifice for the first time, like I was protecting more than a prophecy.

"*Silencio,* Lucas," Huitzilihuitl ordered. He turned to X'Tabay. "Who is your source?"

"Like I said, *years ago.* This was a leak . . . there are no sources," she said.

With a prolonged inhalation, Huitzilihuitl narrowed his eyes and stepped closer. "X'Tabay, the sacrifices are our duty. If we felt something was amiss, we would know. How dare you enter our Council with such nonsense? You have no authority here. Leave now, or face the consequences."

As X'Tabay pivoted toward me, my breathing slowed and my stiffness returned. She watched me with hateful, beady eyes and leaned to whisper into my ear, "Be grateful I can't touch you, otherwise you'd be dead right now. If I am correct, and there *is* a change, I will end your pathetic immortality more quickly than anything I've ever done."

"GO!" Tez screamed.

My body loosened when X'Tabay turned back to the Council, but the tightness didn't ease completely until she snapped her fingers and evaporated, leaving the rest of us in silence.

"What does this mean?" Chac asked. "Is this true? Have you seen something?"

"No, I have not," Tez lied. "X'Tabay has never been up to any good. You can't trust her."

He turned to Xquic, who raised her eyes from her locket with a concerned look. "You were right. X'Tabay is working with someone," she said.

"Have you seen something?" Huitzilihuitl asked, staring at the locket.

Xquic embraced the tiny piece and swiveled it between her thumbs. "I haven't, but I don't open it during the dry years. It's only meant to be opened during the Council."

I moved to the entrance and waited as the bickering I had predicted began. It was fairly common for the Council, and as it escalated, I listened to the sounds outside to escape. Below me, an iguana hunted in the forest, and a refreshing breeze gently blew against my back. I stared back at the Council, irritated with their endless arguing, unchanging each time we met. It was obvious that everyone was sick of this system, but still, no one did anything about it.

First the small god, Chico, condemned Xquic for something she might have prevented, even though he had no idea what he was talking about and was reacting in anger. Then Ix Chel, the old goddess, fought with Tez over something she assumed he would have foreseen. And just like that, one by one, the Council members descended into yelling at one another, fueled now by pure frustration at X'Tabay's revelation.

I couldn't help but notice that Huitzilihuitl stood motionless, avoiding the quarrel and watching me with accusation in his eyes. Had I leaked too much information? I froze within the power of his stare.

"Lucas," he called, arms folded across his chest.

As my defiance shriveled up like a raisin, the room gradually grew silent, and all eyes fell on me.

"Yes?" I answered. I tried to sound brave, but I felt weak.

"I wouldn't have expected you to speak up against X'Tabay. All these times we've met, and you've never spoken more than two words. Why did you speak up? Do you know something?" he asked.

"I haven't got a clue. She's mad."

"Aren't we all?" Chico barked at Huitzilihuitl. "Who are we to decide the fate of the worlds? Every one has reached its end. We've been doing this for four hundred and eighty-five years! Haven't you at least thought that something would change? We aren't the only Celestials out there—X'Tabay could be working with anyone by now."

Mother stepped closer to the Celestials. "Chac, Huitzilihuitl, have you thought of any alternatives if our arrangement with the Underworld comes to an end?"

Chac rocked his head side to side.

"Dylan, what say you?" Huitzilihuitl asked.

Dylan glanced at Gabriella, as he often did to check her well-being. She didn't look good. Her shoulders slouched, and her eyes drooped. Dylan turned back to Huitzilihuitl, his face drawn with empathy. "It's only a matter of time until Mictlan finds another way to get to the Middleworld and take unchartered sacrifices," he said.

Huitzilihuitl's face didn't change as it turned to the right. "And you, Andrés?"

"I agree with Dylan," Andrés said, "but only because we have a different perspective than you. As Watchers, we are forced to see the executioners carry out their task. There have been occasions when an executioner was tempted to take an additional sacrifice. We haven't had to interfere with a mission yet, but I fear we need to start thinking of alternatives to keep the peace, in case the treaty is broken."

My eyes zoomed in on Huitzilihuitl as Father spoke. Judging by his aloof attitude, he still did not trust me, and another piece of my confidence shriveled. I remained still.

"What other options do we have?" Ix Chel spoke up, worried.

"None right now," Huitzilihuitl answered hastily, locking his eyes on me. "We stick to what we all signed up for."

"We need to move on," Xquic said, eyes closed as her fingers wrapped tightly around the locket on her neck. "It's almost time."

When Huitzilihuitl turned to Xquic, my body loosened. "Same kind?" he asked.

Xquic slowly opened the metal locket and focused on the mirror inside. Her brown irises changed to the deepest black. Her face went blank, and her body began swaying.

"Virgins," she began, then she paused. My heart pulsed with adrenaline. "Women. They're young."

Huitzilihuitl turned to my family. "Same rules apply. You get in. You watch. You disappear."

We nodded.

While Xquic waited to see more, Gabriella glanced over her shoulder at me. I clenched my teeth and ignored her, my eyes on

Xquic. At the edge of unbearable anticipation, Xquic finally let out a soft sigh. Her irises grew larger.

"The first sacrifice is Shannon O'Brien from Limerick, Ireland; second sacrifice is Jane Miller from Miami, United States; third sacrifice is Mariama Adeyemi from Bandundu, Congo; fourth . . . Lucie Bennet from Clovelly, England . . ." Xquic glanced up to Andrés with her possessed eyes, making sure he was paying attention, then looked back down into the ornate adornment.

As Xquic spoke the name of each sacrifice, I felt my blood run thick throughout my body. My heart drummed faster, as if she couldn't get through the list quickly enough. It was all I could do not to rip the locket from her fingers and see for myself. I had to settle for pacing back and forth. The citla in my pocket made a star-shaped imprint on my thumb as I pinched it tighter.

"Forty-eight . . . Laily Alam from Rajshahi, Bangladesh; forty-nine is Jiao Gao from Dunhuang, China; fifty is Julia Oliveria from Guimarães, Portugal . . ."

I held my breath to hear the words more clearly.

"Fifty-one . . . Alina Epple from Fribourg, Switzerland. And the fifty-second sacrifice . . . Zara Moss . . . Lake Tahoe, United States."

A new substance pumped into my bloodstream, and the loose pebbles crunched as I fell to my knees. Her name. It was . . . familiar. A fragment from a dream; the memory was too scarce to remember details. Her name stung me. Sharp palpitations cracked my heart's hardened surface and exposed feelings I hadn't felt in a long time. And then, for the first time since my transformation, my heart immobilized me.

I felt the others' stares. Gabriella knelt by my side, knowing danger was imminent if the gods suspected ulterior motives on our part. She had approximately half a second to fix me before the Celestials started their questioning.

It was forbidden for Watchers to show remorse for a sacrifice.

With the exception of child offerings, the rule had never been a problem. Forgetting about a sacrifice came easy. But for the first time in my life, I felt terribly wrong inside, a good wrong—I knew I had to protect this girl . . . Zara.

"Lucas, *levantate*!" Gabriella whispered in my ear. "Get up, now!"

Confused about how this news had affected me so uncontrollably, I wiped the back of my hand against a tear and looked up. Tez's dark eyes were waiting, confirming with softness that *finally* this fifty-second sacrifice was the one of the prophecy.

I felt a spark of the happiness I had wanted for so long, a burst of energy, and my lips lifted in a smile as I stood. Even after hundreds of years of silent nods and shakes, I understood Tez perfectly. It was she, the girl of the prophecy: Zara Moss.

Zara

Chapter Two

Encounter

Nine months later

The roads were wet from last night's drizzle as I drove to the other side of the lake. The warm breeze danced past my open window, feeling sweet against my skin, but my blonde waves were becoming unruly, so I spun my hair into a quick pony and pinned it between my back and the seat.

When I was twelve, my parents moved me to a quaint town called South Lake Tahoe. It's hidden in the mountains in the elbow of the Golden State. Spanning the border with the Silver State, Lake Tahoe is the largest alpine lake in North America, surrounded by granite mountains with impressive snow terrain during ski season. For those two reasons and *only* those two reasons, I'd decided to stay for my first year of college. My friends convinced me I'd be better off enjoying one lenient season with fewer classes and more snowboarding time before burying my nose in books far away from home.

With a quick glance at the clock, I pressed foot to metal in my teal 1994 Acura Legend. It was the last Friday of summer before college and my last shift as a waitress at Lucky Pin, a high-end, state-of-the-art bowling lounge. I had to cross into Nevada and then drive another ten minutes north through the mountains up I-50 to get there, but it was worth it. Even better, I got to work with my best friend, Bri.

I arrived at 5:57 p.m., a few minutes before my shift. I walked past the silvery foyer where the hostess stood into a large rectangular room with purple carpet. It was split into three parts: the bar to my right, the dining area in the center, and the exclusive lounge on my left. The high-glossed lanes were half a level higher in a secluded, dimmed area, each lane complete with couches arranged in rectangles and a two-tiered chandelier hanging above. It cost twice as much to bowl in Lucky Pin's lounge than in any good old-fashioned bowling alley, but it was almost never slow. The place tipped well, and my ambitions for an expensive college kept me working hard for it.

Bri was in the back, filling up sodas. She'd taught me that my brown eyes and chicken legs were a good thing, and that there were actual hair products to tame my seemingly untamable frizz. Basically, in her words, I was "a walking beauty"—if I treated my hair right and wore tight pants to show off my skinny legs, which I did, because a little effort never hurt my tips.

I tossed my purse under the counter and pinned on my nametag. "Hey, Bri. Which tables do you want me to cover?"

Bri was wearing her brown hair in curls today, pulled to the side with a yellow bow. The coils swayed when she moved her head. "You're never going to believe this."

Her excitement surprised me. "What?"

"Well, it's sort of strange since we've never seen them before, but . . ."

"Bri, what is it?"

"There is a family in the lane"—she turned to face the upper floor and began counting from the end, her pointed finger bobbing—"fourth from the right. Do you see them?"

I stretched my eyesight as far as the low lighting would permit and began counting from the right. After many lounge couches and suburban teenagers, I found a family of six, all with dark hair except for one younger blond man. Half of them had their backs to me as they leaned in, listening to a woman with short hair. Just as I glanced at the woman, she stopped talking. Then she aligned her eyes with mine, and her mouth parted, aghast. Our eyes locked for a full second before she looked away and spoke again. Strangely, everyone stiffened and ever so slightly straightened up—except the younger boy. He jolted up and turned slowly toward me. Once his startling blue eyes locked on mine, shock painted his face as well. The woman kept talking. Then chins started turning in my direction. I panicked and spun around. *Is she talking about me?*

"Who are they?" I asked Bri, the hairs on my neck rising.

"Don't know. But they've been here since four o'clock asking for you."

"Have they even finished one game yet?"

"No. In fact, they reserved the table for the entire night, and they were extremely adamant about you being their server. They look like they tip well . . ." Bri said. She looked disappointed.

"Coming from the girl whose parents will be paying her college tuition. All right." I breathed deeply. "I'm going in."

The strange situation tempted me to decline their request, but the promise of a good tip to add to my college fund urged me forward.

The group stared at me awkwardly as I approached. Their skin was the color of old honey; a natural glow shone around them like a guttering candle flame. It was uncomfortable the way they were still, silent—the way I grew lightheaded from the scents of coconut and ginger reaching my nose. I breathed in deeply again. It smelled amazing.

Two couples sat on the couch to my left. One young woman

wore a multitude of turquoise bracelets mingled with metal and dark leather rings that decorated her forearm nearly up to her elbow. A large tattoo covered a good portion of the right side of her chest and continued underneath her shirt. As she crossed her hands over her knees, I saw a large, pear-shaped solitaire on her wedding finger. It was turquoise-colored and rimmed with white diamonds. It looked expensive. Nobody my age would be able to afford that. The blond boy next to her had his arm draped over her shoulder, his bulky muscles shadowing in what little light there was. I looked at his grungy Mohawk . . . they seemed young to be married. It didn't surprise me to see a tattoo on his calf.

The man sitting on the girl's other side had his fingers laced together around his knee, his fingernails painted black. He looked old enough to be my father, but had a large tattoo stemming from the inside of his wrist, a feather headdress at its center over a rush of triangles, zigzags, and dots that climbed up to his elbow. The woman beside him bore a smaller but similar geometric tattoo on her petite wrist. A jade necklace lined with thick gold ringed her neck. She leaned back against the couch and tucked one foot in front of her, then crossed her knuckles lightly over her raised knee and pulled it close to her chest. In her relaxed state, she wasn't studying me like the others did. In fact, though she and the man next to her stared as blatantly as the younger pair next to them, their scrutiny seemed less intrusive.

Suddenly, I became aware of another stare coming from my right.

I didn't know why, but my heart pounded when I turned. My eyes collided with the piercing blue stare of the boy I'd first seen from across the room. He looked close to my age and was a bit smaller than the blond boy, but I still had to look up to meet his eyes. As his slender face stared down at me, his bushy eyebrows rose high with disbelief, like he couldn't believe I was standing right here in front of him. I grew weary of his stare, but I couldn't pull my eyes away from him. He had neat sideburns and a head full of dark hair with waves that swept upward despite its natural unruliness. His nose was perfectly symmetrical—the kind people have surgery to get. There was a groove between it and his top lip. As I stared at its definition, how it perfected his face and set off sparks inside me, his lips parted and a dimple appeared in his cheek as he formed a clumsy smile.

I was momentarily frozen by the electricity of his gaze. I had never seen a boy this beautiful before. I breathed in and looked down, noticing a tattoo underneath his short sleeve. Mazy shapes surrounded a seven-pointed star inside a circle, and a tree coiled deep roots inside the star. The ink wrapped well above his elbow, and I had to make myself look away from his toned bicep to the floor. Blue-laced sneakers covered his sockless feet. I liked them, but I forced myself to look away when I realized I even wanted to stare at his ankles.

"Hi, I'm Zara. May I get you all started with something to drink?" I said.

A low chuckle, soft like a hum, escaped the blond boy's mouth. I ignored it.

"Thank you. That would be more than appreciated," said the man who appeared to be the father. Something made him seem older than the others, though his face was smooth, and he didn't have a single gray hair that I could see. He turned his head and looked past me to the beautiful boy at my right. "Lucas?"

The man started speaking to Lucas in Spanish, but Lucas's eyes didn't move from mine. I couldn't recall if he had even blinked. I felt self-conscious, like a nude model in the wrong classroom. I rubbed the side of my arm uncomfortably while I waited for someone—anyone—to order a stupid drink.

"Honey, I'll take a Coke, no ice," the woman next to the father figure kindly interrupted. She had a beautiful accent and piercing brown eyes. Her jet-black hair, parted down the middle, looked as though she'd poured a bottle of shine serum on it. I scribbled her order on my notepad for a distraction from her immaculate beauty.

"And I will have a Bloody Mary," shot the mermaid-looking girl next to her.

"Gabriella, *por favor*," the woman said to the younger one. She must have been the girl's mother with that reprimanding tone.

"Sorry, I can't serve to minors," I replied apologetically.

An amused burst of laughter came from the blond boy sitting next to her. She shot him an incredulous look and then turned to me slyly. "I am not a minor," she said.

I had no idea if she was telling the truth, but I felt threatened for some reason. *Note to self: mermaid girl is at least twenty-one.*

"No, I mean *I* can't serve to minors. I'm not twenty-one yet," I said.

With her eyes narrowed, she pressed her lips together and pouted. "All right, give me a Coke, *no* ice."

"Anyone else?"

"Yes, I will take a Coke as well, *with* ice." Lucas smiled. His blue eyes sent gratifying pulses down my body. I looked away.

"What do you got, blondie?" the blond boy said.

"*Por favor, amor.*" Gabriella rolled her *r*s dramatically as she rolled her eyes. She seemed more on edge than the rest. I wondered who'd poisoned her water.

"I have all Coke products, lemonade, iced tea, or coffee," I offered.

He let out a prolonged sigh and smiled. "I'll take an iced tea; I'm feeling quite refreshed tonight." He chuckled, looking oddly animated compared to the rest, who all seemed depressed.

"You're such a show-off, Dylan. I'll have a coffee with extra cream," said a voice behind me.

It was the short-haired woman who'd seemed to be talking about me earlier. She sat alone on her couch, smiling warmly at me as if we were old friends. It gave me a funny feeling, as did the tattoo over her neck. This tattoo thing was beginning to seem bizarre.

I looked down at my notes, wishing to get away. "So I have two Cokes with no ice, one with ice, one iced tea, and one coffee with extra cream. Anything for you, sir?"

I looked back up into the father's eyes. Though not as striking as the mother's, they were the same shade of blue as his son's, and he was nearly as good looking. He gave me a puzzled look, scratching casually at the black scruff on his chin. Finally, the leg folded over his lap dropped to the floor and he scooted to the edge of the couch. "Nothing for me, but I have a couple questions for you."

"Yes?" I said.

"How old are you?"

"Eighteen."

"So you are in high school?"

"No, sir. I'll be starting college in a couple of weeks."

He fell silent, and his head nodded as he seemed to ponder what I last said. "Which school will you be attending?"

"Sierra Nevada College," I answered, suddenly wondering why I was telling the truth.

"Do you plan to live at home while attending?"

I swallowed. "Yes."

As I tried to pretend these questions didn't bother me, his expression became disapproving. That bothered me too. He looked tired all of a sudden and shifted in his chair. "You know what? I'm feeling quite parched. Would you be so kind as to add another Coke to the order?"

"Ice?"

He laughed lightly. "*Claro que no.* No, darling."

I walked away, stiff as a board, trying to make sense of them. Bri was waiting in the kitchen by the coffee burners.

"What happened?" she asked eagerly. "You were there for a

long time."

"Well, all I got out of them were drinks. They all seem upset about something. It's weird." She looked confused. I walked to the soda fountain and begun filling up the cups.

"Wait, ice! You forgot the ice," Bri sputtered.

"No, I didn't. They specifically requested no ice."

She squinted at the cups. "Gross."

I poured a cup of coffee while the warm sodas filled. "Were you watching me the whole time?"

"Maybe. Hey, don't forget, I need to catch a ride home with you tonight. Tommy dropped me off."

"Right, no problem." I peeked around the corner again at the family. They seemed to be in conference. "Did this family say anything about how they knew me?"

"No. They walked in here all godlike, looked around, then asked where you were. I told them you wouldn't be in until six. They said that was fine, reserved the table for the rest of the night, and requested that only you serve them." She sounded bored now. "What did you think about the dark-haired boy? Hot, right?"

I stole another glance at the family. Lucas was sitting now, facing me.

"Are you sure you don't know them?" she asked, putting a hand on my shoulder and leaning forward as she stared with me.

I squinted harder in their direction. "Bri, I think I would recognize them if I knew them."

All eyes were on Lucas. As he spoke, he jerked his hands with frustration. Then he swiped a hand through his hair and shook his head, looking exhausted. Suddenly, he snapped his head up again, and our eyes met. Bri and I flew back behind the wall, stumbling into the stacked glasses.

"Why is he so hot?" Bri said, eyes wide with bewilderment.

"I better bring them their drinks. Wish me luck," I said nervously, placing all the cups on the tray.

I crossed the small dining room, headed up the stairs, and went directly to their table. It still smelled like a tropical oasis. I inhaled deeply to fill my lungs with the sweet scent as I set each drink down before its owner. They didn't notice, or didn't acknowledge them as they watched me silently, observing my every move with steady eyes as if I was the most interesting thing they'd seen in a long time.

"Can I get you anything else?" I asked in a rush as I set the last drink down.

"That will be it for now, thank you," Lucas said.

He was leaning closer to me. I got nervous briefly, thinking that maybe we had met before. I couldn't imagine I'd forget a face like his. "Do I know you?"

"No." He shook his head modestly.

I looked to everyone. They all had smirks on their faces.

"The other waitress said you asked for me to be your server. I just assumed we knew each other," I said.

"We don't. We heard you were a great waitress," the mother said with a nod.

She seemed sincere, but I had to force a smile past the bad feeling worming into my stomach. "Oh. Well, again, my name is Zara. I will be back later to check on you."

I felt their eyes on my back as I walked away. I stayed on the upper level, serving tables for people who *did* decide to bowl, but I couldn't help peeking at them throughout the night. The exotic strangers laughed and talked, argued most of the time, but never bowled, all while pretending they weren't watching me. Eventually their inconspicuous glances stopped—except for those from the boy, Lucas. His blue eyes found mine wherever I was. I began to stare back, frustrated, hoping he would get the hint he was staring too much, but it didn't matter. My stare couldn't break his focus.

He was the last to leave at closing. When I went to their area to clean up, there was a crisp one-hundred-dollar bill in the center of the table. My heart stopped. I snatched up the bill and ran out the door to thank them, but only my car and another employee's car were there. I tucked the bill carefully into my pocket and went back inside to clean up.

Bri and I finished putting the bowling balls away, tidied up the dining area, and were free to leave in thirty minutes. It was almost one in the morning when we hopped into my car.

"Since when are you and Tommy together?" I asked as Bri slid into the passenger seat.

"Since two weeks ago. Anyways, what's happening with Jett?"

"Nothing. I don't want to talk about it."

Night in the dark mountains was still and cool. I had just pulled onto I-50 when a deep beat began pulsing somewhere inside me. It wasn't my heart, but something entirely different, like a deep thumping of bass inside my chest. It hurt.

"Do you hear that?" I interrupted Bri midsentence. I could hear myself panting over my rising heartbeat.

"Hear what?"

It swelled inside my chest and pounded again. It felt like a heart attack. When I reached for my chest, my hand slipped off the wheel and the car swerved.

"Zara! What are you doing?" Bri yelled, grabbing the wheel. I slammed on the brakes, and we swerved into the ditch. She looked at me, confused, as I pressed my head tightly against the headrest, my body frozen by pain.

"Are you okay?" Bri asked.

There was pressure under the bridge of my nose, and my chest heaved up and down—then the pain vanished. "I think so."

I stared at the portion of road illuminated by my headlights and took long, slow breaths. Finally I grabbed the wheel shakily and pulled back onto the highway.

Bri watched me, unsure. "You're scaring me."

"No, really. I'm fine," I assured her, tightening my hands on the wheel.

When I looked back at her, blackness began surrounding me, rushing my body into a state of cold oblivion.

I woke on my back on rocky ground, grass poking up between loose stones. My skin burned as the rush of blood returned to my limbs. The air around me was moist, making my skin stick to whatever pressed against it.

It was midday. The sky was orange, and black figures flew in a line overhead like puffs of smoke. Suddenly the sound of a baritone horn filled the air, and the figures turned and headed toward it. I tried sitting up to see where they were going, but my body began shaking hard.

I woke again to a dark street in front of me. "Zara!" Bri cried. She was nearly on top of me as she held the wheel. My vision was hazy, my head pounding as I tried to regain my bearings. "You blacked out! Pull over, now!"

I looked at her: my head was still spinning, but I grabbed the wheel again as she maneuvered her body back into her seat and looked out the windshield.

"LOOK OUT!" she screamed, pointing to the front window.

A black figure stood in the beam of our headlights. I slammed my foot on the brakes, but they locked and the car began to skid. The smell of burning rubber filled the car as we screeched across the asphalt. The man didn't move, and as we neared him, I cranked the wheel to the right as fast as possible to avoid him. We screamed as the car spun out of control.

As we skidded closer to the unmoving figure, I thought he was done for. I expected him to bounce up onto the windshield and shatter the window into thousands of tiny pieces. But the briefest second before impact, my door rushing directly at him, I *saw*—

It was not a man.

When the Acura hit the . . . being, it was like hitting a tree rooted in the center of the road. The metal bent like a straw, and my head slammed into my window. I heard the glass shatter to splinters half a second before the car began to flip. When I looked out my window, frightened, the figure stared back with a grin. It was a thing strung together by woodsy veins; a halo of smoke surrounded it. Half the flesh on its face was missing, distorted by grayish bone, and its beady eyes glinted, deep in dark-hollowed eye sockets. In that split second, as fear ripped through me and blood rushed from my head, I believed it wanted to be hit.

I awoke again, lying flat, my belly against the roof of my car, my head facing the broken window and the road. Agonizing pain pounded relentlessly on the left side of my head. More followed when I tried to move. I was stuck.

"Bri?" I could barely hear myself.

She didn't answer.

It hurt to talk, and it hurt to keep myself awake, but I tried to focus on where I was. The car's headlights were still on, shining at a diagonal into the dark woods. Suddenly, a black shadow darted through the beam, more quickly than I could take a breath, from one corner of the light to the other and into the blackened forest. My body jerked, instinctively trying to wiggle loose, but soon the pain was unbearable.

As my body slipped into coldness, the dark figure reappeared in the headlights' beam. The black silhouette stood unmoving, staring at me. My blurred vision turned it into a living ink puddle, its edges wavering iridescent in the distance. I blinked hard, fear rising as I realized it wasn't my vision that made it blur. There were no clear details to its figure at all—it was simply fuzzy. And its stare alarmed every nerve in my body. Before I could constrain my fear, the thing began moving closer.

I tried to cry out, but excruciating pain stole my voice. My neck felt crushed, like something was on top of me. Warm fluid dripped down it. I whimpered. I was afraid, and it was getting colder.

Then I heard a new noise. I held my breath, recognizing the sound of glass crunching on the asphalt next to the car. It was hope. The sound grew closer to my window, coming from behind, and my spirits lifted. *I'm saved!* But strangely, no one called to me. I was about to plead for help, thinking they didn't know I was there, when suddenly the legs of a mysterious man stopped at the front of my window and faced the hazy creature at the other end of the street.

I trembled as I stared at the legs. They were still as I looked past them to the figure across the road. The thing was looking right at both of us. I tried to wiggle free, but it hurt worse. Couldn't this person see that it wasn't human? I lifted my arm to touch his leg, to warn him, but the weight of my eyelids was getting unbearable. I used all my energy to blink, creating flashes of cold air to keep my eyes open, but my lids slipped shut again no matter how hard I tried.

I forced them open again, my vision doubling shapes, when I heard the man speak in a near whisper. I could sense the threat in his tone . . . and I recognized that voice. I blinked once more and caught the creature disappearing into the forest at a speed too quick to follow.

I felt the coma coming. It deepened into my body, and the world fell silent. I tried to remember where I had heard that voice before, even as unconsciousness settled in. But everything happened so fast. His shoes. Something about his shoes. My eyes turned slowly to his feet. They wore a youthful brand of sneakers, tied loosely, the color blue. Before I could call to him, my eyes slid shut.

I pried them open one last time and saw him bent down, his weight on his hands as he leaned into my car through the window.

Those cerulean eyes had a twinkle in them, even though it didn't match the worry on his face. He was talking to me urgently, fearfully even. But I couldn't hear him over the shallow echoes of my own breath. It was clear who he was, but what was he doing here?

A bluish light blinded my sensitive eyes. It was his tattoo; something was wrong with it. It glowed. I stared at it as the cold began settling in my bones. I tried hard to stay with him, but I couldn't, and the neon tattoo was the last thing I saw before fading away for good.

Lucas

Chapter Three

Triggered

Niya and Malik greeted us as Dylan and I entered our private quarters at half past midnight. They could smell the blood on my shirt, and knew fully that it was her blood. They lingered, sniffing her scent as we ran upstairs to the kitchen. Everyone was seated at the table, waiting irritably for the news.

"Is it done?" Father asked. His fingertips touched lightly, his hands forming a temple. He did this when he was anxious.

I nodded and walked to the sink to wash the dried blood from my arms.

"Any trouble?" he proceeded.

"No, there was only one executioner. I chased him away while Lucas pulled the girls out of the car," Dylan answered as he sat next to Gabriella.

"Did the girls see anything?" Mother asked. She seemed nervous too.

I focused on the blood beneath my fingernails. I hated that Gabriella and I'd had five hundred years to get to know each other. She knew me too well. I wiped the blood away slowly with the white rag and shook my head side to side.

"The fifty-second saw," she spat out, proving my lie. "Oh, this was not a good idea. I knew we should have let her go."

"Gabriella, *silencio!*" Father barked. "Dylan, was she enchanted?"

"Of course. I blocked her memory for good," Dylan stated as he glared at his wife, appalled by her doubt.

"But Andrés, she is the one. She is the fifty-second of the prophecy," Tita argued across the table.

Her face was soft compared to the fierce bone structure my family and I had, like a green apple among elite reds, but she was still like family. I looked at her apologetically, feeling bad that I was the only one who believed her. I dried my hands on the towel and sat next to her at the rectangular table.

"Though you are certain of your knowledge, I am not. Please understand that these are all precautionary measures until we have decided for sure that she really is the one. We are simply buying more time," Father said.

"Time that is not ours, *Papa*. We are not allowed to interfere, you know that!" Gabriella retorted.

"Papa, Zara Moss *is* the fifty-second," I said, though I hadn't any reason to explain my strong feelings for this human. Lately it seemed I was reacting from my heart rather than my head—and they knew it. And I knew that it was wrong.

"Are you sure, Lucas?" Father asked.

I wanted more than anything to say yes. Zara was beautiful, but I wasn't sure yet, even after Tez and Tita assured me she was it. Not sure enough to risk our lives.

Tita turned to me with disbelief. She sensed my hesitation. "Lucas?"

"Tita, I think I need more time too," I admitted, feeling ashamed.

"*Excelente!*" Gabriella laughed. "Let's all just take our time and keep this girl alive. You all are *stupidos!*"

"*Calmate,*" Dylan said softly. He was the only one of us able to talk my sister down. She shot him a glare, but she pursed her lips and folded her arms as she sat down and shut up.

"Gabriella, do not forsake the stars' movement," Father said. "The alignment is happening as was foretold. We will know soon enough if Zara is the one. But for now we wait. No one intervenes with an executioner unless it is on my orders. If we are caught, I will take the blame so that you all may be saved."

"*Amor,* that is never going to happen." Mother rested her hand firmly on Father's and then turned to me. "How was the girl left?"

"I pulled her and her friend out of the car, laid them safely off the road, then called the emergency line. Dylan and I waited in the trees until help arrived. They're safe."

"Very good." She paused, thinking. "I propose that for the time being we enroll the kids in college."

"What?" Gabriella seemed shocked. "Again?"

"Yes. It would be better to watch her more closely there for the time being. Keep her out of danger; get to know what is so special about her. Tita, you can return home so that you may give us news of the portal."

Tita looked to Father with a plea. "Andrés, you are making a mistake. She *is* the one. Remember, the advantage is not ours until she chooses our side. If she were to be taken to the Underworld and Mictlan discovers her true identity, they may form the connection that could kill us all."

"That may be, but we will not interfere unless we are positive. That is a direct order," Father said. Tita bowed her head in submission, and everyone remained quiet.

My chair screeched across the floor as I stood. "I am retiring for the night. Mother, Father, I will go to school, but I am unsure what it is exactly you are looking for in her."

"A connection, of course," Mother replied. "If she is the one, one of us may feel a closer bond with her. Look closely at how your powers feel when near her. Are they weakened? Are they stronger? Or perhaps it is she who will change. Does she see us for who we are? Remember, love is a true characteristic of divinity. If she nurtures such a powerful quality within her for one of us, surely there will be something about her that will be unique."

"*Si, Mama,*" I said as I left the kitchen.

I walked to the telescope by my bedroom window. Out of habit, I looked to the stars, toward the spirits of our people, those who watch over all, who know all. I searched their movements more closely for answers. The Milky Way was approaching, as it was prophesied, but it was too early to tell anything. It was frustrating. I had waited for this moment for hundreds of years, and I still felt left in the dark.

Ahau said I was good at predictions, but the power of conversation with the spirits' realm I had never possessed. I knew Ahau was with them now, watching over me, and I wished more than anything to talk to him.

I changed out of the bloody shirt and flopped on the bed with my arms folded behind my head, worrying about Zara. By now she would be in the hospital. *Tomorrow I will get Dylan to come with me to the hospital to check on her.*

I shut my eyes to meditate. I didn't need rest like I used to, but I still liked the peacefulness that sleep brought. Hours later, I realized I was restless. I needed to be with her sooner rather than later. I went downstairs and knocked on Dylan and Gabriella's door. Gabriella answered.

"What do you want, Lucas?" she asked harshly.

I peeped over her shoulder, looking for Dylan. He sat by the lamp, staring blankly at the television. "Dylan. We need to go to the hospital, now."

"Now?" he asked, already standing, eager to escape his midnight boredom.

"Yes."

"Why?"

"Just get ready," I said, then I walked away.

My relationship with Dylan wasn't always like this. I was once intimidated by his godliness and kept a lot of things to myself. I never made such demands of him. However, I am now immortal, and we are brothers.

I headed downstairs to the large garage and waited in my car. I didn't pick this car, a Lexus LFA; the Aluxes delivered it when we arrived from Switzerland after the fifty-first was taken. Aluxes always chose fast sports cars, usually ones that were hard to get on the open market. We didn't live for money or fame, but a smooth car was one luxury we had, thanks to them. Dylan appeared a moment later, the Lexus's white door soft as he shut it. I revved the engine and backed out of the garage.

"What are you looking for?" he asked.

"Anything," I uttered, plunging the car through the dark woods.

The hospital windows were bright-lit squares in the mountain's darkness. I knew that her parents were there. It was too soon after the accident for me to have come, but I couldn't ignore the force that pressed me forward. I had to see her again.

"How much time do you need?" Dylan asked as he opened the door.

"Two minutes."

We entered through the emergency entrance on the side. Civilians watched nosily as we pushed through the *Do Not Enter* door. Dylan stayed a few steps behind me, enchanting questioning personnel. As we roamed the halls, I overheard a doctor on the third floor say Zara's name and knew right where to go. He rattled on to a nurse about Zara's injuries, how they should have been worse. *Dylan will have to take care of him too. Suspicious humans never amounted to anything good.*

We went up the stairs to avoid any more interactions. The less we were seen, the fewer people Dylan had to trick. He didn't like tricking people if he could avoid it. I opened the door a crack to count the humans on the floor; too many to move at our natural speed. We would hit someone for sure. We would have to walk at a human's pace.

"How many?" Dylan asked.

"Twelve . . . no, thirteen. Zara is in room 321. Follow me, get her parents out, and leave me for two minutes. I will meet you at the car. Anyone who sees us must be changed. No exceptions. And don't forget that nosy doctor and the nurse," I whispered.

Dylan stepped through the door carelessly. "Please, who do you think I am?"

I rushed past him, not in the mood for his games. "Just do it, Dylan."

He followed my trail to her room, down the tile corridor and to the right. Her door was wide open, but we stopped abruptly in the doorway as her parents turned to us.

"Who are you?" her dad asked, his face red from tears.

"I am a friend of Zara's," I answered, walking in without making eye contact. My eyes belonged to Zara now. They locked on to her, asleep on the bed. I passed her father and stopped by her side. There were tubes all around her—one in her mouth, one in her arm, and one in her nose. I wanted to yank them out.

"Just wait a minute!" her father said, his voice rising.

I ignored him. I heard him take one step toward me before he stopped, then both her parents moved in the opposite direction. Dylan escorted them out. The last thing I heard was her mom chuckling at some joke of Dylan's, then I tuned everything out.

The room was dark except for a halo of white light over her bed that made her look angelic. Her blonde hair spread across the pillow and down alongside her arms, rippling in soft waves. The patches of skin not scraped in the crash were perfect. I lifted my hand to touch her, but I stopped. I wasn't sure why I needed to touch her. I'd never had any desire to touch a sacrifice. But I couldn't ignore my pounding heart. I gulped nervously and lifted a hand to hers.

I hadn't felt much physically for hundreds of years, but a sting pricked my fingers and sent weird vibes to my brain. Unfamiliar images flickered behind my closed eyelids. As one image flashed rapidly to the next, my head began to hurt—then I saw the orange sky and let go. I backed away, shocked, and quickly checked the clock. I was almost out of time.

She lay there still, helpless. It angered me that I didn't have time to touch her again and that she would not remember anything. I had lost that argument at Lucky Pin, when everyone decided if we were to save her, it would only be if Dylan could enchant her, a trick to compel humans to believe what he wants them to believe. He wanted her to forget what she saw at the crash. I was forced to settle—it was better than letting the executioner take her.

Footsteps down the hall broke into my thoughts. I swept a stray hair out of her eyes and vanished, the feel of her skin tickling my fingertips as I rushed downstairs.

When Dylan met me at the car, dawn was approaching. The horizon of this city was beautiful above the lake, but it made me miss my own horizon, my home across the ocean.

"Dylan, she's the one," I stated as I sped through the waking town.

"How do you know?"

"I saw something when I touched her."

Her touch, so fresh in my mind, triggered a new drive, and my body tensed thinking of it. It left me wanting the satisfaction of pleasure, another thing I hadn't desired in ages. Now it consumed every piece of me, head to toe. As Dylan opened his mouth to respond, I cringed. I knew his worry, and I knew Zara, my new physical trigger, was bad news. This feeling possessed me. It controlled me.

But he didn't know that with these lustful components came focus and determination, a sense of possession.

"You touched her!" His roar made my jaw harden.

I gripped the wheel harder. "Of course. I'm not afraid." *And damned if I'll let anyone else have her.*

"Don't let your royalty go to your head. We aren't in charge anymore. The Celestials can find out these sorts of things."

"Look, we need to find out, don't we? I'm not going to sit around and wait," I argued.

"Yes, you are. Your father is going to be angry with you."

I ignored him, along with every rule that I had broken. "What color did you say the sky in Xibalba was?"

He turned to me, confused. "Why?"

"Because I think I saw it when I touched her."

"Orange." Dylan leaned back in the seat and shook his head with an unbelieving laugh. "Did you see my brother?"

"No." The tires spun as I turned onto the hidden dirt road that led to our quarters in the woods. "I'm dropping you and the car off, then I'm going for a walk."

"Where?"

"I need to know more of her to make sense of some things. I'm going to her room before her parents get back from the hospital."

He chuckled at my perseverance. "Fine, brother. Don't get caught."

"Never."

I felt unstoppable.

Zara

Chapter Four

The Young Gentleman

A white light overhead woke me from my deep sleep. It was overly bright, with patterns of origami shapes that spiked a prickling throughout my head so intense my eyelids retracted. I squeezed at my temples, trying to relieve the light's biting pressure, and breathed in deeply.

The air smelled funny, like metal and pure oxygen, and my nose itched. When my hand hit plastic, I looked down. A tube ran from my nose to a machine at the side of my bed. Instinct told me to yank it out and run, but my bones felt bruised and unlikely to move; I just leaned my head back, exhausted.

Mother was asleep on the hospital's rocking chair in a tight corner next to the window. My green duffel bag sat on the ground next to her, zipped shut, its bulkiness promising it was full of my belongings.

Jett walked in holding a Styrofoam cup. His round cheeks were sunburned. Using his empty hand, he swiped at the platinum bangs swaying over his brown eyes and smiled.

"You're awake," he said, setting the cup on the bedside table.

He kissed me last weekend. Of course he did. Best friend of my twin brothers, Max and Casey, now off at college in Reno, and I'd crushed on him hard senior year while he was dating a junior named Poppy, a pretty cheerleader monster. It didn't matter, though. Jett broke up with her in March, we graduated in June, and she was out of the picture. We were starting college soon, which meant new competition, and Jett knew that. The kiss wasn't what I expected either. The whole thing bothered me, like it wasn't right, or maybe a little too late. So I'd told him I needed to focus on college and hadn't seen him since.

"Why am I here? What happened?" My voice scratched dryly.

He sat at the edge of the bed, eyebrows arched in confusion. "You don't remember? You and Bri were in a car accident."

"Is she okay?"

"She's been up for days. Went home yesterday."

My head spun. "Days?"

"Zara, you've been out for five days."

"I what?"

He nodded at the table at my side, unplugged my cell, and handed it to me. "Look at your phone—check the date."

Underneath the massive list of get-well texts it said Wednesday. I looked back up at him. "What happened?"

"I don't know." He shrugged. "Everyone's been waiting for you to wake up. Bri doesn't remember anything."

My head ached as I tried to sift through disoriented thoughts. A fleeting memory uprooted a fear with the power to still my very core. A face, split flesh and bone, burned holes in my mind—my breathing faltered—but then lucid blue eyes appeared, and I remembered how they stared down that thing across the street. I turned, not wanting Jett to see the panic stirring in my face.

"What do you remember?" he asked.

I was slow to respond. *Do I tell him the truth of what seems like a nightmare?* My butt was going numb. I tried shifting from one butt cheek to the other, but my arms shook painfully. I looked down and saw raspberry bruises and pink cuts covering my left arm. I winced in discomfort.

"I don't really know," I lied, not sure why.

He frowned, disappointed.

"So what did the doctors say? How bad am I?" I asked.

"You'll be fine. They said because it was a severe concussion, we had to wait until your body was ready to wake up on its own. Other than that, just cuts and bruises."

"How is that possible?" The sound of crunching metal shrieked in my ear, and as it did, my heart swelled with a light electric pulse. My hand shot to my chest, remembering the pain I'd felt that night. "Did they say anything about my heart?"

He frowned. "Why, is it bothering you?"

I nodded reluctantly.

"They ran every test you can think of," he said. "Bri only remembers you passing out, so the doctors did everything they could to find something. She told them that you were grabbing your chest in pain, but nothing turned up. They said it was probably indigestion. You are really lucky, Zara. You know that, right? Everybody's talking about how you should have been dead."

Dead. A riff of chills skimmed over my skin. I shivered, half from knowing I was lucky and half from knowing that the boy's tattoo glowed neon blue. Indigestion seemed stupid. It was not indigestion. Max always got indigestion from splurging on fried food and junk. This was different.

"Zara?" Mom's drowsy voice drifted toward me as she rubbed her eyes and stood.

"I'm fine, Mom," I said. She looked tired. Dark circles surrounded her hazel eyes, which were already swelling with tears. She ran her fingers briefly through her midlength blonde hair and took a big breath.

"Really?" she asked with her Texas twang. Jett moved over as she reached for my arm.

"Yes, Mom. Really."

She turned to Jett. "Go and get the doctor, honey."

He shook his head, glanced at me once more, then walked out without a word. I looked back to Mom as she scooted closer. Her hovering made my breathing pick up. I felt angry suddenly.

"I feel fine, Mom. Really, I do."

"What happened?"

She cupped her hands around mine and stared, longing for answers. Surely she would think I was crazy. *I* thought I was crazy for seeing such things. I looked away, those blue eyes threading themselves deeper into my memory. I pictured them staring through my window. Seeing me there, bloodied and helpless, they showed fear. I wanted to find him, to tell him that I was okay. But wouldn't he already know that if he called the police?

"Mom, how did we get to the hospital? Who found us?" I asked.

She sat back with stern eyes. She never liked that Bri and I worked so late. "Y'all are very lucky now, you hear? God knows I pray on my knees every night for your safety, and you're lucky He answered my prayers."

"Mom . . ."

She paused. "A young gentleman tipped off 911 and told the police where you two were."

"Who?"

"Nobody knows. He wasn't there when they showed up. But that doesn't matter. The good news is that you both are all right."

My lungs were caving in. I started panting. *The boy, that creature, they were real. I saw them. Why would he run?* "Couldn't the police trace the call?"

"They tried, but I guess it didn't work for some reason. Never mind that now. You need rest. You hungry?"

I shook my head. In fact, my stomach was queasy. It was the boy from Lucky Pin who called the police; I was sure of it. And now it was the boy from Lucky Pin who'd made my stomach churn.

I spent the duration of my hospital stay in silence, utterly afraid of what I had witnessed.

It was Friday afternoon when the doctors gave me the okay to leave. My body had healed rapidly enough that I left with only minor scrapes and bruises. It was odd. I should have been much worse.

The chilly air outside smelled of autumn as I got into Mom's car. I stared out the window at the mountain peaks, which had begun collecting caps of white snow. It reminded me why I'd decided to stay home for college my freshman year. Snowboarding. It was Bri's idea, but I suddenly felt disappointed that I hadn't decided to go to college somewhere farther from home. I didn't see myself staying in Tahoe forever, and now, after what I'd seen, I was terrified of this place.

On Lake Tahoe Boulevard, heading east toward suburbia, Mom remained silent as I looked past the boulders into the sparse wood of cedars and fir trees. I imagined logical reasons why that boy's arm would glow like a jellyfish in the deep sea. Nothing came to me.

"Dad and I went ahead and bought your books. Admissions said they will forgive your absences while you were in the hospital," Mom said.

"Thanks, Mom." I'd missed an entire week of classes. Great.

My mind, roving anywhere but in this car, kept me from carrying on a conversation. Mom glanced at me.

"The insurance company called today," she began. "Your car was totaled."

"I figured," I mumbled.

The police had no idea who made the call. I wondered what the boy did after I passed out. Did he leave me there and wait for the police to come? Did he pull me out of the car?

"But your dad and I were planning on something like this happening, so we sort of already bought you a new car."

My repeating thoughts stopped abruptly. "What?"

I felt guilty. Money had been in short supply since my parents opened their photo shop on prime real estate along Lake Tahoe. Now they were paying for my out-of-state tuition and books and car.

"What year is it?" I wondered.

She had a determined look. It worried me more than it should. "Just so you know, your brothers picked it out, and they love it."

Before Mom could sense my fear of what Max and Casey would "love," I turned to watch the rocky landscape merge into the green lawns of our neighborhood. "Thanks, Mom. I'm sure it'll be great."

I sighed sadly at my reflection, disgusted with how I looked. I had a large cut over my left cheek and a black eye on my right. When Mom pulled into the driveway, I tried to contain the flow of emotion that consumed me. Fresh tire marks ran over the lawn, and the aroma of cut grass filled the air as I hopped out. Leaves in fiery colors circled the trunk of the maple tree, and the rosebushes edging the low foundation of our gray stone porch bore vibrant fall blooms. I looked to my bedroom window over the garage. The shades were up, and I could see a vase filled with fresh flowers.

I went inside and started down the mahogany walkway to the kitchen. Light flooded through the large trellis windows, making the robin's-egg-blue cabinets almost painfully cheerful. I'd always liked the color, but it bothered me now. My stomach grumbled as I reached for one of the cookies on the plate in the middle of the table.

Mom opened the fridge. "The boys really wish they could've been here."

"I'll see them soon."

"Do you want me to make you something to eat?" She was shifting glass jars around. The clink of glass shrieked into my ultra-sensitive ears, enough to make me cringe. It was annoying that it didn't stop, and then when it did, it was replaced with the whine of the can opener. The noise tipped off an anger I didn't know I was carrying. I assumed it was because I was tired, but it was uncontrollable, and it came on fast.

"Actually, do you mind if I go to bed early tonight?" I said, squeezing my temples.

She looked at me, stunned. I never passed on a meal. "Are you sure you're feeling all right?"

"Mom, I'm fine! I just need to get some rest!" I hollered. I paused, startled by what I'd done. I stared at her, dumbfounded, then snapped my mouth shut as I rose from the bench. I didn't understand why I'd yelled. It just came out.

Mom cleared her throat. Her face had *I'm going to pounce on you* all over it. I apologized quickly and headed upstairs with my duffel bag before she demanded I go back to the hospital and get more tests.

The dusky light coming through my window silhouetted the flowers on the sill in a shade of dark gray. I fumbled for the light switch and turned on the mini crystal chandelier that hung over my bed. Jewel turquoise was the color of my walls—it had been since I was fourteen. The only thing that had changed was the white furniture I received from my aunt last May. I set my bag on the cream bedspread and sat at my desk, staring into the floor-length Venetian mirror at the creature I'd become. I looked like death itself, and yet I lived.

I put my hands over my eyes and wept. I cried in horror until I noticed that something wasn't right. The room smelled different—but familiar. I sniffed the pillows on the bed, the clothes hanging in the closet, and my tiny bathroom in the corner. It was everywhere, though nothing looked out of place. It smelled tropical.

It felt like I didn't sleep alone that night.

Adjusting back to normal over the weekend wasn't easy. I was convinced that something inside my head had changed the night of the crash—my personality most of all. It split on occasion, making me feel edgy and obsessed with things that never bothered me before. If I rinsed a hand, the other had to get wet. I snapped at Mom and Dad for no reason, and I got annoyed so easily over texts from friends. I wasn't sure what was happening, but the bitterness and nastiness and manic behavior seemed to come with the migraines that started once I returned home; I assumed they were all belated symptoms of my concussion.

So I did what any hormonal teenager would do: I asked to be left alone. Mom and Dad seemed relieved. A lot of things suddenly seemed to have come up on their schedules. Car stuff and work stuff. It felt as if they were avoiding me, but I didn't blame them. As we ate leftover spaghetti for dinner on Saturday, I finally asked what car they'd gotten me. It got Dad to smile, with a little red sauce smeared on his lip, but he refused to tell. I had to wait until Monday when it would be ready.

Monday morning was bright and sunny, cheery almost. Birds chirped on the roof as the sun poked through the shades, but I awoke groggy. I imagined how much reading I would have to catch up on as I rolled the cuffs of my jeans and put on my Oxfords. I went to the bathroom and brushed my teeth. Then I tamed my loose waves into a bun and slipped on a cardigan before heading downstairs.

Normally Mom and Dad would have been at the photo shop by ten, but they'd stayed home to see me off.

Dad, sitting at the breakfast bar, looked up from the newspaper. "Your first day of college, huh?"

I smiled, piling the books they'd bought me into my messenger bag, noticing more gray hair showing on his brunette head.

"Mitch, are you sure she should be driving already?" Mom asked. I supposed it was more my new temper that gave her reason to not let me drive rather than the fact that I actually crashed.

"Mom, if I go with Bri, I'll be keeping her around school for nothing. Her schedule is different from mine," I reminded her. That overachiever was taking eighteen credits; I was taking twelve so I could shoot for the mountain once there was snow. If I'd wanted eighteen, I would have gone somewhere else for college.

"Honey, she's fine," Dad said, pulling the car keys out.

Mom bit her nails a moment before letting out the breath she was holding in. "Oh, all right. Go on. But be safe."

I grabbed the keys and swung open the front door. "Always."

When I stepped onto the porch and saw my new car for the first time, my feet stuck to the ground. I needed a moment to appreciate what my dad and brothers had done for me before my true feelings of not digging this car erupted. As I finally got past the forest-green paint and the ugly wagon style, I knew the only reason why Max and Casey had picked this grandma-looking car: horsepower.

"I got new snow tires for you. I know it's early, but there was a deal at the mechanics that I couldn't pass up. And the engine runs great," Dad said proudly, crossing the lawn and opening the driver's door.

My teeth gritted, but I smiled to hide my embarrassment. I reluctantly slid into the Subaru's weathered tan leather seat, tossing my bag into the back. It kurplunked heavily when it landed. "Thanks, Dad."

The key stuck when I turned it. I had to swivel the wheel and twist the key at the same time. I rolled down the window. When I looked up at Mom, I noticed the flowers at my bedroom window. "Mom?"

"Hmm?"

"Thanks for the roses."

"What roses?"

My forehead warmed with panic. *If she didn't put them there, then who?* I mustered a fake chuckle, hoping she couldn't tell there was a pit hollowing my stomach. "Oh, I must have put them there before the accident. I forgot."

It was difficult raising a smile when I felt so confused. I had no choice but to drive away before my greening face caused a commotion.

Sierra Nevada College was in Nevada, on the northeast side of Lake Tahoe. The lake's woodsy terrain extended up to the school, providing a generous perimeter of large pines and fir shrubs that filled the air with an evergreen scent. Their buildings were few, featuring large windows and cedar beams that looked sleek against the mountainous backdrop.

I parked on the north side, close to the entrance, near a patch of trees between the dorms and the cafeteria. As I walked toward the buildings, my nose buried in the campus map, a rip of pain drove my fists to my temples. My papers fell everywhere, but I pressed even harder against what felt like brain freeze. When the pain subsided, I glanced at the mess, annoyed. I bent down to pick them up, but another sudden throb pushed deep into my temples like icy thorns.

"Ow!"

I was reaching for the papers, squinting against the pain, when I saw another hand grabbing them. I stood up quickly to say thank you, but froze when I recognized the boy from Lucky Pin.

His chin was unshaven and full of dark scruff. I could tell he definitely did not just graduate from high school; most boys my age couldn't grow hair on their faces like that. The smile curling across his face spread from cheek to cheek, too perfectly. I wanted to drool. I gulped and blinked harder. His blue eyes were like quicksand, and I was sinking fast. I felt my heartbeat go irregular when his eyes squinted in sudden amusement. Somewhere in the space below his face, his arm stretched out with my papers. I looked down haphazardly, reminding myself to close my mouth and blink normally as I reached for them.

"Thanks," I said, nervously swiping loose hair behind my ear.

I looked down because staring at him did something to my ability to move, and worried that I looked pathetic. His bare feet wore the same blue sneakers from that night. I drew my eyes slowly upward, astonished that he was here. I could see outlines of muscles underneath his deep V-neck shirt, as well as his tattoo, which was now a bland black marking. I was staring at it in awe, remembering its glowing blueness, wanting to reach out and touch it, when a sudden change of scent in the air caught my attention. It was the scent that had lingered in my room after the accident. I dared to look back up, feeling stunned . . . and violated. My new, uncontrolled anger took over, and I glared at him.

"You." I barely managed the word.

He smiled at my obvious frustration and spoke with a Latin accent so hot it startled dormant butterflies in my stomach. "How are you?"

"You! But . . . how?"

"Me what?"

I tried to remain composed, but no one's voice was that sexy. It made me giddy, which made me angrier.

"The car crash, how did . . ." Suddenly I couldn't remember what I was going to say. In that instant, a tear of pure horror swelled in the corner of my eye. "Were you in my room?"

He scuffed his shoes on the pavement. "What? Of course not." He plastered on a smile, laughing as he held out his hand. "I'm Lucas Castillo."

I must have sounded ridiculous, accusing a stranger of being in my room, and I had very hesitantly inched my hand into his when I got zapped. It didn't hurt—it turned into a soft tingle. It was exciting, even, like the nerves you get from a first kiss, but I pulled away, scared, and looked up. His mouth was agape, and he seemed just as curious as I.

"What are you doing here?" I demanded.

He recovered with a gorgeous grin and swiped his hand through his dark hair. "I go to school here."

My body pounded for answers. "Did you get me and my friend out of the car that night?"

His arms folded, and he stared as if I were mad. "What are you talking about?"

"You're the anonymous 'young gentleman' everyone was talking about in the hospital. Aren't you?"

He dropped his gaze and put his hands in his pockets, shifting from foot to foot. "Look, I don't know what you saw, but I wasn't there."

"I saw you."

He straightened up, cupped his hands behind his neck, and stretched, looking annoyed. His voice was harsh as he stared at the sky. "I've got to go. See you in class."

Then he crossed the parking lot and disappeared. I stared for a moment, baffled, then went on with my day.

As I walked to the cafeteria for lunch, the harsh afternoon breeze chilled me to the bone. I pulled my cardigan tight around me as I entered. I noticed that everyone had turned to stare out the window. Ashley, Hayden, Tana, Tyson, and Tommy all stood in a circle, eyes glued to the far corner of the parking lot.

Bri came up next to me, Jett close behind her. "That's Gabriella Castillo. She's our new English TA," she said, her eyes on the three cats putting books in a car with a Lexus emblem on the back. It was white and, judging by the sportiness, very expensive. "When I'm her age, I want to look that good."

"Bri, she looks the same age as us," I remarked.

"Who buys their freshman kids Porsches and LFAs?" Jett huffed jealously.

"Theirs do," Bri said.

Though I remembered how pretty they all were from Lucky Pin, it was hard not to notice their exotic beauty in the mix of us fresh-out-of-high-school college kids. In the daylight, their faces were even more enchanting, to a degree I knew neither I, nor anyone I knew, would ever achieve. Even their posture was perfect; they were like models posing at a photo shoot for tanning oil.

Gabriella's face was pure loveliness—when it wasn't upset. She had a small nose, and I actually admired her large, accentuating eyebrows when they weren't furrowing at me. The long eyelashes complemented them well. Her collection of gold bracelets reflected the sun's brightness in a shower of light. I was wondering how heavy all that jewelry was, or if it was even real, when I realized that the blond boy and Lucas wore bracelets too. Theirs were finer and made with dark threads or leather.

Out of nowhere they started arguing, as they had at Lucky Pin. Lucas was spitting words at them while the other two stood there and took it.

"What are they fighting about?" Tana looked concerned through the pound of makeup caking her face.

Tommy, Bri's crush, snorted. "Look at all of you—it's pathetic." He slid a trucker hat over his short hair, letting the light brown curls stick out.

I felt a light touch on my arm and flinched slightly.

"You okay?" Jett asked.

"Yeah, why?"

"I don't know. You seem different."

Bri slid to my side and swung her arm around me. "She's perfect; look at her."

He looked me up and down. "That's my point." Bri skipped off to see some other friends, but Jett leaned in so only I could hear. "Shouldn't you still have bruises on your skin, or scabs at least? How did they all go away so fast?"

"Jett!" Tommy yelled. "Let's go. The boat's ready. I want to get as much wakeboarding in as possible before the sun goes down."

"We'll talk later," Jett said. He ran to catch up with Tommy.

Jett was right, but I couldn't let him know that. I flipped back around to watch Lucas, a thousand questions running through my mind.

It was strange how swiftly their composure changed. They were now leaning against their cars in a daze, staring off in different directions. I almost felt bad for how strange it seemed, this lack of recognition of each other. If I had only glanced over briefly, they would have appeared to be waiting for someone, but the longer I stared, the more it seemed they were mourning something.

"They're the family that built that big house on Fallen Leaf Lake," started Tyson, Tana's boyfriend.

"What does their dad do?" Ashley asked, her cinnamon hair falling perfectly straight down her back.

"Nobody knows. My mom works at *Tahoe Review Journal*, and she said that the lady who interviewed them for the welcome column told her that their parents objected to doing the interview. Something about a death in the family made them too sad, so it was Dylan who did the interview," Tyson commented.

"Dylan?" I asked.

"Yeah, the blond with the hot English TA—I mean, wife," Tyson corrected. Tana snorted, and he smacked a kiss on her cheek. "Not as pretty as you, of course."

Tana rolled her eyes and turned her shoulder away from him as she crossed her arms. There was a chill from the window when Bri stepped closer.

"What sort of business do you think they have here?" she asked.

"Probably the illegal sort," Tana retorted.

I watched their beauty more closely. They were too graceful, too fluid, and they definitely weren't here for anything illegal. It was something else entirely, my intuition informed me. Suddenly, Lucas directed his gaze toward me. I froze again. The thought of our skin tingling together frightened me, and I remembered how my room had smelled of him. I was starting to dislike him more already.

He held his stare as his lip curved up crookedly, saturated with curiosity. Still looking at me, he said something that made the other two follow his gaze. I glanced away quickly, but the shiver still came, knowing they were watching. But then his *See you in class* jarred my next step, and I couldn't help but look back.

When he waved to me with a taut smile—as if he knew I would look back—I swung around, somehow upset.

"Hey, Zara, we're all going to the movies. Want to come?" Tana asked.

I couldn't think straight, not with the feeling I was being watched. I tightened my grip on my bag and looked away. "Not today, Tana. I'll catch one next time."

I was on Lake Tahoe Boulevard when I decided Lucas was like a scratch 'n' sniff. There should be a sign plastered to his shirt that says *scratch here*, because you can only scratch so far before you realize you aren't going to get anything in return. Nothing but a bad taste in your mouth.

A migraine formed later that night as I washed the dishes. It had a cold edge to it, like an ice pack left on my head. Mom let me leave the dishes to go upstairs and rest. I had just opened my bedroom door when my cell rang. I leaped for it and stubbed my pinky toe on the hardcover history book I'd left on the floor. I picked up the phone, cursing at myself for the agonizing throb.

"Zara?"

I sat down, reached for the wretched book, and angrily tossed it on the bed. "Hey, Bri."

"Oh my heck. That family, here?" she started, sounding elated.

"Yeah. Imagine," I said, more interested in rubbing my toe.

"I have a theory."

"Theory?"

"Yes. They're cops, the undercover kind. Something is about to go down at our school. You just wait. I'm always right."

"Bri, they are not undercover cops," I declared.

"You'll see. Hey, listen. I wanted to call you and get your okay with this."

She suddenly sounded bubbly. It made me nervous. "With what?"

"The girls and I decided we should do a girls' night at the new club in Reno and . . . we wanted to invite that new TA, Gabriella."

I didn't have a problem with Gabriella. It was her steamy brother who gave me a funny feeling, a deep-in-my-soul bad feeling. I didn't feel right about this.

"Why? You just said you thought she was a cop."

"I did. Don't argue. And besides, I want her to be our friend. And then if she is a cop, she can protect us if something goes wrong. Where do you think she keeps her gun?"

"Bri, one, we don't need protection, and two, Gabriella is married."

"So? Married people have friends," she said. She sounded so naïve.

I laughed, baffled. "Yeah, other married people."

"Well, she said yes. So everyone is meeting at my house on Friday after school. Oh, and we're crashing at my house after," she added quickly.

"Did I ever have a say in this?"

She paused. "Well, not really."

"Then why did you bother to call me?"

"I don't know? Habit I guess. You will be there, though," she insisted.

"Bri, I don't . . ."

"Great, see you then!" Her voice went up an octave as if she'd inhaled helium. "Got to go. Tommy's calling."

I tossed my phone on the pillow, went to the bathroom, and

brushed my teeth, deciding to shower in the morning. After I put on my pajamas, I rolled onto my bed and stared at the white-and-red flowers sitting on the windowsill. Max and Casey must have gone to the grocery store to buy them. Mom didn't have those kind of roses in her garden, and she wasn't the buying-flowers type. They were nice to look at, though, and I fell asleep admiring them.

Lucas

Chapter Five

Tick

I didn't realize how much Zara hung out with Jett. Watching them, though, I realized I was growing fond of her. The way he'd touched her in the cafeteria the other day made me cringe. I'd added myself to Zara's History 113 class a week before. When I found out Monday that he was in the same section as Zara and I, I made Dylan work his godly measure on him after school. Jett changed classes.

Still, that boy was relentless. He rode in her car when Zara went to pick up her last check from Lucky Pin. I knew because I followed them. I never let Zara out of my sight. If I couldn't do it, then someone in my family did.

I imagined how it would go when she saw me in her class. I figured it probably wouldn't be good, since she despised me at the moment, but the girl didn't have a choice. I wasn't going anywhere. I mean, I couldn't because I was protecting her, but I didn't want to either. The prospect of getting to know a sacrifice was too fascinating.

I walked into the auditorium promptly at one o'clock and sat in the first row of stadium seats. In all my years of college, I'd been accustomed to sitting in the last row up top, but I wanted Zara to see me clear as day. I set my only notebook down on my lap and leaned back, rubbing the nubs of hair on my chin as I listened to her footsteps trotting nearer. I smiled, anxious to see her reaction, but when she walked in, her sling bag was sliding off her shoulder, and she fiddled with it instead of noticing me. Her gorgeousness pleased my eyes, and my stomach tensed with desire to be closer to her than I already was. I counted down as she unknowingly stepped closer to me.

On the count of one, when she finally looked up and realized the only empty seat in the room was next to me, her mouth dropped open.

"Hi," I said.

She plopped the heavy brown pleather bag down on the floor and sat silently. I watched her, noting the extreme tension that tightened her body.

"How are you?" I asked.

Her eyes barely grazed mine before her chin dropped toward my arm. "So what's with the tattoos?"

I wasn't ready for that. I swept my right hand over my markings. I hadn't thought about the girl having a personality—much less not liking me. *I'm breaking a tradition that could kill me, and* this *is how I'm treated?* I still liked her, but I glanced away, bothered. "It's a family thing. We all have one."

"Like a crest?"

"Something of the sort," I replied.

"What do they mean?"

I looked back to her and snickered in a way that made her recoil. "Wouldn't you like to know?"

When her gaze wavered, I leaned in, lifting one eyebrow. "Wait, you don't like tattoos, do you?"

She acted like I was a threat. She looked to the front of the classroom, lifted her chin bravely, and swallowed. "I've never been a fan."

My hollowed stomach filled with amusement, and I couldn't

keep the corners of my mouth down. She was a horrible liar. I leaned on the armrest and turned toward her. "And your parents, they taught you this?"

Her short-lived defiance wavered as I gazed at her. She looked away. I suspected it was to hide a blush. "Sort of. Faith, I guess."

"You have good parents."

Abruptly, she shot back, "Why are you here?" There was fire in her eyes.

I raised my eyebrows, pointed to the professor walking in, and stated, "Um, school."

"What are you studying?" she demanded. Her sassiness excited me.

"Generals right now."

I expected her to say something smart after that, but she let off and just watched me. I let her as I pretended to be a good student and opened my notebook.

"Where did you move from?" she suddenly asked.

"A little town near Cancun, Mexico."

"Why would you want to move here?" she said. Now she sounded snobby.

I squinted at her, feeling the low smolder of irony as I held back a laugh. "It's complicated."

"Do you live in the dorms?"

I nodded. I saw her shiver as she leaned away from me.

"So, what part of town did you move to?" she asked.

"We just bought a house off Fallen Leaf Lake."

"We?"

"My parents are retired and moved here, and my sister goes to college here too."

"I thought the government owned a lot of the land around there."

"They do. It's complicated," I repeated, annoyed this time. I had been out of touch with girls for so long I couldn't remember if all girls were this nosy.

This girl's hands were shaking when she looked back up through her lashes. "Look, Lucas—for what it's worth—thank you."

"For what?"

"For saving my life," she whispered.

What little breath my body held was sucked out, and I stiffened. *How does she remember?*

Zara took notice and glanced around us. Then she scooted in closer and whispered, "Why do you keep denying it? I saw you. I know you were there, and I know you saw something else that night too."

Her memory unraveled my calculated thoughts, and my vision dimmed. *How could this be?* Eventually, I narrowed my eyes and leaned in close enough to let her scent drive me crazy. I was careful not to get too close. I wanted to, but it squeezed that physical trigger, wanting to seize control as it had before I was immortal. "How do you remember so much?"

She blinked slowly. "What do you mean?"

I didn't have time to answer her as Professor Tanner began her lecture. So I returned my unwelcome attention to Zara, who was now messing with her hair to create a shield from my glare. I didn't mind because I loved her hair. I could tell when she'd just washed it from the way her shampoo's extracts flowed in the air. Today it smelled like eucalyptus and orange tea, a nice change from her usual strawberry scent.

I expected Zara to look back up—humans are curious creatures, drawn to us by nature—but was pleasantly surprised when she held her ground for a solid ten minutes. When she cracked moments later and tried to sneak an inconspicuous glance, I grinned. She responded with an even more peculiar stare, curious about my amusement but slightly upset, then looked away, shaking her head.

A little while later, her expression shifted to a soft pout, probably annoyance with the awkwardness between us. I chuckled. It reminded me of my sister's attitude and drama. *Women.* Zara scowled at me for laughing before turning back to the professor, continuing her silent game, but I thrived on this reaction.

In the middle of class, the professor assigned us a two-page report and presentation with a partner on the archaeology or civilization of either the Aztecs or Mayans. Suddenly Zara was willing to talk. I didn't like talking about my past, but I especially didn't want to come off as a know-it-all, which would only make Zara more suspicious.

"So, which one do you want to do?" I asked before she could go off and ask someone else to be her partner.

She glanced around briefly. Everyone else was already pairing up. She sighed and turned to me. "Maybe we can do the archaeology one. It sounds easier. Plus, I've got a friend at the library who knows a lot about this sort of stuff."

I leaned back, crossed my arms, and chuckled to myself.

"Is this funny?" she asked.

"No. It sounds like you've got it all worked out."

"Well, if you don't speak up, I won't know if you don't want to do this one."

"It doesn't matter to me. You choose." Her quirkiness pleased me so much that I was letting her do whatever she wanted. *No, what is wrong with you?*

"Okay. Archaeology," she stated proudly.

Hot air escaped me in a second laugh. *The clueless little doll—this will be fun.*

"What?" she asked.

"Are you sure? I mean, the Aztecs were pretty gruesome. Lots of blood." I delighted in rubbing it in as her face washed with disgust. "It might make for a better report. But like I said, you choose."

It was cute how her nose wrinkled. "You are sick."

"No, *muñeca,* actually I'm not."

She gave me a strange look and opened her textbook. "We're going with civilization, so start reading."

I watched her. It was like watching Gabriella make a decision on which bracelet to wear. Zara wasn't upset; she was flustered.

I looked at her book, wondering what wrongful words were in there about my people. "I don't need that."

"Whatever." She slammed it shut and pulled a notepad and pencil out of her bag. "Then let's start with what we know."

The irony was killing me, and I couldn't help but laugh again.

"*Now* what is so funny, Lucas?"

"Nothing, nothing. This isn't going to work. How about you start with what you know, and then maybe I can fill in the gaps," I suggested.

"Fine."

I looked over her shoulder as she wrote the two things everybody knew about the Aztecs.

"That's it?" I asked, unimpressed.

She slammed the pencil down. "Look, you chose this topic!"

"I'm not mad. I told you I would fill in the gaps," I said, laughing as I raised my hands.

"Yes, you did. So feel free to start."

She shoved the paper at me, but my eyes skipped to the pencil sitting on her lap. She sat there, oblivious.

"May I?" I asked, reaching for it.

I knew exactly how to push her buttons; my proximity was one of them. I could hear her heart race as I grabbed the pencil, and I took my time backing away, enjoying the pleasure of teasing her. What surprised me, though, were the hot pulses throbbing through my own body.

I glanced down, ignoring the heat I now felt, and wrote in all caps until I'd filled the entire page. "Done."

Zara stared at it in shock. "Lucas, this is half the report!"

"I know."

"Well, what else do you know?" she asked ecstatically.

"More than that."

"Then why don't we finish it right now?"

"Because."

"Because why?"

She waited patiently as I sat there, thinking. "What's your e-mail address? Maybe that would be better."

"Um, okay." She wrote her address down on a scrap piece of paper and handed it to me. "What's yours?"

"I don't have one."

"Excuse me?"

"I don't have one," I repeated dryly. It was a lie. I'd had *plenty* of alias addresses, strictly for college, in my past. But I wanted to give her one, a personal one—with my name—that had never existed before, but I feared if I didn't watch what I did, I'd be in even bigger trouble.

She chuckled. "Who doesn't have an e-mail address?"

I was working out the mechanics in my head when the professor ended class. I sensed Zara's panic.

"Lucas, how are we going to finish this? It's due next class," she asked.

"*We* are not . . . *you* are." I stood and walked away. I could hear the tile clink as she followed me.

"What?" she yelled. "No! Give me your number at least."

"No," I replied with a sly grin, thriving on her frustration.

When I returned home, Gabriella was in the den. The windows were open, letting the shade of the cool mountain chill the room—not that I could tell the difference. She sat on the leather couch, staring outside at the creek below. I sensed that her mood wasn't any good when I stepped in. Her cell dangled between her loose fingers.

A text from that Bri girl was across the screen, asking Gabriella to go to Reno with all the girls. Gabriella stared out the window as a tear fell from her eye.

"I'm sorry, Gabriella. But we need to be sure. There is too much at risk," I said.

"I have to go out with the girls tomorrow night?" she sniffed, unmoving.

"Yes."

I found myself restless. I walked over to the golden globe and began spinning it.

"Lucas, is there something you are not telling us?"

"Of course not."

"Dylan told us . . . about you touching her . . . and what you saw." There was fear in her eyes when I stared back blankly. "And how you aren't afraid. Lucas, stop it. Stop it all right now. Have you even considered what the Celestials will do if they find out we saved her? Or worse, the war this could start? Please, I beg you, just let her go."

My blood boiled, but my voice strained past an unintentional chortle. "War? Gabriella, everything is too premature to decide such a fate. If we decide to keep her, we shouldn't be worried about war or the Celestials. We should worry about Solstice."

Gabriella stood with a huff and headed for the door. I let her go without argument.

I retired early that evening, but later that night found myself walking past Zara's house, looking into her lit window. There was something about her that I returned to constantly. My ageless body ticked these days in a way it hadn't since the transformation.

When I put my hand in my pocket, I felt a crumpled piece of paper. I pulled it out and saw Zara's e-mail address. I chuckled to myself. I'd never created a personal e-mail account for many reasons, traceable identity being one. But as I looked back up to her window, seeing her on the computer gave me an idea.

I rushed back home and sat on my bed with my laptop. Within minutes I was writing my first e-mail as Lucas Castillo.

To: Zara Moss {littlemissmoss@gmail.com}
From: Lucas Castillo {yoursavior@gmail.com}
Subject: Reno

So what (or who) is in Reno?

Yours,
Lucas Castillo

I tapped my fingers on the side of the laptop as I obsessively refreshed my inbox. For a moment, I thought it would be quicker for me to go to her house and perch right outside her window to just see what she was doing, but then that seemed rather ridiculous. I restrained myself and rolled the citla between my fingers as I paced in my room. On the tenth roll, my computer chimed. It nearly fell over as I stormed to it.

To: Lucas Castillo {yoursavior@gmail.com}
From: Zara Moss {littlemissmoss@gmail.com}
Subject: My savior. Really?

Reno is none of your business and I wouldn't know. I have to do a report all by myself so I'll probably miss out. My partner sucks.

I'm not yours,
Zara

. . . .

To: Zara Moss {littlemissmoss@gmail.com}
From: Lucas Castillo {yoursavior@gmail.com}
Subject: Report

Ungrateful. Do you not remember that I practically wrote the entire thing already?

Yours (whether you like it or not),
Lucas

. . . .

To: Lucas Castillo {yoursavior@gmail.com}
From: Zara Moss {littlemissmoss@gmail.com}
Subject: NOT YOURS!

How am I supposed to know if what you wrote are true facts? If you're not going to help, quit e-mailing me.

I left the e-mails at that. I didn't care if she was upset with me, but I didn't want to make her hate me. I cared too much about her for that to happen.

The next day, while Zara met her friends inside the cafeteria to keep out of the cooling weather, I stayed with Gabriella and Dylan out at the cars. Gabriella's braids kept the wind from flapping her hair as she yelled about why I was wrong to save Zara. I argued back, of course, but as I did, she turned to Zara and scowled at her as if she was going to kill her on the spot. My muscles tensed with anger. It was one thing for me to treat Zara coldly, but I would not tolerate Gabriella doing so.

"Gabriella, *párate*!" I commanded.

She looked back with a cheap, satisfied grin. I ignored her and checked the cafeteria. By Zara's startled expression, I knew she'd noticed the death threat. I glowered at Gabriella.

"What?" Gabriella snickered and smoothed a loose strand of black hair away from her eyes. "It's only fair. She has no idea how miserable she is making me right now while we keep her safe. The good news is that the redhead caught the flu. Heard it in the TAs' office today. Now I don't have to go out with the girls until next weekend," she said, sounding relieved.

When I saw Zara coming toward us, I turned toward the lake and began walking. "Nobody can make you miserable except for yourself, Gabriella," I yelled back.

Dylan straightened from his conspicuous boredom. "Where are you going?"

"A walk. And honestly, Gabriella, you're going to let a human get you all worked up like this? The poor girl has no idea, give her a break. By the way, don't wait for me after school. I'm going to get meat for Niya and Malik."

After I returned from the lake, I walked aimlessly around campus, waiting for Zara to go home. When she did, I left for the market.

When my family arrived in Tahoe, the first thing we did was find a butcher we could trust. We met Joe at the supermarket off Lake Tahoe Boulevard, a smuggler trying to make extra coin for his family. I usually went straight to the alley behind the store for special orders, but I didn't need too much, so I went inside to pay civilly.

"Hey, Lucas, what can I get you?" Joe said, dropping his customers. The husband and wife waited for a second, confused, then walked away, muttering, when they realized Joe wasn't going to help them.

"I need twenty pounds of sirloin steak, two turkeys, and six racks of ribs," I said.

He smiled as he did every time. "Ever going to tell me what you do with all this meat?"

"No."

He laughed overdramatically and disappeared behind the thick hanging plastic doors. He returned with several packages wrapped in butcher paper, tied tightly with twine.

"Your special order should be here by November," he added under his breath as I handed him flaps of cash.

"Great." I didn't care.

Afterward I decided to go down the dairy aisle for a kick. When I passed the produce, I made a note to never buy avocados from there. They were pathetically small, not like the ones at home, which looked like large squash. I was still wandering the aisles, bored and thinking about how I missed eating like I used to, when I saw Jett staring at me and all the meat I carried. I turned away and left the store to avoid an unnecessary confrontation.

Niya and Malik were waiting for me outside the garage. They drooled as I laid all the meat on the ground and unwrapped each package one by one. When I was done, I threw each piece of meat far into the woods. Niya and Malik had disappeared hundreds of feet into the trees before I could tell them to go, so I sealed the bloody butcher paper tightly, discarded it in the trash, and went in through the garage, wondering if Zara had e-mailed me back.

Zara

Chapter Six

Best Interest

Lucas was insane. Why didn't he e-mail me back? That arrogant jerk. What, did he think that I was *really* going to pull this off on my own?

When Ashley caught the flu and canceled our Reno trip, I was tempted to do the rest of the paper myself, but I bit my lip and set the project aside, assuming that he would e-mail me back. But Sunday night came, and he never did.

After dinner I went to my room, crossed my legs on my bed, and flipped open the thin, glossy pages of my history book to chapter 1, "The New World." In history class sophomore year, we'd brushed briefly on the subject of the New World; unfortunately, it had not advanced my knowledge of the subject. I vaguely remembered Spain, explorers, and Pocahontas, who I was sure was not a real person. Or was she?

As I skimmed for ideas on what to write about, a black-and-white painting of a stele caught my eye. It was a large, flat stone with a warrior carved in its center, facing sideways, holding a club or a head. It was strange, but what stood out to me was the tree standing next to it. I thought its spiraling roots looked familiar.

The next image showed Hernan Cortez, the famous Spanish

explorer, in a metal breastplate. The caption read, "The Aztecs and Mayans survived amidst bloody battles between each other until the arrival of Spanish explorer Hernan Cortez, who set in motion the fall of their primitive empires."

I was yawning, already bored, when my phone buzzed against my pillow. It was a text from Bri:

Everyone is meeting at the slaughter house Wednesday morning to catch some rays before it gets too cold.

The slaughter house was the spot we went to all summer. It was a foreclosed house Bri'd found along the lake earlier that summer. The balcony was right over the water, so we bought cheap folding chairs and left them there for when we decided to go back. I yawned again and rubbed my eyes as I set the history book on the floor.

You should invite that boy from Lucky Pin.

What was Bri on? Lately she seemed like a hippie at Woodstock—too much of this free love.

Funny. I was just thinking how much I couldn't stand him.

Why are you always so upset lately?
And just do it . . . he's HAWT.

No.

I put my phone on silent and rolled over, then an idea came to me. I sprang to my desk and shook the mouse to take the computer out of sleep mode.

To: Lucas Castillo {yoursavior@gmail.com}
From: Zara Moss {littlemissmoss@gmail.com}
Subject: Lake House

Some friends of mine are meeting at Lake Tahoe tomorrow, at a vacant house on Baldwin Beach. You can't miss it. Why don't you meet me there and we can finish the report.

Zara

I didn't expect him to e-mail me back, so I was shocked when I heard the new-mail alert whistling on my computer a minute later.

To: Zara Moss {littlemissmoss@gmail.com}
From: Lucas Castillo {yoursavior@gmail.com}
Subject: Doesn't sound fun . . .

And I hate the water.

Ew. Ew. Ew! I clenched my fists and screamed into the pillow. When I'd caught my breath, though, it took minutes to fall asleep.

A rainstorm swept in that night. The wind scraped the branches against my window so loudly that I woke up. The whistling gusts prevented me from falling asleep again, so I lay on my back and let the wind play its song, wondering what Lucas would be like if he were bearable to be around.

When I woke up the next morning, the sky was black. I could hear thunderstorms coming in. Jett called to cancel the lake party and instead came over with Bri and Tommy to watch a movie (in a friend sort of way). On Tuesday, despite the gloom, the girls resumed planning for Reno, hoping the skies would clear by Friday—so they could wear their slutty clothes, of course. But the odd, omnipresent storm stuck around until Wednesday, and it didn't look like it'd leave us any time soon. Tahoe's weather forecasters had no idea where it came from or why it hovered, unmoving, over Lake Tahoe.

"Well, it doesn't look like it's getting any worse, so we're all still going to meet at the slaughter house today in one hour." Bri had called bright and early. Wednesdays were our off days.

I glanced out my window. It was gray and drizzly. "To do what? Nobody is going to get in the water, and we'll all get soaked."

"Why do you always have to be the party pooper? Who cares what we're doing? Everyone is going to be there, so it'll be fun."

"I might stop by. I have to deposit my last check from Lucky Pin and work on my history report that's due tomorrow."

I could hear Bri yelling at her little brothers on the other end. "One hour," she said before hanging up.

I checked my e-mail, curious if Lucas had happened to e-mail me back. Zip. Now I'd have to stop by the library too. *That lazy piece of . . .*

I cursed under my breath as I dressed. With the storm, everything had cooled off a ton. The leaves were changing colors quickly and falling in flurries that left the branches bare. I slipped into a light sweater, not understanding why anyone would want to go to the lake to hang out. The water would be freezing. But I hopped in the Subaru anyways, turned up the heat, and headed to my bank at the edge of town.

It was a small building surrounded by towering pine trees, just off the 89. Thunder had gradually become constant, and the underbrush rattled as I stepped out into the empty parking lot. I ran inside, out of the drizzle, deposited my check, and went back into the grayness. Then I heard a suddenness of soft whispers carrying on the wind.

I froze in my tracks and checked around for other people, holding my breath. But there was no one. As I looked back at my car, a shower of simultaneous lightning bolts struck the mountainside just past the bank. It was unnatural and terrifying, but amazing—I counted at least fifteen bolts at one time. I stepped out from under the bank's awning, watching in astonishment as the barrage continued for seconds, then minutes. And then, before I knew it, my ears were listening to musical rain tapping on the asphalt, the lightning had stopped, and the whispers were gone.

I hustled to my car, slammed the door shut, and fumbled for the locks. It was a false sense of safety, but I did it anyway. I revved the wagon and took off toward the lake, not wanting to be alone anymore. When I hit Baldwin Beach and found the gravel-covered driveway along Route 89, I turned in.

My stomach immediately twisted into knots. Poppy's red sedan was parked next to Jett's black truck. Bri's car was there too, and many others I didn't know. I shifted into reverse quickly, backed out, and headed for the pier. Why was Poppy there? It was midday. High school didn't let out for a few more hours.

I drove to the pier, furious, feeling blindsided by Jett. The windshield wipers were working double time, but the rain poured down in sheets, and their tiny blades couldn't work fast enough. The parking lot was empty when I pulled in. I parked by the staircase that led down to the dock between the library and the coffee shop, where I intended to go first.

As I stepped underneath the eaves and out of the rain, I heard my name spoken in a way that gave me shivers. I stopped and turned. The sexiness in it excited me, but I felt an uncontrolled rage coming when I saw Lucas walking toward me.

I was about to give him a mouthful for pulling the no-show on me when suddenly a pounding rose in my chest, rhythmic and hard.

"Were you always like this?" Lucas asked as I grabbed the doorframe to steady myself. He clearly realized he was done for, even though I'd grabbed my chest to stop the pain.

"Like what?" I snarled, out of breath.

"Angry. You are angry a lot."

The pounding spiked, and it was too hard to stand. I bent over and braced myself, clutching my fingers over my knees. "No. It started after the accident." I hated that I was telling him this.

"What started after the accident?" Lucas leaned in and put his hand on my back.

I focused on his blue eyes through short breaths. They were blurry, so I squinted as I wheezed, "The moodiness, the obsessive compulsiveness, the migraines, the heart pain."

The worry that consumed his face sharpened. "Zara, are you okay?"

"I'm fine, Lucas," I snapped. As luck would have it, the pressure lifted and I could breathe. I straightened up and breathed in deeply. "What were you doing all week? Our report is due tomorrow. How can you not care?"

His eyes flickered to the coffee shop doors behind me, and he laughed coldly. "I'll save you some trouble." My heart nearly stopped again when he reached past me. The scruff on his face shadowed the dimple in his chin so handsomely, but I wondered if he ever shaved. He noticed and smiled softly as he opened the chiming door. "I do care."

My mouth flew open as he backed away. I improvised by pausing in the middle of the doorjamb to buy more time.

"How?" I grunted.

My body blocked his way, and we remained wedged together between the smell of hot coffee and the chilly rain outside. His face was only inches from mine when his grin widened.

"I only care when it's in my best interests." His mystical voice urged me to move closer, but his strong hand pushed the hollow of my back, forcing me into the coffee shop.

I huffed and spun back to Lucas, laughing incredulously. "In your best interests?"

"You ask too many questions." He closed the door with a teasing smile, delighting in my confusion. "See you later."

"You're not getting coffee?" I lashed out.

His perfect smile melted me into giddy goo, and I could tell he knew it from the soft laugh that escaped his kissable lips. "No, *muñeca*."

I stared at him as he walked away, hating that arrogant smirk of his. But for some reason, I couldn't stop thinking about it as I waited for my coffee.

The rain was settling as I walked to Tahoe Pier Library at the end of the strip mall. Mae sat at the circulation desk reading a book as I walked in. Though she was old, there was nothing about her that reminded me of my own grandmother. Her white hair was short and stuck out straight at the back of her head. She hated perms. And her frail body looked lost in the large, chunky sweater she wore.

"Well, hello there, Zara," Mae said, setting her book down.

The library was small, the size of two of my bedrooms. It was dark inside; today the large windows only brought in the outside gloom, but the marigold walls made it feel cheery anyway. The place was old, with the original sixties sparkling popcorn on the ceiling, and the stagnant air smelled of old pages and dust, but I loved to come here. Near the window sat two high-backed chairs, a place I used to sit in summer and read books with Mae.

"Hi, Mae. It's been too long," I said as thunder boomed outside.

"I heard about your accident. Are you okay?"

"Oh yeah, of course," I answered. I didn't want to talk about anything that reminded me of Lucas. "Hey, listen, I need your help with a report on Aztecs, and I know that you like to read books about that sort of stuff."

She giggled lightly to herself.

"What?" I asked.

"*Stuff*. You say it like you are completely lost."

"You're right. I am. But can you help me? My partner began writing some things down. I have it right here so you can see what we have so far." I pulled the sheet of paper out of my purse and unfolded it. I had to admit, his all-caps handwriting was sleek.

Mae grabbed the paper and took a moment to read. Her head started to shake.

"What? Is it bad?" I pressed nervously.

"This is very interesting."

"Good interesting?"

"This"—she held up the page—"is not freshman-level reading."

"What do you mean?" I snatched the paper from her hands quickly and searched it for answers.

"Have you read it yet?" she asked.

"Not line for line."

She pointed to the paper and picked up her book again. "I'll give you a moment, honey. You need to read that."

I brought the paper over to the window and sat down to read. Hairs rose on my arms as I finished the disturbing contents. Kidnapping women and children to be slaughtered didn't sit well with me. I shoved the paper back into my purse to distract myself from the slime stirring in my gut.

"Did you know all of this?" I asked.

"Some of it, not all."

Mae disappeared among the bookshelves. She came back with an old book, twined together by thin thread. "Here. This will help with your report."

As she set the burgundy book down on the counter, I worried it would fall to shreds on contact with my fingertips.

"What is it?" I asked, afraid to touch it.

"A book on the New World."

I continued to stare at it. The old paper was a burnt-yellow color on the edges, and rips marred the sides of the volume.

"Where did you get it?" I asked.

"My great-grandfather was a geologist who studied Mesoamerica." Mae chuckled. "This was just one of the many crazy things he had that he didn't want the government taking. So he passed it on to me when I was a girl. It looks like it's made of skin or something—it's always given me the jibbers."

"Mae, I can't take this," I said, scooting it closer to her.

She shoved the book back quickly. "No. This is an emergency."

"No, it's not. I'll just do my research on the Internet," I insisted, taking a step toward the door.

"You will do no such thing. Listen, right before my grandfather died, he told me that a Maya Indian gave it to him when he was in Guatemala during the Depression. He never told me why it meant so much to him, only that it was very important. Maybe you can find out why it's so special. I've tried to find books similar to this, but I can't find anything in print. As far as I know, this is the only book of its kind."

I looked to her for permission before snatching up the book and nestling it inside my bag. "I will take good care of it, Mae, I promise."

"I know you will, honey." Her face filled with excitement as she looked over my shoulder. "Hey, will you look at that. The rain stopped."

I turned around, confused. There was no blue sky just moments before. "It has. I guess I better go before I get stuck driving in it again."

"Take care, Zara."

I was treading in the small puddles at the top of the stairs leading to the dock when my heart pumped again. Sharp pain rocketed through my body, making me jerk upward.

"Augh!"

I grabbed at my chest and tried to rub away the pain as I staggered over to the railing. Between breaths I calculated the distance to my car. If I ran I could get there quickly enough; I could sit down before another attack. But then the agony spiked higher than ever before, and I collapsed to the ground.

I was lying in darkness on sharp rocks and broken branches. I had turned my head up toward the moon that shone frothily in the dark blue sky when a loud scream shattered the silence.

"No, NO!"

There was pure fear in the voice, which came from a place I couldn't see. Thick trees surrounded me, but I cocked my head, searching for it. Then the sound of a deep horn filled the air. There was sudden movement above. I looked up, past the tall trees, and my heart stopped.

There were hundreds of puffy clouds flying low toward the horn, except within the clouds I could see figures, their skin ropy with bones. There were no whites in their black eyes, which were set back in hollow sockets. I heaved, knowing that they were like the creature I saw when I crashed. I wrapped my arms tightly over my stomach as the voice—a girl's—screamed again.

"NO!" More urgent now.

The thread of fear froze me, but when those black creatures dropped in the distance, I followed. I crept quietly over the rugged terrain, afraid I would be noticed, but as another horn blared I sped up. I was running steadily, dodging rocks and ducking under branches, when I saw a clearing a few paces ahead.

I stopped atop a hill, above the valley where the creatures had gone. A massive pyramid crouched in its center, its tiered levels growing smaller as they rose, with steep stairs that climbed up one side. I snuck down the hill through a thick forest to the lake that surrounded the pyramid city. Ahead, a stone bridge stretched across the water, joining the land and the floating town. I moved along the trees until I reached the edge of the bridge, and when the last canoe had passed me, I ran as fast as I could over it and into the city.

Canals wound through the smaller buildings that surrounded the pyramid, cut right up to the foundations like the channels of Venice. As I passed an odd tree with tangled roots that coursed above the hard dirt, I caught movement out of the corner of my eye—three of the city's inhabitants walking toward me. I hustled to the shadow of one of the buildings. One walked almost close enough to touch, a male, I thought, speaking some unknown tongue to the other male-ish figures walking with him. I sucked in tightly and held my breath. Too mesmerized to shut my wide eyes, I saw the undead clearly. *I am doomed. I am stupid. I shouldn't have come.*

The men appeared human, skin wrapped around their bones as it should be, but in full light, the skin appeared thin, and I could see formations of bone underneath. The tall one, his face covered in war paint, paused briefly. My heart stopped; my back burned as I forced it harder against the wall. *Where can I run if he sees me?* I looked over my shoulder to the right and then the left, then cursed silently. I had been so busy observing the three men that I hadn't noticed that there were creatures everywhere: on the steps, in doorways, in canoes on the canals, and on every corner. There was no place to run.

I glanced back to the one who had stopped. The other two had turned toward him, waiting as he bent down and messed with the back of his calf. Something was wrong with it. It was more sinewy than the other parts of his body. I squinted harder. His skin was completely transparent. I gasped, quickly throwing my hands over my mouth. None of them seemed to have noticed me. His long fingers massaged at it while he yelled in irritation. He slapped it a couple times, then straightened up. He balanced on his good leg and started shaking his leg. The ligaments and muscles underneath the skin of his calf began to fade away, and the skin became visible again.

My sweaty hands slipped against my mouth. I didn't move, though, as the three undead walked past me. As they turned a corner, I stepped away from the wall, surprised to have gone untouched and unnoticed. *Can they not see me?*

Suddenly stale smoke stirred in the air, and my gut wrenched. I'd never smelled anything worse in my life, but somehow I knew this stench. My hands flew back toward my nose to block the smell of burning flesh.

A line of black smoke grew in the air near the pyramid. I swallowed against my heaving and stepped out of the shadow and into the orange light. A group of half-naked children with excited faces rushed past, showing no sign they had seen me. *How?* I could feel the hairs on my arms swaying in the wake of their movement as another cry circled in the air. *That* cry. And it was coming from the place the boys were running to. Wait. The whole town was moving toward the scream, toward the main pyramid.

I moved on the outskirts of the crowd, staying as far from them—and their shifty skin—as possible. When we entered the hollowed-out space surrounding the main pyramid, I could see the smoke rising from the right. The crowd gathered in tightly at the base of the temple and faced the ascending steps. I moved around them more easily now that they were focused on the pyramid, but stopped abruptly when I saw the smoking pile. Though already charred, the dismembered bodies, pieces of white bone shining through, shocked me. The limbs were small—my size—and I couldn't stop the strong pulse deep within my stomach; the chest cavities looked as if they'd been ripped open. *And where are the heads?*

I stepped back. Two men sitting on the ground a few feet away, their faces half covered in a thick red paste, were chewing noisily on something. My nostrils flared, and I could feel chunks clogging my throat as I watched one bring half a human arm to his hungry mouth. The other gnawed a piece of a leg already pocked with bite marks. I looked away for relief, but instead found the heads. They had been impaled on the spikes of the fence behind the two cannibals. There were too many heads to count, the fence extending deep into the trees, but I could tell which heads were the newer prizes by the fresh, dripping blood seeping from the necks. They were all young women, some with short, curly hair and others with long locks now matted over their faces with dried blood.

I have to leave, now.

I turned and ran.

This isn't the way. No, it's this way. When I ran into the same canal by a large rock formation twice, I knew I was lost, but at least the streets were empty. Then an abrupt screech echoed off the narrow stone walls. I needed to escape, but instead I was returning to the death trap, looking for higher ground. I climbed a short stone wall stained with deep burgundy streaks from the top down to the dark soil. The girl screamed again, louder.

The hovering creatures had landed at the base of the pyramid before the gathered crowd. The haze around them vanished, and their forms shifted to the unnerving, humanlike shape of the others. A few members of the crowd came forward and welcomed them with hugs and kisses.

Then, as one, the crowd turned to stare at the entrance to the temple courtyard, parting to form a walkway. I was squinting, trying to make out the approaching figures, when the scream rang out again. Chills raced up my neck. It was the girl, dragged through the dirt by two of those creatures and followed by two more. The parted crowd watched; some cheered. She screamed and squirmed, thrashing against their grasp, but their grip was firm, and they began climbing the pyramid. Eventually, her legs weakened and dragged behind her, and I noticed the color of the steps. They were red and slick with wetness. *That's odd—the girl didn't look bloody.*

A man with long black hair, a bare chest, and large cape stepped out from the small room at the top and met them. The feathers bordering his collar were long and stiff; they poked some of the creatures that bowed before him. They held the girl still as he circled her.

At his nod, the workers threw her onto the stone slab in the center of the pyramid's peak. She flailed, but each grabbed a limb and yanked hard.

No, please! Don't!!

The feathered priest moved to stand behind her head and, without flinching, raised a dagger above her. Tears swelled in my eyes as he plunged the knife down and her pleading cry turned to an unbearable scream. I looked away just as her screams ceased. I covered my mouth, trying not to vomit as the cheers rose from below. When I wiped my tears and looked back, I wished I hadn't. Her body was rolling down the steps, a fresh, red streak trailing behind her.

I hopped off the ledge and hugged myself tightly as I backed away—and my shoulder was suddenly pushed back as if I had been hit. I stumbled for balance, but looked to see who pushed me all the same.

"Zara!" There was another voice in the air, much softer than the horrifying screams that still echoed in my ears. I shuffled around, shaken, looking for the person touching me as my feet searched for solid ground.

My other shoulder jerked back, my feet slid on the loose gravel, and I began to fall.

"Zara!"

My eyes closed when I landed, but when they opened Lucas was there, close enough for me to smell his minty breath.

"Zara!" His voice shook. "Are you okay?"

It took me a moment to realize I was back at the pier, lying in Lucas's arms, of all places. His arm was a firm bar under my back, supporting my weight. Cold sweat drenched my head, and I suddenly felt embarrassed.

I tried to sit up, but my head spun painfully.

"No, stay down for bit. You look really pale," he ordered.

I tried to look around through the spinning. I wasn't on the upstairs parking level anymore; I was at the bottom of the stairs near the water's edge. "Did I . . ."

The inner corners of his eyebrows slanted together. "Fall down the stairs? Yes."

"How long was I out for?"

"Only a minute."

My hand throbbed. I tried to get a closer look at the red, swollen knuckles but whimpered in pain when I flexed them. Lucas moved in carefully, his eyes on the plump bruise, and without asking, he reached for my hand.

A tingling sensation zapped me the instant our fingers touched. I jerked at first, causing his hands to press more firmly around my fingers, but my muscles eased as I watched him survey the damage. He gently turned my wrist a couple of different ways and then was quiet for a short second. Annoyed that I was still lying in his arms, it occurred to me that this guy always showed up when something bad happened. Thankfully, he finally let go, and my growing panic eased.

"It's not broken . . . that's good," he said.

"How do you know?"

"No bones are popping out in abnormal places. Can you move your fingers?"

Despite the pain, I flexed my fingers slowly. "Yes."

"You're okay, just a bruised hand. Do you think you can get up now?"

I nodded. He was helping me to my feet when a soft ring sounded in his pocket. I jumped, still shaken from what I had seen. Lucas just let the phone ring as he gazed at me. I stared back, concerned about his guilty look.

"Aren't you going to get that?" I asked.

"It wouldn't be a good idea."

Before the voicemail could beep, the phone rang again. It sounded urgent. But this time Lucas irritably grabbed the phone, shut it off, and buried it deep in his pocket.

"It sounded like it was important," I said, brushing off dirt.

"You're more important; they just don't get that yet."

"What did you say?"

"Family stuff, don't worry about it." He paused and shifted his feet, avoiding my gaze. Then he rubbed his hand down his neck as color rose in his face. "Ah, dammit."

"Excuse me?"

He shook his head as if I'd misunderstood him and pinned his gaze on me. "You going to be okay?" His blue eyes showed only honest sincerity, but with the urgency of needing to leave.

"Of course I'm going to be okay. It's not like this hasn't happened before," I said, taking a tiny step up the stairs. *But it hasn't. Not this bad. Not this real.*

I was trying to leave him behind, but Lucas moved after me with a sudden interest. "Blacking out?"

I turned to him, frustrated that I felt safe sharing my secrets with the one person I didn't trust. I sighed and looked away, wondering why I was going to tell him this. "I don't just black out. I see things."

"What sort of things?"

I looked at him defensively. "It's only happened twice."

"What happens?" he pressed.

I paused, picturing the ways this could go badly, how stupid I must seem. *I'll keep it simple.* "I go to a place where the sky is opposite of what it's like here. And there's a huge pyramid, like the ones in your country. I've seen them in our textbook."

Lucas's eyes grew wider, as if I'd startled him. His urgency was with me now and not the missed phone call. A warning burned inside me for some reason. *Leave, Zara.*

"The sky, you said it's opposite of how it is here?" he asked.

"Yes."

"What color was the sky?"

I rolled my eyes, wondering why he cared about my weird hallucinations. "Orange."

He paled, and he was suddenly very preoccupied with the ground and scratching his head. I was about to say something, but he cut me off, an urgent note in his voice. "We better get going. Do you feel well enough to drive, or should I drive you home?"

I backed away from him when he came closer. My knees stung. I looked down. My skin was ripped to shreds. I brushed the dirt off my knees carefully and took another step up. My left ankle was sore too. Luckily, after a few steps it felt better, and I could walk without feeling humiliated by a limp. But Lucas followed me anyway. I was mad at myself, that I couldn't resist looking at his face, which was too beautiful to go unnoticed even now, twisted with emotion.

When Lucas remained silent, pondering, I felt my new anger rising. I wondered things myself. He nearly stumbled into me when I stopped. "Were you following me?"

His glare, which normally angled down on me, now shot up from the step below. "Of course not."

"So if you're not following me, what were you doing out here?"

"You're going to turn this on me?" His smile was attractive; he looked almost proud of my rebuttal, but there was caution there, and awkwardness.

"Yes, I'm curious."

"About what?" he asked.

"You."

His stare went solid, the smile on his face slipped, and then he coughed. "You going to get that?"

"Get what?"

Just then my phone buzzed in my pocket. I stared back to Lucas as I reached for it. *How did he . . .* It was Jett. I huffed and hit silent. I would deal with him later.

When I glanced back down to Lucas, his jaw had hardened and his blue eyes looked anywhere but at my own. "It isn't safe to be alone."

I laughed because it was just too funny. "You don't know Tahoe that well then. This is the safest town ever."

His eyes flashed to mine so harshly I felt weak. "Go home now and stay inside with your brothers. I prefer for you to be with people in general, but if Jett is whom you choose to run to after you're done with me, or your lame party, so be it."

How did he know I had brothers? Fury exploded within, and the blood started to sizzle in my veins. No boy had ever been so rude to me. And who was he to decide whom I hung out with? *Talk about control issues.* I wondered why his face, for all its demeaning ferocity, also showed the immense sadness I knew I'd seen.

"Is that what you want?" I asked angrily.

He stepped away, pivoting his body so I couldn't see his face, though I knew it was nearly exploding with frustration. He clenched his fingers tightly in his hair, then ran them through it until they stopped at his neck. He squeezed hard as he craned his head back. Underneath his madness, he looked . . . exhausted?

He blew out a puff of air. I stared with disbelief at his strange reaction. Then he turned back to me, raising his voice through gritted teeth. "Promise me."

The discomfort in his contorted face proved he was interested in me. But why? Why wouldn't he hang out with me when I asked? And why in heaven's name did he not like the water? Who doesn't like the water?

Everything just felt too weird, and the anger swarmed in with a vengeance, surpassing any fear I felt.

"Whatever," I said, taking a few steps up the stairs before turning back to Lucas. "You know what? You don't get to call all the shots. What if *I* don't agree with you? I can do what I want. I was here first. *You* leave."

His authoritative stare sparked a pinch of cowardice in me, and I felt my squared shoulders flinch. "This isn't your call to make. Now go home and do as I say."

This time I was afraid of the power in his voice and the way it made my stomach curl. I whipped around and stomped up the stairs to the car, flinging my arms dramatically in the air with each step. I didn't look back until I got to the wagon. Surprisingly, he was right there behind me, watching. Why did he care that I wasn't alone? What was he doing, babysitting me? *Weirdo.*

The loathing I felt for Lucas was immeasurable. I shot him one last enraged glance before dropping into my car and pulling away.

Chapter Seven

The Way It Was

I parked at the curb of my house minutes later and surveyed my injuries. First I looked at my knees and their shreds of broken skin. Vertical red streaks covered my kneecaps as if I'd been butchered with sandpaper. My palms were covered with cuts too, a deeper gash near one pinkie stinging worse than the others. I winced in misery.

Now that my muscles were cold and the adrenaline almost gone, I had to force my weak legs to swing out of the car. I walked to the house with every muscle begging me to stop. I had stopped midway across the grass and arched my back in a stretch when I noticed Max and Casey's unwashed Civic in the driveway. My intestines knotted with embarrassment about how I must look. When I got to the porch, I could hear the boys' obnoxious cackling inside. I cracked open the front door quietly and then stepped in when I thought it was clear.

I had one foot inside when the door miraculously opened. I jumped at the sight of Jett standing inside. He looked me over, from my feet up, his expression saturated with ridicule.

"What happened to you?" He tried hard to keep a straight face, but a large smile spread cheek to cheek. "Max, Case, come see Zara!"

"Where's Poppy?" I pushed past him and headed straight for the medicine cabinet.

Jett swiped the blond hair out of his eyes and straightened, looking confused. "Poppy?" I heard him close the door and follow me into the kitchen.

"I saw both your cars at the slaughter house."

"You must have got there right after me. I didn't even get out of my car. When you didn't show up, I left. I tried calling you. I didn't know she was going to be there. Promise." He grasped my arm lightly when I tried to nudge away. "Are you okay?"

My hair fell across my face as I glared back. A red leaf was stuck in the frizz. I yanked it out just as Max and Casey walked around the corner. They stopped at the sight of my disarray and erupted in laughter.

The twins were tall and thin, with dirty blond hair and hazel eyes. They had a way with words that annoyed me, as their little sister, but endeared them to others. When they fought as kids, they always called each other ugly. They weren't idiots. They knew they both had the same ugly face. I just never knew that you could fight with someone and love them all at the same time. Lesson well taught. However, such pitiful goofiness came off as bullying as they got older, and they often found themselves in fights. It seemed, lately, that Max's unfiltered arrogance most easily distinguished him from Casey.

"You look like Eve, Zara. Figs and all," Max crowed as I searched the cupboard for bandages. My lip began quivering as the stinging got worse.

"Enough, Max," Jett intervened with a frown.

"Thanks, by the way," I shouted over my shoulder, hands meddling with bottles, "for asking how I was after my car crash."

"Negative. Not going to happen," Casey said. "Too much bro mush."

Jett looked stumped. "Bro mush?"

"Look at you, Zara," Max mumbled, nachos and cheese spilling out of his mouth. "You're perfectly fine, just like Jett said. Why would we need to ask how you were?"

"And the flowers? Don't act like you don't care." I asked. I was getting upset now.

"What stupid flowers?" Max snapped back.

Pure terror slowed my breathing. I moved slower now, feeling a prickling sensation in my toes as I rummaged through my thoughts. *How did those flowers get there?*

Max rolled his eyes. "Anyways, Jett, what do you want to do today besides hook up with our sister?"

"Max, stop!" I yelled.

"Not cool, Max." Jett shook his head, but I couldn't help but notice him laughing. When I threatened him with a crazy stare, he sobered and stepped closer. "Zara, what happened? Don't tell me you tripped."

Finally. The bandages. *Who put them underneath the athletic tape, the rubbing alcohol, and the ibuprofen?* I snatched one up, annoyed, grabbed the antibiotic ointment as well, then went to the sink. When the water ran warm, I dipped each wound under the faucet one by one and scrubbed furiously, as if it would erase my memory of Lucas—and the girl's body bleeding out as it rolled down the steep pyramid steps.

The work of tending my wounds made me forget about the utter humiliation of the boys' stares, but I also grew more terrified. What if I passed out again? I bit my lip, trying to stop it from quivering harder. It was difficult until the thought of Lucas made me want to scream.

"Zara," Jett called from somewhere distant, but when I looked up he was standing right next to me. His eyes flicked from the bloody scrapes to my eyes and back to my unnecessarily hard scrubbing.

"What, what did you say?" I mumbled.

"Where'd you go?" he asked softly.

"I went for a hike," I lied, resuming my cleansing with more gentleness.

"Were you attacked by an animal or something?"

"Ha. Not exactly," I muttered under my breath.

"What did you say?" Casey leaned over the bar across from me. I stopped so that I could look at him clearly.

"I said, not ex-act-ly. Gosh, what is with you guys? Lay off me for once."

"Wow-oh-ho!" Max snickered. "Eve to Medusa. You're killing me, Zara."

"Let's go. We need more ammo for tomorrow," Casey said.

The boys were never up to any good when ammo was involved. But today, my heart was ultrasensitive. So much death, so much blood.

"You're going shooting again? You just went. And you're going to get caught one of these days, watch," I reprimanded.

Casey tilted his head with a grin. "Nah. Wilson Canyon is the best desert for it."

"And there's not going to be any more animals left if you shoot them all!" My voice rose as if I had a megaphone pressed to my lips. The boys looked at me funny. "Just leave those poor rabbits, squirrels, or anything else you want to shoot alone."

The twins froze, looked at each other, then broke into their obnoxious laughs. "It's coyotes," they said as they walked away.

Jett stayed at my side. His eyes drooped when the first tear formed in my eye. "Want to talk later?"

I didn't look up at him, only scrubbed. He waited a second, then dropped his head and walked away. Everything hurt. Thinking of Poppy and Jett hurt. Thinking of Lucas hurt. My damn knees hurt.

After I had tended to every tear in my skin, I suddenly felt that everything on me had to be cleaned. I lifted my shirt up to my nose and took a sniff. *Ugh, I even smell like Lucas.* I went upstairs to my room, stripped off the rest of my clothes, and stepped into the shower. The fresh water stung the open flesh, making me cringe in pain. I hurried, washing away the remaining dirt and picking the black rims out from under my fingernails. Once my body smelled fruity and the cuts had turned a soft pink, I let the water fall on my back while I crossed my arms tightly over my chest.

I squeezed my eyes shut when the memory of the girl's scream echoed in my head. I shivered. Next came those black eyes, those creatures that looked like the one at my crash. I felt a wave of sickness inching upward as I imagined that somehow Lucas was involved.

I tried to finish the report later that night, but I was too exhausted. The report would have to be composed of whatever I could pull from Mae's book in the morning. I threw my hands over my chest as I lay down and listened to the drizzle with unfocused eyes. *It's strange how often it's been raining*, I thought. And then I prepared something to say if Lucas dared to show his useless face.

I woke to yellow light shining through the window. I shot out of bed, excited to feel its missed warmth, but shivered instead with achy bones. It was chilly. Then I remembered it was already the last week of September.

The wet streets smelled of oil as I drove to school an hour later, my bag packed with snacks for the day. I was hoping to get something written before class, but sitting there in the empty campus library, I couldn't focus. There was a gritty feeling in the pit of my stomach, and I questioned why I was still in town when I could be attending another college, away from home.

At noon I met Bri at the sub shop inside the cafeteria. She was twisting her hair and avoiding her lunch as I walked up.

"You're not eating?" I looked at her full plate as I sat down.

She stuck up her nose as if repulsed by her turkey sandwich and batted her eyes. "No. I am on a new diet."

I looked at her, amazed. "Why? You're skinny."

"Not as skinny as you." She pushed her food to the edge of the table and folded her arms. "So, what happened to your hand?"

With the way Bri stared at my hand, I was glad I'd worn pants to cover my knees. I glanced down at it, then stared myself, dumbfounded. The purple had already turned to a soft yellow. It was nearly healed.

"I fell," I said.

"Since when are you clumsy?" She chuckled.

I looked up and folded my arms over the table. "Bri, have you been feeling normal since our crash?"

"I feel better than normal. You, no?"

I felt the opposite. Avoiding her gaze, I occupied myself with pretending there was something in my bag I needed. "I'm good. Just tired still, I guess."

Bri slouched, uninterested again, slowly picking at the bread of her sandwich. "Anyways, I can't wait for Reno. It's going to be so awesome. I bought the perfect dress to wear, I just hope the stupid rain doesn't come back." She left the sandwich and started searching for something in her purse.

I picked up a fork and played with her Jell-O to occupy the nervous energy twisting through my veins. "So, what's the story with you and Tommy?"

"I don't know." Her speech was slow as she examined her nails. "The boy sure does move like a snail." She glanced at her watch and stood. "Crap. I didn't realize it was so late. I've got to go. See you tomorrow, right?"

"Right." I waved good-bye and played around on my phone until my time of doom arrived.

I was surprised that Lucas wasn't in class when the hour hit. Part of me actually thought he'd show up. I was pulling out a piece of scratch paper when he slid onto the edge of the chair next to me. He smiled casually, as if nothing was wrong, though a second later his right leg started to shake, and he tapped his pencil on the armrest.

I looked away with a roll of my eyes and reached into my

backpack, where Mae's book was sandwiched between textbooks. I pulled it out and pried it open, looking for interesting facts I could add to my speech. I was grateful that the grade was not based solely on our written report, which I was sure we were going to bomb. As I swiped a strand of hair behind my ear, I saw Lucas do a double take at the book on my lap.

"Where did you get that?" he asked, pointing to it.

"The library."

"Which one?"

"The one on the pier." I folded my arms over it as if to protect it from his protruding stare. "Why?"

"Can I see it?"

A funny feeling ballooned inside me. I watched him suspiciously, holding him responsible for my uneasiness, and inched away slightly. "No."

"No?" That demeaning tone made me feel ten times smaller.

"Because it's not mine," I blurted. "And it isn't the library's. My friend let me borrow it."

"Who?"

"You wouldn't know her."

Lucas pondered this as the creases between his eyebrows deepened. "You said the library on the pier?"

I nodded weakly, my mind incoherent. The furrow of his eyes, the freshly shaven face—he *did* shave—the unruly hair; it was all hot. I had squeezed my eyes shut and then opened them wide to wake up when Professor Tanner called my name. Panic washed through me, and I looked to Lucas.

He smiled slyly and handed me a sheet of paper.

"What's this?" I asked.

"Our report."

My fingers went stone cold as I stared at the sheet between them. "You did our report?"

He chuckled. "Don't you want to read it first before you get up there?"

"Ms. Moss?" Professor Tanner called.

My hand shaking at the risk I was taking, I walked to the front of the room and cleared my throat. Lucas spread his arms across the chairs on either side of him and grinned boyishly. I was either going to regret this or cherish this. I looked down at the typed page and began.

Everything flowed until halfway through, when the details became gory—and very similar to what I had witnessed. Sights and sounds from yesterday—even scents—flooded my senses. My body shook enough to make me clip my words midsentence, and I had to stop. I glanced around the class, mortified, as I wiped my perspiration from my brow. Nobody cared. Half were looking down at their phones, and the others were either doodling or checking the clock. As I further stumbled over words like *scalp* and *dismember* and *cannibals,* I made an obvious effort to scowl at Lucas. When the torture was over, my body trembled with fury as I sat next to him.

"What?" he mouthed, as I glared at him.

"You're just sprinkled with surprises, aren't you?" When he didn't respond, I blew out all my hot air like a pricked balloon. "Of all things about their civilization, *that* is what you decided to put in it? Blood-crusted hair, beating hearts, dismembered bodies, cannibals!"

His usually animated face suddenly showed no emotion. "Yes, because *that* is how things were."

I leaned back quickly, my body pounding for some reason. "Why couldn't you have put something about their calendar or native vegetation?"

"What's the fun in that?"

My mind ran a million miles an hour after reasons why Lucas would know so much about that—or why I saw what I did. I had begun to wonder if there were still tribes of them today, hiding and doing those things in secret, when Lucas chuckled weakly.

"Those Aztecs don't exist anymore," he said.

I was stumped. "Ancestors, maybe?"

His lips sealed with a pinch, and he looked downward. "How's your hand?"

I glanced at my hand and let out a slow breath of astonishment. The swelling and redness were gone, and the knuckles were bony again. *That's weird.* I twisted my hand and made fists over and over again. Just an hour ago it was a yellow plum.

"It's, uh, better," I said.

"I see that." His bushy eyebrows were raised, but not in a pleased way.

I tucked my hand under my other arm, out of his view, and nodded. "So what's the deal with you?"

His blue eyes moved to the burgundy book on my lap. "Find anything interesting?"

"I haven't really read it yet."

"I had one similar years ago. But it's all fake, only legend."

I didn't understand why his attempts to discredit Mae's book vexed me so badly, but they made my blood sizzle. Disagreeing with Lucas would probably always be the norm.

"How do you know?" I asked stubbornly, petting the rough cover.

"Because, I told you, I had one just like that, but I lost it."

"That can't be true. I think this is the only copy."

"No, there were more." His voice held a hint of dishonesty. I stopped, perturbed by his arrogance. It was insulting. Did he really think I was that gullible?

I packed the book back into my bag and zipped it shut. "Listen, Lucas, now that this whole report thing is over, we don't have to pretend to be nice anymore. I have my own thing going, and you *clearly* have your own agenda as well. Okay?"

"Okay what?"

"Stop talking to me."

He folded his arms and laughed, amused yet again. "What's my agenda?"

"Don't know, don't care."

He leaned in close enough to let the curl of his dark eyelashes send my body into shivers, and he flashed a closed smirk. "Oh, Zara, but you should. Deeply."

I stared at him as I inched as far away from him as possible, and I turned my back and leaned toward the professor. As class ended, I watched Lucas leave without a good-bye or a glance or a wave. Maybe ignoring him would mend our fake relationship.

When I stepped outside, the last cold breezes of the storm had covered the parking lot with rust-colored leaves. I breathed in. The crisp air finally smelled like autumn. I sat in the wagon with the windows rolled down and studied my hand, baffled that there was no sign of injury.

As I drove home, my thoughts turned to Lucas, as they usually did lately. After the report disaster, there was no way I was going to trust him. Then I remembered that Gabriella was coming with us to Reno. I squeezed the wheel tighter, hating that she would probably report everything I did to her stupid, hot brother.

Chapter Eight

Night Games

The next day, I forgot about Lucas long enough to get laundry done. In between loads, I helped Mom bake an apple pie. As I packed the last of the necessities for beautifying myself for Reno, I glanced down. My duffel bag was overflowing with every item I owned. I zipped it anyway, shifted my hip to the side, and yanked it up, yelling bye to Mom and Dad as I opened the front door.

Lucas was standing on the porch, dressed all in black. When he smiled wide, I saw straight, gleaming teeth. It was heart-jerking, yet irritating that he could be so beautiful. It wasn't fair.

"Are you here to kidnap me?" I joked.

All pretense of happiness left him. His face went blank, and his body tensed.

Well, that didn't work. "What are you doing here, Lucas?" I asked as I shoved past him.

"I'm sorry."

"For?" A memory of him at the accident surfaced, though I pretended I hadn't a clue. He'd denied it completely, been a jerk to me all along. Suddenly I felt he shouldn't be apologizing, he should be *explaining*, starting with how he knew where I lived.

"For not being straightforward with you. Here." He pushed a rose toward me. The stem was wild with thorns; blood red rimmed each petal over a solid white bloom. It was perfect. I looked back up. Underneath his dark lashes I saw grief, and exhaustion again, as though he hadn't slept in days.

"What's this?" I asked.

"It's a rose," he said, managing a snarky smirk. "You know, most girls would take it and say it's okay . . . or throw it in the guy's face."

"I'm not like most girls."

He snickered. "Trust me, I know."

"Do you? Because you didn't seem to care when I tried to work on the report with you. And why the hell do I feel like you're always lying to me?"

He shrugged. Now he looked as though he really didn't care. "Zara, nothing can excuse how I may come across."

"You're right, but an explanation would, starting with this rose." I swung it like a magic wand.

"If I could, I would, but I can't," he pleaded.

"What do you mean?"

His hand fidgeted around in his pocket. "Look, I didn't come here to disturb you."

"Are you going to explain the roses in my room?"

"What do you mean?"

I shook my head at him, incredulous. The boy had a lying problem. I mean, he was only offering me one of the same flowers I'd found in my room. I gripped my bag and walked past him.

He turned after me. "I was hungry. Thought you might like to go grab a bite to eat."

"Are you asking me out?" I laughed.

It was hard to act tough when my bag was digging into the bones of my shoulder. It slowed me down. I tried to push it along with my hip, but it started to hurt, and I stopped and dumped it to the ground.

"No!" His voice was high, playing it off. "No," he repeated, though it sounded like he was reassuring himself. And then he sighed, looking at the grass. "No."

I raised my eyebrows, waiting for an explanation.

He glanced up, looking innocently—subtly—through his dark lashes. "So?"

"I can't. I'm going out with the girls tonight. Your sister is coming with us, didn't you know that?"

"No, of course I did. But there's been a change in plans."

"What?" My voice jumped an octave when my cell vibrated in my pocket. "It's Bri."

Lucas watched as I listened to Bri ramble on in one long sentence. Tommy and the rest of the boys wanted us to go play night games with them, and of course Bri had accepted. Everyone was to meet at Bri's house at dark.

"You were right," I said, dropping the duffel bag at my feet. "Ever played night games?"

"What's that?"

"I'll explain while we eat," I said.

As I levered up my bag, which now seemed to be full of cement, Lucas snatched it away, disregarding my nasty rejection, and carried it effortlessly to the house.

I walked to his expensive car, shocked that I'd actually agreed to go with him. When I sat down inside, it was like being on a beach, smelling the ocean. It was very clean, and the light gray leather still looked brand new. I looked around. The buttons on the dashboard were all futuristic looking compared to my wagon.

"Where are we going?" he asked, sliding noiselessly into his seat.

"Hamburgers?"

I had a ten-dollar bill folded in my back pocket; it would buy me one bacon cheeseburger, fries, and a drink at Lamplight's Diner. I was impressed when he said he didn't need directions. Then again, Tahoe wasn't that big.

We drove to the pier's strip mall in a silent bubble, mainly because our togetherness was awkward. Last time we were here, he'd caught me as I fell. I kept thinking of the phrase *Boy meets girl, boy likes girl, girl hates boy, girl likes boy,* wondering strangely if the last part would happen. Luckily, Lamplight's Diner was only a few minutes away, a few stores down from Mae's library, and we arrived there before I said something dumb.

When he pulled into the small parking lot, I watched people at the lake docking their boats amid the long, towering shadows cast by the setting sun. Lamplight's filled the larger space in the back corner of the mall. It was still a small diner, but they had a fairly decent patio on stilts over the water. I usually sat there.

Lucas and I followed our hostess through the restaurant, past the vintage streetlamps set at each booth, to our table outside. The air was cooler over the lake—a crisp chill that gave me a running shiver. I slipped my cardigan on and sat down. The waitress lit the gas heat lamp next to our table, letting her eyes wander to Lucas frequently.

"So, what are night games?" Lucas asked, looking away toward the lake.

My spirits lifted, despite my annoyance with the server's obvious stare, and I couldn't help but smile. "Are you ready to run a lot?"

He sipped his water, clearly suppressing a laugh. The sunset sparkled in his eyes when he looked back up. And then I noticed his beard—it had to have been a week's worth of growth, but he'd just shaved yesterday. *That's strange.*

"Don't worry about me," he said, smiling still, letting me dissect him in my mind.

I reminded myself to look past his unblemished handsomeness, past the butterflies now fluttering in my stomach. The waitress cleared her throat. I looked up, but I could feel his eyes on me.

"Two bacon cheeseburgers, two fries, and two strawberry shakes," Lucas said.

The waitress and I simultaneously looked at him.

"That is what you were going to order, right?" he asked.

I shook my head silently.

"You got it," the waitress said, walking away with her head down as she scribbled.

When she had disappeared, I started explaining. "The first thing you need to do is wear all black"—I briefly looked down at his clothes—"which, apparently, you already are. Then we split into two teams. One team runs, the other finds. Usually we start at Bri's and finish at the gondolas over at Heavenly. The finders' team will give the running team a five-minute head start. Their goal is to run on foot to Heavenly without getting caught. The team that makes it there with the most players wins. And, I also should tell you that anything goes: backyards, alleys, you name it."

He seemed very interested, though with a wise smirk. "Why all black?"

"Because you can blend in with the night." Duh.

"Ahh," he exhaled, his smirk turning to an amused smile.

I wondered what his secret humor meant as minutes passed in silence. Lucas let me be, looking around at other tables or toward the mountains across the lake until the waitress set the greasy food in front of us.

"Anything else?" she asked Lucas.

"No, thank you."

Lucas seemed too polite for someone my age. Normally my friends would just grunt, or look down until the server eventually walked away, recognizing they were being ignored. I liked his manners—it meant I wasn't feeling embarrassed, the way I always was with my guy friends.

I remembered something important as I shoved a fry into my mouth. "Oh, and I should probably warn you: Tommy and Jett can get a little crazy. They've been known to drive the truck on sidewalks and lawns to find someone."

He watched as I loaded my hamburger with ketchup, then leaned in. "That was going to be my next question. How do you guys see in the dark?"

"The cars' headlights mainly, but Jett has a searchlight, so watch out for that. And sometimes they'll get out and chase you down on foot with a flashlight."

"Right." His smile appeared again. "So, have you ever made it to the end?"

It wasn't hard to catch the sarcasm in his question. I frowned. *I don't look that helpless, do I?* "Only once. I always get outrun if I'm being chased on foot. But if they're in the cars, you can hide behind bushes or fences."

He nodded, somehow gloriously. "Got it."

I looked down and shoved another french fry into my mouth. "It's easier said than done," I assured him.

"I think I can handle it." There was a tint of laughter in his voice.

I watched as he took his first bite. The juices ran down the burger to his hand, then splattered onto his plate. It was interesting watching Lucas get dirty. He was somehow the cleanest person I knew, even if he did always seem to have scruff on his chin.

"Do you like it?" I asked hopefully.

"Very good."

Lucas's hair spiked messily upward, a dark terrain that seemed untouchable. It was stunning how his short sideburns moved halfway down his ear, drawing my eyes to his defined jaw. I looked around at other tables impulsively. My suspicions were confirmed when old ladies giggled in our direction a few tables down. I rolled my eyes and looked back to Lucas, who hadn't moved his eyes from me.

"So, you never told me . . ." I began, but he pointed a finger to his cheek and tapped.

"Oh!"

My free hand instantly flew up and found ketchup on my cheek. I was sure my cheeks flushed the same color as I wiped it off. I looked down, embarrassed, and noticed his hamburger, or what was left of it after a few bites.

"Are you even well enough to be running after your blackout?" he asked.

I looked back up quickly. "Lucas, I'm sorry. I shouldn't have told you any of that. It's so stupid . . ."

"Saying I'm glad you did," he interrupted, "would be an understatement."

"What do you mean?"

His gaze dropped suddenly. "Your hand's all better."

"I've been healing fast lately," I joked. He didn't laugh.

"Is that normal?"

"Not really. But when I got home from the hospital, my injuries went away really fast. And now these ones did too."

His stare lingered before he spoke. "What do you remember about that night?"

My heart picked up. The memory of Lucas yelling outside my shattered window flashed through my mind. "I . . ." I was suddenly confused. *Why is he asking me this when he denied it?* "Why are you curious all of a sudden?"

"For starters, you're welcome."

"For what?" I asked, perplexed.

The sunset silhouetted his straight nose perfectly. His face was carved stone, symmetrical and perfect. He leaned in closely. "For saving you that night."

There was a bump as my stomach dropped to my feet. "I knew it," I whispered. "But why do you want to know what I remembered? You were there."

"It's not the same."

I leaned in with chills. "I don't care what you say. I know you saw what I saw."

He sat up straight. "You weren't supposed to remember anything," he mumbled under his breath, looking at his glass as if he were talking to it. When he glanced back up he looked more confused than I felt. "But you're healing really fast. It doesn't work like that."

"What are you talking about? You're freaking me out."

He scooted his chair closer. "Zara, don't you think if I were any other person, I would look past the quick healing and say that it was just that you heal fast? Nobody heals that fast; it's unnatural."

"Gee, thanks."

"And your blackouts are not right, either." He looked away. "It shouldn't be like this—if you were normal."

"Earth to Lucas: you're scaring me. And two, the sun is almost down. We better pay and get going."

The mountains across the lake had become black peaks against the streaked colors of the sunset. I couldn't talk about what I saw in my blackout to anyone, especially Lucas. He must have realized I wasn't going to say anything more, because he lifted his head in a regal fashion and with two fingers motioned for the waitress to come. She was at his side, batting her eyes, in three seconds. It was pathetic.

"More water?" she asked him.

"No, thank you. We are ready for our bill."

She looked disappointed. As she fidgeted with her apron, I looked back toward the sunset. The gnats flittered over the water in busy, transparent clouds.

"Here you go. And please, let me know if I can get you anything else," she said.

She clung to the folder. As her hand lingered on the black leather, it tempted my jealousy, and I felt my rage brewing again. When Lucas's eyes left her to scan the bill, I somehow felt better.

I pulled out my ten, but before I could get it inside, Lucas slipped a fifty into the folder and stood.

"That won't be necessary," he said, waving my money away.

"Thank you." I felt foolish putting my money back into my pocket, but something told me he wouldn't take it anyway.

I rubbed my hands along my arms to warm them as we walked back to the car. Thanks to its altitude, Tahoe always cooled by around fifteen degrees at night. My shivering deepened in my thin sweater, and my teeth actually chattered as I waited for him to unlock his Lexus.

"You cold?" Lucas asked.

"A little," I answered, trying not to sound needy as I sat down on the firm leather seat. "You?"

He snickered to himself as he cranked up the heat. "Nope."

His voice held that sarcasm that always put me in a sea storm of confusion. I suddenly didn't know what to say that would sound intelligent or proper, so I stared out the window as the town's lights turned on.

When Lucas pulled onto Main Street, though, the suppressed urge burst. "Lucas, did you see another man at the crash?"

There was still enough light to see the muscles underneath his shirt tense. "Did you?"

"Yes, and I'm pretty sure I hit him too," I said—it was more information than I wanted to share, but everything spilled out naturally at this point.

"Have you told anybody this?"

I shrugged in my seat. "They wouldn't believe me if I did."

Lucas was silent until he pulled up to my dark house. Maybe he thought I was crazy.

"I will wait for you to change," he said, and just like that, it was like I hadn't even asked the question.

"Really?"

"It's no secret Jett doesn't like me, so it doesn't really matter if we show up in the same car," he concurred.

"Right. Be right back."

I skipped up the stairs and ran to my closet. It was full of clothes, but not so much black. I didn't want to wear what I always wore for night games, a grungy hoodie and tight yoga pants, but there were no other alternatives. I threw the baggy sweater over my head and wiggled into the stretchy pants, sprayed myself with a flowery scent, and headed downstairs.

My jitters only intensified when I stepped outside. Lucas's white car looked frosty in the dark as it idled, but the smell of a warm paradise blossomed when I opened the door. I sighed.

"Thanks for waiting."

Lucas was unmoving, distracted with the rearview mirror. I didn't understand. There was nothing but the blackness of the mountains past my house.

"Any time," he finally said, shifting gears slowly as he took one more look at the woods.

Bri's house towered on a small hill the next street over. It was the largest house in the neighborhood, with multiple turrets. It had a long, winding driveway and enough evergreen trees to look like Santa's village at the North Pole. Her dad was a plastic surgeon and liked things ritzy.

I saw Jett's black truck parked along the curb when we pulled up. Ashley's yellow Bug sat behind it on the downgrade of the hill, and then there was a car I'd never seen before. It was champagne colored and said *Porsche* on the back. I turned apprehensively to Lucas.

"Gabriella's here," he answered promptly.

"Oh."

Suddenly I wanted to disappear. Showing up with Gabriella's brother was the last thing I wanted to be doing.

Jett was leaning against Bri's car in the driveway when we pulled up. He stood up when he saw us and moved his blond hair out of his eyes to stare. I could see he was wearing his black prescription frames. He usually wore them at night to see better. I couldn't help but look away from his jealous glare to Gabriella, who stood on the lawn next to Dylan. With her thick hair pulled up into a high bun, she looked like an hourglass. Just as I started to look away, my breath stopped: the bombshell was smiling nicely at me.

"Finally," Tommy said, hopping out of the truck's bed as Lucas and I joined them on the slanted driveway. "Alejandro and Zara are here. Did Zara explain to you how to play?"

"It's Lucas, and yes," Lucas answered.

"Good. You're on my team. You look like you'd be of good use."

Lucas didn't seem honored—he clenched his jaw. "All right."

"Then we get Dylan," Jett yelled back.

Gabriella was suddenly next to me, talking softly in my ear. "And the girls?"

"They pick which boys are on their team first, and then the girls go on the team their boyfriend is on," I answered, as the boys picked.

"So then, will you be on Jett's team or Lucas's?" Her question took me off guard.

I recovered first with a blink before I turned to her and answered plainly. "Jett's. But he isn't my boyfriend."

"Right, because you practically can't stand the fact that he waited around a few short years to decide that he liked you."

"Gabriella, look, whatever I did to you, I'm sorry."

Her playful chuckle confused me. "Zara, I'm only joking. I would be upset if Dylan waited around that long too. Though, if I had any say in this, I think it would be cool for you and Lucas."

I wanted to make her finish her sentence. "For me and Lucas to what?"

"Gabriella!" Dylan hollered.

"Looks like you're on my team," she said. She delicately moved to Dylan's side.

I followed her to our team. Jett casually put his arm around my shoulders, making sure Lucas was watching. Lucas's eyes were locked on Jett's all right—but not the way they had locked on the rearview mirror—this way practically defined *If looks could kill*. Jett looked away more quickly than I expected.

"We're running first," Jett said, once we were huddled as a team. "Gabriella, Dylan, you guys know where to go?"

"Of course, man," Dylan answered.

"Just checking." Jett raised his head out of our circle slightly. "And Tommy, no cars in the alleys."

Tommy and the others on his team laughed. "You're funny. Look at you, you're shaking in your pants."

"Shut up, Tommy," Jett remarked before turning to us. "All right, guys. They have the searchlight on my truck, so stay off the streets. If you see them coming from a block away, hide in the bushes until they pass you. Got it? Oh, and if you get to the gondola first, call me."

"So, we go alone?" Gabriella wondered.

"Every man for himself. Is that a problem, Barbie? No offense, Dylan," Jett said.

"None taken," Dylan said, chuckling.

Gabriella ignored them, but glanced over at Lucas with worry. When he nodded, she glared back at Jett. "Just stay out of my way," she replied harshly.

"Gladly. When Tommy counts to three, you run the hell away from here."

"We know, Jett." Tana giggled.

"Just making sure. And be careful on Main Street. Getting out of the neighborhood is the easy part; it's crossing Main Street that's tough, so don't be stupid about it."

"Jett, I think we all got it," I remarked, pulling away from his arm.

There was a clunk when Tommy hopped up into the bed of Jett's truck. We all looked over at him. He was standing on one leg, the other braced on the sideboard.

"All right, you little babies, time to get running. And if we call your name, you're out. Let's go. Five, four, three, two . . .!"

Jett ditched me at once and sprinted across the street. I stood a moment, watching everyone take off in different directions. Tana ignored Jett's advice and followed Tyson to the neighbor's yard across the street. They disappeared in the shadows. I decided to run east, toward the next street in our neighborhood—there was another exit on the north side. I searched for Gabriella and Dylan as I crossed the street, but they were nowhere to be found.

The streetlights were out on the next street. I was suddenly scared to be alone, so I took my chances and ran in the open on the sidewalk, hoping the moonlight wouldn't give me away. By the time I passed the fifth house I was out of breath, but close enough to see the entrance to our neighborhood and Jett's back running away from me. I ducked behind a bush and waited when headlights appeared behind me. As the car passed, a scratchy rustle started in the leaves. I jumped up and charged as fast as I could toward the exit.

When I reached Lake Tahoe Boulevard, it was packed with cars, which made it impossible to know which was Jett's. To stay clear of all of them, I kept to the side of the road with no buildings, hiding behind boulders and shrubs against the edge of the woods. The boulevard eventually turned to Interstate 50 at the city's edge, and soon I was alone on the road. After a mile, I was halfway and also out of breath, but the mountainside along the edge of the road was getting too steep. I needed to cross the road.

My foot was almost on the asphalt when I heard Tommy's laugh. I retreated behind a large boulder, then peeked out enough to see them approach. Hayden drove slowly while Tommy directed the searchlight in the back, shining it right at me. *Crap.*

I turned around and crouched down, leaning my back against

the cold rock. The blinding light was only inches from my toes, and I could feel my feet slipping on the pine needles beneath me. I tightened my muscles and breathed in sharply through the burning. Finally, Tommy yelled to Hayden to keep driving, and I released my aching muscles with a sigh.

Snap.

I flipped my head toward a sudden cracking in the trees. It was deep in the woods, where I couldn't see beyond the first few rows of trees. I didn't care if I got caught. I charged toward the street and crossed it as fast as I could.

I didn't stop until I was standing in a small alley behind the local tattoo shop. Its flickering neon lights barely lit the back. I couldn't see well, but I knew I was close. I'd been to Heavenly hundreds of times; its entrance was only a few blocks east. I decided to stay in the alley, behind the trash bins, until I reached the road between me and the entrance. I thought I was moving smoothly along, keeping hidden, when I stepped on a small bump. A loud hiss rose and a cat on its nightly rounds ran away and jumped the wall. *Stupid cat.*

As I turned my back, cursing that it nearly scared me to death, I saw movement in the shadows behind me. A familiar shadowy figure stepped out into the open. I nearly fainted as the blood rushed away from my head. I dug my nails deep into my skin to stay conscious and turned to sprint, but hit my shin on a garbage can. I kept my balance somehow and fled, half hopping from pain.

As the pain eased, I didn't look back—I just sprinted harder. At the end of the alley, a sliver of yellow light from the streetlamp gave me hope. I bolted across the street to the parking lot entrance, trying to get to the gondolas as quickly as possible. But I had forgotten that there was nothing here, only another stretch of poorly paved asphalt that led to the parking lot, and *then* the gondolas. And how could I know that anyone from my team would be there already? I could end up alone.

Dela

I spun around, searching for an escape route. The reflective glimmer of the dark lake caught my eye. As I pivoted toward it, multiple whispers carried on the wind.

"Lucas?"

No one answered, so I took off toward the lake.

My legs burned, but I didn't dare stop. Through the frenzy, I tried focusing on what the whispers were saying. It was a strange language, like what I heard when I blacked out. The voices chanted the same thing over and over, in a unison that was almost tangible, making me wild with panic. When I finally reached the edge of the lake, my lungs were rough like sandpaper, and I coughed horribly as I tried to catch my breath.

A few feet away, the rocky cliff dropped straight down to water far below. I turned my back to the water, not wanting to face what my mind was telling me to do. Tears filled my eyes when the figure glided from the forest into the open. I took a step back. Another emerged out of the forest at my left, closer than the other, and I took another step. With each gliding step they took, I took another one back, praying for another way out. I remembered what they did to that girl on the pyramid.

Soon I was on my toes, my heels teetering over the edge. The glistening water beckoned me to jump. I looked back up, scared, hoping for another way. The creatures were getting nearer—ten feet, seven feet. They were only three feet away when I decided to jump. As my feet lifted into the air, I saw timeless blue eyes behind the predators, stricken with fear.

"Lucas!" I screamed, reaching for him as I fell backwards into the water.

CHAPTER NINE

Safe

Air howled in my ears as the bloodless undead rushed after me, their thirst for death bright in their glowing eyes. My arms flung away from their outstretched bony hands—they promised to reach me, but the dark water caught me first.

Needles of cold glass stabbed along my side. I fought the pain and kicked to stay afloat, but I was sinking, the pressure intense in my ears. A charley horse cramped my calf, and I thrashed my arms, desperate for breath but unable to stretch my leg to kick.

I could see the surface just for a moment, but my lungs drew in water as I raised my hand toward the blurry moon in one last farewell. As my body surrendered, something in the water cinched my waist from behind. A current pressed against my head, and then I emerged headfirst. I gasped and took a breath of the cold air as if it was my last.

"Zara," Lucas said. "Hold on to my arms."

I coughed out water instead of thanks. He held me tighter and swam around the cliff, toward the beach. When I felt rocks underneath my feet, Lucas let go. I stumbled over their smoothness to the beach, collapsed, and coughed up lake. When my heaves eased, I turned to Lucas. He stood on the shore, leaving a careful distance between us. Distress was clear on his face, and I noticed a dim bluish light glowing through his soaked sleeve. Every nerve told me to run screaming, but I didn't. I pushed the dripping hair off my face and observed his arm, remembering its freakish glow at the crash. He stood still, letting me stare, and then he moved, his apologetic expression changing to one of guilt. I struggled to understand what he could be guilty of as he pulled his fingers through his hair, sweeping wet strands off his face, and began to pace nervously.

As he walked back and forth, spinning something small between his fingers, relentless shivers overtook me. The bluish light under his shirt dimmed, and his figure faded to a black silhouette. My bewildered stare went unnoticed as he continued pacing. I wrapped my arms around my legs and curled into a helpless ball, listening to my teeth chatter as I waited for him to say something.

My stomach roiled with doubts that Lucas was human. I uncurled enough to squeeze my sick stomach tightly. He still paced, saying not a word to me. It was only when the clattering of my teeth grew louder that he snapped around to look at me.

"Zara!" He rushed over to place a hand on my shoulder, but I jerked away, scared.

"You're freezing. You need to get warm. I know this is the wrong time to ask, but I need you to trust me," he said.

An uncontrollable shiver turned my nod into a cringe, but Lucas bent down and slid his arm under my shoulders. In a fraction of a breath I was cradled against him. The heat radiating off his body warmed mine instantly, and without asking, I pressed my head against his chest.

Hardly disapproving, he lowered his chin to my ear and whispered, "Shh."

I scanned the dark woods where he was looking, trying to figure out what he meant, and then realized we weren't alone. As he watched for movement in the trees, he kept me tucked against his chest protectively. He waited, and when the trees were still, he took off.

An unexpected blast of wind whipped my face. The tree line rushed past in a black blur against the city's glow. Icy wind froze my wet body. I squeezed my eyes tightly, nestled my cheek against his chest, and breathed in. His tropical scent was ecstasy, perfection. And then I noticed his breath was soft and easy as he sprinted.

Heavenly appeared in the distance across the street, barely visible under the moon's glow. I felt the blood rushing through me now that we were safe. But Lucas stopped abruptly behind a tree.

"What are you doing? We have to get out of here!" I yelled as he peeked out at the dark street.

"No, not like this. Here she comes."

My neck cranked stiffly in that direction. Gabriella and Dylan were running toward us, but it was hard to follow them when they moved at the same velocity as Lucas.

"Zara, you mustn't say anything about what you saw to your friends. Do you understand?" Lucas asked.

My lip trembled. "How do you know about the shadows?"

"There will be time to talk later," he rushed. "I need your word."

"Okay. I won't."

It was easy to give in when his lips were so close to mine, but they moved farther away as he looked back up.

"All right . . ." his voice trailed off as his sister approached us.

"Zara!" Gabriella cried. She turned to Lucas angrily. "Where were you? You were supposed to be on her trail."

"I was until one locked me down," he argued back.

"What?" Gabriella gasped.

Dylan looked past our shoulders to the lake. "They know."

"Know what? Who?" I asked.

"Nonsense," Gabriella snorted. "All they know is that this is the third time we've impeded. *Hijole!*" She threw her hands up in the air in disbelief.

"Gabriella, we don't have time for this, nor is this the place. You have to change clothes with her now; she's freezing," Lucas directed.

Before the initial shock of what he was saying settled in, Gabriella's clothes were on the ground and she was in her bra and underwear. Lucas set me down and turned around, creating a false wall of privacy. *Was he serious?*

"Dylan," Lucas yelled sideways. *Oh, he is.*

Dylan chuckled, then folded his arms as he gave us his back.

Gabriella peeled my clothes off in layers. I tried to help, but my numb fingers wouldn't move properly. When the sweater came off, the wind bit at my skin. It didn't stop until Gabriella's long pants and sheer shirt were over me. She handed me a light jacket that smelled like roses.

She stood. "Now what?"

Lucas spun around, his gaze criminal enough to make me wonder how ridiculous I looked in Gabriella's clothes, but his smile was dangerous. "Good."

Before we could speak, headlights shone through the base of the trees. Loud, reckless laughter followed. We turned simultaneously.

"Gabriella, Dylan, go! Tell them I followed Zara to the edge of the lake, we started messing around, and she fell in," Lucas schemed.

The height of their raised eyebrows implied their assumptions. I blushed.

Lucas only smiled a little though, half-serious. "Not like that. Tell them I will be bringing Zara home. Then go to Bri's, get my car, and meet us here."

"In my bra and underwear? You're funny. Dylan, you do it. I'll meet you at home," Gabriella said.

Didn't they live at Fallen Leaf Lake? Before I could say this was a highly impractical plan, Dylan nodded, and they ran back to the other side of the road. My head spun, wondering not only how long they would take, but also how Gabriella would make it back unnoticed in only a bra and underwear. We weren't too far from home, but it was a good walk, farther if she was going to Fallen Leaf. Plus, I was still freezing with my wet hair. Gabriella had to be freezing too. I leaned back against a tree and looked to Lucas anew.

"How have you been keeping this from me?" I asked, overwhelmed.

He focused on the ground and paced, two fingers rubbing a circle on his temple. "When I heard that you girls were going to Reno, I had Gabriella go to make sure you would not be alone."

"No," I corrected. "Bri *invited* Gabriela. She didn't come because you planned it."

He looked down at me, a clear expression of confidence in his version. My mouth dropped.

"Who are you?" I asked.

"I am . . . the good guy." He smiled and gave a light chuckle. "For lack of a better word."

"Compared to who?" I asked, grabbing my head, which was now hurting badly.

"My life, it's complicated, Zara. I am the good guy compared to those shadows, all right?" he said, frustration coloring his words.

I laughed. "You're comparing yourself to shadows? Seriously?"

"They aren't what you think. *I'm* not what you think."

His head snapped in my direction as I muttered under my breath, and yet he still knelt easily by my side.

"Look, I like you. But I don't want you to get involved with me because of this," he said.

"You could have had me fooled," I said, turning my face away.

"I'm serious, Zara. You shouldn't joke."

"Don't flatter yourself. I was *talking* about the shadows."

Lucas seemed stumped for the first time. It felt nice.

"They were chasing *me* tonight, not you. But you already knew that, didn't you?" The evidence was clear in his frozen face. "Why are they chasing me, Lucas?"

A line of white light blazed through the dense trunks. Lucas shot up, ignoring my question.

"They're here," he said as his car and Dylan's convertible spun around the corner.

"Great," I groused, trying to figure out how they got here so fast. I tried to mask my disappointment. I was angry, but suddenly I didn't know what I wanted. I felt safe with Lucas and wanted to stay. As I stood up and brushed the dirt off, Lucas held a hand out to stop me.

"No, we're staying," he said. It almost sounded like a command. Chills ran down my spine, and yet I loved the thrill.

"Did you have any problems?" Lucas asked as Gabriella handed him the keys. She had changed into a skirt and short top that showed off her midriff. *How was she not cold?*

"Nothing, brother. But we can't be sure you're safe tonight. Mother said to come home soon," she replied.

She gracefully slid into the orange convertible, and they sped away in screeches and smoke as Lucas opened the door of his car. There was a dry set of clothes folded on the passenger seat. He pulled shorts and a T-shirt out and set them on the hood before briefly looking back up with a grin.

"Turn around, please," he said.

I obeyed, trying not to think too much about the fact that Lucas was changing out of his clothes, and at very close range. When he finished, he stuck the keys in his pocket and headed down the unmarked path toward the lake a few steps before he turned. "You coming?"

Adrenaline spiked through me, and I jogged after him. "Where are we going?"

"I need to show you something."

He walked fast. It was impossible to see anything in the dark without a flashlight. My ankles were weak on the uneven ground, and I knew I was slowing him down, but he was patient and even gentlemanly, pausing to hold branches out of my way. My fear receded when there was humanity visible in him.

"Has Gabriella seen those shadow things before?" I asked Lucas's back.

"Yup." I could practically see his smile as he popped the *p*.

He held the last green curtain out of my path, revealing lake before us, clouded by fog. He reached for my hand, and I jumped at the familiar rush of tingles.

"Relax. As long as you're with me, you're safe. I would never let anything happen to you," he said, lowering his thumb over the back of my hand. A beat of warmth swirled inside me suddenly, and I felt weaker.

As he led me to the shore through the wall of opaque cloud, I saw fireflies flying above the water, glowing in the fog like twinkling fiber-optic stars. My heart started racing. He was taking me to a place where, if anything happened, no one would see.

"I'm sorry. It's been a really long night, and I have a terrible headache, and I . . ." I began to explain dizzily, slowly resisting his pull toward the water.

" . . . have plenty of excuses," he finished, pulling me with more effort.

His blunt response took me aback, and I wondered if I could trust him. I mean, I wanted to, as enticing as his handsome Latin features were. But there was something inside me, something dark, that lurked in anger.

"Look, I'll take you home in a moment, but please, I am running out of time. Give me five minutes?" he asked.

I shook with the rush of different emotions, but mostly fear as my heartbeat intensified. *What if I don't like what he tells me?* I folded an arm across the hard pounding and bit nervously at my fingernails. He left me and walked toward the water.

"Can I trust you?" he asked, stepping onto the light film of cold, black water covering the river rock. I watched him in the haze as he crouched down.

"Yes," I hiccupped nervously.

"Very well then, come here."

His voice magnetized me, flattening my fear as I walked to him through the swirling fog. My heart beat erratically as he waited, calm, his elbows on his knees.

When I was close enough, he checked that I was watching, then touched the lake. He raised his dripping fingertips and ran them gently over the black markings on his left arm. The hieroglyphic tattoo glowed turquoise. It was extraordinary, but scary, and left my body tingling with strange excitement.

"Lucas, why is your tattoo glowing?" I asked, freaked out.

He watched me steadily. "It does this to remind me of where I come from and who I am."

I backed away when he stood.

"Who are you?"

His intimate eyes were cautious when he took another step closer to me. I looked down, unable to remove my eyes from the neon glow rising from his arm. "Those shadows and I are from similar realms." He paused. "There are things in this world that aren't what you would call normal."

"Things? Others besides those shadows?" My lips moved, though I was unsure of what I was saying, much less believing. My blackout was *only* a blackout. It couldn't be real—that girl *couldn't* be dead.

"Yes."

"Are you human?" I blurted out, steadying a foot behind me.

He chuckled, taking another careful step toward me. "Hardly. But would it count if I said I was human—well, sort of—at one point in my life?"

"Why are those things after me?" I rushed, taking another blind step back. His tattoo was dimming, or his arm was drying.

"I'm curious." His eyes squinted in speculation as he continued to close on me. "I am going to try and say this as politely as possible: have you been with anyone before?"

"Excuse me?" I asked, offended.

"Have you ever been with a guy before?" His feet finally stopped, and his jaw went hard as he gulped. "Intimately?"

I was suddenly glad for the fog to cover the rush of color to my cheeks, though it seemed he was blushing too.

"What does that have to do with anything?" I asked, recalling as I did that one night I'd made it to second base with my friend Adam.

All I heard was a sigh of relief. "Good."

"I didn't answer you!"

He grinned tolerantly. "You said enough."

Whatever he was, he was clever. But it scared me that I might actually have feelings for him. I looked away to mask my feelings, upset with myself.

"So what now?" I muttered. But it was only a moment before I found myself goggling at him once more.

"I haven't figured it out yet," he said, his face void of any expression. He picked up a rock and skipped it far over the water, too distant for me to see where it finally sank. "But we should probably take you home."

I nodded.

When we got in the car, my breath stuttered as Lucas leaned over toward my door. He looked up with a naughty smile as if he fully knew the effect he had on me. "Seatbelt."

"Right," I said stupidly.

I had a bazillion questions to ask, but did I dare ask? Should I wait? I couldn't get over my nerves or the knots in my stomach, so I kept quiet and stared out the dark window. When we pulled into my neighborhood, I expected him to start shedding some light on the evening's events, but when he pulled up to my house, the only thing he said was, "Are you going to be okay?"

The deep-rooted anger erupted.

"Define *okay*. If *okay* means bumps and bruises, yes, I will be fine. But it's more than that. You know things that I think I deserve to know," I said, overwrought with exhaustion. "And what did you mean when you said you were running out of time?"

"You shouldn't know this much. It's not safe."

I ignored him. "You said you were from the same *realm* as the shadows. Are you an alien or something?"

He chuckled. "No, I am from Earth."

"Can I trust you?"

Sadness took over his eyes. "You probably shouldn't."

"And Gabriella and Dylan—can I trust them?"

His smile twisted as he shook his head, contemplating. Then he grinned widely, knowing already that I'd hate his response. "Probably not them either."

I threw open the car door.

"I get it," I said, bending over to see his face.

He rested his elbow on the steering wheel casually and looked at me. "You do?"

"Yes. You are trouble, and Gabriella is trouble. Wherever you are, those *things* will be. Just leave me alone, Lucas. Stop following me . . . I don't need your protection . . . and . . . I don't need you to pretend to care."

I slammed his door closed before he could reply and stormed to the porch. Once I was on the other side of the front door, I leaned against it for strength. *What did I just do?* I wasn't sure what had just happened, but now I was more scared than ever.

Chapter Ten

Abandoned

I hid in my room all weekend like a lunatic hermit, afraid to leave as theories of who or what Lucas could be rained down in my head. Eventually my confusion drove me to pure madness. I felt weak and vulnerable until, abruptly, as I got ready for school Monday morning, one idea began a constant ticking: *Staying away from Lucas might* not *be in my best interests.*

The frost on the grass didn't really surprise me, not in early October, but the rumors at school did. People were saying that Lucas had moved.

"What?" I blurted, almost choking on my carrot at lunch.

"Yeah, their dad got another offer back in Mexico," Ashley said, combing her fingers through her red hair. "Heard all about it in English when Gabriella didn't show up."

"But what does his dad even do?" I asked.

"No one knows at the *Tahoe Review Journal,* and *they* know everything," Tyson said, popping a tater tot into his mouth.

The news tightened the knots in my stomach. Within an hour, they were so big that I had to make bathroom runs throughout class to wet my face. As I leaned over the porcelain sink and splashed the cold water on my cheeks, I looked at myself in the mirror. A pale face, almost green, stared back when I realized I had been wrong.

Dela

Without Lucas, I feared for my life.

Every day without Lucas I was more on edge, believing that the rumors were actually true. After school on Friday, as I drove home past the pumpkin patch, watching the pickers get wet in the light drizzle, I suddenly remembered the book Mae had given me. My gut told me it was a good place to start investigating my suspicions—whatever those were. When I got home, though, Max and Casey's car was not what I wanted to see.

"Hey, sis. Miss us?" Max said, leaning back on the breakfast bar as I walked through the door. His hair had grown shaggier, and he was chomping repulsively over a large plate of nachos.

It was disgusting. Imagining his stomach as a bottomless pit, I looked away and started for the stairs.

"Is Jett going out with you tonight?" Max yelled. I ignored him and kept ascending. "What is that kid doing tonight, Case?"

"I don't know. I'll call him," Casey said.

I closed my bedroom door and crossed to my desk. I picked up the burgundy book, wiped off the collected dust, and opened it slowly. The hardbound cover creaked as I turned to the title page, *Legends of the New World*.

A couple of pages in, I knew this wasn't a mass-produced book. Blotches of ink spattered the pages as if cast off a quill, and the fine paper was filled with drawings and tiny notes underneath that looked handwritten. It was scribbled cursive, as if the author was in a hurry, making it look more like a journal than a book. I skipped to the back cover to search for sources or an author, but there was nothing.

I flipped back through the book until one picture caught my eye. It was a set of twins. The caption read, "The Hero Twins." I leaned in closer, focusing on the small drawing. The artist's notes called these twins gods, but they looked like savages in breechcloths, one with a Mohawk and the other with long hair in a ponytail. The

Mohawk twin held a ball the size of a grapefruit, while the other held a tomahawk.

Something about their broad physique and the way they stood seemed familiar. The boy on the left I was almost positive I recognized. Then suddenly my breath cut short and I choked. My eyes widened with bewilderment. It couldn't be. I pushed the thought out and pressed my fingers hard into the book to read the names underneath the drawing: "Hunahpu and Xibalanque." I looked back into the eyes of the boy on the left, unbelieving, and determined that his face belonged to someone I knew . . . Dylan Castillo.

I threw the book shut and scratched my chin. It couldn't possibly be Dylan. That would be ridiculous. But my finding fed a curiosity I couldn't ignore. I hesitated, but before I knew it, I was turning back to the page. I stared at it hard. *How are the drawing and Dylan so close?* I turned the page to another picture, skipping a few paragraphs of writing. It was a sketch of a city set on the edge of a tall cliff overlooking an ocean. It was beautiful. The caption called it Tulum.

As I moved to the next drawing, my anxiety intensified. It was an entire page full of pictures I knew I'd seen before. There were six distinct drawings, similarly mazy, but each different in itself. One I was positive was an exact replica of Lucas's tattoo. It had the circle, the mazelike lines, the star, and the tree. My eyes zoomed to the scribbled cursive above it: "Markings of the Royal Gods." *Gods?* I quickly looked underneath the picture. The caption read, "Aztec Prince." I blinked hard, closed the book quickly, and sat up, stumped.

Before I even considered accepting Lucas as an Aztec prince, sure that I was losing my mind, I needed to leave. I aimed for the grocery store to purchase something—anything with high sugar content. But under the grim sky on my way home, with a seat full of candy, I thought I saw movement through the forest. I pressed my foot against the gas pedal without thinking, hoping to reach home before something else reached me.

Dela

By the time I turned onto my street, the late sky had cleared, creating the perfect cloudless dusk. Jett's car was parked on the curb, dewy from the afternoon showers. I shifted to park with a deep breath, still imagining I was being followed, and braced myself for the run from my car to the front door. I counted to three, then opened the door and fled for the house.

I was surprised to find all the drapes drawn when I stampeded inside. It was dark, with the kind of quietness that raised the hairs on my arms.

"Jett?" I called out, slowly taking a step toward the stairs.

I scanned the front living room through the dimness while I waited for him to say something. But I heard nothing.

"Jett?" This time my voice was trembling as I tried to speak up. *Maybe he didn't hear me.* "Jett?"

I didn't see any movement in the living room, so I moved on to the family room like a victim in a horror film. *Where's that stupid light switch?* My hand fumbled along the wall as I got past the stairs, feeling around for the plastic cover. Before my hand could flip the switch, a loud "BOO" sounded at my side.

"AHH!" My arms flew to the sides, knocking over some pictures on the end table. Jett laughed.

"I'm going to kill you! Why'd you do that?" I screamed, practically feeling my veins popping out of my neck.

I didn't wait for an answer. I was already rushing up to my room as the first tear fell. I didn't want Jett to see me emotional like this, but a knock sounded on the bedroom door the second I slammed it shut.

"What?" I hollered. I flipped on my light and sniffed. The air smelled like Lucas, as it had when I returned from the hospital.

"Zara, it's Jett. I'm sorry. Look, don't be mad. We just thought it would be funny."

But I wasn't listening. I stepped away from the door and

followed my nose. The trail brought me closer to the window, and then I saw it. There, sitting on the windowsill, was another vase with a single fire-and-ice rose. A piece of ripped parchment paper was tied around the rim of the glass with twine. My hands trembled as I reached for the paper.

I'M SORRY.

I swept the shades away from the window and searched the street for him. When I saw nothing but the gold light of dusk, disappointment and fear settled in. The rumors at school were true. I was utterly alone.

"Zara, did you hear what I said?" Jett called through the door.

I strode to the door, ready to kill that boy, and threw it open, creating a wall of wind that blew through Jett's hair. He took a step back, looking scared.

"You have no idea what I've been through the past few weeks, so please, spare me the stupid games," I said.

"Well then tell me, because I don't like who you are right now. What happened?"

I puffed exhaustedly and retreated to my bed, where I fell on my back and stared up at the ceiling. "Never mind, forget it."

"No. Tell me." He stepped through my parents' invisible *do not cross* tape between the hall and my bedroom and joined me on the bed. "I'm concerned about you."

He looked to the rose on the window and put some pieces together. "Did Lucas do anything to you when we were playing the night games?"

I felt stiff as I turned my head to him. Eight years had passed since Jett was last in my room. He sat there hunched over, with his elbows on his knees, a boy who was sincerely concerned and confused. His brown eyes were soft when he asked me again. "Did he?"

I looked back up to the ceiling again, not able to bear Jett's sudden love for me. "No," I answered. "Lucas didn't *do* anything."

Once I said it, I shook my head incredulously, and my shoulders shook as I started laughing. Lucas *didn't* do anything. Not literally, and yet I held him responsible for everything. Jett had no idea of the measure of trouble I had been in since my car crashed that night. He had no idea of my migraines, the visions I had when I blacked out, or the creatures that had been chasing me. All of it was too unreasonable to explain to him . . .to anyone.

"I have just been a little spooked lately, that's all. Your joke came at the wrong time for me. Sorry, I shouldn't have flipped out on you," I lied.

"Really?" he asked. He seemed to doubt me at first, but eventually his squint went away, and he looked down at the ground. "I had no idea."

"Well, now you do," I said, resting my hands across my ribcage.

Mom appeared at the door, looking at us sternly. "Oh, good afternoon, Jett. You know the rules."

"Yes, Mrs. Moss," he answered as he shot to the door, where he leaned for a moment. "I planned for us to do a bonfire tonight, but we can reschedule it for another night if you want."

"No, that's fine. I just don't want to be alone," I said.

"When can you be ready?"

"Twenty minutes?"

"All right. I'll go pick up Tommy and Bri, get the wood and lighter fluid, and come back to get you," he said before fleeing downstairs.

By the time I got off the bed, there was a warm dent in the shape of my body. I dressed warmly, pulled a beanie over my head, and walked to Jett's truck without enthusiasm. Tommy and Bri were in the back of the cab, and Max and Casey sat in the truck's bed, whistling obnoxiously at me as I got into the truck. The only thing good about leaving was watching the twins freeze as Jett accelerated onto the freeway.

The 52nd

The last bit of sun was setting as we entered our usual bonfire area, a little clearing flush with the lakeshore, filled with soft sand and fallen logs. Loud music and laughter swirled in the cab, but I stared out my window at the brilliant streaks of orange, purple, and pink in the sky, dreading its darkening. It was black by the time the fire was lit. I was paranoid, checking over my shoulders and across the lake for any movement, constantly observing my surroundings.

Then, out of nowhere, headlights shone on the fire. I followed the hazy beam to the approaching car as it parked next to Jett's truck and its lights went off. At once I recognized the red sedan, and fumes ignited at my core. All four doors opened, and five snobby cheerleaders stepped out.

"Who invited them?" I looked meaningfully at Jett.

Max got up and walked toward them, smiling. "I did."

"Why, man?" Jett asked, sounding truly upset.

"I hate you," I yelled at Max.

"Relax, they don't mean any harm. Ladies!" Max held his hands like a circus ringleader, inviting them to come to the fire.

Poppy spotted us and snickered as she walked over to the twins.

I stood. "Jett, get me out of here right now."

"What about Max and Casey?"

We looked at them simultaneously. The twins were sitting on a log, each with a girl sitting on each leg. Jett turned back to me and nodded. "All right. Tommy, Bri, we're leaving."

They were cuddled together on a log, maybe a little too comfortable for an audience.

"Bri's parents aren't home. Can you take us there?" Tommy asked.

"Yeah, sure. Let's just leave . . . now," Jett said.

Without a word, Tommy stood and pulled a giggling Bri toward Jett's truck.

When we got back home, my anxiety didn't get any better. I was surprised to see the house completely dark. Jett followed me inside and watched as I dashed through the house, obsessively turning on every light.

"You going to be okay alone?" he asked.

My feet froze. *Alone?* I pushed past Jett and ran outside to the driveway. My parents' cars were gone.

"I'm coming with you to take Tommy and Bri home," I stated, marching back to the truck.

"Um, okay." Jett nodded without argument.

When Jett pulled up to my house a second time, I was relieved to see that my parents had finally come home.

"Thanks for the ride," I said as I opened the door.

Jett's hand reached for my arm. "Hey."

I looked from the hand clasped around my arm to his face, which was grim in the light from the green dashboard.

"I just want you to know that Poppy has nothing on you," he said.

I looked away. This was neither the place nor time for a heart-to-heart with Jett. "Good night, Jett."

The moment the metal of his door clanked shut, I had the feeling something was following me in the dark. I speed-walked up the grass until Jett's car drove away, then sprinted to the porch, my hands already reaching for the handle of the front door. I stormed into the house and slammed the door shut behind me, but stopped short when I saw Dad in the living room reading a book by the lamp. He cast a funny look at me over his reading glasses.

"Oh, hi Dad." I laughed awkwardly.

"*What* are you doing?"

"Nothing. I just hate being in the dark by myself."

"Since when?"

"Since now. Good night," I called, skipping steps upstairs.

The only thing calming when I walked into my room was the lingering scent of Lucas. I walked to the window and sat down on the windowsill. I picked up his good-bye note once more and wondered why he'd left. Then I saw Mae's book peeking out of my purse. In a flash his note was falling to the floor and I was running for the book, desperate for answers. I sat at the desk, flipped the light on, and began reading from the beginning.

It wasn't until my head knocked against the desk that I realized I'd fallen asleep. So I walked to the bathroom, brushed my teeth, and washed my face in an attempt to stay awake. I slipped into my flannel pajamas and rubbed my neck as I settled back down at the small desk.

I decided to skim through the pictures and leave the rest of the reading for morning. First I returned to the page with the picture of Lucas's tattoo. I was certain it was an exact replica. But the way the roots twisted and curled around the trunk of the tree also reminded me of the one I saw in my blackout. I didn't want to look at it anymore—or didn't want to see the connection—and instead hopped over to the page with the twins, realizing that the ball the god was holding looked similar to the one in the tattoo on Dylan's calf.

I flipped the pages more quickly now. Halfway through was an odd sketch of a map with one half missing. A few pages later, I found a drawing of a barefoot woman with short, spiky hair. When I looked into the friendliness of her beautiful smile, I paused, cupping my hand over my mouth as my head began to spin. This woman had a tattoo, just like all the other members of the Castillo family. I found my eyes drawn to the caption underneath: "*La bruja.*"

I fumbled for the Spanish–English dictionary at the corner of my desk, near the bottom of last year's book pile, and opened it quickly to the Bs. When I saw the word *bruja*, I jolted back to the sketch, unable to withstand the anticipation or the turning of my stomach. It read, "witch {charmer, sorceress; a person who cast spells on others}." I zoomed back to the woman in the drawing, who didn't look anything like a witch. Her friendly features were young and playful, but the evidence pointed me toward an unexplainable conclusion. I'd seen her with the Castillo family at Lucky Pin.

I had to move on, but when I turned the page, I immediately closed the book, afraid that the creatures shown there would come alive and get me. Although it was absurd, I placed another book on top of Mae's to weigh it down and went to bed for the evening, with the lights *on*.

When I woke up the next morning it was sunny, but a darkness seemed to hover over the burgundy book. I felt tricked when I found myself sitting down again to open the leather-bound journal. My shaky fingers turned the frail pages with caution until I reached the page where I'd stopped. The drawing seemed less scary in the daytime, although I still envisioned it coming to life.

The sketch of two entities filled an entire page. The one on the left was a shadow identical to the ones I'd seen during the night games. Its hazy shape was precisely what I remembered, a human figure with hollow eye sockets and long fingers. The picture to the right showed a skeletal man, the same size as the shadow, but only partially covered with skin, with his innards on the outside. The identical midnight eyes proved that these were the same monster—and worse, the creatures of my blackout world. A shredded breechcloth was wrapped around the naked skeleton's waist, and he wore strange armor over his head.

Only a few words were written underneath these drawings: "*Demonio de mundo terrenal.*" In seconds I was searching the dictionary for a translation. I shuffled through the pages to the letter *D*. There, *demonio*—I followed the typed words to the right: "demon." I jumped back and started shaking my hands as if I could ward the knowledge off.

No, no, no. Demons do not exist. The words repeated in my mind. Suddenly I felt an awful flow of fluid heaving up my throat, an upswelling of filth. I rushed to the bathroom, threw my hands down for support, and splattered the toilet with rancid liquid. *Right, I missed dinner, didn't I?* My stomach cramped with nauseous hunger as I wiped my mouth and swiped my toothbrush through it. Then I went downstairs to raid the kitchen, leaving the old journal for another time.

"Hey, Mom," I moaned, rubbing my stomach. I opened the fridge and pulled out the first thing I saw, a carton of orange juice.

Mom flipped a blueberry pancake on the skillet and looked at the oven clock. "You're up early."

"I couldn't sleep well."

"Are you sick?" she asked, observing my pale skin.

"No." I tried to sip the orange juice, but it didn't sit right in my stomach. I left it in front of me untouched, my attention drifting out the kitchen window to the flying leaves in the backyard. Max and Casey were outside, hunched over in the dirt. "*What* are the boys doing, and *why* so early on a Saturday?"

"We got a call from jail last night." Mom didn't move her head, but her eyes swept to the back window and over the twins. "Your dad had to bail them out at three in the morning; he put them on family community service to pay him back."

I laughed, feeling a little better.

"You should have seen their faces when we picked them up." She laughed.

"Wait *we*? You left me alone last night?" I panicked.

"Yes, you were asleep."

"Why didn't you wake me up?" I asked frantically, my forehead sweating.

Mom laughed again as she sat down at the bar. "And wake you up? You're hilarious." Then she buried her nose in a fashion magazine. As a retired pageant queen, she was religious about keeping up with the latest styles, even though our funds didn't allow her to buy Gucci. "Why on earth would I do that?"

"Because it's irresponsible." I pounded the counter, raising my voice. "You'll get child protective services called on you!"

Mom looked up from the colorful pages and laughed again. "You are seventeen, Zara. You're a big girl."

"Ugh. Don't do that, Mom."

"Dad said you were a little on edge last night. You're not tripping, are you?" Her eyes stopped dead on mine, searching suspiciously. I lost my appetite.

"What? Mom, no. That's disgusting," I said, appalled.

I glanced at the twins once more. As much as I wanted to be entertained by Max and Casey pulling weeds at seven on a Saturday morning, I felt drawn back to my bedroom and the mulch of my depression and self-pity. Maybe I was in denial or just scared stupid, but either way, I was not picking up that book ever again. It didn't matter. I had been abandoned.

CHAPTER ELEVEN

Hallow's Eve

It was mid-October, and a thin white film crunched underneath my feet as I trekked across the lawn.

"What is that awful smell?" I asked, hopping into Bri's car. The sun sparkled through the frost-webbed corners of my wagon's windshield as we passed it. I sighed.

"It's my new caramel lotion, and if you don't like it, you can drive your own damn car." Bri stared ahead without the slightest glance at me. "Tell me again why you don't want to drive yourself? You're going to flunk your history class if you never go."

"Like you care about my classes. And besides, I don't need to show up to pass. I can study from the textbook on my own."

"Why can't you just drive your own stupid car?"

Bri's annoyance with me over the past couple of weeks was finally erupting, and I took full responsibility. My headaches were constant, I complained whenever I wasn't being a jerk, and I was spooked to death that I would be chased again, or maybe even black out while I was driving. Bottom line, I didn't want to be alone. I was upset that Lucas had left. I needed him, and while I thought of him often, I also thought of the vomit-inducing book that continued to collect dust on my desk.

"I told you, I can't drive because of my migraines," I lied.

Bri pinched her lips and remained silent. I wondered how much longer I could hitch rides with her.

"After the party," she said.

"What?"

"After the Halloween party—you know, big shindig, costumes, punch, keeps the students from driving drunk?—after that, I'm done. Your car is perfectly good to drive, and you *obviously* are perfectly fine too. I'm not buying your crap. You have until Halloween to figure your mess out and make your life normal again. This carpool thing is not good for our relationship."

I looked out the window, feeling ghostly as the blood left my head. "Okay."

When I woke on Halloween morning two weeks later, I knew something wasn't right. The hair on my arms stood up. A new headache began midmorning and then, at lunch—just my luck—nausea joined the party. I took medicine for the headache and tried to shrug the nerves away, but the sickness was relentless. The bad feeling that came when Lucas left, which never went away no matter what I did, now grew exponentially.

Going out that night made me feel doomed. I didn't feel human. My fingers were cold and unresponsive, and it took nearly two hours to get ready. I stared at the crimson silk dress Bri had brought for me and clutched at a lurching feeling in my stomach. I kept its contents down long enough to tug and squeeze and suck into that silk.

Spicy fumes made their way into my room. My stomach grumbled payback for boycotting food all day, but I ignored it, even though my mouth watered desperately. I looked into the mirror, emotionless, vaguely seeing the historical dress encasing me. The corset was tight, not only pushing my breasts up but also making it hard to breathe, and I fell into a daze. An irksome voice rose from the depths, where my worst fear resided: *so this is what I will look like when I die.*

the 52nd

A noise scratched in the air. It vibrated over and over until I finally recognized Bri's voice downstairs.

"Zara, you up there?" Bri called again.

My eyes strained on my reflection as I choked out a feeble response. "I'm here."

"Hurry. It's a good forty-minute drive."

A new shiver went down my spine as I hiked my skirt out of the way and sent my body downstairs to what felt like my funeral.

It was dark in the house except for the mini lights wrapped around the banisters, which sent clusters of orange and purple light ricocheting across the stairs.

Bri fretted at her cakey face in the mirror. Most of her hair was pulled up smoothly into a bun, leaving tight curls falling down to frame her face. Her pale yellow dress had much more intricate detail than mine, with bone-colored buttons and white lace edging the sleeves and corset. And by the look of her bulging breasts, I could tell it wasn't her seamstress but Bri who decided to make the corset extra tight.

"Really, Bri?" I asked, briefly comparing our chests.

She looked down at the round pudginess below her chin and shrugged innocently. "What?"

"Remind me why we all decided to dress as Sleepy Hollow characters."

"The girls chose and the boys just did what we said. You would know if you'd get your head out of the clouds and listen for a change."

I rolled my eyes to the door. "Let's just get this over with."

Farther down the road, Bri turned on the radio. Her singing was like screeching in my ears. Later, when she started squealing the high notes, I shut off the radio.

"Hey, I was listening to that."

"No, you were killing it. Bri, come on, you can't sing," I said, looking at the speedometer as she entered the freeway. "Slow down!"

It wasn't just the speed that coiled my fear. My stomach cramped when I realized that we were past the city lights, and tall, black trees now surrounded us. I hugged my arms snugly around my belly and wheezed.

Bri looked at me strangely. "I'm only going five over the speed limit."

"Well, you're freaking me out."

Her foot let off the gas. "Happy?"

"Thank you."

Bri kept her face forward and didn't say a word the rest of the drive. I didn't mind. I kept my eyes on the dark trees. She exited the El Dorado Freeway and joined a train of headlights snaking toward a canyon. The party was in a barn in an abandoned pasture between Angora Lake and Echo Lake. The deeper Bri drove into the canyon, the more my sickness built up and my breathing became shallow.

"We're here," Bri said. The brake lights of the car in front of us glowed red on her face as she coasted to the shoulder.

I felt clammy. I rubbed my palms on my dress and squirmed in my seat. Feeling panicked, I turned to look at the narrow, tree-lined road that led to the barn. It was nearly black under the trees. The sick worry in my stomach grew into a stabbing sensation as my corset's deathly grip suddenly pinched out every ounce of air I had. *I have to go in there?* I started fanning my face with my hand, feeling hotter by the second.

"Can you breathe in that thing?" I squeaked.

"What are you doing? It's fifty degrees outside." Bri sounded annoyed. She reached into her backseat, grabbed a paper, and starting fanning me. "Get a hold of yourself; you're embarrassing, for crying out loud. And yes, I can breathe in this thing."

She hopped out of the car and leaned back in, her breasts threatening to fall out of her dress. "You've been all weird ever since Lucas left. Whatever creepy fetish you two have with each other is between you two. *I* prefer to remain normal." She straightened up and looked around.

I hauled myself out and shot back, "*You* aren't normal, and I *don't* have a fetish."

A draft of mountain air frosted my breath, and I reached for my jacket.

"What are you doing?" Bri hissed. She ran around the car with a repulsed expression and snatched it away.

"What? I'm cold."

I reached for it, but she tossed it into the car. "These dresses are *not* supposed to be covered up by jackets."

I ignored her and grabbed it. As I slipped it on, Bri turned and waved to the arriving cars. Boys in strange costumes leaned out of windows, cheap beers in hand, shouting random words to people standing around—like us. *This is ridiculous. I shouldn't be here.* Bri was bobbing up and down, her hands clapping rapidly together. "College is so much better than high school," she crowed. "Ooh, there's Jett. Let's go catch up."

He was in a crowd of kids heading down the small trail. Stretchy white fabric clung to his calves.

"Are you wearing tights?" Bri laughed as we came up behind him.

"Yes," he groaned. "Who the hell chose Sleepy Hollow? Worst idea ever." His hand moved to his tight leggings and began shifting parts around.

"Gross." I gagged.

"Where's Tommy?" Bri asked.

Jett pointed up the line. "Up there with Hayden and Ashley. They wouldn't wait for me." Another shift. "Man, my crotch is killing me."

Bri chirped, did that weird clapping thing again where her hands flapped like a hummingbird, and ran ahead.

"If I'm going to be walking with you, leave your crotch out of it," I said.

Jett laughed, glancing down. "What's wrong with my crotch?"

I rolled my eyes. "You talk like it's your baby."

"Good point. So, I've been writing some new songs."

"Oh yeah?"

"My EP is doing pretty good. I've been getting pressure to start an album."

"From who?"

"I thought you were following me on YouTube," he said, surprised.

"I haven't really had time," I said, feeling that the forked fingers of the black branches threatened to reach forward and snatch me. I edged closer to Jett.

He put his hands in the pockets of his jacket and stared at the dirt. "A couple of my songs have gone viral. Someone pretty big I guess saw me and wanted to see more."

"So are you going to do it?"

He laughed. "It's not like that, Zara. You don't just make an album with no intention of pursuing that career."

"That's not what I asked."

We took a few more steps toward a dark covered bridge. Slivers of moonlight hit its roof through the trees. Eyeing just how dark it was inside, I stepped on the heel of the person in front of us as I maneuvered myself between Jett and another schoolmate. I looped my hand over the crook of Jett's elbow and leaned my cheek close to his shoulder. As I set foot on the first plank I squinted.

"What's with you, Zara?" Jett asked, squeezing back.

Out of nowhere, amid the rush of water in the stream below and the others' talking, I heard a deep chant, a whispering tune that seemed to echo in the wind.

"Do you hear that?" I asked.

He raised his chin enough to look around. "Hear what?"

Fear spread through me, and the corset pinched my organs as I squeezed Jett's arm harder. I closed my eyes and let him lead me across the bridge. When the sound beneath my feet changed to dirt crunching, I opened them and relaxed. We were descending into the open meadow. There was the barn, barely visible through the unmown grass. It was lit festively with vibrant lights, and as we got closer, I saw that it was two stories high. The large front door was cracked open, and light escaped through it into the night as a thick beam.

"Don't leave me tonight," I said.

Jett's hand overlapped mine. "I won't."

A stream of colors welcomed us as we followed the kids inside. The barn had a dance floor with live music, colorful spotlights, and cheerful swaths of streamers. The single room was huge. I had to crane my neck to see the ceiling.

Bri and Tommy poked through the crowd, holding hands.

"Zara, Jett!" Bri called.

Tommy dropped a shoulder and leaned into Jett. "Are you good, for later?"

"Good for what?" I asked.

"It's nothing," Jett responded.

"They're going to play a prank," Bri said.

"Guys, no," I said frantically. They looked confused. "I mean . . . the dean is here. What if you got caught?"

"Zara, come on, it's just a fun joke."

"No, it's not. Nothing ever is with you guys. You'll take it too far," I argued.

Tommy looked to Jett. "Jett, take care of her."

"Excuse me?" I said, taking a step closer to Tommy.

Jett stepped between us. "Zara, go get a drink with Bri, and by the time you're done, I'll be back."

"Back? Where are you going?"

"Nowhere. I'm just stepping out for a minute."

"Don't go alone," I asked.

I felt Bri's hands slip around my shoulders. "Come on, Zara. It'll be quick."

Yes, it would be quick. As Bri pushed me along, all I could think of was how quickly those demons almost had me.

"I'm not going alone," Jett assured me.

I shrugged Bri's hands away and looked him square in the eye. "You have two minutes."

I watched as Tommy disappeared to the back of the barn while Jett exited through the front. Then I walked to the punch bowls with Bri while she rambled on about some sort of lipstick. After she poured our drinks and began talking with someone in her English class, I snuck out a side door and searched for Jett. I could hear the rest of the boys giggling near the back, but Jett I saw up the hill, standing in the overgrown grass. He was far away, and there wasn't a soul around him.

I felt the anger rising. He was farther than I thought he'd go, and he hadn't taken the road. I went after him, to catch him before he reached the bridge's darkness. If those demons came after me, I wouldn't be surprised if they came after him too.

"Jett!" I shouted. "Come back!"

Finally, after a long drifting moment of despair, he turned. He began to walk toward me, looking confused, shouting words with his hands that shooed me away, but my heavy breaths drowned out his voice. I looked back, mentally calculating my distance from the barn. I was a lot farther than I liked, but Jett and I could make it back in a couple minutes if he was willing to run hard.

"Run," I yelled, but he didn't.

I waved my hands frantically, desperate for him to come faster, but my shoulders were confined so tightly in the silk that it hurt. Then it occurred to me that Jett couldn't hear me.

I watched angrily as he walked back, taking his time. I was nearly at a run now.

"Jett, run!" I screamed, feeling the hairs on my skin rise as a hushed whispering grew out of the wind's soft rustle.

I looked around, my knees going weak with the feeling that the demons were here. But the night's ravenous darkness was too deep for clarity, and between my skirt and the grass up to my knees, I couldn't see where I was stepping. Just as I twisted my ankle on a hidden rock, a blackish figure stepped out of the bridge and into the moonlight. I froze, and as my legs went numb, it transformed into a ridged cloud and sped after Jett.

Before I could stop myself, I kicked my heels off. I waved, hollering at Jett as I raced toward him.

"Jett! Behind you, RUN!"

I didn't know what Jett saw in me, but when he finally looked behind him, he turned back to me in a run-for-your-life sprint. Pure horror covered his face.

I ran toward him. "Jett, hurry!"

The tall blades cut my arms as I pushed through. Jett chanced a look back and tripped, falling out of sight in the deep grass. The demon submerged itself in the pasture, and another form of panic struck me as a trail of blades swayed, nearing Jett. At the place where he'd fallen, the grass went still. Then there was a bloodcurdling scream.

My tear ducts burst. I froze, half-numb. My mouth gaped open, creating endless puffs of frosted carbon dioxide. The gasping dried my throat until an excruciating cough formed deep in my lungs. I choked, trying to keep my attention on the location of Jett's scream.

Through the brittle wetness in my eyes, which were nearly frozen in the cold mountain air, I stared, horrified, at the patch of grass shaking unnaturally from side to side. Jett's screams suddenly subsided, and the trail of rustling grass moved back to the bridge.

A second later, his body slid out onto the open road in front of the bridge. The demon pulled him swiftly across the patch of packed dirt by one leg. Jett's other leg kicked through the air, his fingers fighting for purchase in the dirt, but it was no use. His body went grayer in the shadow, and he looked at me, pale and aghast. My stomach sank to my feet. My cheeks were wet and cold, and I couldn't breathe.

"ZARA!" he screamed as his fingertips disappeared into the bridge's darkness.

I sprinted toward the bridge. Tears blurred my eyes, and I wiped them as best I could without stopping. Sharp points of pain cut through my feet as pebbles found places to embed themselves in my skin. The stinging brought still more tears.

I stopped abruptly where the grass ended, staring across the patch of dirt to the bridge. I could hear the whispering growing stronger inside the black arch, beckoning me to enter. It was nearly impossible to stop the heaving that almost made me vomit. I ran a palm over my forehead while I swore to myself. Jett was dead because of me . . . I knew it. I wiped my eyes, looked back at the barn one last time, and sniffled. There was no going back.

Adrenaline pulsed through my veins, giving me new strength. I saw everything so clearly now. It was these creatures that had chained me down the past weeks, making me afraid to do anything. I was sick of it, sick of running.

My first step onto the packed earth was difficult, like kissing death. My shredded feet stung like a whip's lash with each step. But I could feel my fingers tingle as the shadows called me in, their voices growing louder with each step I took. As I approached the bridge, shaking, I felt the chains from the past few weeks lifting. This was the end.

When I entered the bridge, I didn't expect the whispers to stop suddenly, leaving only the noise of the stream. I waited, confused.

"Jett?" I called softly.

Nothing.

I took another cautious step, then another. I couldn't stop my hands from trembling as the flaky wood squeaked beneath my steps. "Jett?"

His moan came from the other side of the bridge. He was curled into a ball on the wood floor.

"Ouch," he moaned.

"Jett!"

I knew I would be stupid to go farther in, but I couldn't leave him. I ran toward his crumpled body. I had only gone a few steps when a flash of black struck and a form appeared, blocking my way to Jett.

Even in the murkiness of the bridge, I could see his shift from smoky wisp to a very pale human. I sensed a delirious anger when he snickered. But something about his human form seemed off, as though he had once been muscular but was now weak and thin, but not undead like the others I had seen. His light skin was dirty, like he had rolled on the forest floor. Twigs stuck out of his filthy blond hair, and he was barefoot and shirtless. The only thing covering him was a torn piece of fabric around his lower waist. I looked up into his eyes. They were like black diamonds, glaring at me in a frenzy, but I studied him, wondering why he looked so familiar.

"Let him go. He's hurt," I pleaded.

The dirty thing didn't speak; he held his hand out to me and twisted it. He smiled, and my body flipped over, first my head slamming against the planks and then my belly. I tried to sit up, but everything spun, and I dropped down to the bridge's damp floor. Warm fluid oozed down my temple toward my cheek. I tasted blood.

"Zara," Jett mumbled.

I heard the fear in his voice's rawness. He called my name over and over as I tried to keep moving toward him. But there were black stars each time my eyes stuttered open. I feared I was blacking out again.

"Ow," I moaned, limply rolling onto my side.

Jett shrieked in pain. The pitch shook the molecules of my blood and made me cringe. I tried twisting my head in his direction, but when the yell stopped suddenly, I couldn't look. My hair fell in my eyes as I wept. When I had enough courage to look again, I straightened my head, but as I did, a deep noise came from the opposite direction. I pretended it was the boys coming after us, but the louder it grew, the more I feared it was something large and animal, and very upset.

I'd heard a lion roar on TV before; this was different. It sounded like a deep cough. The muffled whispers responded with a competing, synchronized tune. As both the roar and chant approached, fear drained my energy, leaving me a bag of bones glued to the bridge.

But I knew that if I was going to have any chance of surviving, I needed to get out now.

Just as I started to sit up, an invisible force slapped me down like a flapjack. My chin jerked upward, and my eyes rolled back at the explosion of pain. I saw the man still there across the bridge, unmoved, staring at me with fury. I tried to curl up into a ball, but my body wouldn't give in to my command. My limbs were painfully stiff, arms by my sides, legs glued together at the knees. Something I couldn't see held me down. Then, as his bare feet moved across the bridge with a cracking of splinters, my stomach hollowed.

"Ahh," I moaned again, trying to squirm out of the invisible bands.

My back arched in agony, popping as I tried to slide sideways toward the barn. I couldn't get free. I had collapsed back with exhaustion when a black ball of smoke appeared by my side. It floated in midair, two glowing eyes buried in its fogginess. It exuded a deep chill as it waited for the footsteps to get closer. This was the type of demon that had tried to take me earlier, I was sure of it. But why wasn't he taking me now?

I gasped. *They want Jett.*

"Jett?" My throat was an old washboard, and my voice scratched down it as I called his name.

He didn't answer.

Ten, nine, eight, I counted down the footsteps to my side. The low snarl came again. I endured every tortured pain to twist my head to see what he was, but the man somehow kept me pinned down, loosing an eerie laugh. Finally, when I saw his foot from the corner of my eye, panic took over.

In that moment, a blurry black shape flew over my body and struck the cloud of smoke at my side. The shadow released a high-pitched shriek and retreated swiftly into the trees by the stream.

The figure landed by my side, and my eyes widened. I was staring at a jaguar with a coat as black as night. It looked at me like it knew me, then disappeared into the trees after the shadow. The man's feet remained by the crown of my head. He would see me dead soon enough.

I lifted my chin skyward. I had to see the face of my killer. As I looked into the psycho's eyes, a horrifying recognition imprisoned me. I had seen him in the burgundy book—the man who looked like Dylan, *exactly* like Dylan, only grimmer. His jagged teeth showed in a greedy grin, and his hollow black eyes were crazed with an obsession with prey. He smelled like death.

"Who are you?" I asked.

He crooked his ear to a bony shoulder, and that demented smile broadened. "The question is, my little darling, who are you?"

Blood seeped into my mouth as I coughed. "I don't know what you mean."

Observing me now with curiosity, he crouched by my side.

"Don't, please. You don't have to do this," I cried.

His eyes promised violence. "Yes, I do. You have no idea how special you are."

His cold fingers ran through my hair; he lifted a lock to his nose and sniffed. He snickered under his breath. "You are going to make me very happy."

My eyes felt dry, but a single tear ran down my cheek as they skidded shut. I couldn't bear to look at him directly. His face was gruesomely contorted.

When his unnaturally cold hands grabbed my wrists, I jerked and screamed as much as I could, hoping that someone would hear me. As I fought with the little movement I had, his rough laugh stopped. There was a thud, his slithery fingers vanished, and then there was silence. A second later firm, warm hands enveloped my shoulders and shook.

"Zara! Zara, it's me," an angelic voice said through the darkness.

I unhinged my stiff eyelids slowly and peered through slits. Lucas's face was centimeters away. My eyes flew open, and I frantically searched around us. The man was gone.

I panted, looking back to Lucas in confusion as he sat me up and threw his arms around me.

"I won't give up," he said, anguished.

I closed my eyes, shaken and lost, and pressed him closer. His hand moved up and held the back of my head closely. I winced at the pressure, but he only squeezed me tighter so that I could rest my chin on his shoulder. His warm scent of coconut and ginger comforted me, and I broke down and sobbed.

"I'm so sorry," Lucas said into my shoulder.

When he let out a long sigh of agonized relief, I noticed Gabriella standing behind him. A glimmer of blue burst like a star over the char-black lines of her tattoo. It was beautiful, with feathers and flowers. Her eyes were on us as she calmly stroked the coat of the jaguar at her side.

The man and woman from Lucky Pin stood next to her—his

parents. The woman looked alarmed.

My head pounded. I held it as I tried to stand.

"Where is Jett?"

"Jett?" Lucas loosened his grip just enough to study my tormented face.

"They got him. He was just right over there." I pointed to the opposite side of the bridge.

Alarm flashed on Lucas's face, and he yelled in Spanish to his parents. At once they moved faster than I could even imagine, disappearing into the shadows of the trees in a blink.

"Zara, how are you feeling? What hurts?" he asked, drawing my hair back to survey the damage.

"My head," I admitted. I tried to rub the soft spot in the back, but his hands beat mine there and gently moved them away.

He picked through my hair softly, observed for a moment, then looked at me. "Don't rub it; it'll get worse."

"Why are you here?" I asked, confused.

Before he could answer, Gabriella had bent down next to me.

"I have to lie down," I begged. My head did feel worse. His hands were already firm against my back, pressing me up as I tried to lie back again.

"You need to sit up, Zara." He pulled me against his chest, and I rested my head against his rib cage. It felt wet and sticky.

"What's wrong with my head?" I cried.

"You just cut it . . . you will be fine." There was a slight stutter in his response that made me feel he wasn't telling the whole truth.

I ignored his orders and reached for it, but again he grabbed my hands, this time insistent when he pushed them down on my lap.

Lucas turned to Gabriella. "Go get Malik. Leave Niya with us."

Gabriella disappeared where the first jaguar had run off, somewhere by the river. Moments later, Lucas's parents appeared at the other end of the bridge. His father held Jett in his arms. The limp body was bent unnaturally.

"We found him in the woods. He's still breathing," the mother said, her accent beautiful, as the man carefully laid Jett next to us. I leaned over Jett and cried. His face was pale and scratched.

"Zara, this is my mother, Valentina, and my father, Andrés," Lucas said.

Before I could speak, Gabriella returned to the bridge with the jaguar. "Malik and I are here too."

I couldn't help but stare at the large black cat that heeled next to her. His spotted coat was clean enough to shine in the dark. He watched me closely, as if he was reading me. I squirmed, a little uneasy, and moved my eyes from him to the other jaguar, Niya, who paced back and forth with random hisses. Though she would not sit, somehow I didn't feel threatened by her.

"Where's Dylan?" I asked.

The calm jaguar, Malik, looked up behind me and released a violent roar. I jumped, but Lucas shot up so quickly it was as if I'd never sat next to him, my legs and arms perfectly supported on their own. Lucas followed Malik's gaze to the tree line, to a dark figure moving toward us. I heard the voices again in the rustling of the trees, and I was anxious for Lucas to come back to me. The demons were returning.

"Put Zara and Jett in the middle!" Lucas yelled, angling himself in front of me.

Without argument the family formed a circle to shield Jett and me. Lucas faced the approaching demons, guarding me with his arms outstretched. His tattoo glowed a faint bluish-green through his sleeve. Valentina stood next to him. As she stretched out both of her arms in front of her, palms facing down, her tattoo blazed turquoise on the inside of her wrist.

Thunder crashed above, and both jaguars roared. I forced my eyes to look beyond the luminous blue into the dark woods near the stream. In the shadows of the forest, multiple clouds of black smoke moved slowly toward us. Their whispering chant grew louder. Malik's ears pointed up, but he and Niya remained in place, flanking Gabriella, ready to pounce, lips curled back to bare sharp teeth.

We were all staring at the same spot on the bridge when Dylan unexpectedly stepped into the small clearing. Enough dim moonlight reached him to show that he was breathing hard, a blueness ablaze on his calf.

"Where's Xavier?" Valentina asked as he approached us.

"I ran him out. He disappeared before I could get him," Dylan replied. He stopped and pulled Gabriella into a tight hug. She kissed him fast and hard.

I gasped as the roaming shadows suddenly attacked. I almost didn't see Valentina move, but I caught a glimpse as she lowered her hands. A round of lightning struck every shadow, eliciting high-pitched shrieks.

I grabbed my ears as they popped, turning to Jett. His chest was rising and falling slowly. I looked again and saw that we were outnumbered. Lucas's solid muscles tensed as more thunder sounded overhead. Dark clouds swirled over us in dark shades of gray. I squinted through an unexpected wind.

"Mom, you got this one?" Lucas asked, narrowing his glare to one demon.

"I got it," she yelled back as the storm growled.

The hard wind whistled past us. It whipped and stung my skin like a wet towel.

"Okay," Lucas roared. "I got twelve o'clock. Dylan you got two, Gabriella five, Dad you get nine. Malik, Niya—you two take out the leftovers. Got it?"

I blinked, bewildered that he was talking to jaguars, and fumbled at the hair flying into my eyes.

"On three . . . make this quick, or the boy will see everything."

Lucas hunched slightly. "One, two, . . . three!"

An explosion of air knocked me back. In less than a fraction of a second they were gone. Andrés and Gabriella ran toward the left side of the bridge, each chasing after a demon. Lucas didn't run, but jumped far, colliding with the demon across the bridge and wrestling him to the ground. The demon's black cloud shifted into a human shape as it wiggled and squirmed to get out of Lucas's grasp. But Lucas was stronger. He kept him pinned as he rammed his arm into the black chest and withdrew it in the same millisecond. He held something in the palm of his hand, a blackish blob, then tossed it to the ground. The demon shrieked and evaporated into black, glittery ashes.

Lucas burst through the ash cloud and headed for another form, going straight for the chest. He punched his hand in and out swiftly, yanking out another clump of matter. Another shriek, and the second demon vanished into dust. Lucas moved on with a dizzying speed, slaughtering the demons that moved along the bridge.

Beyond him, there was a snap near the bend of the river. Dylan was holding a demon against the trunk of a large tree, which threatened to fall, its roots rising from the ground under the pressure. Before it could topple, Dylan punched through the demon's chest just as Lucas had. There was another high, ringing hiss and more ashes.

Niya's deathly roar caught my attention on the other side of the river. I watched, sickened, as she bit off a part of a shadow—a head or a limb, I couldn't tell. Its shriek and its black dust disappeared into the wind like magic.

Suddenly, a demon darted across the bridge toward me. Without thinking I threw my hands up to cover my face, but before I could scream, Lucas pinned him from behind. They fell to the ground, and the black night glittered with more ashes.

Lucas rose, wiping off the dirt on his pants, and looked up. His gaze froze on me, worry creasing his forehead. But then one cheek plumped upward into a tender smile, and his eyes softened, probably amused by my wild stare. He chuckled and winked. Then, too quickly for me to follow, he took off after another demon.

After the last speck of dust blew away, the storm lifted and the wind died. My body shivered as the Castillos returned to the bridge. The jaguars were at their heels, still watchful, glancing toward the dark areas of the forest.

Lucas knelt at my side and began searching for injuries. "Are you hurt?"

"No, just my head." It pounded, but I felt weaker now that he was next to me.

His hand rustled in my blood-crusted hair, checking once more. When he was satisfied, he slid his palm down my cheek—just as Jett moved.

"Owww," he moaned, stirring in slow movements.

"Lucas, *ven aca,*" Andrés called.

Lucas obeyed his father and joined him a few feet away, where the rest of the family had congregated. Their tattoos weren't glowing anymore. Andrés spoke urgently in Spanish as Niya folded her legs and settled on her belly next to me. She started licking my arm. I didn't like it, but I was too afraid to move. Then Lucas knelt again next to us.

"Thank you, Niya." He petted her head and looked to Jett. "Gabriella and Dylan will take care of Jett."

I found myself smoothing Jett's hair off his face as Gabriella and Dylan appeared behind Lucas.

"Is he going to be okay? Shouldn't we get him to a hospital?" I asked, straining as they pulled Jett away from me.

"No." Lucas looked beyond me as I watched Gabriella and Dylan surround Jett. "Dylan will fix him, and then they will take him back to the party."

"But those things, they'll come again for him."

Lucas shook his head. "They won't go after him again."

"How can you be so sure?"

His face clouded. "Because they want you."

My head spun, and a new form of nausea hit my stomach.

"He won't have any memory of what happened," Lucas said.

"But he's hurt!"

Lucas pointed to Jett, who was balanced under Gabriella's arms. Dylan stepped in front of him, talking. Jett's head rolled back, his eyes half-shut as he moaned, and Dylan backed away. What happened next I wouldn't have believed if I hadn't witnessed it with my own eyes. Jett's injuries healed in seconds until there wasn't a scrape left.

Dylan snapped his fingers once, and Jett's clothes changed from torn and bloody to clean and whole. Niya and Malik leaped over the bridge, and Lucas gently twisted my shoulders until I was looking at him.

"I need your word that you won't say anything, or Dylan will have to do the same thing to you," Lucas whispered. He paused, then lifted a pleased half smile. "Though I suppose that won't work on you."

"I won't say anything. I promise," I reassured him as Dylan came to kneel by me. "I promise, I won't say anything!"

Dylan chuckled and snapped. A pocket of air hit me and left as fast and precisely as it came. The rips in my dress vanished. The dirt on my skin was gone, I had shoes on my feet again, and my headache had disappeared.

"I thought you said it wouldn't work on me," I said, perplexed.

"I did. I wasn't talking about the appearance part." He glanced at my head. "I was talking about the mind part. He can't make you forget for some reason."

Behind him, Jett was talking to Gabriella, asking confused questions. Lucas cringed.

"What's wrong with my head?" I wondered worriedly.

There was a tender touch near my elbow. Valentina was there. Her dark porcelain fingers felt like feathers as they lingered. I felt undeserving of her graceful touch.

"Nothing is wrong with your head," she said. Then she broke contact and joined hands with Andrés. She looked at Lucas. "Don't be too late, son."

They turned together and headed down the dark trail to our cars.

I turned to Lucas in a panic. "Who was that man on the bridge? Who's Xavier? How come he didn't look like the other demons?" It was a quiet outburst, but it made Lucas stiffen and look away.

"He said something to me," I continued.

Lucas turned back to me, curious. "What did he say?"

"That I was going to make him very happy."

Lucas stayed quiet as his eyes wavered from my left eye to the right. "That man is Dylan's twin brother. I'm afraid that's all I can tell you right now." His eyes flicked over to Jett. "It's not safe to talk here. You must go home with Jett now."

Brother? A knob cranked, and I remembered where I'd seen him. That horrible old book said Dylan and his twin were gods. They called them the Hero Twins. My eyes burned as I stared at Lucas, wondering what he was. And then every fiber in my body went numb. I paused, unblinking, half frightened by him, half fascinated. My gaze held his eternal eyes differently when he grinned. He was called the Aztec prince, a royal god.

"Who are you?" I wondered.

Our heads turned as voices approached from outside the bridge. There was a group of kids walking toward us. Lucas straightened up hurriedly. "Please, Zara, go home with Jett."

I was appalled. He was still avoiding me. "Just leave me alone, Lucas, at least until you decide you can answer."

Lucas held his hand out. "Let me help you up."

At first I stared at his palm with disbelief, but some force flooded me, saturating my nerves with a desire to be with him. I looked elsewhere before I gave anything away.

"I can help her." Jett was at Lucas's shoulder, reaching for me. After he helped me up, he looked at Lucas jealously. "What are you doing here, Juan?"

Lucas's jaw tightened, and any innocence he had washed out of his face. "I didn't know you had to be a prick to go to a school dance."

"Come on, Zara. Let's go home," Jett said.

As we started toward the cars, Lucas locked his hand on mine and tugged me back. My heart galumphed when he wouldn't let go. Then without a word, he lowered his chin, pressed his lips to the back of my hand, and gazed up at me again. "Be safe."

I pulled back slowly as the particles of my body melted.

"I will," I mumbled.

Jett pulled me, but I stiffened as the gravity of Lucas's stare bored in on me the farther we walked away.

"He is so weird," Jett started.

I didn't answer. My lips pressed into a smile. *He's back,* I thought—until something sucked out my happiness. The entire way home, I wondered why a god would be after me.

Lucas

CHAPTER TWELVE

Tez

"That was too close," I said to Gabriella and Dylan as Zara and Jett walked away into the darkening trees.

"You were right, brother. I am so sorry I doubted you," Gabriella said.

"So what do we do now?" Dylan asked.

When the pair had disappeared into the blackness, I turned back. "We follow her, never let her out of our sight. You two go home. I will make sure she gets home safely."

"Be careful," Gabriella warned.

I sped through the pathless woods and reached my car long before they arrived. I sat inside, spinning my citla between my fingers, waiting for them. Once they hopped into his truck I followed, keeping enough distance to avoid any suspicion. When they exited the freeway, I took another route and parked across her street, six houses down, turned my lights off, and waited once more in the dark for them to arrive.

When they pulled up, Zara didn't leave his truck right away. I hated waiting for humans. They were slow and their manners were cold, like the fluid that ran through my veins. But my temper boiled with every minute she spent with him. What was taking her so long to leave his truck? They weren't kissing. I knew because I could hear them. But I still had to put the citla down because it wasn't working as a distraction, and I clenched the steering wheel to stop myself from going over to yank her out of his car. When she finally was safe inside her house, *and away from Jett,* I felt my lungs open back up.

What is wrong with me?

I was rolling out of her neighborhood before Jett could even back out of the driveway.

At my house, the lights glowed all the way to the perimeter of evergreens. I could hear Niya and Malik roaming the forest as I pulled into the garage, but I ignored them, preoccupied with this new drive I felt. It pulled and tugged as if attached to me with strings. It was then, as my heart revved, that I knew I was determined to do everything in my power to keep that girl safe.

I don't know why my family still bothers to whisper. I could hear everything they said, even from the garage, and I recognized a smooth voice in their midst that made me tense. I went inside the house, afraid that its presence was not good news.

The study was dim when I entered. Everyone stood still as I looked around for Tez. He was standing next to Father across the room, their backs against the blackened window.

"Lucas," he said.

"What are you doing here, Tez?"

Mother turned toward me and looked up from the couch. "Tez has taken a great risk coming here."

"Do the Celestials know what happened?" I rushed, looking back to Tez as my heart raced.

Tez shook his head. "No."

I sighed with relief.

He walked over to me and set his beverage on a small gold table. "Lucas, do not be alarmed. I carry good news with me as well."

"Let's have it, then."

He straightened his suit jacket and cleared his throat. "The Underworld's fury grows, and with the executioners coming back tonight empty-handed, their suspicion grows as well. I have seen new visions of the future." He paused. "If they do not return with the girl by Solstice, they will go to the Celestials."

"Then we must close the portal."

Tez held his hand up and shook his head. "Lucas, I am not done. There is more that makes this matter more complicated. You have seen Xavier recently, have you not?"

I nodded. "Tonight, with the executioners."

"Yes. X'Tabay's working with him."

"But . . ."

"I followed her after the Council and saw them together. They didn't know who the fifty-second was, but after learning that Xavier was with the executioners tonight, I am positive he knows now who she is. And I believe he's planning to use her to break his curse."

"How?" The word stormed out of my mouth.

Instead of being cross with my short temper, Tez's face softened apologetically. There was a concern in his eyes that I wished wasn't there. "That, my young boy, I do not know."

I screamed and pulled at my hair. "Does Mictlan know who she is?"

"Of course not. Mictlan would not let Xavier tamper with his belongings," Father said.

"That's where the good news comes," Tez said. "Your parents tell me that the girl suffers from blackouts in which she sees glimpses of Xibalba, and that Dylan can't reshape her mind like other humans."

"And her body heals more quickly than normal. How is that possible?"

"Because as the girl of the prophecy, she has been given a divine calling, which apparently gives her strength to heal quickly. This proves that my next theory may work."

"Theory?" I asked, perplexed.

He nodded, circling the room as he spoke. I wished he wouldn't. His calmness was causing turmoil in my guts. "If the girl heals quickly, she should be strong enough to learn to control who is in her mind. The girl suffers these blackouts because Xavier's awareness is unintentionally penetrating her mind. It must be our top priority to stop that invasion."

"Tez, if Mictlan is unaware, then how is Zara even seeing Xibalba at all?" Mother asked.

Tez stopped moving. "The prophecy said both worlds would love her."

I nearly gagged. I tried so hard years ago to forget that part of the prophecy. I recalled the next part, hoping it would neutralize the acid flooding my stomach . . . *but through a deep connection with one of either world, a balance could be restored.* I stared back at Tez. My *world*, I thought. This was the beginning of the end, and I was going to prove that I was more a part of it than he knew.

Tez looked from me to Father. "It is clear to me, as it surely should be clear to you . . . the girl has a connection with Xavier."

I went numb picturing Zara with Xavier, knowing this part of the prophecy—Zara's choice of love—was out of my control.

"But Xavier isn't even a Xibalban god," Gabriella stated, confounded.

"No, but his mother is, and he resides there. It makes sense," Tez replied. "Should we keep the girl, there must be a plan for when they come back to take her."

My immortal family was unresponsive as statues, still, but attentive nonetheless. I would have been corpse pale, if my body could lose color. When I recovered, my muscles flexed as he casually talked about what I felt was *my* property. The girl belonged to *me*.

I swallowed hard and broke the stagnant silence. "No, of course.

But if Xavier wanted her for his plan, why didn't he come after her earlier?"

"Lucas, my dear Lucas. Even after all these years, you still do not understand the Cosmos. There is much power to see in the stars above. Never turn your back on your enemy, for he is a trickster, and a smart one. Xavier waited all this time because he had to wait for the end of the Long Count."

A wave of frustration drowned me. Xavier couldn't have come unless the Milky Way had moved simultaneously with Winter Solstice, and only at the end of a Long Count, a term of five thousand one hundred and twenty-five years.

"How could I have read the stars so wrongly?" I roared, tugging harder at my hair. I *knew* this.

"*Hijo*, do not be hard on yourself. Remember, you had your entire family to convince. It could have easily been missed," Mother said, reaching over the couch to touch my forearm lightly.

I turned my back to her. I was the one who had been waiting for this moment, not her. *I* was the one responsible. It already felt like Zara was slipping through my fingers. It hurt.

"I haven't much time," Tez interrupted. "We must move on. Lucas, are you ready to face the consequences of keeping this girl?"

My chin, which had dropped as I looked at the floor, now rose, and I spun to look at the one god who had been ahead of me all along. Tez watched me with an enduring patience as I regained my senses, sniffed, and nodded silently.

"Very well," he said, turning to my parents. "Andrés and Valentina, you shall begin intervention with the girl's parents as discussed. When it is time to close the portal, you will invite them to your home in Mexico so that the girl is not left alone, even for a short breath. Dylan and Gabriella, you two will go to school this week to keep an eye on her while Lucas prepares the basement for training."

"Training?" I interrupted.

"Yes. As your family and I discussed before you arrived, the girl needs to teach her mind how to keep the gods out. Without this control she is weak. This training can protect her from blacking out during Xavier's unintentional projections. Dylan will be her instructor." Tez was talking, but looked completely uninterested. He moved along, swiping his fingers on furniture, checking for dust, looking outside at the black, glistening stream, brushing his tailored suit for lint; all this until he finally glanced back at me.

I stared incredulously, but it gave me time to see Dylan's excitement at the idea. I gritted my teeth and glared at him. "And how do you suppose he does this?"

"The truth?" Tez wondered.

I nodded again, ligaments tightening down my neck.

"In the most extreme circumstances." He pulled a sheet of paper from the inside pocket of his blazer. "I have the plans here."

Tez handed me the folded paper and then smoothed a hand back through his sleek hair. The paper had drawings of cages, poles, rings suspended in the air, and weapons.

"Are you serious?" I laughed.

His fine features looked inquisitive. "Do you have another plan?"

My jaw poked out as my teeth clenched, and I submitted a subtle shake no.

"Right, we haven't much time. Lucas, you have until Friday to get your basement to look like that. Then comes your next task, the most important of all from here on out." He stopped and focused harder on me than he had all evening.

"What?" I wondered in dread.

"You are to beguile her."

"Trick her?" I replied, outraged.

"No. Beguile her. They are two completely different words."

"You would have me beguile Zara as our ancestors once did their lovers? It's absurd . . . it's vile!"

"You swore that you were ready to do what it took."

"That is taking her freedom away! You know the effect I have on human girls if I so much as bat an eye at them," I argued. "I don't want her throwing herself at me."

"Why not?" Dylan asked. Gabriella nudged him.

"Are you an idiot?" I said, turning to him. "A connection isn't made under false pretenses. It's deeper. It requires more work, and I can't control *us* if she is acting like a . . ."

"Like an eighteen-year-old girl?" Gabriella said.

"Yes!"

Tez stepped closer to me. "We need you to win her over. Don't act like you haven't romanced your share of women."

My chest filled with steam, and I took a step closer. I would not beguile Zara like *that*—that was part of my old mortal days, when women flocked to me. I was immature then and gave in to physical desire at a moment's notice. Zara was different, and should she throw herself at me, I wouldn't lie with her as I had with other women. I would wait until we were filled with a sweetness to satisfy our hearts and tongues, and it would be lasting and eternal. It wouldn't be crude, and she wouldn't be beguiled.

"Come again?" I asked, wondering if I'd heard him right.

"Lucas, the girl must be on our side, or else we will all perish should the Celestials find out any of this. I am as much a traitor as you are. I need to know if you can do this." He asked evenly, though it sounded like an urgent plea.

I breathed in deeply to cool my rage. "I feel it may not be necessary. I fear I am beginning to feel a bond with the girl already, which is why we don't have to be sucking tongue to get anywhere." I took a long breath, and the memory of the sensation I felt when I touched her gave me the confidence I needed. I put my hands in my pockets. "She will be won over. I promise."

Father and Mother stared at me with wide eyes.

Tez smirked. "Good. Next, most unfortunately, is the bad news. We cannot close the portal unless Xavier is in the Underworld. As long as his body roams freely in this world, we cannot close the portal that leads to the other. His body *must* be in Xibalba, where his soul resides. This will ensure he cannot go after Zara in the future."

Father cupped his hands over Mother's shoulders. "How do we keep track of his whereabouts?"

"We don't," Dylan answered, looking nowhere but out the midnight window. "He returned with the executioners tonight, and I am sure he will join them again at Solstice. We wait until after Solstice, when he has returned to Mexico with the executioners, to close the portal."

"Are you sure?" Father asked.

Dylan twisted toward us, grief evident on his face. "I know my brother better than anyone here. Trust me, he won't see that one coming."

"Tez, thank you," Father said.

"Don't thank me. I am in this for my own reasons, as you are. Should your efforts be successful, I will call on you once more. Good luck."

He nodded and evaporated into the air.

"Well, that went well," Dylan joked.

Gabriella rolled her eyes and stormed off.

Mother stood and faced Father. "We shall join the club where her mother plays tennis and her father plays golf. Perhaps we can also run into them at the restaurant they like to eat at on their dates."

"Very well, *amor*. That will be fine," he said.

Mother left the room to focus on her new task. Dylan rose from the chair and turned to me. I couldn't take my eyes off him, *the trainer*. It was absurd.

"Don't worry. I'm not going to kill her," he remarked easily. It was too light for my liking.

I gritted my teeth. "I will do this *only* because Tez thinks it will help her. Don't think for a second that I am going to leave her alone with you. Every second she is with you, I will be there, watching. If I think you are harming her, I will stop you."

"Lucas, I wouldn't. Trust me when I say I want to protect her as much as you do." He glanced down at my tense posture. "Maybe it is not wise that you watch her train."

I waved the piece of paper still clenched between my fingers at him. "What do you plan on doing to her?"

"Whatever it takes to make her strong." He shrugged.

"That's where you are wrong, brother." I shoved the paper at his chest. He clung to it, confused, as I walked away. "You can't. She's only human."

There were flurries in the air Monday morning, but it wasn't cold enough for snow to stick. I envied Dylan and Gabriella as they went to school, while I had to go to the hardware store and the sporting goods store and the hunting store. My list detailed a ridiculous amount of lumber, steel poles, rope, bolts, screws, and rubber balls. I rapped out my requests briskly at each store and hired a delivery service before going home and waiting nearly two hours for them to arrive. The deliveryman eyed me suspiciously and asked what I intended to do with all the supplies. After I told him I would unload the supplies on my own, his chattiness stopped. He stood there stupidly until I ordered him into the taxi waiting on the roundabout beneath the graying sky, confused with the prearranged transportation.

"Your truck will be at your office in one hour," I said as I closed the door of the taxi.

I was again amused as the human sputtered, driving away in a taxi instead of his truck. It only took me ten minutes to unload enough wood and equipment to train an army from the twenty-six-foot truck. I was grateful when Father offered to return the vehicle while Mother was out with Zara's mom at the club. I wanted to get as much done as possible before night fell so I could spend my night watching Zara.

We had kept the basement empty, knowing we wouldn't be here long; I couldn't have imagined it'd be used for this. I grabbed a two-by-twelve from the lumber pile I'd created near the stairs and leaned it against the wall in the back corner. As I ran across the basketball court-sized room to fetch more wood, I noticed the folded paper Tez had handed me on the ground. Somewhere between the meeting and now, Dylan had strategically placed it on the floor, knowing I might need it.

Although I vividly remembered what they wanted and didn't need directions on how to build the rope climb or the pyramid of stairs or the hanging bars, I glanced at it out of boredom. I was embarrassed to be putting Zara through this, but the boys were right. Zara needed training to survive. I tucked the paper into my back pocket and got back to work.

Hours later, I was sweaty, so I took off my shirt, which only made my smooth chest clammy. Any rope burn or slice I endured while working vanished almost the very second it came.

As I was sawing a wood beam, I heard them return from school. I left the project and zoomed upstairs, covered in sawdust. They were getting out of Dylan's convertible. It was getting too cold for a topless car now. We'd have to change to something more suitable for winter.

"How is she?" I asked. They took their time getting out.

"Upset." Dylan smirked.

He brushed past my shoulder. I followed him through the house to the kitchen while Gabriella trailed behind, snickering under her breath.

"Really upset," she added, pouring herself a glass of water.

"I knew she would be. I will explain everything to her on

Friday," I said, remembering that the first rule of women was to *never* make them upset.

Dylan laughed, swallowed a piece of chocolate, and surveyed my appearance. He looked amused. "How's it going down there?"

"Don't worry about me, just be ready to do your job. It'll be done by Friday," I called, returning to the basement.

When sunset came, I had only mitered a few more angles of wood, but I called it a day anyways. I was progressing more quickly than I'd expected. I had completed one of the cages and the platform for the rope climb and only needed to add the rope. On my way up to the main floor, I stopped at a thought and turned to survey the new arena. The distance from the floor to the platform was too high. Should Zara fall and hit the concrete floor, she would surely break a bone. *Not a good thing if I want her to like me.* Tomorrow I would buy a tumbling mat.

Later that evening, out of nerves, I showered, dressed, and was in my car, on my way to Zara's, in a short five minutes. When I saw her bedroom light on and the shades open, excitement fluttered in my stomach. I parked a few houses down and sped soundlessly on foot through the shadows. When I reached her house, I glanced around for peeping bystanders and, in one quick leap, jumped up to perch myself in the darkness of the roof.

Zara was near the window, sitting at her desk. By the way her face leaned toward the bright screen, I gathered she was intrigued with something on her computer. I wasn't surprised to find she was researching her observations of us. It was only literature off the Internet, so I hardly called it credible. She looked dissatisfied when a herd of unicorns and fairies showed up as results for her search on *mythical creatures.* She hit delete. Her attention went to my old journal, sitting on the corner of her desk. After tapping her fingers a few times, she hesitantly propped it open and typed *demonio de mundo terrenal.*

I was amazed at the extent of information given on personal websites. The translation, "demon of the terrestrial world," brought up websites that called the executioners "phantoms" and "spirits of the dead." One website had pictures fairly close to what she had witnessed, noting that it was more common for these "Aztec ghosts" to appear as puffs of black smoke or dark clouds than in human form. She was smart to abort that search after she ran into vampire myths. Aztec ghosts—yeah, right.

I liked her persistence, though, and she looked back to my burgundy journal. Finding something of interest, she hurriedly typed it in the search engine. She didn't back down even when it called me "Vanquisher of Evil." Rather, she went back to the journal, gathered another phrase, and typed "legend of the cosmic balance." She weeded through the junk quickly, but I stiffened when she stopped on a website with tiny cursive print. I read it, feeling rather paranoid at how I was now being perceived.

> *Our world is living on the brink of destruction after Celestial gods descended to Earth out of fear. . . . Underworld gods ambitious for blood. . . . The cosmic family have become immortal warriors to protect us from these ghosts of hell and keep the cosmic balance . . .*

I looked at the bottom left of the screen. The author of this site was just an old man, but it was jolting how accurate he was. He was right to say that the imbalance of heaven and hell began when Cortez overthrew the Aztec empire. That scum. Hell, the writer was good enough to throw out the fact that the damage Cortez caused the New World was so unimaginable that it immediately became a myth. No one would have believed that Celestial gods descended to Earth out of fear of losing their idols and temples.

Zara's gasp was audible through the closed window, although

she clasped her hand over her mouth.

Great, based on this website she thinks we are here to save everyone.

As she went on reading, curiosity about what she really thought of me started killing me. I wondered if she and I would ever be possible—for me, not her. I'd never been into someone as young as she was, or anyone so uneducated, or even anyone considered average financially. Money buys you freedom to not worry about the day-to-day logistics of saving money or paying bills. In my case, it buys privacy. For others, it buys status or fake friends. Zara's house was decent, and they had enough to get by, but I wondered about it. What made them happy, when they had none of the security I had?

I continued to observe Zara, turning my back only when she changed for bed. The waves in her blonde strands highlighted the frame of her face when she turned around. She was stunning. In fact, I couldn't recall if I'd ever met a human as pretty as her. She had a raw beauty; her lips puckered even when they were still, looking plush and full, and her thick eyebrows arched innocently. She looked harmless, but there was a fierceness in the depths of her dark brown eyes that sucked me in, and my eyes stayed on her until I had not a second left.

The heavy clouds overhead began to drop light patters of rain on the rooftop, just as Mother had said they would. I peeked through Zara's window one last time. She had lain down in bed; her eyelids were closed, and she breathed smoothly as she started to fall asleep. It was peculiar, this feeling inside me, that I thought I'd like to wake up next to her—if I slept like I used to. I stared back with envy, bothered with that thought, and left her to sleep in peace.

On my way home I imagined for the briefest second what horrific things Zara must think of me—a monster, a demon, or even a ghost—but I executed that train of thought quickly and focused on the training facility. After all, I would see Zara on Friday, when I would make everything perfectly clear.

But I couldn't overcome my curiosity and went to her window every night after that. I *had* to go. I passed several sunsets watching her fall asleep. A mortal life was simple. Wake, eat, and dream. I had never cared about losing that cycle when I changed, but I did now. Watching Zara made me miss its simplicity. She was a pretty sleeper, and the desire for there to be an *us* worsened a deep-rooted fear. I could get lost in her, and I would lose sight of the consequence of what I was doing . . . and I, or she—or both of us—could get killed. I would have to break with tradition first, without any blood; otherwise I feared she would never forgive me for what I'd done to be free of it. War and killing came easy for me because of my past, not so much for her. She was too fragile, too clean to be involved in or even equipped with a way to cope with the ugliness. I had to protect her from that, or I feared the hurt would be unfixable.

Mother protected her throughout the night while I worked on the basement—wondering what she was dreaming—and then I returned in the dewy sunrise to see her wake up. As I watched, I tried to separate myself from her, reminding myself that I was nothing like her anymore: physically, mentally, or financially. But the more I watched her, the more I wanted a new life. The more my money didn't matter. The more my years of education—which, combined, added up to her mother's age—didn't matter. The more I didn't want my old life anymore, but rather a new one, complete with aging and a job and a relationship.

I finished Tez's project in the middle of the day on Friday, leaving more than enough time to shower, polish my already shiny car, and show up at Zara's house before she left for the evening. The gloomy clouds Mother had brought in remained, shedding a heavier rain as I pulled up to Zara's curb. I stayed in my car, listening to the fabric of Zara's shirt rustle as she slid it over her head. I was confused. My body was pulsing in places dormant since I had turned immortal as I wondered what she was wearing—or, rather, what color her bra was.

When I heard the crushed fibers of the carpet as she walked downstairs, I suppressed my personal feelings and brought my focus to the task of swaying her to our cause. As her hand twisted the doorknob, I flew across the lawn in a millisecond, stood up straight, and put on a smile. The door swung open, and she jumped.

CHAPTER THIRTEEN

Cosmos

"How do you keep popping up like that?" Zara asked, startled.

She wore a green cardigan underneath a small peacoat. From the way she looked me up and down, I gathered that my summer attire was unacceptable.

"Where's your coat?" she asked suspiciously.

"Never mind that." I handed her my cell phone. "Here, call Bri and tell her I will be escorting you to school from now on."

I was preparing a reason, but she grabbed my phone and began dialing. "How do you—" She stopped, covered the earpiece as the other line buzzed, and snarled, "Is that why you showed up uninvited, to arrange my traveling arrangements for school?"

"Would it matter either way? Do you want me to play the good guy or the bad guy?"

Bri's answer cut off Zara's rebuttal. Bri sounded confused about why her caller ID read *Private,* but Zara made up a lie that left out any details about me. I was surprised when Bri didn't put up a fight, but then her questions turned to my and Zara's relationship. I held back laughter as a pretty, rosy color surfaced on Zara's cheeks. That was when Zara ended the call.

She handed back the phone, her other hand playing with her hair. "Here."

"Zara, who's there?" When her mother stepped into the doorway, her hand rose to her chest and a large smile appeared on her face. "Oh. You've got company."

Zara rolled her eyes as her mother made herself comfortable against the weathered doorjamb.

"Hey, are you Valentina's boy?" she asked.

If she could see the resemblance, Mother's gambit was clearly paying off. The plan was panning out perfectly. *Don't mess it up,* I thought, and I smiled more widely.

"Yes, I am. My name is Lucas. Nice to meet you, ma'am." I leaned in to give her a small kiss on the cheek, which is what we do whenever we greet someone. It wasn't anything special, but she suppressed a giggle.

"Oh, I'm Lori, nice to meet you too. I just adore your mother."

Zara finally unfroze, shifting her weight to acknowledge her mom. "Wait, how do you know Lucas's mom?"

"She joined the club where we play tennis. She is so sweet," Lori said, flapping her hand at me.

"I hope you don't mind that I came here uninvited, but I was just about to ask your daughter out to dinner," I said.

Lori's mouth struggled to stay closed as she held back a chuckle. "Not a problem at all. Zara has no plans. She was going to join her dad and me for dinner in town, but I'm okay if she goes out with you."

"Perfect!" I beamed. Zara looked embarrassed, irritated, and shy all at once as her mother practically threw her at me.

It was Lori who moved first, taking a step back into the house. "Well, you two have fun. Curfew is twelve, young lady."

"Mom, it's just dinner," Zara muttered. "And I'm not in high school anymore."

"Oh, okay. It's one."

After Lori closed the door, Zara stood still, eyeing me. She looked scared—debating whether she should get into my car. I pressed my hand gently to the hollow of her back.

"You ready?" I asked.

She jumped subtly away from my touch and folded her arms across her chest as she crossed the lawn. When I opened her door, she stopped abruptly and held on to the door for support.

"Where have you been?" she asked.

I suddenly realized the toll my abandonment had taken on her this week. *She needed me.* It pierced my conscience, a task not easily done. I didn't understand how she could make me feel so wrong, but in a nice way. I felt sick for creating a training arena designed for strong men, not petite girls. And then I suddenly felt guilty for having to involve her in this dangerous plot.

My connection to her was a weakness, a thorn in my side that needed to be removed, but I was very much intrigued by her—and I didn't want to resist it or ignore it. I wanted to act on it and see where the tenderness would take me. It was then that I knew for certain I wouldn't need to beguile her; it would come naturally over time. So I tossed out Tez's rules.

As she stared at me, I dazzled her with a grin. She muttered under her breath and got into the car. I would give her the answers she desired sooner rather than later, but I took my time closing her door and walking around the car. I breathed deeply and smiled, enjoying the simplicity of the moment. I would open the door for her a million times more.

As I slid into my seat, pretending nothing else mattered except for this moment, her stomach grumbled.

"Is takeout okay with you?" I asked. "I know it's nothing fancy, but I've got somewhere I want to take you when the sun sets." I watched her breathe in and out through her nose. A small smile parted her mouth, but I grew self-conscious. *Do I smell?* "I will tell you what you want to know there," I added, casually pretending I was scratching my leg but really sniffing my armpit.

She looked sick, but she said only, "That sounds great."

"Any recommendations?"

"Chinese?"

I shifted gears and accelerated down the sleek blacktop. The glare from the late sun blossoming through the clouds made her blushing cheeks more golden.

"I've got a question," I said.

"Funny, I was thinking the same thing," she said. The edge of anger in her tone exposed her frustration, and I felt that thorn wedge itself deeper into my side. *Don't let it control you.*

I gripped the wheel tighter. "Do you believe that two enemies could ever work together to fight off a bigger cause?"

She laughed. "What?"

"I'm being serious. Can two people who hate each other be civil enough to join forces and be stronger for something that's bigger than them?"

She shrugged and looked out the front window. "I guess." She didn't look back, but calmness spread over her face. "I think my brothers are like that. One minute they hate each other, the next minute they love each other."

Love? Hah! The Mayans and Aztecs will never love each other. "I wouldn't say *love*, but a mutual understanding that they want the same thing."

"Oh, I get ya. Yes, I suppose so."

"You suppose?"

"Yeah, you know. Like you and me."

I laughed. She was a feisty one. "Like you and me?"

"Yeah."

"Who's the hater and who's the lover?"

"Oh." She looked down at her knees with an embarrassed grin. "Why are you talking about us like this? I don't hate you."

"So you love me?" I chuckled.

"No!"

"Don't worry, I wasn't talking about us . . ." I leaned closer to her shoulder. "And I don't hate you."

The tension in her upper body relaxed, and she leaned back in the chair.

"I'm asking you this because the answers you want go deep. I'm talking centuries of human history, and explaining the nuances would take days."

"So?"

"In short," I said, pleased with her eagerness, "two groups of people that I knew a long time ago joined forces to fight off a bigger threat. Sometimes I think I still don't understand it, and I wonder when they're going to explode."

"Still? I thought you said you knew them."

"Knew, know, it's not relative," I said.

The skin on her powdered cheeks tightened when her eyebrows lifted. "Lucas, who are you talking about?"

"Aztecs and Mayans." I studied her face, watching for her fear, but there was none. Only silence. "An elite group with members from each tribe was formed to ward off a greater evil."

"And you're one of them?"

"No . . . thank goodness." She didn't reply, but she stared at me like I was suddenly an open book. "So, how long have you known Jett?" I asked to take her attention off me.

She suddenly looked uncomfortable and made a temple with her fingers as she stared out the windows into the grayness. "Since I was twelve."

"And you two never tried the dating thing?"

"No."

"He's an idiot," I said.

"Jett . . ." She finally looked at me, tongue-tied as she searched for words. "He's not an idiot. He's just . . . comfortable. So comfortable with having me as just a friend that I guess he never thought about us being together. At least, not until a few months ago."

"Why the change?"

"He said it was graduation that got him thinking. I don't know, is this what you want to be talking about?" She shrugged.

"No. I've just always wondered about that."

She pressed the palms of her hands together and tucked them between her knees. Her thighs distracted me from the road; I had to look upward to the steeples of the fir trees to distract myself. Now more than ever, because we were alone, I needed to focus. No risks.

I cleared my throat and clenched the wheel tighter, fighting back my immoral, primitive self. I'd grown closer to her during my night-time watch than I thought I had. *Problem? Nah.*

"Where are you from?" I asked.

As if she needed a distraction as well, she began twirling her platinum hair around her little finger. "Originally Las Vegas. At first my parents were fascinated with Howard Hughes's vision of the desert, but it didn't take them long to get sick of the dry heat."

The Lexus's headlights glistened against the fogged-over window of the Chinese restaurant, detailing every fingerprint and smudge as I pulled up.

"What do you like here?" I asked, talking over the rain that tapped against the car.

She scrunched her nose. "Anything but seafood."

"Okay, wait here," I replied, locking the doors behind me.

As I waited for the food, my eyes were locked on the steamy window, looking through the rain and past the crossing windshield wipers to the inside of my idling car. Zara sat there, examining the interior as if she'd never seen the inside of a car before. She stiffened when I came out a few minutes later, holding two paper bags stuffed with food. The drizzle wet my back as I placed the takeout on the backseat. Though the chilly water didn't faze me, the billowing exhaust of my car told me the temperature was dropping.

We drove back to Zara's place in painful silence. I knew that Zara wanted to talk only about the one thing that I did not want to talk about—not yet, at least. I diverted my attention to keeping the temperature inside the car at a comfortable degree of warmth. Every minute or so, I checked the hot air leaving the vent. I was sure humans didn't do this when they turned the heat on, but I couldn't tell what was too hot or too cold. My new habit seemed to distract Zara from her disappointment in me.

"We're not going to your place?" she asked as I pulled into her neighborhood.

"No."

I stared at the horizon, where the sunlight had poked through in the final minutes of evening, pouring a rosy gold color underneath the puffy gray clouds. I parked at the flooded curb and shut the engine off. Zara stepped out into the downpour and ran for the cover of the porch while I grabbed the food and followed her. She directed me to a small loveseat on the front porch.

"My parents aren't home, so we're eating out here," she said.

I admired her for respecting her parents even when they weren't home. The older women I knew didn't have such rules, but Zara had this maturity that made me want to break the rules with her even more. I was about to set the bags down on the small coffee table when she shivered.

"Want a blanket?" she asked.

"What for?"

"Oh." Her face changed, and I suddenly felt embarrassed that I couldn't feel the temperature. "I mean, I'll go get a blanket for *me*, then."

While she was inside, I emptied the bags and arranged their steaming contents neatly across the table. I was leaning back against the wicker seat before she returned with an old quilt and sat down by my side.

"I didn't know which one you wanted," I said. "Kung pao beef or almond chicken?"

She bit her bottom lip as she decided. When I felt my bad qualities poking around, wanting to take advantage of her purity, I looked away. *Damn it. I can't do this.* This virgin had no idea how much power she had over me. She was like a black widow, *una viuda negra,* luring me into her web of lustrous desire. Her pinched lip was hot, and I tried to focus on anything other than wanting to bite it with my own teeth and tug it into my mouth.

"Kung pao beef," she finally said.

I piled mounds of saucy beef onto her plate next to the huge piles of fried rice and chow mein I'd already served. She took it graciously and loaded a large forkful.

"So, how did your parents meet?" I asked just as she put the heaping fork into her mouth, steam and all.

I watched with great pleasure as steam escaped her mouth through the hand she covered it with. I couldn't tell if it was because the food was too hot, or if she was trying to be modest while she spoke, or both. But there was nothing modest about her mouth, opened wide and breathing steam. I took a bite quickly to fill my mouth, which I couldn't seem to keep shut.

"At college. And yours?"

"Nuh-uh. I'm not done." I smiled, relishing her frustration at my refusal to give over any answers at all, though she had no idea how crazy she was driving me.

"This is so not fair; you know that, right?"

I swallowed my bite and grinned. "Favorite food?"

"Mexican."

"Really?"

"Yes." She chuckled, a sound that trapped my emotions and made me dizzy—if a pleasurable dizziness existed.

"Favorite animal?" I asked quickly.

"Horses. Although having a pet jaguar would be pretty cool."

I smiled dangerously as I eased further into her web. "Jaguars *are* pretty cool. Favorite course at school?"

"Photography . . . easy A."

Zara answered my every question instantly, waiting anxiously for the next—or for the part where I would tell her about me. When the rain finally lifted, and the clouds rolled out of the valley, leaving a clear sky streaked with pink and purple, I knew it was almost time to show her the Cosmos. I pondered the darkening sky for a moment before turning to her. Her plate was almost empty.

"Would you like some more?" I asked.

"No, thank you. I'm full."

I suddenly became restless with what I was about to tell her. I had never dreamed, in the five hundred years I'd lived, that I would be sharing my life story with anyone.

"Zara, I need to know that I can trust you. I will fully disclose to you what you want and need to know, but it stays between us. Trust me when I say it's not just for your protection, but for the protection of everyone you know as well. I must have your word that you will never reveal to anyone what I am about to tell you."

For the first time that night, my *viuda negra* smiled easily and turned back into the *muñeca* I loved—my doll, so clean and pure and trusting—as she said, "I promise."

"I was hoping you would say that," I said, relieved, and I stood. "Then we'd better be on our way. There is much to tell you."

Her elation flared and lit an ember in my heart, a new sensation. I stared at her in awe, wondering what else she was doing to me, until it blew up into sparks and I realized it was the feeling of companionship. *So this is what it feels like.* I offered my hand, unable to let go of my smile. "*Muñeca?*"

Her hand was shaking in mine. I lowered my thumb over the

back of her hand and squeezed gently to ease her nerves. Looking into my eyes with a blind trust that made me fall even harder for her, she tossed the blanket on the loveseat, never even looking back as we headed to the car.

"Have you ever seen Venus?" I asked as we turned onto Tahoe Boulevard.

"Venus?"

"I sort of grew up watching the stars and planets. There was a priest who taught me how to follow it when I was a boy. I used to wake up almost every morning before the sun rose just so I could see it for the few short minutes that it was there."

There was a pleasant silence as we drove along the lake toward the canyon. The sky was now darkening to blue, forcing me to turn on the headlights.

"Lucas?" she asked.

"Yes?"

"What does 'vanquisher of evil' mean?"

I considered her determination through the red glare of the dashboard. I knew she would not budge on this, so I tried to answer as simply as possible. "It means *I* am not the bad guy."

"I didn't know there were *bad guys* and *good guys*," she joked.

I laughed. "And I didn't know there was a human so interested in the dangerous undiscovered."

We both smiled, and she turned to look out the window.

"Where are we going?" she asked, watching the city lights turn to black tree trunks.

"To a clearing where we can see the stars better."

Zara's heart was pounding louder than the engine.

"Are you scared?" I asked. I was ready to turn the car around.

"No. Well, a little."

"How about you tell me what you know, and I'll fill in the gaps," I offered, trying to ease her stress and her abnormal heart rate.

"All right." She wiped her hands along her lap, sat up, and inhaled deeply. "First . . . those shadows are demons from hell." She shot a glance at me, but when I only looked amused, she went on reluctantly. "I read somewhere that they're Aztec ghosts who come to Earth to take people for sacrifice. I suppose I don't understand why me . . . or why anybody."

When I didn't respond, she pointed up two fingers before continuing. "Next is about you, but you're tricky. Obviously you are from the same realm as the demons, like you said, but I also think you are a god." She paused to watch my unchanging expression. "I read about Celestial gods who came down to Earth, so at first I thought you were one of them. But then I read about a different type of god . . . one I've never heard of before . . . a vanquisher of evil or a warrior god. Those gods have markings on their skin like your tattoo, which is why I think you are one of them. Although no one has ever believed that they even exist. Anyway, if that's what you are . . . you're a legend." The first difficult steps taken, she continued without fear.

"You're supposed to protect Earth by saving the victims taken for human sacrifice, which is why you came here, to protect me. But I don't understand why the demons keep coming back."

"And lastly," she said, holding up a third finger, "there is a witch involved in this somehow. I saw a picture of one in the burgundy book, and she looked identical to the girl that was with you at the Lucky Pin."

Her light body bumped into the passenger door as I fishtailed on a sharp corner, my landmark for the small group of trees ahead that disguised my little road.

"Sorry. I'm not used to driving with anyone else in the car," I admitted as she rubbed her shoulder. "Your story sounds pretty good, but you're wrong on a few things."

"What do you mean?"

"Your discoveries are skewed."

Suddenly, looking at Zara made my throat swell, and I started to choke. It was time to take the plunge. I focused on turning onto the hidden road, lowering my speed as the track turned to mud. I felt sick saying this.

"Zara, I didn't come to Tahoe to save you."

I let there be silence, but I wished I hadn't. Even with the small rocks banging against the undercarriage, I could still hear her when she gulped, eyes not budging from my face.

"You are right. I am from that legend. My entire family is. But they are wrong about us. Zara, do you remember that night at the Lucky Pin?"

"I remember you fighting with your family a lot."

Keeping my face aimed at the road, I rolled my eyes to her. "We were arguing about you, about whether or not we should let you go. There is something you should know about yourself that I will reveal to you by the end of the night, but for now, just know that you were special in my eyes. For that reason, I felt that I needed more time with you, so I convinced my family that night to allow me more time."

"What are you saying? That I was supposed to die?" she asked fretfully.

I nodded, ashamed.

"Well then, how come you waited for my car to crash? I almost did die!"

"I didn't know I'd be cutting it that close. My family and I were coming to agreements."

"*Agreements?*" she asked, sounding appalled.

"Yes. If I were to save you, Dylan would be allowed to erase your memory. Except you proved us all wrong when you retained very specific recollections of what occurred that night. After that, my curiosity about you kept me around. I knew I needed to interfere . . ."

"During the night games," she finished for me, her face now blank.

"I thought that if I showed you my tattoo, you would say you'd seen it before, or maybe it would bring out certain feelings I was looking for. But when you were shocked and scared, I realized I didn't have the concrete evidence I needed to persuade my family to let me keep you safe, and I was too weak to watch the demons take you. That is why we left after that night."

"You . . . you left me . . .to . . ." Her sentence trailed off as shock washed through her. "But . . . why did you come back on Halloween?"

I raised my eyebrows. "Because somebody told me that something I've been waiting for a very long time finally *did* come to me."

"What?"

"You."

It was quiet while Zara tried to get her bearings. I kept a cautious eye on her as we neared the top of the mountain.

"Wait, let's just pretend for a second that I miraculously understand the tiniest bit of what you're saying. I still don't understand who *you* are."

I cackled. "You are asking the wrong question, *muñeca.* I just told you that I knew who you were before we met, and you want to know who *I* am?"

"Yes," she answered, and she held her breath. Her face looked hurt, but there was an edge of candidness that twisted my heart. It felt nice, so I smiled.

"My family and I weren't always this way, you know. We were called to do this."

She folded a leg onto the seat and turned to face me. Her face glowed in the darkness. "Do what?"

I wanted to stretch my hand out and cup her cheeks, kiss the fullness of her mortal lips.

"I am not a god, Zara. Never was . . ." I looked away, feeling the burden of telling the truth. "I was a demigod."

I couldn't resist looking back, and I anticipated her next question.

"My mother I can thank for that. She's the goddess, which naturally makes my father the human—well, *made* him the human. I was only a demigod until I reached twenty-three. That girl from the Lucky Pin, Tita, she's the witch. Her, my father, my sister, and I all became immortal when we were called to do this. Ah, we're here."

For the first time in twenty minutes, Zara tore her eyes from me and observed her surroundings. We were underneath a blanket of stars, parked on an unmarked overlook up a little from Inspiration Point. Emerald Bay spread far beneath us. I hopped out and walked to the trunk, noticing that I had blundered through enough wet dirt to give my white car a new paint job. I didn't care. I removed my telescope, threw the blanket that covered it onto the backseat, and carried the black cylinder to the far edge of the cliff, positive that she would follow out of curiosity.

One, two.

"What's it like?" she called from her seat as I strode away.

I looked up at the burning stars and then down to the glass lake, bewitched by the delicate glow. Tonight was more than perfect; it was romantic.

"What's what like?" I asked.

"Being immortal." Her enthusiasm drooped noticeably when the icy air reached beneath her coat as she got out. Her body tightened, and she clamped her arms around herself.

"Not what you would think. Over here." I motioned her over with a jerk of my head and turned to my scope's settings as she tiptoed across the mud.

"So a priest taught you how to watch the stars?"

"How to *read* the stars," I corrected. I squinted into the telescope as I adjusted the lens. "Ahau was like a godfather to me. He used to tell me that the stars and the galaxy were sacred, and that they could reveal many things to us. Venus is the easiest to track because it arrives just before the sun rises and just after the sun sets. Ahau called it the morning and evening star. Take a look."

I backed away, pointing to the scope. She loosened her grip on her shivering arms and leaned over to squint into the eyepiece.

"It's amazing. Vegas was always too bright to see the stars." She stared a long moment and then backed away. "What happened to your godfather?"

I left her and walked back to the car. "He died a long time ago."

Zara watched, amazed, as I jumped soundlessly onto the hood. She walked noisily across the gravel and leaned her elbows on the hood next to me.

"I'm sorry," she said, staring bewildered at the view before her.

I fixed my eyes on her. I reached for her hand and circled the pad of my thumb over it. She tensed but didn't move, so I continued. "Don't be. He was old and way too smart for his own good."

"So what was the deal with his obsession with the stars?" she asked, watching my thumb move over her hand and then looking toward the sky.

I followed her gaze upward, remembering the way of my old life. "It wasn't just his obsession, it was everybody's. It was how we lived."

"I don't . . ."

"The stars are a calendar, as much as the paper calendar you use today. Any sort of galactic movement is what we call Cosmos. Where I come from, they used the Cosmos as a tool for scheduling."

When I glanced back, she was looking at me as if I were a creature she'd had nightmares about as a young girl. I let go of her hand and paused, hating the way she looked at me, but I realized just how badly she needed to get past this fear. I scooted closer, smiling when she jumped and then froze. I was a mere foot away from her, not close enough to be tempted, but near enough to read her spiking emotions and relish the fact I wasn't the only one.

"Scheduling what?" She stared back, wide-eyed.

"The usual. Ceremonies, rituals . . . wars."

I figured this would shatter the block of ice she'd become. I was right, almost. She thought for a few seconds before inhaling deeply and displaying a mocking grin. "Wars? You determined wars by the stars?"

She chuckled incredulously, but I couldn't take my eyes off the purity that sparkled in her eyes in the moonlight.

"Well, when you say it like that . . . Actually, we had to. There isn't much choice when everyone believes the same thing. It actually made it easy to predict when someone was going to come after you . . . it sort of prepared you."

She still stared at me dumbly.

"Don't girls your age read horoscopes?" I pointed out.

"I guess, yeah."

"Same thing. The Cosmos can predict things that may come to pass."

Zara relaxed, and I scooted closer, but her body tensed again.

"So, what does this have to do with me?" she asked.

I adjusted my weight, leaning back a ways to give her the space I had just closed. I was the one who suddenly felt uncomfortable.

"I lived during a crude period where beheadings and bloodletting were common," I started nervously. I grounded myself in her steady heartbeat and went on. "As a young child, I wanted to understand why people made human sacrifices. My mother explained to me that the bones and blood of the Underworld gods created the Middleworld, and over time, they wanted repayment in the form of blood. So they created a creature that could feed off humans, drain their blood, and bring it back to the Underworld."

"That sounds like a vampire."

"So they were called. But they don't exist anymore. They haven't since AD 800, when the vampires revolted and kept the blood for themselves. The gods were angry and destroyed all the vampires.

Then the gods came up with another way to get not only the human blood they desired, but also human hearts. They compelled the Aztecs to sacrifice humans and extract victims' hearts as they were still beating. This compulsion worked every day for hundreds of years—until the day Hernan Cortez came."

"Why?" she asked, stretching her legs in front of her as she leaned back.

"Because he destroyed everything, every ritual, every tradition."

She stared back blankly, and I knew she needed more. I started playing with the zipper of one of her boots as a distraction. "Do you mind?"

She shook her head, and I continued.

"In my culture, the Celestial gods use two Mayan calendars, a religious calendar of two hundred and sixty days and a solar calendar of three hundred and sixty-five days. If you combine these two, the least amount of time between repetitions of the same two days is fifty-two years. It's called a calendar round."

I pinched and rolled the metal between my fingers as she watched me.

"The year Christopher Columbus landed in the Americas, 1492, was the same year the calendar round ended. Remember, we were a superstitious people, and we believed calendar events were foretelling. Twenty-six years later, Cortez came. And when word spread fast throughout all the tribes that a white man had appeared on the shores of Vera Cruz, my people believed he was Quetzalcoatl, a god who was supposed to return to us at that time. This single event upset the balance of Cosmos between the gods of the Underworld—what we call Xibalba—the earth, and the Celestials."

"Upset?"

"Don't you see? Cortez's arrival caused a collision between three worlds that were never meant to be together in the first place. Cortez set off one of the most unforgettable clashes of civilizations in history, and Xibalba and the Celestials were affected as well. Xibalba's compulsion to make human sacrifices no longer mattered because the human believers were dying in large numbers, in battle against Cortez and from the diseases his people carried. There was no one left to perform the rituals."

Her chest rose with distress under her peacoat. "Why do you blame Cortez?"

"Because of his immature inability to accept another culture," I grunted. "His wrongful pride led him so far astray that he never questioned why the Aztecs were sacrificing humans every day. He had no idea a dark force compelled them; he only saw barbarism. He destroyed anything to do with any religion other than his own. Anyone or anything that stood in his way was killed on the spot, and the rest of the believers were branded like cattle. A lot of blood covered the dirt roads in those days."

I looked toward Zara, waiting. She was silent. Her light hair rippled down in waves like the petals of a white rose in a dark abyss. She wasn't running through the woods screaming, so I presumed I hadn't scared her yet. I looked back to my hands, remembering how much blood had been shed on them—and by them. Feeling disgusted, I let go of her boots and tucked my fingers under my arms.

"Cortez had many weapons and armor made of metals we had never seen before. It made his warriors strong, which is another reason our people at first believed him to be Quetzalcoatl. When tribes fought against him, he wiped out hundreds of our men, whereas we could only wipe out a handful of his. But Cortez had his eye set on my father's city, Tenochtitlan, because of its wealth and size. It took just under two years, but it seemed that Tenochtitlan went from population twenty-five million to one million almost overnight."

When I paused, I heard the quiet chattering of her teeth. I fetched the spare blanket from the backseat and wrapped it around her.

"Thanks," she said, snuggling inside the wool. "What

happened next?"

I settled next to her more comfortably.

"Every city that fell to the Spanish throne meant fewer people offering human sacrifices to Xibalba. So the Underworld gods decided to come to Earth themselves to take the sacrifices. The Aztecs suffered these abductions while at the same time being under attack by Cortez. In desperation, the humans begged the Celestial gods to salvage what was left of our lands and population. The Celestials negotiated an agreement to provide human sacrifices to the Underworld, and my family accepted responsibility for seeing that everyone abides by that agreement."

I waited anxiously while she studied me. I could almost hear her mind working. "What was so special about you guys that you were chosen?"

"The Celestials saw my family as a different breed. We represented Aztec and Mayan, god and human. My father was a member of the Aztec royal family and my mother a Mayan goddess. It was pretty much a done deal for us to become these 'vanquishers of evil,' especially when the Celestials learned that my mother had kept her identity secret from the humans for all her years on Earth."

Her gaze was perfectly still. I lowered my chin and raised my eyebrows.

"Which is hell, by the way—watching humans fall when we have the power to help them," I added.

I felt uncomfortable in my skin as she pushed hair out of her face with an arm still carefully tucked underneath the blanket. She was so beautiful. I never imagined that telling the truth about myself would have a beguiling effect. She looked at me differently now.

"My parents met by accident. At the time, my father was the prince of Tenochtitlan and had been sent by the king to trade with the Tabascans, a neighboring Aztec tribe on the east coast. While he was crossing the mountain pass outside the city, he was captured by locals and taken for sacrifice. My mother found him locked up in one of their cages. He was weak but well enough to walk. She helped him escape, and they returned to Tenochtitlan. During that time, Mayans and Aztecs were not allowed to marry. Even though my mother had saved my father's life, the king despised her because she was a Mayan. But it was only a matter of time until her nurturing love, a rare commodity in those times, made everyone adore her for who she was. She never admitted to being a goddess, and eventually they were allowed to marry.

"After they married, my mother told Father that it wasn't safe to be in Tenochtitlan anymore. They moved east toward the coast and settled in a lost city called Tajin. My earliest childhood memories are of playing Tlatchi and throwing spears in the marshes near the city. Mother ordered my sister and me to keep our demigod natures a secret, saying it wasn't safe for others to know, that dark times were ahead. And then, shortly after that, we learned why Tajin had been abandoned. It was the place of Mictlan, who is one of the rulers of the Underworld."

She looked confused.

"The name means 'place of the dead,'" I explained. "Today, the Underworld can take people from anywhere in the world. But then, before the agreement, Tajin was where the Underworld took its sacrifices. We didn't know this until people in the city started disappearing. The abductees' family members complained to my mother and father that they were seeing their missing loved ones in the smoke of the incense in their home and in the shadows of night."

I could sense the chills rippling on her smooth skin as she buried her nose under the blanket. "Like ghosts?"

I nodded. "My parents discovered that it was the executioners, those shadows that have come after you, snatching people. The Underworld gods were angry that humans were giving them fewer hearts than they were used to receiving. But at the time, my parents didn't know that Cortez was destroying cities and disrupting the daily ritual. When they did hear what Cortez was doing, they became fearful. They knew our city did not have enough warriors to fight him, especially after they learned that our Tabascan neighbors had been massacred. They had twice the population we had. I was fifteen when my parents decided we had to leave Tajin. They warned our people what was happening, and that they were leaving the city. Every individual had the choice to stay or go. Those who chose to stay—which was most of them—were sacrificed by other nearby tribes who still had temples, or forced to fight against Cortez."

She poked her head out, turtle-like, and pulled the blanket more tightly around her shoulders. "But where did you go?"

"A historical site now infested with tourists." I hesitated as I remembered, sadly, how it once was. "Tulum."

"You actually lived in Tulum?" She looked funny, wrapped tightly in the blanket and yet radiating energy, and my desire to touch her greatly increased.

Still, I laughed to think that my story was enlightening. "Actually, yes. I lived there until I turned—until I became immortal. It wasn't until Tenochtitlan fell, with millions of casualties, and the crusades were moving south to the Maya territory that the Celestial gods finally realized the cosmic balance was getting out of control and decided to act."

"And brought you into it, right?"

"Instead of the entire platoon of Aztec and Maya Celestials getting involved, a council was formed to oversee the welfare of all. The Council knew that if they were going to make rules, they needed someone to make sure the Xibalban gods did nothing they weren't supposed to. They knew my mother's secret. She had lived in the Middleworld longer than any other Celestial god. So they chose her to be a Watcher—but then they had my father and us to think about. They decided that if we were worthy, they would transform us into immortals in exchange for our aid in monitoring the gods of the Underworld."

"But what about Tita? She's like you, isn't she?"

"Tita, yes. She helped us carry out our task so that we could become worthy, and in return for her cooperation, the Celestials decided to keep her with us."

I slid down from the hood, crossed my feet in the grainy mud, and leaned back against the car. I talked into the sky as I recounted the part of my history I hated most.

"The first Council was the eve of August 13, 1527. I cannot forget the date: six years exactly since Cortez besieged Tenochtitlan and the beginning of the Mayan massacres in the south. The Celestials summoned us that night to Tulum and explained what we were to do, and then one of them touched each of us. The touch is what started the transformation. The Council didn't stay. They left my family and I to deal with it on our own, knowing we'd see them again . . . in fifty-two years. I hated them for a long time after that. My mother and Dylan didn't need any changing. They were already gods. It was my father, Gabriella, Tita, and I who withered in pain."

I found my voice shriveling before the anger combusting inside me. The mere memory of the torture I endured that night put me in the zone where nothing else existed except the memories of pain. The sort of pain that sweeps all happiness from under your feet, drowns you in hopeless misery, and leaves you parched with despair.

I wish I had known then that the torture of my transformation was only a step toward another prolonged session of torture, living my immortal existence in isolation from the world I guarded. Relationships were forbidden, love was unattainable, and I was alone. My eyes, dry for centuries, now watered in an unnatural way.

I saw Zara shift subtly and awoke from my reminiscence. I turned to her, wiped my eyes swiftly, and fiddled with the frayed hem of my shorts. "In any case, this agreement restored the balance after the chaos Cortez brought, and it keeps the human race safe to this day."

"How?" she breathed.

If there was a part I hated more than my unnecessary immortality, it was this. I cringed inside at what she would think of me. I froze, looking down at her, and then said with plain precision, "The balance isn't that we save every human . . . it's that we let them go."

Silence. I wasn't aware that humans could be so still.

"In order for the balance to be kept," I went on, wondering if she heard me correctly, "I have to watch them take fifty-two people every fifty-two years."

Her eyes moved first, showing disgust. "How do you know who is going to be chosen?"

I sighed with relief when her feet remained planted on the ground next to mine instead of jetting away.

"The sacrifices are revealed to us in a Council."

Zara's body shook next to me. "How many more are left after me?"

"There aren't any. You're the fifty-second."

The beat of her heart accelerated instantly. It made me sick to be the cause of such fear. I watched guiltily as her chest heaved. "Who else was taken?"

I bit my lip, nauseated. "Other young girls like you."

Her hands flew to her mouth. The whites of her unblinking eyes were stark in the darkness. I wanted to cradle her in my arms and whisper to her that everything was going to be fine, but I knew the effect that would have. I wanted her to fall for me as humans fall for one another. I wanted it to be normal. I quashed my urge to touch her by crossing my arms.

But when she looked away stiffly, and a tear glistened as it fell down her cheek, I hurried to clasp her hands between mine.

"I'm not *going* to let them take you, Zara. I'm keeping you."

Her hands were ice as she angled her head to me. Her expression was soft and complicated and scared. *Oh,* muñeca, *don't cry.* I wiped a tear with the back of my hand and then let go even as more tears fell.

"Why me?" she wondered.

"Because you're the girl foretold in a prophecy." I stuck my hands in my pockets and began to pace as guilt ate me alive. "Early in the eighteenth century, just after the fourth round of sacrifices, Tita came to me one morning saying she had been kept up all night by images racing through her mind. I thought it was ridiculous at first because they showed a time and place so far in the future that many important details were lost. But when Tita showed me how it could better our lives—everyone's lives—if it were true, I felt the goals of my eternity change. It made me seek out every fifty-second victim . . . seek out you.

"I wasn't convinced it was you when we met—and I regret so badly that I ever doubted. I hope that you can forgive me someday."

Zara crossed weak arms over her belly and slumped over, staring at the dark lake. "The roses on the windowsill, the note," she whispered with a voice stripped of any emotion. "What changed your mind about me?"

When she turned to me, weary, her face had paled, and I knew her stomach couldn't take much more either.

"Tita," I responded quickly. "She was outraged when we came home early without you. For weeks she yelled at me, telling me I had to get back to protect you. When I was convinced it was you, I was livid because everything I felt about you, everything I knew about you, was right; I just kept denying it. I felt so foolish for not having paid attention to the movement of the Cosmos."

"How is it that she knew and not you?" Her eyes drifted away into memory while her elbows curled harder into her stomach. "She knew at the Lucky Pin. Didn't she? I could tell by the way she looked at me."

I nodded, embarrassed by my doubt. "Tita said it was you she saw in her dream. We couldn't have known because it wasn't our dream. And it was difficult for her to convince any of us because she saw the visions hundreds of years ago. After the crash, when Dylan's trick worked on your friend but not on you, my family was more susceptible to the idea that it was you, but it wasn't concrete. They needed hard evidence. Once I learned what you saw when you blacked out, I had that evidence."

She shot up and blurted, "That place exists?"

"Zara, that is Xibalba, the Underworld, that you are seeing. I went home that day and shared the news with my family, but it still wasn't enough. They were searching for one more thing, one very important factor that the prophecy talks about."

She bolted off the car and grabbed her head. I was at her side without thinking, before her warm heart pumped one more pulse. It was more difficult than I thought to get her to calm down. Though her feet were planted, she moved all over the place, twisting to the right, then left, then right again.

I leaned down to look her in the eye. "Are you all right?"

"Lucas, I don't know. My body is shaking, but I'm not cold."

I wrapped my arms around her shoulders, reminding myself not to squeeze too hard, and carefully brought her against my chest. I rested my chin on her head, thinking fast for something gentlemanly to say, a human thing to say, as I breathed in the strawberry scent of her hair.

"I can take you home if you need to," I offered, almost taking it back instantly. Dylan would have a fit if I failed to tell her about the necessity of training.

"No, just give me a sec." She sniffled on my shoulder.

I bit my tongue. My impatience was growing as the moon neared the mountain peaks. I was losing precious time before her curfew. But when I let go of the schedule and realized she was in my arms, I breathed in and smiled, relieved that she couldn't see how much I enjoyed holding her. Zara was smaller than anyone in my family; even with her enfolded in my arms, I could still grip my own biceps. And her hair rubbed softly against my chin, something I could get used to.

Eventually, after a nice, long, *human* minute, her heart slowed and her wobbly knees locked. "Lucas?"

I loosened my hold enough to see her face. "What?"

"What else did Tita see in the prophecy?"

I sighed, then took her hand in mine and guided her to sit down on the car's hood.

"She saw that the virgin girl chosen as the fifty-second sacrifice would be able to shift the balance between heaven and hell, should she be saved." I curled my index finger underneath her chin and rubbed her dimple with my thumb, staring at it as I told her the rest. She was so beautiful I could barely keep focused on what I was saying. "But you won't do it alone. Through love you will set in motion things that can return peace to all of us, or destroy everything we love."

She didn't flinch as I moved closer to her, smelling her breath. Her eyes stared hard at my lips.

"But I should tell you . . ."

Her eyes fluttered as I moved in closer . . . just one taste.

"Tell me what?" she whispered, startled. I closed my eyes and sniffed hungrily. I wondered how a prophecy could predict that such an innocent girl could have the power to destroy me if I were the recipient of her love. I wished it were wrong. And then I remembered Tez. *Xavier loves her too, and I know he will fight*. I backed away suddenly.

"I'm not the only one you may have a connection with. There is one more, in another realm, who wants you."

Her head shook as fear glossed over her eyes. "Lucas, this girl you talk about. She isn't me."

She was beginning to lose her cool again. I gave her space but then stepped forward again, afraid she'd flee and I'd have to chase her down.

"Yes it is, Zara," I said. "You were chosen at a time we believed that Earth would be renewed. It's called a Long Count, and it only happens every five thousand one hundred and twenty-five years. The prophecy said certain astronomical phenomena would take place during its time. That's why I have been paying close attention to the planets, the sun, the stars, to all the movement of Cosmos. It's supposed to occur during Winter Solstice, when the sun aligns with the dark rift in the Milky Way."

She nodded, uncomprehending. When she didn't move from the hood, clenching her hands around her knees for dear life, I felt it was safe to move on. I hopped up and knelt by her side, pointing to the starry sky above us.

"Look," I said, "a galactic alignment is coming, and it only happens every twenty-six thousand years." I paused, feeling her heart racing. "It's going to happen *this* December, Zara. And when it does, it will open another way from the Underworld to the Middle-world. It's the darkness that will cloud our world, as the prophecy says. And you—" She stole my breath away when I looked into her chocolate-brown eyes. "You are the light, I am sure."

She uncurled and jumped off the car again to pace back and forth frantically. I followed after her. She bumped into me when I blocked her path. She looked up in confusion.

"Lucas, I . . ." she stuttered.

I shook my head. "Shush."

I felt guilty for what I was about to do. Not because she would want more, but because I would. I glared at her like a predator. Silver snowflakes drifted from the sky as she stood motionless under the iridescent moonglow. Her breath came as dreamy white puffs in the night, but I had to disrupt it. I needed her to feel what I felt, that our connection was real. Nervously, I stepped closer, until the outer layers of our clothes touched. Her knees shook. When I reached to cup her cheeks, her eyes widened. I held my position long enough for her to inhale once and then went in slowly.

Her lips were like red velvet cake, smooth and sweet. I kept my lips tight, resisting the urge to be free, to taste. All I needed was for her to feel that spark, to know we had a connection. However, it was I who tensed first as the tickling sensation ran wild. My limbs stiffened as I fought the urge to part my lips and devour her purity. Afraid I would lose control, I backed away, flinching at the sound of our broken kiss.

"I'm sorry, I just . . ."

There was a new color in her cheeks. The cherry flush calmed my insecurities, but I couldn't fight how my body pounded for more. It promised to ruin me if I didn't give in. *So long have I waited, just one more.* I swept her into my arms and kissed her hard. She gasped for air at first but then rested her arms around my neck and plunged her tongue into my mouth. It played with mine for a moment, but when her hand slid down my front, pushing against me as she panted, I had to back away before I ripped off her shirt. I wasn't accustomed to stopping at only a kiss, and my body was aching.

"I'm sorry," I repeated, wiping my lips with the back of my hand, troubled with this new pain I felt.

"No, I . . . um." She looked at her feet as her thin fingertips brushed her wet lips. When she looked up, it was my breath that stopped. "I felt something."

My body was nearly exploding. "You *are* the girl the prophecy talks about. The connection it talks about, with one of the worlds, is with me."

"And my connection with the other?"

Though her remark stabbed a spike of jealousy through me, I was impressed with her strength. But I couldn't answer her. It killed me to imagine her having a connection with anyone other than me, of having a physical relationship with anyone other than me. I ignored her question for now and looked down at my watch. It was getting late.

"There is much work to be done," I said. "I will explain on the way home."

She looked upset. I pretended I didn't notice and opened her door. Though she shot inside like a fireball, I closed it softly behind her and turned to retrieve the telescope.

A moment later, I pulled a sharp U-turn and headed for the canyon road. Finally, I said into the silence, "When I returned home Halloween night, there was a Celestial waiting for me. He is a god, not to be taken lightly in any sense, and I hold the highest respect for him. Therefore, what I am about to ask of you is . . . unfortunate. It brings up the issue of your blackouts."

"My blackouts?" Her skeptical voice bobbled from the uneven road.

I looked at her. "You saw more than just the orange sky in Xibalba, didn't you?"

Tears were forming in the corners of her eyes, proving I was right.

"It doesn't matter," I said, wondering how much she had seen that I wished she hadn't. "The executioners have until Winter Solstice to retrieve you, and your blackouts prove that the connection with a god in the Underworld exists. When you black out, it makes them stronger and us weaker. We need these blackouts to end. In order for that to happen, you must come home with me so that Dylan can train your mind to keep the gods out of your head."

"How?" she squealed as the tires screeched through a turn on the slick road.

She grabbed the emergency handle as I accelerated. My jaw tightened, and I wondered how I was going to tell her. It was ridiculous even for me, and I was embarrassed to say it. It would sound stupid no matter what.

"It's simple, really. Just an obstacle course Dylan needs you to practice. But you don't have to worry—I will be with you one hundred percent of the time." I studied her in the dark. She kept quiet, watching the roadside reflectors blurring by.

As minutes passed, the windows began to fog up, and snowflakes glittered in the car's headlights. When Zara turned to look at the clock, I instantly tried to understand what her expressionless face meant. Was she upset? Was she scared? Did she think I was absurd?

"It's late," she finally said, rubbing her arms.

Unthinking, my hand was messing with the heat again. "Are you cold?"

She chuckled. "Why do you keep doing that?"

"Doing what?"

Her eyes flittered to the vent. "You're obsessed with the temperature gauge."

"No, I'm not."

"Yes, you are. How come?"

I hesitated. "I can't feel fluctuations in temperature."

"Oh." Her hand gently pushed mine over to feel the airflow. The immediate tingle was soft like soda fizz. "This is better," she said, turning the glowing red knob to its hottest and leaning back with a prolonged sigh. "What sort of obstacles?"

"I think it's better if you see for yourself. I don't want to scare you."

She laughed. "I think our relationship is past that point, Lucas."

"True." I chuckled. "How do you feel about starting tomorrow?"

"He can get rid of my blackouts?"

"As much as you're willing to let go."

I was worried she was going to explode any minute, tell me she hated my very existence and wanted nothing to do with me. In which case I'd ignore her, possibly kidnap her until after Solstice. And even then, I wasn't sure I'd give her up.

Instead, she responded, "Let's do it."

Zara

CHAPTER FOURTEEN

Fallen Leaf

The November weather had turned very cold, but I awoke feverish. The carpet's fibers were cold against my toes as I walked to the window. White powder covered the entire street, except for a pair of black stripes that ran down the middle. A burst of hot furnace air intoxicated me as I got ready—or it was Lucas's lips last night? Their sharp lines, plumper than I'd expected, wouldn't leave my mind.

Lucas had said to dress comfortably, so I slipped on my black leggings and a loose sweatshirt I dug up from the dresser. I grabbed Gabriella's clothes, neatly folded, from my dresser and went downstairs to wait. Mom was making oatmeal in the kitchen when Lucas knocked on the door promptly at seven.

"Who's that?" she asked as she turned, looking disheveled in her bathrobe.

"It's nobody, Mom. Just my ride," I answered, rushing a donut into my mouth and guessing it'd be the last thing I ate for a while.

"Well then, why doesn't Bri just walk right in?"

"Well, Mother, because it's not Bri." I brushed a hand down my thighs to wipe away the powdery crumbs. "I won't be home until dinner."

I could see Mom's head poking out of the kitchen as I went to the front. I sidestepped to block her view and opened the door.

"Hey, you ready?" I pretended the strange, leaning mother behind me didn't exist.

His head was down, his hands tucked in the pockets of his red jeans. He scuffed the porch with his black sneakers and looked up. "You're unbelievable."

"What?"

"I'm taking you to my house to learn how to keep a god from penetrating your mind, and you're asking me if *I'm* ready?"

I stepped out, pretending to ponder his statement as I closed the door behind me. "Yes."

Actually, I couldn't think about it unless I was close to a toilet. It made me nauseous. I walked through the cottony fluff covering the grass and slid into Lucas's car. I took in slow, deep breaths of the exotic-oil scent floating in the air and felt more serene.

"You didn't tell your parents it was me picking you up, did you?" Lucas asked, shutting the door silently behind him.

"No. I don't want to raise questions I'm not ready to answer."

"I understand. But that won't do."

I leaned back uncomfortably and pointed my thumb toward the house. "You're right. Shall I go back in right now and straighten things out?"

The car started before I could see his hand twist. He was shaking his head, lips pursed in a pleased smirk. "Later. We've much work to do."

Lucas drove south on Lake Tahoe Boulevard until it deepened into forest, then turned west toward Fallen Leaf Lake on a small, unnamed road walled in by ancient trunks. Lucas said nothing as we drove down the tunnel of shade, swerving around potholes hidden beneath the snow. I clung to the side of my seat, fighting a yawning pit in my stomach and praying we wouldn't spin out and hit a tree.

Dela

By the time the uneven road smoothed out, I had lost feeling in my knuckles. I flexed them as we rounded a curve, and large iron gates appeared between the firs, reaching half the height of the grandfather spruces. Scrolls and swirls adorned the doors, which were flanked by an equally tall brick wall camouflaged by the new snow. As Lucas rolled up, the gates opened automatically, and my fingers loosened in awe as we entered.

"Welcome to my quarters," Lucas said, sounding indifferent. I couldn't shake the feeling that something was wrong.

"Quarters?"

"This isn't my home. My home is in Mexico."

"Of course," I said, feeling stupid.

I looked back out the window, suddenly rethinking my decision to come. This place was a fortress. Inside the gate, webs of silver pine needles and naked branches hung over the road, weighed down by heaping piles of snow that glistened in the kiss of sunrise. The white-tipped evergreens stretched as far as I could see.

As we neared the lake, the trees became fewer and the road turned black, probably thanks to expensive heaters underneath. It gave me a clear view of the house, whose grandness against the fresh winter landscape was breathtaking. I expected to see a stone castle of some sort, like something from Europe, but instead a pleasing, cream-colored villa with gray roof tiles sat over the rocky lakeshore.

Lucas pulled through a white marble portico and curved around to the double front doors, still unresponsive. My eyes traced up the pillars framing the door to a crystal chandelier hanging in the vault, then back down to where the marble steps stopped at my door. *Still worthy of a king*, I thought. Evergreen shrubs dusted with iridescence crept up from the earth and along the outermost side of the stairs.

Then, through the tableau of silver and white and icicles, I spotted two still black figures. They sat upright at the foot of the doors, jade eyes glowering at me.

Lucas let the car idle, a disgusted look rising on his face.

"Look, Zara, I don't want you to think that what I did yesterday was okay."

"The kiss? That's what this is about? All the moping this morning?"

He looked away guiltily. "Yes. That can never happen again."

"You're confusing me. I felt something, didn't you?" Instead of my stomach knotting the way it did whenever I felt a guy was breaking up with me, the fever came, this time with anger.

"The connection we feel is only a false sense of love," he claimed. I found it unconvincing.

"Who are you to tell me what I feel? You don't even know me."

"It's just lust, Zara. That's all."

I huffed and gazed out the window. "When is Solstice?"

"December twenty-first."

Lucas was opening my door before I realized he'd gotten out. I stepped out, annoyed, figuring I'd rather take my chances with the unleashed jaguars than in an argument with Lucas.

"Fine. We just have to put up with each other until then, and after that we can go our separate ways. Where is this stupid training center?" I mumbled, feeling I'd like to die about now.

"This way."

I followed him up the marble steps as his head dropped even lower between his shoulders. We stopped next to the jaguars.

"Niya, Malik, this is Zara," he said.

Sleek black heads turned slowly and locked large eyes on mine. It startled me at first, but a moment later, I knew these animals would never hurt me.

Their uneven spots were visible in the daylight. Niya, the female, sat on the left, her spots gray and black and beautifully shiny. She was a little more restless than Malik, who sat motionless except for his eyes. His fur was black as night, with larger, matte splotches.

I raised my hand to pet them but then retracted it quickly, wondering if they'd bite it off. Lucas chuckled despite his gloom.

"Niya and Malik don't hunt around here. In fact, they never hunt. We bring them fresh meat from the markets," he stated. He watched me closely and somehow anticipated my next question. "They're like us. They don't need to eat as often as they would if they were . . . what's the word . . . adequately mortal? They were given to us for protection at our turning, and they have been a part of our family ever since." He patted Malik's head roughly, drawing a low purr through the jaguar's sharp teeth.

"Do they understand you?" I asked, perplexed.

"Perfectly. Shall we go inside?"

The lack of interest or excitement in his voice reminded me that I was here on a mandatory basis. "After you."

I knew that he had noticed my effort to avoid eye contact, and I could see his sadness deepen. I waited for him to move and then followed, not caring that the jaguars were at my heels.

We walked into a great room with a two-story wall of windows showcasing the white-and-gray lake. Inside, the room was vibrant with color, stonework, and gold. There were old artifacts and murals and a life-sized statue of Andrés by a grove of green plants—something I wondered about. Lucas gave me no chance to ask, but instead veered left into a narrow hallway that curved toward a single door.

We entered a study with lemongrass-patterned wallpaper and denim-blue paint trim. It was chilly. The windows that rose from the dark wood floor to the soffit ceiling across the room were cracked open, the draft enough to feel as though I were outside. Beyond the windows, the room seemed to float in a sea of green and snow. I crossed my arms and stepped closer. Below, the foundation sat on a large, flat crag of rock that stuck out past the house, suspended in midair. A thin stream of water trickled over the side and cascaded down into a stream.

"I like to spend my nights here because the water drowns out a lot of the nuisance noise I can't shut off," Lucas said. "Dylan and Gabriella will join us shortly."

As chilled as I was, I turned and found the room warm in rich browns. A tufted leather couch with a deep sepia hue faced the window, and beside it sat a peculiar side table with exquisite gold trim. Atop it were old books stamped with gold foil and a sheaf of parchment paper bearing scribbled cursive text. On the other side of the couch was an antique-gold globe on a stand. Cartographic maps had been tacked up on every available wall space between tall oak bookshelves with intricate trim. Ancient-looking books, tattered with age, were grouped together on one side, while newer, shinier books were bunched together on the opposite side.

The room looked staged. Everything was in its place—there was a desk with no computer, and even the linen drapes folded across one another perfectly. It all looked human enough until I saw strange objects of metal and stone tucked into the open spaces of the bookshelves, antiques that I knew no human historian would ever have a chance of obtaining.

"What are these?" I asked, touching a round engraved stone.

Lucas followed me closely, not allowing less than two inches between us. "Nostalgic mementos."

My hand left the stone and traced over the grooves carved into what looked like a piece of driftwood. I realized it was shaped into a weapon, a club of some sort. "Old?"

"Very," he said, watching me more closely. *Nervous are you, Lucas?* I thought, delighting in his edginess.

Footsteps echoed in the hall as Lucas lifted my finger and pulled it away from the piece. Gabriella and Dylan walked in just as I stubbornly pulled my hand away from his. My attention fell on Dylan first; I was already intimidated by his unearthly might.

"Zara, you decided to come after all." Gabriella smiled and

greeted me with a kiss on one cheek. "You know, we've never had a human over before."

I waded in with sarcasm. "Well, I didn't really have much of a choice. The blackouts, the prophecy—the world's going to end."

Everyone laughed.

"I brought you your clothes back," I said, speaking fast out of nerves. *I'm not that funny, am I?*

Gabriella glanced at my attempt to make them look professionally folded, then looked up. "That's very kind of you to remember," she said, placing them on the table behind me.

Dylan suppressed a smile as he studied me up and down. I picked at my nails, hoping my trainers and capri leggings would do. No fashion blog ever advised on how to dress when your personal trainer was a god. He stepped forward. "You're funny."

Feet moved evenly along the hall's marble floor, casting musical echoes. Valentina glided through the walnut door first, her arms stretched wide. She wore a tight dress that made her curvy immortal body look Photoshopped to perfection.

"*Bienvenido*, Zara," she greeted me in her beautiful accent. Her sleek hair tickled my cheek as she embraced me gently and kissed my cheek.

Andrés followed and kissed my other cheek before I could resist. I stiffened nervously as they all stood staring at me, suddenly uncertain of how I got here, a house full of gods and immortals. I was probably doubly red from shock. I let my hair fall to cover my burning cheeks, feeling unworthy of their regard.

"Thank you," I finally muttered, remembering from Spanish class in high school that *bienvenido* meant welcome. She made the word sound so elegant.

"Would you guys like to come back to the kitchen for some hot chocolate before you get started?" Andrés asked.

I accepted for both Lucas and I without question. Lately he

didn't seem to know what he wanted, and a warm drink sounded comforting.

"Lucas, I will be waiting for you in the basement," Dylan said.

Lucas shot Dylan an enraged glance as we walked away. I looked in the other direction, sensing a long feud there that I didn't want a part in.

I wanted to look more closely at the rare items in the front room when we returned, but I couldn't take my eyes off Andrés. He moved as a king should—back straight, chest lifted—and Valentina followed with her shoulders back and chin high. My trotting steps fell heavily as they flowed up the spiral staircase. They didn't seem to notice, or pretended not to hear, as we headed toward the back of the house.

Gray light flooded through another wall of windows into their vast kitchen. Without the barricading trees, the sense of floating was even more intense; the lake was their backyard. Two crystal chandeliers lit a spotless granite island. Every surface was stark white and squeaky clean, including the lacquered dining table. The only spot of color was the red rimming the familiar fire-and-ice roses in a white vase on the table.

Andrés pulled out a Lucite chair by the glass wall and motioned for me to sit. As I did, Lucas dropped into another chair by my side, but turned away from me. I gazed out at the cold whiteness frosting the large boulders in the water. *Dad would kill to photograph this wintery manor,* I mused.

"Zara, honey, how are you holding up?" Valentina asked kindly as she checked the whistling teakettle. I thought about her question until she handed me a white hobnail mug steaming with a cocoa bean aroma. The contents promised to be thick and creamy, and my mouth watered.

As I parted my lips to answer, Lucas shifted his gaze to me in a calculating sort of way, and suddenly I couldn't remember what I was going to say.

"I am, umm . . . can Dylan really get rid of my blackouts?" I asked.

Andrés lifted his chin as I sipped the froth. "Lucas, did you have a chance to tell Zara what's going on?"

Lucas tilted his head and shrugged, looking offended. "*Por supuesto*, Papa." He turned to me with more liveliness in his face than I had seen all day. "Didn't I?"

"Yes, yes, he did, Mr. Castillo," I stuttered. I wiped my mouth. For some reason, I felt I should be saying *Your Highness* or *Your Majesty*.

"Please, call me Andrés. And I am curious: what do you think about all of this?" His thick eyebrows furrowed. I froze at his blunt question, confused.

"What do I think about you?"

Andrés's laugh was casually powerful. The dangling crystals on the light overhead shook. "No. What do you think about you, the fifty-second, the prophecy, the training?"

I gulped, not really finding the drink pleasant anymore. "It's a lot to take in."

"And what do you think about us?"

I was beginning to see similarities between Andrés and his son. Both had sharp-cut jawlines masked by a grayness I knew would be darker by evening, and both were exceptionally forward. But the attention of all three flawless beings, intent on my words, still made me feel like a lab rat.

"I think you guys are amazing." I let out an awkward chuckle and shook my head, swiping hair behind my ear. "I don't know how you guys do it. How you can watch people being taken."

Andrés scratched his chin and turned to Valentina with a disapproving grin. *Did I say something wrong?*

"Zara, honey, it's never easy. How do I explain?" Valentina pondered for a slight second. "Imagine our world held at ransom. If we didn't allow all fifty-two sacrifices to be taken, the Underworld would come and take more. And the end result of *that* would be tragic."

I nodded, still processing.

She lowered her chin, squinting as she deciphered my churning emotions. "I mean a war, Zara, a war I'm afraid we haven't got the power to fight. Do you understand?"

My eyes widened as I fought a sudden tide of tears. Lucas reached for my hand and squeezed. I didn't want to look at him because I knew it would make me cry, but I appreciated his gesture.

"Mama, *por favor.* You're scaring her . . . *apurate* . . . tell her the rest," he urged angrily.

"What, *hijo*? I'm just making sure she understands what's going on. Now, Zara, I didn't mean that we're going to watch you be taken, because it's obvious that we're not. You are a precious thing to us," she said as her bold eyes dissected me.

I gulped.

"See, you are not just the fifty-second sacrifice. You, my dear, are without a doubt the girl in the prophecy. And with that, we are all confused. We have been waiting for you for a long time." She took a sip of hot chocolate with her lips gently pressed together, frowned once, then spoke. "You're the gambling chip that changes our game. But all chips are at risk."

I felt a surge of regret as she paused and watched me, thinking further.

"However, if what Tita says is true, than we could rid ourselves of the sacrificial ceremony forever," she said.

"How?"

Niya and Malik walked in. It was unsettling having wild cats roaming around without chains, and yet strange that they heeled at Valentina's side.

"That's the problem," she said. "We don't know yet. We just need to focus on one thing right now, and that's keeping you alive until Winter Solstice. Saving a sacrifice is a first for us. You understand that, right?"

Though I appreciated what she said, pressure tightened my lungs. "Yes," I managed.

"And as such, I am afraid this change brings the chance of retaliation. That being the case, you mustn't be left alone until this situation is settled."

She paused another moment and looked to her son, her finger bobbing back and forth between Lucas and I. We glanced at one another, confused. His hostility, so clearly visible, hurt me, and I squirmed in my seat.

"I'm aware of your relationship," Valentina said, "but Andrés and I decided that it would be best if Lucas stayed with us at night and someone else took the night's watch. Until we can understand the force that connects you two a little more, we need to be careful to not take anything too lightly."

"All right," Lucas agreed rather too quickly. I wanted to kick him underneath the table for being such a jerk. Instead I sat up straighter and pressed my hands together.

"That's probably a good plan," I agreed, a little relieved I didn't have to see Lucas twenty-four seven. His moods were exhausting. "Valentina?"

"Yes?"

"This connection that Lucas and I have . . . is it the one talked about in the prophecy?"

"Yes."

Lucas straightened up, his eyes boring into me. I pretended not to notice, even though amazing tingles flooded my body.

"Well, haven't you ever thought about the consequence of that force . . . of me?" I wondered.

Valentina froze. "Of course. It scares me to death. But how do you feel when you are with Lucas?"

The balloon in my chest that had been popped by Lucas's uncanny behavior was inflating again with giddiness. Lucas waited wide-eyed for my answer. This was on another level than the ordinary *Do you have a crush on my son?* question.

"Like there is an invisible force that wants to push me to him, like he's the one I chose. I can't explain it," I responded. I felt embarrassed, but I hoped it would comfort Valentina's worries about the prophecy. Lucas just looked angry—almost disgusted—and the tingling had started to sting badly.

Andrés moved from his statue's pose. "But you have not been faced with the Underworld yet. They are very powerful and very convincing. You may wince now, but it may be that you have a connection with the Underworld like the one you have with Lucas. It could be just as strong," he warned.

My stomach turned at the inconceivable thought. I felt the immortal royal eyes on me and wondered whether I was actually turning green.

"That will never happen," Lucas interrupted, partly to comfort me. But partly he looked . . . jealous?

"We hope not," Andrés said. He reached for my free hand. His nails were polished black, but his warm smile was the complete opposite of Goth. "Zara, we aren't going to let anything happen to you. We promise. We've never seen Lucas this happy, and we have lived long together."

Lucas, happy? That has to be a joke. Hostile, yes. Angry, yes. Moping, sure, but not happy!

Lucas stiffened and stood, coughing under his breath. "We'd better get started."

I shuddered when he placed his hand on my back. I jumped to my feet so that I could brush his hand away.

"By the way, Tita will be here tonight. She'll be attending school with you as a precaution," Valentina noted.

"Tita?"

"Very well," Lucas said, stretching his hand over my back again to push me gently out of the kitchen before Valentina could answer.

I shrugged Lucas's hand away once we turned the corner. "Quit touching me."

Lucas nodded. I noticed his jaw muscles tighten as we descended to the first floor, through another door, and down another flight. Beyond a corner landing, a room opened before us. I placed my hand on the wall to steady myself. *This isn't a room. It's a training facility.*

"Just a few obstacles?" I joked sourly, staring at the corner pyramid. It reminded me of the one in my dream in miniature, with only ten steps, each the height of two normal stairs. There was a rope wall, metal trapeze bars and rings dangling from the ceiling, mats, weights—and racks of weaponry ranging from bows and arrows to spears and wicked-looking knives.

Lucas walked ahead of me into the weird arena. I watched his back incredulously. I wanted to storm back up the stairs and call Bri to have her pick me up.

"Zara, Lucas, you're here. Finally," Dylan said. He sounded bored.

Lucas approached Dylan, his back blocking my view. Next thing I knew, Dylan threw his hands up and backed away.

"Wow, brother. Relax." Dylan chuckled as he turned to me. "Zara, you ready?"

"What did Lucas say?" I asked, pretending Lucas wasn't here as I approached them.

Lucas spun around. His blue eyes were hard. "I said if he did anything questionable, I would stop it before he could finish it."

I shivered, wondering again what I'd gotten myself into. But I couldn't let Lucas know that. I squared my shoulders and laid my jacket on the floor.

"I'm ready, Dylan," I said.

Lucas looked shocked at my defiance. I smiled as Gabriella

shooed him and his livid look to the stairs.

"Ignore him," I whispered to Dylan. "I don't know what his problem is."

Dylan laughed harder and glanced at Lucas. "I like this girl," he said. Then he turned to me, leaned in, and winked. "And he heard everything you just said."

I pivoted around, frightened at first, then embarrassed when I saw a smirk on that mad, fascinating face.

"Let's just get this over with, please," I said.

"Right."

Dylan walked to the corner opposite the pyramid, where a cage woven of two-inch rope sat beneath a platform ten feet above the floor. A rope ladder hung from the platform. Above it, I realized, the dangling rings made a path across the room to another platform.

"If you want to live, you have to be more than what you are. Forge yourself into a weapon. Got it?" he asked.

I nodded.

He looked up to the platform above him, then back to me. "Your blackouts have a greater chance of occurring when your emotions are high."

"Why is that?"

"Because it makes you vulnerable. A god can exert mental power very easily over someone who is swayed by strong emotion. So, we start by making you vulnerable. I want you to climb up to the top of the platform and swing across the rings to the other edge of the room."

"I'm not sure I can even do that," I argued, staring at the rings ten feet above my head. I probably couldn't reach the end even if I was fast. The room was too long.

"Vulnerable," he reminded me.

I grunted and headed for the platform's ladder.

It looked a lot higher up once I was looking down on everyone's heads. I placed a hand on a ring and waited. Dylan had his arms folded.

"Waiting for you," he said.

Lucas was still there, just a body in the room, good for nothing, watching me too closely for someone who said he didn't care. I stared angrily at him as my knuckles tightened around the metal. And then I swung.

It was like I was in elementary school. I gripped each ring tightly and swung from one to the next. It was a breeze—until my skin started to burn underneath my fingers. The burn became a sting when I touched the metal. Then I started to sweat. It made my fingers slippery.

I stopped midway and looked at my feet. Ten feet felt much higher when my shoes were dangling aimlessly in the air. Dylan watched me with a grin. I tried to catch the next ring, but I had no more momentum. As I clung desperately to one ring with both hands, my head started to pound.

"Ow!" I yelled, fingers slipping.

"Feel that?" Dylan said. "I am inching my way into your head. When I do this, it sends an abnormal rush of electrical impulses to your brain, until eventually your blood vessels dilate and the blood drains from your brain."

"Well, how do I stop it?" I barked.

He circled underneath my body. "Focus. Concentration."

"Ow!" Frost shrouded the left side of my brain.

"Dylan!" Lucas yelled from afar.

I looked for Lucas, but there were black flurries in the air, shifting in the same direction as my irises.

"Zara, you must fight back. I want you to find the image I'm transmitting to your brain and crush it. If you don't, you will black out," Dylan yelled.

My arms shook. I closed my eyes and focused on what I could see. There was nothing, only pitch-black behind my eyes. Sweat slimed the metal rings. I flung my eyes open, scared. "I can't hang on!"

"Destroy it!" Dylan ordered.

"I can't!"

"Focus, Zara!" Lucas shouted.

"Zara, you can do this!" Gabriella added.

"I can't!"

The lights were going dim, and my head was getting colder while my body sweated streams.

"Do it, Zara!" Lucas ordered.

"But I can't see anything!" I spat back.

I could see Dylan, calm, looking straight up to me. "Zara, fight to see the picture I'm putting into your mind so that you can crush it," he said.

Pressure snatched my breath away, and then the lights went out.

I awoke on the mat, with Lucas holding my feet up. The pounding, coldness, and dizziness were gone. It was as if I had never fainted.

"She's awake," Lucas noted.

I pried my legs away from his hands. I couldn't let him know he had upset me with his foolish words earlier. I avoided eye contact while I fixed my hair into a ponytail and cracked my knuckles.

"Again," I said, and I climbed back up the ladder.

This time, Dylan didn't let me get as far. I was crossing the rings easily when a blunt prick of ice in my head indicated that Dylan was tampering with my mind. It progressed swiftly, and next thing I knew, I was in Lucas's arms. He grinned. I rolled my eyes.

"Again," I said, jerking out of his embrace.

For hours Dylan and I repeated the same routine while Lucas sat back, watching blankly as I hammered myself, but always there when I fell. Each time I rolled out of his arms as fast as I could, wondering why he was doing this.

Finally, when my palms were open blisters and my arms were

jelly, I had my first vision before blacking out. I shrieked, and then I woke up in Lucas's arms. It took me longer to get up this time. Even after I staggered to my feet, I found myself leaning on Lucas for support as the room spun.

"Really Dylan? Ding-dong ditching?" It was something I did for fun long ago—when I was ten, maybe—ringing doorbells and running away.

He chuckled. "One of my greatest pastimes in the sixties. That's beside the point. You finally acknowledged that someone was in your head. You passed the first step." He looked at his watch. "Only took you three hours. I think we're off to a great start."

"She needs to eat, Dylan," Lucas said harshly. He guided me toward the stairs.

In the kitchen, Lucas aimed me at a chair and prepared a light sandwich and another mug of hot chocolate for me. There was no setting for him when he sat.

"You're not eating?" I asked.

"It's unnecessary."

"You ate Chinese."

"Ever since I became immortal, my body hasn't needed to eat on a daily basis. It's not life or death for me, so I eat when I feel like it."

I took a bite of the sandwich and looked away. "When you feel like it?"

He snickered coldly at my mockery. "You're going to make me eat?"

"No. I can't control you."

"I beg to differ."

His response gave me chills, asking questions I didn't want to pursue, and I remained silent, staring out at the lake as I finished the sandwich. After lunch he insisted I take a longer break when I admitted my muscles hurt. Of course, I had to decline. I couldn't show him that I was weak, though I wasn't sure I was fooling him.

The 52nd

I regretted my decision when Andrés, Valentina, and the jaguars watched from the sidelines while Dylan had me climb up and down the pyramid's steps. I felt stupid holding onto each step, struggling for balance and heaving at the same time. Thankfully, just when I thought I was going to puke up my sandwich, Dylan decided to switch to the cage.

My legs cramped inside the small, scratchy prison as he tried to penetrate my mind. After the image appeared of an orangutan scratching his butt with his hand, sniffing it, then falling off his tree, the blackness drowned me out. Gabriella was by my side when I woke up, pressing an ice pack to my head.

"Gosh, what is with the images?" I asked, rubbing my head, which was aching not because I'd bumped it, but because Dylan had pushed his way in one too many times.

"Would you rather I showed you beheadings or people's limbs being cut off? Because I guarantee that is what you will see next time you are pulled into the Underworld," Dylan said. He snickered under his breath. "Besides, it's one of the funniest things I've ever seen."

Dylan was right; the Underworld was exactly what I *didn't* want to see. When the image of the two men eating human limbs resurfaced, I nearly gagged. I climbed back into the cage without another word, but paused as my foot spasmed. "What is the point of the cage?" I asked as I reached for my foot and pushed my thumbs into the painful cramp.

"Are you uncomfortable?"

"You have no idea," I said, more sharply than I intended.

"Then you are vulnerable. Your discomfort makes you weak. All you can think about is getting that cramp out of your right arch, right?"

I ignored him and kneaded the screaming muscle.

"If you get taken by the Underworld, you will not die right

away," he continued. "They will lock you up in a cage similar to this one and leave you there until they are ready to sacrifice you. That's the point of the cage."

"Fine, I get it," I said, hugging my knees close to my chest when the cramp went away.

CHAPTER FIFTEEN

PROSPERITY

"She's done for the day," Lucas said. Seeing the weariness in his beautiful face, I didn't dare shrug away when he reached for me in the cage.

"One more hour," Dylan retorted.

"No."

Lucas dragged me away without another word. Sticky sweat glazed my hand, but he didn't let go until we reached another walnut-colored door upstairs.

He pushed it open. "This is my room."

The lights were dim, and it was hot. There was a gas fireplace in the corner, and judging by the amount of heat radiating out of it, it had been turned on some time ago. Its orange light flickered on the navy walls and the chocolate velvet headboard running up to the ceiling. There was a high-back chair in the corner, upholstered with funky printed fabric, and panels of camel-and-white chevron textile hung at each side of the black French doors to his balcony. It was getting dark outside, but it was light enough to see the fog that had begun bubbling in the brittle air, obscuring much of the lake.

I could feel his eyes on me as I moved farther into the lion's lair.

"Where are your pictures?" I looked around at the bare walls.

"We don't really take pictures."

"Why?"

He shrugged. "Evidence, I guess. And for obvious reasons, we didn't have cameras when I was a boy."

There was an awkward silence. As I shrugged my overstretched shirt back over my shoulder, I noticed he was struggling to say something. I wanted to push him to talk, but I bit my tongue.

After a moment, he cleared his throat. "How are you feeling?"

"I'm okay. Dylan wasn't as bad as I thought he would be."

"Yeah, well, this is only the first day," he reminded me.

I raised my eyebrows and nodded, wondering suddenly why I was in Lucas's room.

"Would you like to sit?" He motioned to the rug.

He relaxed a bit after we sat. As he focused on the fire, I hiked my knees up to my chest and rested my chin on my kneecaps, waiting for him to speak.

"I gather you're wondering about school on Monday," he started, leaning back on his elbows.

"I'm wondering a lot of things, Lucas."

He looked away and cleared his throat. "After I took you home last night, I came back here and thought about you for three hours. When I realized that it wasn't three hours but actually the entire night, and I'd ignored my family and every responsibility I had, I felt there was a problem. I was so consumed with you mentally that everything around me went away. And I fear that neglecting my instincts is very dangerous." He paused and looked into the fire. "We can't get close like last night, ever."

"You're a wreck," I said.

"I know."

There was another long moment where I thought Lucas had something else to say that would make my heart feel another little tear, but it never came.

"Tita will be registered in all your classes," he said.

"Oh." I didn't care.

"She likes to stay at home when it's off season."

"Off season?"

"You're the last sacrifice. After you, there wouldn't be any more abductions for another fifty-two years."

Imagining the recent abductions, I wrapped my arms around my legs again to hide my chills. Right at this moment, there were families searching for their missed loved ones. I gulped against a deep pressure in the back of my throat. "Why can I hear the shadows' whispers?"

The muscles in Lucas's face tensed, creating a shadow above his jawbone in the dim flicker. His beauty burned hotter than fire into my heart. It hurt.

"It's your connection with the Underworld," he whispered, picking at a loose string in the jute rug.

He wouldn't look at me as I remembered the distorted faces. The warped bones twisting like tree roots over their smoky skin haunted me. "What are they . . . the executioners?"

"They are dead, soulless creatures, the fallen Aztec and Mayan kings."

I was sure Lucas heard my heart leap into gallop—he focused on me more cautiously.

"And no other sacrifice can hear them?" I asked weakly.

"No."

He looked so peaceful leaning against the small coffee table, while I felt my lunch climbing upward. He scratched his bicep softly, exposing more of his tattoo. Then he pulled a tiny wooden star out of his pocket and casually twirled it between his fingers. It matched his tattoo.

"What does your tattoo mean?" I asked.

"You are the most peculiar little creature I've ever met," he said, smiling as he looked down at his markings and then back up, his eyes smoldering yet soft. "The star symbolizes perfection. The rooted tree depicts the three realms: heaven, Earth, and hell. And the circle that encompasses both symbolizes their eternities."

"And what's that?" I pointed to the star.

He held up the piece to observe it closely. "This was a gift Ahau gave to me when I was born. He said to never let it out of my sight, that it would bring me great prosperity someday because it would never guide me wrong."

"And has it?"

He looked up at me with an expression that warmed his coldness. "It's brought me to you."

I looked down quickly and fiddled with my fingers while my pounding heart gave me away. "Why does everyone in your family have tattoos?"

"They appeared on our bodies during the transformation."

"How?"

He shifted uneasily. "Maybe we should talk about something else." Anguish danced through his voice as he gazed into the fire. His skin seemed polished, the way it mirrored the light from the logs. *I bet he's never had a pimple his whole life.* And then I noticed his chin; it was darker, like Dad's three-day no-shave runs.

"Do you ever shave? I've never seen you without facial hair."

His teeth sparkled against the fire when he smiled. "I did this morning."

"No you didn't. You had stubble this morning."

"I can't help that," he said. "That's a part of me now."

I wondered what he meant but didn't want to pry further for some reason. "So, what's going to happen after Solstice?"

He started picking at the rug again, more quickly now. "I know that you desire to be rid of me as soon as you are saved, but it can't happen right away. After the executioners come for you and are unsuccessful, they will return to the Underworld through the portal to report. My family and I must close that portal to ensure they do not come after you again. When the time comes, your family will travel with mine to Mexico. We can keep a better eye on you there, should the executioners attempt to come for you once more. Only then, when the portal is closed, will you be free of me."

"Free of you? Who ever said I wanted that?" His answer cut open painful memories of how sick I'd felt when he was gone. *I don't want Lucas to go, ever.*

I looked around the room to hide the tears surfacing in my eyes. There were funny items on the bookshelf and the small bedside table. They were old looking, all made of polished stone or leather. A large headdress hung in a glass case on the wall by the door. It reminded me of an Indian war bonnet or a Roman warrior's helmet, the way the metal wrapped over the head to the ears. Faceted green jewels and turquoise surrounded its tarnished bronze crown beneath a spray of tall black feathers that fanned out like a peacock's tail.

"What is that?" I asked.

"What I wore when I was human."

I laughed. It was half the length of the door. "It's huge."

"I *was* the prince." He had a Cheshire cat grin, the kind that no doubt attracted lovers to his bed.

I blushed and looked away. There were a few more pops in the fire as Lucas got up. "We'd better get you home. Gabriella will be there at six thirty for the night watch."

As I started for the door, he unthinkingly interlocked his fingers with mine. I didn't back away, except try to keep a straight face as he guided me to the garage.

The parked cars in front of my house sat beneath a foot of fresh snow. I didn't realize how long the day had seemed until my body started to ache. Looking at the sparkling pathway the porch light made in the dark, I was suddenly disappointed I wouldn't see Lucas until Monday.

Dela

"Someone will be watching you this weekend. I will be here Monday morning to pick you up for school," Lucas said in the dim red glimmer of the dashboard. "We will pick up training where we left off after class."

He was perfect in the darkness. The shadows on his face outlined the beautiful groove that ran down the middle of his upper lip. My chest hollowed with disappointment when I realized he was waiting for me to get out.

Lucas's car idled after I shut the door, collecting new snowflakes until I was safely inside the house. After dinner I checked my bedroom window as snow danced downward from the black sky. Gabriella's gold car was parked underneath the lamppost across the street.

I stepped away and looked at my phone. It was crowded with missed calls. I shut it off. My head was on the verge of exploding. I took ibuprofen and dragged myself into the shower. The shredded skin of my palms stung. *They'll probably be better by tomorrow,* I remembered, and I ignored them.

I closed the blinds and pulled the drapes. I felt safe for the first time in weeks and fell asleep peacefully.

I was sitting in my car, late at night, in my dream. I was at a park. The headlights were shining down a grassy hill toward the swings. A young boy, maybe five years old, smiled at me as he ran up the hill in the stream of headlights. He was happy, but as he ran to me, an executioner swooped through the beams and grabbed him. The terror on that boy's face, looking me straight in the eyes as the executioner snatched him with clawed hands, burned in my mind as I wrenched awake.

My room smelled like Lucas when I inhaled the cool air. A blue sticky note fluttered slightly on my lampshade.

I came to check on you. Gabriella said you were screaming. I put my number in your speed dial. Call me when you get this.

Lucas's name glowed at the top of my phone's quick-dial list. *Number one. Figures.* The phone rang for approximately 0.2 seconds before he picked up.

"What happened?" He sounded worried.

After I shared my nightmare, the line was silent.

"Do you think they took this boy?" I asked, flashes of his horrified face running through my mind.

"Of course not. We would know about it," he responded, offended.

"You're not mad at me?"

"Why would I be mad at you?"

"I don't know, because I'm weak?" I said.

"Zara, you've only had one day of training. Do you feel okay?"

"Yes." I felt more guilty than pained by the few muscles that were still sore, but I wasn't going to tell him that. "Was this real?"

"No." He paused. "Or, at least, it's not happening right now. I think your dream was another form of your connection. It gave you a perspective."

I frowned. I didn't know what I expected to hear, but "a perspective" wasn't it. I could barely handle the blackouts.

"What you saw in your dream, Zara," he said when I didn't speak, "is what I've seen hundreds of times. It's possible you had this dream because, well, you and I are close right now. Your dream allowed you to see our world from my perspective. I've seen this happen hundreds of times." There was another long pause on his end. "I'm sorry you had to see that."

I bit my nails and nodded, forgetting that he couldn't see me.

"There probably will be more dreams," he added apologetically.

The phone slipped through my fingers. I caught it before it hit the ground and banged it back against my ear.

"Are you sure you're okay?" he asked.

"I'm fine."

A light tap on my door startled me. "Zara?"

"What?" I yelled, covering the earpiece.

"Who are you talking to?"

"To Lucas Castillo."

"Valentina's boy?"

"Yes, Mom, what other Lucas do I know?"

"Invite him over for dinner on Monday for family night. I'd like to meet him properly."

I knew Lucas had heard her. I could practically see the arrogant grin on those kissable lips of his.

"Are you going to answer her?" he asked after a few moments.

"Fine." I covered the earpiece out of habit and yelled through the door, knowing he could hear everything. "Mom, he said he'd come."

I wondered if he could sense my reluctance too. I didn't want him over for dinner, but there was no way out of this.

"Tell him to be here at five thirty," she responded.

"I'm not going to bother telling you what time. You probably heard her better than I did," I said.

He cackled. "I'll pick you up tomorrow at seven. Oh, and you might want to tell your mom this time that you've arranged for me to drive you to school every day. Humans' imaginations tend to make them suspicious for no reason."

My mouth dropped open at his presumptuous accusation. *My* idea to have him pick me up? *Suspicious for no reason*! The blatant lie crawled beneath my skin, steaming through every pore. *This was all his idea!*

"I'm driving myself tomorrow. I'm not going anywhere with you."

I could hear the rustle as he scratched his chin. "When I come to get you tomorrow, bring my journal. I want it back," he demanded.

"I said I'm not going anywhere with you, didn't you hear me? You can't put me in this cage. You can follow me, and I'll be just fine."

"This isn't a debate. I will see you tomorrow in front of your house . . . don't try anything stupid."

Me against the determined immortal—not even fair. I grunted. "Anything else, Your Majesty?"

"No."

I slammed down the phone before he could fit another command in. But there was no room to breathe when I realized that Lucas now consumed my daily life. My throat felt parched and scratchy. My old life, filled with wonder about what college would be like, had dissolved, and the new unavoidably revolved around a conceited immortal's secret world. I curled into a ball beneath the sheets. How was I going to tell Mae she wasn't getting her book back?

CHAPTER SIXTEEN

Beguiled

I met Lucas outside Monday morning, feeling grateful that my torn palms had gone from stinging to peeling to pink so quickly. It was dawn, but dim, and the streetlights still cast their yellow halos on the street. I shoved the old journal hard into Lucas's chest as he stood on the greasy snow lining the road, opening the car door for me. He didn't budge as I got in, fuming.

A light song in Spanish played in the background as he backed out into the black slush. I watched my abandoned green wagon with longing as we left. It didn't matter that Lucas didn't have my exact schedule; I wasn't allowed anywhere alone since the decision to "keep" me. My freedom was gone; I understood that, but did circumstances have to be this bad?

"You do realize you're going to have to talk to me sooner or later," he said as we pulled onto campus fifteen minutes later.

"I prefer the latter," I finally answered.

"I'm sorry to hear that, because it looks like it's going to be sooner."

I shot him a glare to cover my confusion, but he wasn't looking at me. I started and banged an elbow against the door when I saw his family staring at us from outside the car. Gabriella had her apocalyptic bracelets of diamond-cut turquoise and jade and squares of onyx hiked up her arms. She wore a matte-gold sequined miniskirt and pumps in the low-forties temperatures.

Tita, whose head only reached Gabriella's chest, wore the same warm smile she'd had at Lucky Pin. She had short, fine hair the color of coal and a duskier complexion, and a pale pink flush on the apples of her cheeks that made her innocently desirable. Over her neck, behind the small plastic binder pressed against her chest, was the black etching that marked her as one of them.

Who was I fooling? Lucas could never be with me, and I could never be one of them. Why would I want to? Immortality had taken a toll on Lucas, clearly. And I wouldn't want to be a miserable person moping around like him, even though he did it beautifully.

Lucas's engine went soundless, putting a hum of stillness in my head. I expected Lucas to hop out, but he stayed.

"We have an alibi," he said.

"There is no *we* in this equation," I reminded. "*You* have an alibi that *I'm* obligated to follow."

He pursed his lips when I lifted my chin stubbornly. "If you desire to return to your normal life," he said, "you will. But not until we close the portal. For now, you will cooperate." His hand reached for the door but stopped abruptly. "It would be a lot easier if you acted like you didn't hate me."

"No, it would be *easier* if you didn't exist."

His whole body turned toward me ever so slowly, his disgust slithering over my skin, making me shiver. "What did you say?"

I shrank in that instant, wanting to take it all back. "Look, I can't forget about how I felt in the mountains. And I know you felt something too. So why are you ignoring all that?"

His face was hard, his forehead furrowed in concentration. "Who said I was ignoring all that? I'm only ignoring you, and for good reason, which I told you in my room. You should be more careful whom you kiss if you can't control your feelings."

His words sucked the breath out of me and wrung my pride dry. I sulked in the seat as he fluidly exited the car, his expression changing to false cheer. I was stunned that he could act so happy while I felt incarcerated by all his rules. I was only human, and I deserved a human moment to adjust my attitude. I was living in *his* mythical world now, and feelings aside, I knew he was right. Which bothered me. He was only trying to protect me, or himself, as Valentina would think.

I watched them. Their smiles lit up the frozen space around them, drawing wondering eyes from all around as they conversed in the golden tint of the sunrise. I wondered what Lucas had meant when he said Tita *helped* them to become worthy. She looked so pure.

I grabbed my bag and muttered nervously under my breath as I let myself out. It was freezing, and worse, my friends pointed fingers in my direction. *I've been a bad friend, ignoring their calls.* I pretended I didn't notice and burrowed my chin into the collar of my red jacket, feeling the gazes of the unusually gorgeous immortals on me as I approached.

"Hi, I'm Zara," I said shyly.

Tita's dark irises were powerful in the icy air. "I know who you are."

"Tita will be in all your classes. If you need to use the restroom, wait until class is over so Tita may escort you. If she tells you to leave class, you do it," Lucas commanded. He put on a pair of black designer sunglasses and turned to the others. "Do we need to go over anything?"

"What are you talking about? We are *just* going to a couple classes," I pointed out. Dylan and Lucas snickered, and Lucas slid an arm over my shoulders, saying slyly, "Don't hate me, Miss Moss."

Then he flicked two fingers, and Dylan, Gabriella, and Tita were off, gliding east over the slippery white powder toward school.

"I am going to regret this, aren't I?" I said into Lucas's shoulder as we started after them.

I'd never fully acclimatized to his exotic scent. It brought warmth into my joints, making it a little easier to walk. But I was so focused on the glares my friends fired at me that I slipped. As if it was second nature, Lucas grabbed my shoulder and supported me, so tightly his fingers began crushing my shoulder.

"Ouch!" I shouted.

"Sorry." He winced as I rubbed my shoulder.

He stopped rushing as we approached the snow-covered tables in the courtyard where Tita waited. Soft snowflakes fluttered past Lucas's nose as he lifted his glasses.

"Don't deviate from the schedule. I will be waiting for you in the cafeteria at noon. If you're not there by five after, I'm coming to look for you," Lucas said to Tita, angling his back so that I couldn't see his face. She nodded, and he walked away without another word.

I stared balefully at him until Tita grabbed my arm.

"Come on, we'll be late for class," she warned kindly.

A sudden sharp pain wedged into my ribcage. It stabbed anew with every breath I took for the rest of the day. When Tita and I arrived at lunch, Lucas was waiting in the cafeteria. As he sat down by me and watched me eat, he never stopped moving: his fingers ran through his hair again and again or picked at the fringe of his shorts. I couldn't read gods, but I could read men, and Lucas was doing what every normal man would do if he was nervous around a girl. I didn't want to believe it because it only hurt more; I looked away, pretending I didn't know, and finished my meal.

"Zara!" Jett called in the parking lot after school, sloshing toward me through the snow.

Tita was at my side, and Lucas had a fair ten paces on of us, but I was positive his cocked head was listening.

I ignored his rules and turned to Jett. When Tita did too, I was suddenly slightly jealous of Jett's freedom.

"Yes?" I asked.

His eyes wavered back and forth between Tita and me.

"Some of us are hiking on Saturday—backcountry snowboarding before the lifts open. Wanted to know if you'd want to join."

"I can't," I lied. "I have plans." *This* was why I stayed home for college. *THIS*, and I couldn't go.

"Well, then how about the next Saturday?"

"Busy." I turned before my *help me* face gave everything away.

The snow crunched behind me as he followed. "And the next?" There was a hint of anger in his desperation.

"Busy," I repeated blandly.

He rushed in front of me, glanced at Tita, then spoke angrily. "Can I have a word with you, alone?"

I was surprised when she backed away, even if it was only five feet, to where Lucas had joined her. Tita was pushing against his chest, shushing him as he tried to push past her hands. I wondered at that moment if she was as strong as the others. My answer came when Lucas's brow furrowed as he pushed against her, but she didn't budge. Her feet were planted in the snow as she whispered something to calm him down. I let him notice my glare before turning my back to him, delighting in how little I had to do to make him mad.

"Yes?" I said, demanding attention when Jett didn't remove his eyes from Lucas.

He looked back finally, concern evident in his gaze. "So, are you and Mexico . . .?"

"Lucas?"

"Yeah. Are you and Lucas . . .?"

"Are Lucas and I what?"

"A couple?"

The answer was already rising to the air before he finished, and I said it as loudly and harshly as I could. "No."

the 52nd

What I would give to see Lucas's face. Jett loosed a relieved smile and settled the prescription glasses over his eyes.

"Well then, what are you doing Saturday?" he asked curiously.

"Something. But you don't have to worry about it. It will all be over once the new year starts. Promise." And at that, I patted his shoulder and left.

The drive to Fallen Leaf was especially slow. I was paranoid about what Lucas was thinking when he drove only forty miles an hour. I imagined it was about the Jett incident earlier. I felt ashamed that I was the only one addicted to our connection. I couldn't stop thinking of his lips on mine or the way his hands softly held my head.

"Over here, Zara," Dylan called from the back corner when we entered the basement.

Niya and Malik were pacing near him, but I felt comfortable. Their bodies seemed relaxed. Dylan had changed into basketball shorts and training shoes. Of course he had to look like a sports model. The tips of his fingers lightly bounced together and apart as he waited for me to reach him.

"Demons and gods have supernatural senses and abilities. Immortals have preternatural ones," he said. "This means that your lover boy over there could never do this."

I only saw Dylan's hand rise after I heard Lucas scream behind me. I turned and found him rubbing the side of his head. A dark leather ball rolled on the floor at his feet. My spirits lifted.

"A god can do supernatural stuff like controlling things without physically touching them, a type of telekinesis. Lucas, though, cannot. He's only exceptional, that's all."

"Only exceptional?" Gabriella laughed as she came down the stairs.

Dylan winked at Gabriella, then turned to me. "My point is that it is vital you break this connection with the Underworld. Right now, your blackouts are a side effect of the connection. Imagine if the Xibalbans found out: you would experience much worse than blackouts. And it worries me that it could be more powerful than your connection with Lucas. So, are you ready to begin round two?"

My nod was feeble. They trusted me too much. What if I wasn't enough?

"Good. Let's start with the rope net."

I looked over my shoulder to a third platform almost as high as the ceiling. It was discouraging, but so was the way to get up it. I stepped in front of Dylan and placed a foot on the first tier. It wobbled uneasily beneath my feet. I waited an eternity, it seemed, to steady myself. I glanced once more at Lucas, unable to resist. He barely looked at me, and when he did, his eyes were stone.

I started to climb. I was wondering how far Dylan would let me get when my calves caught fire.

"You can do this, Zara!" Gabriella cheered below as I reached the halfway point.

Suddenly, cold poured into my head and hardened, freezing knives of ice in the right side of my head. A new image began forming. It webbed out like crystals until it shattered, bringing blackness to envelop me.

Once again, I was in Lucas's cradling arms. But this time I was grateful his gaze wasn't on me—it glared at Dylan with almost tangible disgust.

"What is your problem?" Lucas yelled, though he set me down gently.

I backed away.

"Don't be weak, Lucas," Dylan said, glancing over his shoulder. "You ready, Zara?"

Lucas stepped in front of me and blocked Dylan's view. "No, she's not. Quit being so hard on her. You have to ease into things, and you are not easing into things!"

As they argued, I timidly retreated to the steps and took a drink of water.

"Don't worry about him," Valentina said, sitting down next to me to watch the two argue.

"What do you mean?"

"I see what's going on between you two. He's afraid."

"Afraid?"

Her dark eyes met mine. "He is distancing himself from you because he is afraid what the prophecy foretells about you destroying our side. He is only protecting himself."

"Protecting himself from me," I corrected. The ball of hope that we'd ever be together detonated, leaving me empty and scared. "Does he think I would choose the other world over him?"

"Perhaps," she turned to Lucas. "Or protecting him from himself."

"Himself?"

"Mm-hmm. He's never cared for anyone. I think you may be the first. Perhaps he's afraid he'll hurt himself if things go wrong."

"Is this your supernatural sense?"

She smiled tenderly with a slight parting of her lips. "No, honey. It's my motherly sense. Don't be too hard on yourself. Lucas cares for you more than he lets on."

My head cranked back to Lucas when her shoulder nudged me softly. "Best get back to work."

As I returned to the rope climb, Dylan and Lucas continued to quarrel. My thoughts were stuck on Valentina's expression. She thought I was strong. She believed I could do this. My breathing was jagged as I clenched the rope, thinking about Lucas's fear of me choosing the other side over him. I would not be the one to bring the world to destruction. It would rot and die before I had anything to do with such abandonment. I would prove him wrong.

As I climbed up the thick twine of hemp, my determination made the cold penetration muted, barely noticeable as Dylan's image surfaced. Dimly, I saw him standing with me in a tropical forest, barefoot. The leaves were luscious and green like pillows beneath my feet until something pricked my heel, bringing my focus back to home.

I found myself clinging to the rope with aching arms and legs as Dylan's image tried to resurface. My head pounded with waves like static. I glanced up, desperate to escape the blizzard in my head. I was only a couple of feet from the platform. When I focused on the edge above me, the image dimmed, and I slowly inched my way to the top. When my spent body collapsed on the platform, the excruciating pounding disappeared.

There were claps below. I looked down and saw a faint smile on Lucas's face.

"Excellent," Dylan called up. "Let's call it a day."

Tita joined the others while I climbed down.

"Who's got night watch tonight?" she asked.

"Andrés," Lucas said, with a startling harshness that made Tita look curiously at him before glancing over to me.

"See you tomorrow, Zara," she said. Surely she noticed the awkwardness as Lucas escorted me upstairs. I mustered a smile over his shoulder, and her face said a thousand times, *I'm sorry*. Tita understood.

By the time I changed into my school clothes and slid into Lucas's car, the sky was already darkening. I couldn't resist looking at the prince through the red glow of the dash. I wanted to study him and his past, but he kept his proud face turned to the road. He pulled up to my house right at five thirty. Though the sky was a light indigo, every light was on, including the second-floor floodlights, which were only turned on when we were expecting guests.

"Are you sure you want to do this? I have no idea what my parents will say," I warned him.

He looked toward the house, determined, and reached for a

cardigan in the backseat. "Not a chance I'd miss this."

I braced for parental embarrassment, but Lucas was already opening my door. He slipped the black cardigan over his shirt, and we trekked up to the house and wiped the snow off our shoes on the porch. The house smelled like a roast had been simmering all day. It made my stomach grumble.

Mom emerged first from the kitchen. Her strawberry-blonde hair was curled, and she wore the gold necklace Dad gave her for their ten-year anniversary. It looked like it came from a different planet entirely than Valentina and Gabriella's gaudy jewelry. The fragile, thin chain blended with the color of her flesh.

"Mitch, she's here!" she yelled upstairs. "Thanks for bringing her home on time, Lucas. I hope you guys are hungry."

"Thank you for inviting me over for dinner tonight, Mrs. Moss," Lucas replied.

"Not a problem. We love to have company."

"Want some help, Mom?"

"No thanks, honey. Everything is ready. Will you just get Lucas something to drink? I'm going upstairs to fetch your dad."

I had started toward the kitchen when I noticed Lucas in the living room, staring at the black-and-white portraits hanging on the wall.

"Is this you?" He pointed to a picture of me when I was six. My two front teeth were both missing, my hair was in pigtails, and I was wearing a swimsuit.

"Yes." I blushed.

He snickered quietly. "You were . . . cute."

"You don't have to be nice."

He faced me with a sincerity that filled the room, leaving no trace of annoyance. "I meant it."

While I was caught off guard, he looked at the next and the next. His smiled changed a level at each picture. It made me anxious, and my humiliation crystallized the moment he laughed out loud.

"So this is the Lucas Castillo I have been hearing so much about," Dad said as he walked down the stairs, unbuttoning the collar of his shirt. "It's nice to finally put a face to the name."

He extended a hand, which Lucas shook firmly.

"Nice to meet you too," Lucas said. He pointed to the pictures on the wall. "Did you take all these pictures?"

"Lori and I did. We're a bit obsessive with the camera, if you couldn't tell. Didn't Zara tell you we have a photography business along the lake?"

Mom nudged Dad's shoulder and looked at Lucas. "You don't have to answer that. Come in, come in. The food is getting cold."

We followed them to the kitchen, where Mom tried not to smile as Lucas held my chair out.

"So, Lucas, how did you and Zara meet?" she asked, passing the roasted carrots.

The task of scooping baby carrots onto a plate was simple, but Lucas did it bewitchingly, so graceful and handsome were his smooth hands, and for a moment I wished I was those baby carrots. He knew exactly what he was doing and turned to me innocently. "Carrots?"

I yanked the glass bowl away from him. He was doing that thing again that made me stare for no reason. How come I didn't have *that* kind of voodoo? If only he gawked at me like I did at him.

"Actually, Zara and I met at Lucky Pin," he said, smiling as I looked away in annoyance.

"Oh? Do you go there often?"

He chuckled quirkily. "I don't really see a need to anymore."

Mom's eyes lit up, but I was worried about Dad. He took his time chewing, and after he swallowed, his mouth worked silently, like he had something stuck in his teeth.

"I must say, I've noticed a nice change in Zara's behavior since she's been hanging around you," Mom said. "After the crash, she was so moody and angry."

"Mom!"

Dad coughed. "Where do you live, Lucas?"

"I live just off the Eighty-Nine on Fallen Leaf Lake."

"Isn't that government property?"

"Our land? No. It's been in our family for years."

"Sounds beautiful," Mom interjected as she sliced her salad. She looked kind of manic. *Who slices salad?* "So, your mother tells me you also have a sister, and she is married?" Her pitch rose, fishing.

"Yes. Dylan and Gabriella grew up together. He proposed to her as soon as he heard that we were leaving the country. I guess he couldn't stand to live without her," he said. His eyes flicked to my plate, making the food in my mouth catch in my throat.

"What are you studying, Lucas?" Dad asked.

Lucas chugged a large gulp of water before answering, "Public affairs."

Mom shifted in her seat. "Oh, that sounds nice. Political maybe?"

"Pardon me for asking, but why did you guys have to leave?" Dad interrupted.

"Dad!"

"What? It's a perfectly normal question."

"It sounds like you're accusing him of being exiled or something," I said.

Dad looked to Lucas. "Were you?"

"No, I wasn't." He chuckled, his dimple showing in his uneven smile. "We moved because my dad wanted a change. He's been retired for a few years, so there was no job holding him back."

"What did your dad do for work?" Mom asked.

I used my finger to scrape salad and stroganoff into one bite, hoping it would make the contents on my plate disappear faster. *This dinner must end, the sooner the better.*

"He was in trade and exports," Lucas responded.

"Exporting what?" Dad wondered.

"Stone."

"Stone?"

Lucas set his fork down and wiped his mouth clean. "Yes."

"Natural stone?"

"He traded both, natural and faux stone, sir," Lucas said, resting his arms on the table.

"Anything in particular?"

"Well, any kind of stone."

"Stone from where?"

Oh, Dad, are you serious? At this rate, dinner would last all night. I laughed with unbelief. *Come on, Dad, stone. Stone means stone. Who cares where it comes from?* Lucas seemed unmoved by the nosiness, as if he expected it—or enjoyed it.

"Well, mainly limestone from Mexico." Lucas was suppressing a smile.

"Huh. I would never have guessed. Interesting." Dad finally put a bite into his mouth. "Well, if your parents ever get bored of being retired, you tell them to stop by our shop anytime. We'd love to show them Tahoe."

"That's very nice of you. I'm sure they would love that."

I looked at Lucas's plate. It was untouched.

"Lucas, try the rolls, they're my favorite," I urged dramatically.

He managed to take a few bites as Mom and Dad ate. His bites were larger, which cleared his plate faster.

"So I bet you two are just the cutest at school. Young freshmen. I remember . . ." Mom said unexpectedly.

"Mom!" I mouthed *stop* to her, but she just shushed me. "We're just friends," I insisted.

Lucas sipped his water with a grin visible through the clear glass and then glanced at his watch. "I should probably get home."

I shot up quickly. "I will walk you to the door."

"Thank you for your hospitality. Thanks for dinner, Mrs. Moss. It was very good."

"What was that?" I whispered, once we were at the front door.

"That was great," Lucas whispered back. I couldn't tell if his meek expression was sarcastic or just plain naïve.

Snow gusted in when he opened the door. I crossed my arms to block the bitterness.

"I'll be here at nine to pick you up," Lucas said. He lingered a second, his eyes wavering, then unexpectedly leaned down and kissed me on the cheek.

"Good night," he said before disappearing through the door.

Once he'd driven away, I stood on that doorstep for a solid minute. The warmth of his lips lingered on my cheek even as I helped wash the dishes and later as I got ready for bed. I peeked outside, secretly hoping it was Lucas's car across the street, and felt disappointed when it was a black Mercedes-Benz. Lucas had told me one day which series Andrés's car was; I vaguely remembered S, but I wasn't sure. There were numbers, and although Lucas didn't tell me the exact total, I distinctly remembered that his car was worth more than my house.

The kiss that probably meant nothing still excited me enough the next morning that I raced to get dressed.

"Be home later, Mom. I'm going to Lucas's after school," I said.

"Again?" I could hear the *human suspicion* in her tone as she peeled a banana.

"Still just friends, Mom."

A thin fog greeted me outside, but its sheerness promised it would leave by early afternoon. Lucas was leaning against a white Range Rover in a black T-shirt. He had a wide grin.

"Is this yours?" I asked, sliding onto the stiff leather as he held the door open.

"Yes."

Inside was a futuristic red dashboard and custom gray leather, just like his Lexus, except that this car was unused. The new-car smell was nice, but I missed the tropical scent of his other car.

All the way to school, Lucas's cheeks were locked into a permanent grin. He maintained this peculiar expression all day. I worried that something was stuck.

"All right, what is it?" I asked as we left school.

"We need to go shopping for some meat," he finally said.

"Meat?"

"Niya and Malik are hungry. We need to stop at a supermarket so we can feed them."

"Again, there is no *we* in this equation," I said, lighter this time. He seemed kinder today.

"*You'll* be the one feeding Niya and Malik," he fired back. I felt sick.

Still, I laughed. "Seriously?"

He chuckled as he shifted gears. We rolled through the glorious white mountains, but the calm and beautiful creatures kept popping into my mind—the meat-hungry wild animals that were for sure going to kill me. I was surprised when Lucas pulled into the ordinary local supermarket, bypassed the parking lot, and parked in the alley in the back by the empty pallets. He left me inside the running car and knocked on the dilapidated back door. A fat butcher with a bloody white apron answered. The man watched as Lucas spoke, then nodded. Lucas pulled a roll of bills from his pocket and passed it into the butcher's hands.

The butcher disappeared inside and reappeared dragging a brown bag the size of a cow. By the way he struggled, I could tell it was heavy. With no attempt at disguising his strength, Lucas picked up the heavy bundle and threw it with ease to the top of the car, where it landed with a thud. The butcher said nothing. He nodded once and retreated back inside the building.

Lucas opened his door and stepped up to tie down the meat before getting back into the car.

"What was that?" I asked, disgusted by the large carcass above. The more I thought about it, the more I felt the urge to gag. Lucas noticed and grinned.

"A zebra. I ordered it a month ago."

When we reached the gates to his house, I noticed two dark, spotted figures against the stark white snow, charging through the trees. They followed us all the way through the woods to the side of the house, where Lucas parked just outside the garage. In the passenger mirror, I could see them jumping furiously to get the meat.

"You ready?" Lucas sounded too enthusiastic.

"Are you crazy? I'm going to die out there!"

"No, you'll be fine."

Lucas jumped out and practically skipped to my door. The jaguars didn't even glance at him, too focused on the fresh, bloody meat above my head. They jumped fiercely for it as Lucas opened my door and held out his hand. I leaned away—these were not the animals I knew.

"I'm not going out there!" I yelled. "They're hungry! They'll bite me!"

"Come on, don't you trust me?"

"Not right now."

"Look, I'll show you." He turned to face his pets. "Niya, Malik, *sientanse*!"

To my amazement, the spotted jags sat. Still, their lips pulled back to show jagged teeth and release hungry growls. Lucas ignored them as he pulled the bag off the car and set it in front of my open door. A patch of black-and-white fur peeped through as he unwrapped the burlap. The zebra's head was missing, and the rest of the body had been dismembered. It was a heap of bones, juicy red meat, and sparse patches of fur.

"Watch." Lucas slid his cardigan sleeve up to his elbow and bent down. He picked up a leg and threw it into the woods, out of view.

Niya ran after the meat, and Malik stayed, waiting. Lucas waved me out of the car, but I couldn't move.

"Come on, Zara. Honestly, would I make you do this if it wasn't safe?" he asked. He held his bloody hand away from his side as thick drops of blood fell to the loose pebbles by his sneakers.

I inched reluctantly outside until the smelly pile of flesh was at my feet. I stared at the pile, trying to find a piece that didn't look so big, or so bloody. But it didn't exist. I settled for a leg. As I pulled my sweater up on one arm and bent down to grab it, Malik growled. I jumped.

Lucas didn't intervene. He waited patiently, coaching me with steady eyes to move. I let another moment pass before going in for the leg again. Meaty muscle squished between my fingers, and the blood dripping down the back of my hand was cool. I chucked the leg as hard as I could, but I wasn't surprised to see it fall far short of where I'd hoped. Which is to say, it plopped down on the gravel of the driveway a few feet away. Malik sprang for it anyway, picked up one end in his teeth, and dragged it off into the woods.

"Where's he going?" I asked. Lucas was chuckling softly. "What are you laughing at?"

"Nothing. You did it. I didn't think you would." Lucas cleared his throat and pretended to have a serious expression. "I like a girl who isn't afraid to get her hands dirty."

I looked at the pile and then my red hand. The stench of butchered meat rose, and I had to turn my head away to breathe. The gagging was nearly uncontrollable. I squeezed the bridge of my nose with my clean hand.

Lucas stepped in. "Allow me."

He grabbed another leg and a part of the body and chucked both into the woods. Then he threw the smaller pieces after them. The jaguars were nowhere to be seen. The only evidence was the bloody bag at our feet.

"Isn't that going to attract bears?" I asked, my voice distorted through my pinched nose.

"Nah. That meat will be gone in ten minutes. And Niya and Malik like to bury the bones. Sometimes their mutt behavior is really strange. Let's go clean up."

I turned, but stopped in my tracks as I finally *looked* at the garage. I knew that every member of his family had their own car, but it was overwhelming to see them neatly parked together in pairs, black and red, gold and orange, and finally white, where the Lexus stood alone. I'd never seen so many cars with some type of turbo exhaust on the backend in one place. I thought of Max and Casey first, and then I thought of that one word: *horsepower.*

Lucas got to the door before he noticed I wasn't behind him. "Ah, you got me. I was trying to not show you the garage." He walked around and started pushing my back with his clean elbows. "Because I knew this is the reaction I'd get."

"Do you own all of those?" By now the blood on my hand was freezing—a unique, new kind of nasty discomfort.

"A perk of being ageless, I guess. The Aluxes picked them out for us."

"The what?"

He pushed me along more quickly as the blood crusted in the toasty house. Lucas turned on the faucet in the kitchen sink and made me go first. I scrubbed at it harshly, aiming the spray under my fingernails as my gag reflex worsened. The water ran red.

"How'd it go?" Dylan asked in the middle of a heave.

I scrunched my nose and shook my head as I held my breath, hoping the bile would stay in my body.

"Me neither," Gabriella said. "It's disgusting."

When I finished, I moved over and let out my breath. Lucas's tattoo glowed brightly underneath his shirt as he scrubbed.

"You ready?" Dylan asked, breaking my stare.

"Sure."

I wanted to wait for Lucas, but I knew he'd probably beat me down since I still had to change.

"Where're Andrés and Valentina?" I asked as we passed the large stone statue in the great room.

"With your parents, setting up Mexico," Dylan said.

"Are they . . ."

Dylan chuckled. "No. Andrés still has humanity in him. He doesn't like to brainwash people unless he has to. They'll arrange it over dinner."

Dinner? I was scared to think of my parents' reactions. *Hey, Mitch, hey, Lori, demons are chasing your daughter, and we need you to come to Mexico for a little while.* Dinner would be a disaster. They would never allow me to see Lucas again.

I swallowed bile and went up to change.

Lucas was the only one who watched me every time I trained over the following weeks. I got stronger as things got harder, but Lucas became unbearable. He was now the one pushing me physically, repeating *again* after each blackout. He was harder than Dylan, and I hated it. I didn't know what I'd done to make him think I was this strong, but I wasn't. I could never forget that *I* was the one who chose to walk toward the screams when I blacked out. I should have gone the other way, but I didn't.

Friday after Thanksgiving, while everyone I knew went shopping for the holidays, I hung from a steel pole fifteen feet in the air, blisters open and seeping, staring at Lucas in a silent plea for mercy. My body was weak, and I knew I only had seconds before I fell again. Dylan caught me for the first time when Lucas didn't budge. When I came to, I glared at Lucas angrily.

"Again," he said, a soulless statue.

Later that night, as the snow fell, I cried, and the next night, and the next. I knew whoever had night watch heard me, but no one related it to Lucas. It was hard going to school each day, hearing what the others did on the weekends while I trained with gods. And it was hard that my mom didn't believe me when I told her Lucas and I were only friends. But it was harder still that Lucas never admitted what I knew he'd felt under the starry sky.

The Castillos and Tita watched me sadly as I returned to the house each day after school for training, their eyes apologizing for Lucas's behavior. I realized that I respected them because they kept my crying jags a secret. It was the honorable thing to do.

One afternoon, after I had just returned home from training and two hours before our parents were to meet for dinner, Lucas unexpectedly called.

"Get ready. We're going to dinner with them," he said. Not an ounce of pleasure rippled in that sweet voice.

I looked down at my sweat-sticky sternum. It would take me a while to get ready, but I didn't dare disagree. I ran for the shower. Afterward, I sucked into a mint pencil skirt and a striped shirt and braided my natural waves for speed.

"Mom, you *do* know that it's an hour away, right?" I called when I went downstairs and they weren't there. I figured they would be a few minutes, so I walked to the mirror and glanced at my new figure. My waist had shrunk with all the training, and I had curvier muscles. I turned to the side and glanced at my butt. It was firmer. I smiled, but then I frowned as I brushed the wrinkles out of my skirt. My stomach cramped with guilt. *I don't deserve to be saved. I'm a traitor. This shouldn't be me. I shouldn't be here—I should be dead.*

Moments later, as the lawns and streetlights were replaced by dark trees against the purple sky, images of the Underworld haunted me . . . burning piles of half-eaten limbs, heads on spikes dripping lines of fresh blood to the ground, trails of blood running down the temple's steps . . . The blood—so much blood—had a scent that wouldn't leave my mind, no matter how hard I tried. Over time, it had infused my brain and painted a picture of sweet desire—as if I wanted to go back! It was disconcerting. I pushed my elbows deeper into my hollow stomach, hoping it would ease the edge of my treacherous thoughts.

We drove south in the black forest for forty minutes. I recognized the headlights of the orange car that trailed us all the way. It was Dylan's Porsche Cayenne, which only passed us when we reached Carson Pass and turned into a small lake valley lit by the bright white lights at the base of Mount Kirkwood.

As we turned the bend of Kirkwood Meadow, a large wooden sign twinkled the word *Pearls* in globe bulbs. It was staked into the snow at the turnoff that led us up a hill dotted with smaller aspen trees. The restaurant overlooked the vast blackness of Caples Lake from atop the hill. Andrés, Valentina, and Lucas, dressed in evening clothes and fine jewelry, waited underneath the black awning near the prelit potted greenery.

Dad let out a prolonged sigh as he pulled into the carpeted valet drop. Lucas was opening my door and reaching for my hand before the engine died.

"*Buenas noches,*" he whispered, kissing my cheek softly.

He wore a slim, tailored beige suit and a black skinny tie. His hair had been gelled down, and his smooth skin seemed impossibly fine. Surprisingly, the images of blood vanished, and I remembered to breathe as we joined the others.

Andrés kissed Mom gently on the cheek. "I'm Andrés."

Valentina put her arms around Dad, kissing him lightly before embracing him. "And I'm Valentina."

"Nice to meet you," Mom and Dad said simultaneously, both stiff and unsure of this new custom.

Andrés gestured toward the entrance. "Shall we?"

We shuffled through double doors into a large room. The ceiling was high and draped with ivory fabric that fanned out from the center to the outermost edges of the room. Ivory wax candles topped candelabras and sat in votives on every flat surface, and some even flared in wall sconces so subtle they appeared to be floating.

As Andrés passed a small desk, the young receptionist, dressed all in black, stood and motioned subtly to each of us to continue. But then, as Lucas passed, her lingering eyes became voracious. I looked back in time to see her whispering into the other receptionist's ear, glancing at me with a conspiratorial look.

"You look gorgeous," Lucas noted from the side of his mouth, over a distance he had carefully measured between us. The compliment seemed odd when he didn't even look at me.

"You're not too bad yourself," I said, likewise distant.

Andrés stopped at a round table near the back, next to a wall featuring a shimmering indoor waterfall. Lucas drew my seat out. *Going through the motions,* I noted. I pretended not to care. It only hurt worse when I did.

"Valentina, that is a nice necklace you're wearing," Mom said. It was fifty times wider than her own, full of jade and red stone.

"Thank you. It was a gift."

"From Andrés?"

Valentina smiled humbly, her hand brushing the stone. "No, from a dear old friend."

"Dinner is our gift tonight. Please, don't be shy. Order anything you'd like, but may I add that the oysters here are my favorite?" Andrés said with a grin.

I opened the heavy menu expecting multiple pages. There were only two. The cheapest thing on the menu was fifteen dollars, and that was for a house salad.

After the waitress brought our drinks and we ordered, Andrés and Valentina made ordinary talk. It was nice, but I felt sick with worry about how my parents would handle the invitation. Dinner was one thing, but a trip to Mexico was completely different.

I barely registered what I ordered, and it might have been McDonald's for all that I tasted. But as the plates emptied, I knew it was nearly time.

"Lori, Mitch, you know, Andrés and I have been thinking a lot about something," Valentina started, and then she looked to the king. He was a fox in the dim light, and I could see the thin tracing of black eyeliner that rimmed his lower lids. It reminded me of the people of the Underworld, only their shadowed eyes came not from a tube, but from death.

He spoke with a rich, heavy accent. "We would like to extend an invitation for your family to join us for Christmas this season at our home in Mexico."

I couldn't move my head fast enough—I caught only the tail end of Mom's jaw dropping open. Dad was in a different reverie: his eyes wouldn't lift from Andrés's black nail polish.

"Well, honey, what do you think?" Mom asked, nudging Dad in the ribs.

"Well, of course, you two can go home and think about it," Valentina added. "We would really love for your family to join us, and there's plenty of room in our house, so the twins would be welcome to come too."

"That's very nice of you to offer. Did you have a certain date in mind?" Mom asked.

"We were thinking December twenty-second. Stay for a week and return right before the new year," Valentina suggested.

Dad downed his water in a gulp and wiped his mouth. "That's very generous. We'll talk about it and get back to you."

"Please consider our offer," Andrés urged.

I sat back in my chair, amazed at Andrés and Valentina's knack with people. They were smart and funny and very humanesque. Mom nearly giggled whenever Andrés said anything. Everything went more smoothly than I could have dreamed—until a cold, unwanted prickle crawled up the side of my head.

It startled me, and I couldn't stop a subtle jerk, like it was something I could throw off. Three pairs of Celestial eyes were on me before I could recover. I smiled nervously and looked down. My right hand was trembling now, and I dropped my fork. The sound of metal on the flagstone floor made Mom and Dad look too. I reached for the fork, annoyed, avoiding their eyes at all costs and mumbling under my breath.

When the tickling expanded into a painful, frigid web over my brain, I chuckled awkwardly. "I'm just going to go outside for a little breather."

Lucas was half out of his seat when I reached for my head. "I'll go with you."

I knew it would be pointless to try to get him to stay. His parents would insist he go. I didn't bother to make eye contact and just walked toward the exit. It was freezing outside on the patio. The icicles hanging from the roof were sparse but sharp. I stepped up to the railing and looked beyond to the black lake below.

"Are you okay?" Lucas asked.

I turned to him, upset. Cold pierced my head as I moved, pinning an image into my brain. *No, not now!*

"Why did I have to come here tonight?" I asked. I couldn't stop the tears rising in my eyes or the flash of images seeping in.

"Because I wanted you to."

I pressed my palm hard against my head as the invasion drained my strength. I didn't want to go back to that place, ever. It was changing me into someone horrifying, but I couldn't help it. I was weak, and I was disgusted with myself. "What is wrong with you? What changed from that night you told me everything?"

His eyes softened as he concentrated on me. I wondered briefly if he knew how much I needed him. "Nothing did, Zara. Yes, I understand there is an unknown connection between us, but love is dangerous, especially in this matter."

It sounded thoughtfully planned out. "You're a coward."

"You're wrong," he charged, though his gaze seemed less steady. "On the contrary, I find myself completely taken. I just choose to not act on it. You are better than this, Zara." He sounded disgusted with himself.

The right half of my head was now all ice. "What are you afraid of? That you'll use me, or that you'll lose me?"

He was quiet.

"Can't you just let me be, Lucas?" I cried.

He chuckled, but it sounded exhausted. "About as much as you can let me be."

"Then if that's the case, why am I even fighting? You don't want to save me, Lucas." I glanced down; I couldn't remember the last time I'd dressed up. This outfit was stupid. This dinner was stupid. All of it—all the cover-up lies—and I was the worst one of them. I brushed the palms of my hands along my thighs, pinched the fabric and pulled at it. "This isn't me." I looked through the windows into the restaurant. "I don't belong here. And this skirt—I've only worn it once in my life—and the chauffeuring, and the fancy cars, and the special attention. I don't deserve any of it. Maybe you should let me go . . ." He stepped closer, but I backed away. "No, don't. I can't be who you want me to be, because that isn't me. I don't want you to waste any more time on me. I'm ugly inside. I'm a horrible person."

He poked his chest and then waved his finger at me. A horror struck me, the way the creases of his mouth dropped. His eyes showed deep distaste. "And this isn't me, either. Do you have any idea how hard it is to break a tradition you've followed nearly your entire life? Half of me is saying, 'Take what you want, Lucas, you deserve her'—which, by the way, is another struggle, because I don't even know what to do with your frail little body—and the other half is saying, 'You do this, you die.' I'm scared of you. I've never wanted something so little and so badly at the same time. It's damn confusing!"

And the tears rolled. "Why? I feel like you make it that way."

"No, Zara, there's no way around it. Before I met you, I was eager to break the sacrifice tradition, but now . . ."

"What? You regret it?"

"I realized when I kissed you how hard making the right decision can be. I realized the risks it brings . . . the fears it brings. Back then I was pompous, and I didn't care about anyone but myself, which made my decision to break the sacrifice tradition easy. But when I . . . when I kissed you . . . I knew that I wasn't caring only for myself. I care for you, Zara. More than you know, and I need you to trust me."

The low light from the restaurant hit him straight on, shaping a symmetrical shadow along the center of his face, which hadn't changed at all, except for the slightest droop in his eyelids. His blue eyes flicked away and then back to mine, and then he stepped close. In the startling nearness of him, I forgot to shut out the cold knives for a moment, and the contours of his face dimmed. I tried to regain control and focus on him, but a flash of blackness shot through me.

I awoke to the familiar orange sky. My skin, which had been ice cold, now burned with the rush of blood returning to my limbs in the hot, moist air. I was standing barefoot on green leaves. A beetle squirmed by my toes, and I jumped away, glancing around me. I was on that same hill, above the city and the large pyramid. And then I heard that low, deep noise calling through a conch shell. My gut jerked. *Not another one.*

My feet jerked suddenly and walked toward the city with

a mind of their own. I pulled at my legs, trying to stop, and a bloodcurdling scream filled the air. I didn't know what to do. A controlling power flooded my body, and I found myself walking more quickly toward the sound.

I was climbing over a branch, crying because I couldn't stop, when the pyramid came into view. It was the same scene: a girl trying to get away and a man at the top waiting for her. *Go, Zara. Go now. See what's there.*

I was taking my first step toward the small town over the lake when my body seized up and I fell backwards. Before I could rise, it happened again, and blackness began to cloud my vision. I fell on my back, paralyzed by a bitter cold that pricked at my toes and fingers and spread throughout my body.

"Zara, Zara! Can you hear me?" The familiar voice rose through the frozen darkness.

When I opened my eyes, Lucas was there, his face tormented.

"I hear you," I answered. I tried to raise myself up, but my head spun and I fell back, winded. I whimpered into Lucas's shoulder as he held me. "Please, help me. I don't want to go back there. I don't want to go back."

His breathing was rough as he hugged me more tightly. "We're taking a break from training tomorrow."

He helped me to my feet and wiped my tears with the pad of his thumb. I could tell his helplessness frustrated him by the way his eyes narrowed underneath his dark eyebrows. Our parents were merrily finishing up slices of chocolate cake when I returned. Valentina's smooth face turned worried with once glance at me. Andrés gracefully rushed the after-dinner coffee along, and soon we were saying our good-byes and heading home.

I rode home with my parents, and as we rolled through narrow bends past large, white-topped boulders in the dark woods, I rested against the door. I wondered what she looked like, the sacrifice whose screams echoed in my ears, and where her family was. *How long was she held captive until she finally met her fate?* I glanced at the rear-view mirror and watched the beam of Lucas's headlights through snow drifting like white confetti. They followed as far as the hidden turnoff to his house, where they disappeared and a new set emerged to follow us all the way home.

I peeped out the window when we got home. Dylan's orange Cayenne was parked across the street atop a new layer of snow. I lay back on the flannel sheets and pressed my palms together, wondering what Lucas could possibly want to show me.

CHAPTER SEVENTEEN

UTOPIA

A raspy ringing shot through the silence again and again, vibrating against my belly. Still more than half-asleep, I fumbled my hand under the tangled sheets and found the bugger.

"Why are you calling me at six in the morning?" I moaned to Bri.

"You're busted. Come outside right now."

"No."

"Zara Moss, you come outside right now, or I will go upstairs to your room and dump cold water on your face. I know where the spare key is," she reminded me.

I groaned. My feet were still asleep, and it felt like needles were spiking through my heels as I trotted to the window. Bri was standing in the middle of the lawn in her robe, hair in curlers, snow piled to her ankles.

"Bri, what are you doing?" I looked behind her. Dylan's car was still parked across the street with a light layer of cold cotton on top. I feared he was laughing inside it.

"Ten, nine . . ." she began.

"Okay, okay! I'm coming, geez."

I chucked on my boots and fled downstairs in a mere cami and boxers. It was pearly outside as the sun peeked above the horizon, but the frost nipped hard at my body.

the 52nd

"Are you crazy? It's six in the morning!" I yelled, hunching over from the cold.

"Friends tell! And you're not telling me something!" Bri said, her nose a bright pink.

I looked past her shoulders to the orange car. "Okay, come inside. We'll talk."

"No. I'm not going anywhere until you tell me right now."

"Why right now?" I whined. My feet were freezing in my boots.

When she didn't budge, I glanced over her shoulder once more, then back to her, and stomped immaturely. "Dang it, Bri, you'll be the death of me."

"Try me."

"What do you want me to say? Lucas and I sort of have a thing, and I didn't tell you because I'm not sure what it is."

She stood there dissatisfied. "It's not just a thing, is it? You really like this guy."

I nodded sheepishly, knowing the god across the street was prying with his perfect hearing.

"Have you told Jett yet?"

"No! Don't, please. I was waiting to tell him, maybe when it's more official. And don't blab this to Tommy either. I know how your mouth works," I added with a sneer and a shiver. "Now, can we go inside? I'm freezing."

"I've actually got to get home. I've got plans with Tommy later today."

"What are you doing up so early then?"

Her face turned absentminded. "I don't know. Just woke up and couldn't go back to sleep. Misery loves company." She shrugged.

"There's something seriously wrong with you," I hollered as she walked away.

"Ha! And just so you know, I like Lucas for you. He makes you vulnerable."

Dela

There was that word Dylan loved and I detested. It made the strings in my gut snap. "What did you say?"

"You've finally let your guard down."

No response except cottony puffs moving skyward as I exhaled.

"Oh, come on. Don't act like you don't know what I'm talking about. Every guy who's dated you knows you're a hard shell to crack."

Now I couldn't move. My throat dried out, leaving me gasping for breath.

"Are you okay?" she asked.

"Very," I muttered scratchily.

I needed both hands to close the front door after she left. *Is she right? Is Lucas right about us not being together?* I didn't feel vulnerable, but when was the last time I'd thought about life after all this? Where would I go? What would I study? I was too consumed with my feelings for him.

My cell was going off again in my room, much more loudly now that a body wasn't covering it. I skipped steps upstairs to catch it before it woke the house.

"Please don't tell me Dylan just called you?" I asked Lucas, already mortified.

"He didn't need to. I heard it for myself. I'm at your doorstep."

I ran back downstairs, panting, to let Lucas in. He had changed into a blue sweater and denim. He assessed my apparel and my hair before bringing his eyes back down to mine. It was clear from his expression that I looked rough.

"Want to talk?" he asked.

I crossed my arms over my chest, suddenly feeling naked.

"I need to change first," I said, touching my gnarly hair. "And maybe brush my hair too."

He smiled. "Dress warm."

"Like going-for-a-stroll warm?"

"Like going-to-be-outside-all-day warm."

the 52nd

He waited on the living room couch while I unearthed my warmest street clothes. I layered two shirts under a buff sweater and pulled my skinny corduroys on over a pair of tights. Then I braided my hair to eliminate the tangles and powdered blush onto my cheeks.

I left a note for Mom and Dad on the kitchen table, letting them know I'd be back by early afternoon, though I always felt those notes were more lies. What if I never returned? When we walked out, Dylan's car was gone, and the Rover was parked along the curb. The sky graduated into a blossoming blue as the night's fresh snow crystallized in the morning rays. Light sparkled in every direction.

"Where are we going?" I asked after settling into his car, grateful for the heated seat.

"A special place I like to go to for clarity. You could use a little of that right now."

With the town still asleep, the unplowed boulevard was deserted. We drove west past Emerald Bay, continued north on the 89 as it curved along the lake past Sugar Pine Point, and then drove deeper into the unpopulated mountains. A familiar pop song played on the radio as the flocked fir trees breezed by the window.

After what seemed forever, Lucas finally exited onto a side road and drove another twenty minutes along switchbacks up the wintry canyon.

"We're almost to the first point," he said as we pulled onto a narrow shoulder.

I looked around for a mile marker or even a trail, but he didn't stop. He plowed through the foot of snow into the untamed underbrush of pine trees until suddenly the trees gapped. They opened into a tiny clearing where the sun shone down, creating a circle of glistening snow. In the middle waited one snowmobile.

"Is that yours?" I asked.

He grinned with unfiltered excitement. "The only way to get where we're going. Bundle up—it's going to get a bit cold." He grabbed his jacket and left me in the car.

"Splendid," I said to myself.

It bewildered me, in these winter conditions, that he wore only a jacket the weight of my underwear. I imagined it was for show—when he threw it on, he only fastened the first three buttons. Then he put on a loose beanie. As he waited on the snowmobile, I dutifully wrapped my green scarf over my head, concealing everything except my eyes, and put on my mittens and peacoat and beanie.

Lucas's magnetism was inescapable. His eyes twinkled when he half smiled, and an exciting sense of danger stirred in my gut as he dangled a helmet off one finger.

"Are we going far?" The scarf caught my breath, warming my nose with moist air as Lucas removed my knit hat, tucked it into his back pocket, and slid the helmet over my head.

"You won't freeze for very long, if that's what you're asking." He grinned as he snapped the buckle and lifted a pair of goggles. "Put these on."

I was grateful that the merino hid my scowl as I strapped on the goggles.

"Put your arms around me and hold on tight."

I obeyed the prince nervously and molded my arms to his firm core.

"Just remember that I'm breakable," I added.

He tilted his head in a subtle bow as the machine roared to life. "Of course, *mi muñeca*."

Before I could wonder again what that word meant, I was thrown off balance by a flash of glacial air. It knifed through my layers and crawled along my skin as the countryside passed by. We sped over collapsed logs, frozen rivers, and deep rolling hills. At some point, specks of wet dust gathered in the lower corners of my lenses, shattering my view of the trees into sunlit kaleidoscopes. And then Lucas stopped.

He pointed to our right. "Look."

The aspens and fir, a barrier of white and brown bark, parted before an expansive clearing around a pond. Across the solid ice, flush with the edge of the frozen water, were broken steps leading to a very small building with a steeple. The remaining steps were frozen under the water.

A soft sunburst filtered through the silvery foliage around the spring. Its chalky streaks held snowy flecks, like crystals woven into the air. I looked more closely at the ruin and gasped. White-winged butterflies flew in and out of the milky water lilies at its base, and birds chirped a morning tune on the iced branches above.

"What is this place?" I asked. I breathed in and tasted the purity in the air.

"This is my sanctuary."

He grabbed my hand and led me around the pond to the chipped steps.

"Wait here," he said, and he disappeared into the chapel.

He came out holding two blankets, a thermos, and two Styrofoam cups. He laid the plaid tartan over the pine needles on the cold slab, then handed me the Sherpa throw, which I draped over my crossed legs as I sat down.

"How did you know about this place?" I asked.

He smiled, seeming pleased, and passed me a cup of steamy hot chocolate before sitting down across from me.

"I discovered it when we moved to Tahoe," he replied. "For some reason, I feel the spirit of Ahau more here." He looked to the sky, seeming more at peace than I'd ever seen him.

I let the rising steam thaw my face for a second as he remembered his old friend, and then I let the near-scalding liquid coat my throat. The rich flavor of cocoa and cinnamon immediately took the edge off the shivering in my bones.

"Are you warm enough?" he asked. There was such sweetness

in his face, but I sensed the torment and hesitation as he kept me at a small distance.

"I'm fine."

His timeless eyes glinted like gems in the silver light and imprisoned me. When he forced himself to look away, the scary idea of his age broke my reverie.

"When were you born?" I asked hesitantly.

He watched me cautiously for a moment. "June eighth, fifteen-oh-four."

It took more effort to swallow, especially to keep my shy gaze on his ageless eyes. "What do you do with all that time?"

He released a relieved chuckle and leaned back, playing with the Sherpa as he stretched his legs. "Part of me is Mayan, which means that for the past five hundred years, I've been a dreamer, hoping that a mystical utopian community will come to be, somewhere in a distant time."

I didn't follow. It probably showed on my face.

"As I told you earlier, it's not easy watching people being abducted, knowing they are all going to die a horrible, painful death. Wherever I am, I find a sanctuary. A place I can come to alone and think, and be at peace. Dream of a better life, pray that those sacrificed will pass on to a better life too. You should try it. It helps a little."

"Try it for what?" I wondered.

"To help with your blackouts. I've seen you overcome them before, but some obviously come on stronger than others. You need something to root you down. A dream, a place, or a person." He faltered on the last word, and I noticed how much closer he had moved to me. Our bent knees were nearly touching.

I picked up a piece of snow and threw it at him playfully. "Thanks, Dr. Lucas."

He wiped it off his shirt with a pleasant smile, but he was silent, confused by my friendly fire.

"But seriously," I said. "Thank you for all of this. I appreciate it."

He blinked hard, twice, and his statue stare tweaked into a shocked expression.

"Well, before all of this *dreaming*, what did you do as a prince?" I asked, uncomfortable beneath his stare.

His tight face loosened into a dimpled smile. "As a royal, I did three things every day religiously: I studied, I fought, and I ate."

I tried to act sophisticated, but he disarmed me as always. I pretended he didn't notice when my breathing faltered, though I suspected I wasn't fooling him when he smiled again.

"What did you study?"

"Astrology and war."

I must have looked disappointed, and he chuckled.

"What did you expect for royalty, law? Medicine? Back then, those jobs were for shamans and priests. As a prince, you were nobler if you excelled in war. And besides, a lawyer was as good as dead. There was no diplomacy between cities of the Maya. The Aztecs at least had one ruler who oversaw the smaller cities near them and handled taxes and such. Where I grew up, in the Yucatan, we ruled only one city, the one we lived in. There were a lot of fights between cities for power."

"Was it really that bad?"

"I don't understand why people think they have bad neighbors. Do their neighbors try to kidnap them, remove their hearts while they're still alive, cut their legs and arms off or behead them, or drink their blood for fun?" He looked up sharply and let out a deep breath. "Anyway, I guess my protective instincts come out a bit strong when it comes to you. Sorry . . ."

"Don't apologize," I rushed out. "Please, don't do that. It's not you. It's me. Trust me, it's all me." I rolled my eyes to the silver pines, annoyed with my inability to control my mind or emotions, and now my actions as my blackouts worsened. “If it wasn’t for you, I wouldn’t be here right now.”

“But . . .”

“No, don’t. Lucas, you have every right to be like that. I’m not angry with you, I promise.”

“You’re not?” He looked relieved, but I didn’t like the way that doubt showed in his brow.

“No, I’m not. Look, we all know I’m weak compared to you.” My fingers fidgeted with their placement over the cup. “I need to tell you something, but I’m afraid you’ll be angry with me.”

When he didn’t respond, I nestled the cup of hot chocolate shakily into the snow.

He studied my hand and looked up, worried. “What?”

“I haven’t been completely honest with you . . .”

“What?”

I breathed deeply and looked across the pond. “My blackouts haven’t been as nice as I’ve made them out to be. I see things. A lot of things. You already know that. But lately, when I’m there, instead of fearing what I see or hear, I walk toward it.”

“You what?”

I tightened the blanket around my legs, worried about what he thought. “At first it was uncontrollable—I couldn’t stop walking toward it . . . the screaming. But the more I go there, the more my fear of that place goes away, and I feel curious.”

He looked betrayed, and I felt guilty.

“I can’t explain the crazy feeling, but it scares me to death. It’s that emotion, Lucas, that desire that makes me afraid. I’m afraid it would control me again for Solstice. I feel dark inside.”

His body was against mine before I finished my sentence. He wrapped his arms around me tightly. “I promised you I would never let anything happen to you, and I won’t, even if I have to protect you from yourself.”

I drank deeply of his tropical scent and tried to control my pounding heart. "Thank you."

He squeezed me somewhat more tightly, his hands beginning to slide down my body, but then he backed away suddenly with an apologetic look.

"Sorry. That was wrong of me. I shouldn't have—" he began quickly.

"It was *just* a hug," I said incredulously.

He shook his head. "Do not tempt me, Zara."

"You came on to me!"

"Aztecs one-oh-one. Because of the nature of my living being, of my very existence, I feel I have to devour everything virtuous about you."

"Your godlike nature, or your Aztec nature?"

"Both!" he replied. He stood to pace in frustration. "After the transformation, every human feeling I ever carried increased exponentially, while everything I felt physically went dead. But now, for some reason, every fiber of my being is on fire."

My eyes followed him as he moved. "What do you mean?"

"When my body became immortal, I could sit at the bottom of a frozen lake for over an hour and be perfectly okay. I only need to eat every other month or so, I sleep two hours at most a week, my facial hair grows out of control, and I could bleed for days but never die. My body would heal itself, and I would go on living. Absolutely no limits to my physical state, never have been, until now, with you. Something about you makes my insides crazy—a crazy you've no idea of."

"Then give me an idea." I hoped he'd kiss me again.

But he froze, his inner struggle growing clearer when his eyes hardened. Instead, he picked a piece of crumbling stone out of the snow and chucked it. As it slid across the frozen pond, he bent and picked up another piece, repeating the same throw. It was a good distraction.

He spoke with his back to me, throwing stone after stone. "I am anxious, jittery, and nervous."

"You, nervous?" I didn't mean to laugh out loud, but it came out whether I liked it or not.

He turned to me and cocked his head. "Yes."

My butt froze to the tartan as he sat back down and stared at me intently.

"But mostly, the hole I felt my whole life, the longing for . . . something, has now been filled, and I can't satisfy it the way I want to. And it's burned me like fire since the day I met you."

I felt brittle before his honesty, afraid to move. He chuckled—perhaps I was turning the color of my scarf.

"Aren't you going to say something?" he asked.

A nerdy laugh slipped through my lips. "Come on, Lucas. Being you can't be that bad."

"Zara, for five hundred years, I've felt nothing but emptiness. There's nowhere I can go to find someone who shares the same life. If I could have seen then what I see now, a life damned to solitude and unhappiness, I'm not sure I would have chosen this path."

"Don't say that."

"Why not? It's true. And now that I've finally found something special, I still can't have her."

I blushed and looked away, at a loss for words.

"I'm sorry. I didn't mean it like that," he added in a rush.

"Yes, you did. You're choosing not to have her." I couldn't believe I'd pressured him—or that I'd referred to myself in the third person.

This time, it was the immortal who froze while I took my turn staring at him hard. "You're just as afraid as I am, aren't you?" I said when he lowered his head toward the blanket.

He looked up through his lashes, his voice so close but so distant in its softness. "You and I . . . it's too dangerous."

"More dangerous than me and the Underworld god?"

He looked away again, to the tree line, where the sunlight was strengthening. The snow crystals seemed to have been embedded in the branches.

"My feelings for you have grown, so much that I feel as though our relationship should be forbidden. The kiss on the mountain was because I was selfish. I was used to taking what I wanted. I wasn't thinking right that night. But I care for you more now than I did then, and us being together is too much of a risk, as I keep trying to explain. It scares me, Zara, because *they* have the power to destroy our world if you make *me* weak. And you can get seriously hurt. Don't you see that?" He said it, finally, what Valentina had presumed all along. His voice, his own hellish destruction: he would choose not to love. And it made him a sad sight. I saw only remorse and longing in his eyes. Longing for what? For hope? For companionship? He only needed to reach out to me and I would be his, but he didn't.

This was the truth, and it hurt, and now I was offended.

"I get it, all right? We don't need to talk about this anymore," I said sourly. He couldn't know that my heart was peeled back and exposed, bleeding out as we spoke.

Or could he?

He couldn't even look at me in that instant. "Fine."

Feeling colder, I took another sip of the cinnamon cocoa, but it suddenly tasted bitter. I gave up on it and set it back down in the snow.

"Why won't you talk about what happened when you transformed?" I asked.

"Because. I just won't," he said curtly.

At this rate, I would know more about the Underworld than I would about Lucas. I didn't want it this way, but I feared this was the only open direction, and I feared when I would black out next. Moments passed while I regained my courage, and then I asked carefully, "What will you do then after the portal is closed?"

He picked at some strands of grass poking through the snow, hardly acknowledging me as he stared across the pond. I imagined that this was the type of prince he was, cold and snappish, but a part of me denied it. That part imagined him kind and respectable and desirable.

"Stay in Progresso, deal with the Celestials." His voice was sour.

"Will you come back to Tahoe?"

He paused, thinking, then looked back to me. "I don't think so."

I didn't know what to do with his response except snuggle my hands under my arms, hoping it would tame the tightening in my chest. I wondered if time would ever change Lucas. He stressed over fear of the future, like I did, but I didn't suffer from the decision to risk everything to change an old and binding tradition like he did. His pain hung before my eyes: guilt, resentment, unforgiveness, anxiety, worry . . . I didn't want to feel it anymore, but it flowed out of him so easily and broke like a wave over me. I slumped and looked at my feet.

"Zara, I didn't bring you here to upset you. I brought you here to help you. Let's not talk about me anymore," he suggested.

"But I want to . . ." He was too preoccupied with what had been done or needed to be done to look at me straight on. I watched him remove the beanie from his head and swipe his hand through his hair. It rose nearly two inches from his forehead. "What's your real name?" I asked. I pictured something fierce.

He looked back up to me. "Mulac."

It sounded nice, properly divine. "How come you chose Lucas?"

He fiddled with the laces of his shoes. "Because he was a doctor to Saint Paul in the Bible. We all chose names that would be acceptable to the Spaniards. To prove we had converted to their beliefs."

I imagined the Spanish friars in the sixteenth century and the methods they used for conversion, which we'd read about in school.

New names to avoid the brutality turned on those who resisted. It was horrible.

"Does Xavier always come to help kidnap the sacrifices?"

"No." He sighed, his eyes on the pale blades where his fingers played. They were delicate with the frail grass at first, but the grass snapped the moment he was distracted. I understood, suddenly, the frustration of supernatural power, breaking everything too easily. He threw the shredded grass to the ground. "The executioners are the ones always sent. We believe Xavier is involved in order to break his curse, but I suspect it's also partial revenge for what I did to him."

"But why would Xavier come now and not hundreds of years earlier?"

"Because it's the end of the Long Count calendar, and you are a virgin. The only time possible for him to break a witch's curse. He needs pure blood."

Blood rushed to my face, coloring my cheeks the same cherry red as my nose. I looked down, embarrassed. "Honestly, does *that* really matter?"

His gaze was steady as I hid under the blanket.

"It means everything. Without that purity, it would never break a curse as black as his."

"What did you do to him?" His complexity—his past—scared me, and I wondered if I was smart to ask such detailed questions.

Lucas hunched over his crossed knees and rested his elbows on the caps. "Xavier and Dylan come from a strong lineage of Mayan gods. They were known as the Hero Twins. Dylan was called Hunahpu, and Xavier, Xibalanque. Together they were very smart and very powerful. But unlike the other Celestial and Xibalban gods, they lived on Earth. They tricked people so potently that their victims self-destructed, destroying their own lives with things like crime, dishonesty, and infidelity.

"Gabriella was only seventeen when she met Dylan. She saw the good in Dylan. They fell in love. Next thing you know, Dylan was telling Xavier that he wanted to change. But Xavier was furious. When he found out Gabriella was the reason for Dylan's change of heart, he tried to trick her to her own death so he could get his brother back. Nobody knew that Gabriella and I were demigods, so when Gabriella jumped off a cliff just as Xavier had coaxed her to, he presumed she was dead. Gabriela waited for him to leave so that he would believe she was dead, and then she went into hiding. By the time the Celestials approached us to be Watchers, Gabriella had been in hiding for weeks. It was obvious what we needed to do to become worthy. The Celestials didn't like Xavier because he disturbed the peace on Earth. He couldn't let humans be. So Dylan helped Gabriella and I plan his destruction. And it was this act that gave us our pass to immortality."

"But . . ."

"How did we do it?"

"He's a god. Aren't gods indestructible, curse and all?"

"All gods have a spirit that is worth far more than their physical body. Spirit is what makes a god powerful and vulnerable."

"I hate that word."

Lucas's lips curved up silently. "We figured that if we could curse his soul to Xibalba, we would be rid of him. But of course we needed a witch."

"Tita."

He nodded. "That summer we received word that the Incas in Machu Picchu were going to sacrifice a witch. We saved her and brought her back home to Yucatan, where we planned our attack on Xavier. His arrogance was his weakness. When we heard he was going to make an offering up north at Tajin, a Mayan woman who looked similar to Tita, we swapped Tita for his captive victim. Tita bespelled herself so that when Xavier tried to kill her, his spirit would be cursed to Xibalba and Tita's life would be preserved.

Since then, Xavier has been locked in Xibalba, trying to get out."

"How come I saw Xavier on the bridge if he isn't allowed to leave?"

"That's just his rotten physical body. It's been deteriorating for five hundred years. While his spirit is trapped down there, his physical body is weak here. Because they aren't together."

Xavier had been feeble and thin, his pale skin almost translucent. Lucas noticed my shudder.

"Don't worry, his physical form really isn't that powerful without it," he said.

"But he had power over me." I remembered the way that Xavier's fingers flicked and slammed my body into the bridge that night.

"But not over us. That is why he fled when we arrived."

"You cut it too close sometimes," I joked nervously.

His smile played with my heart, controlling me in a very different way than Xavier had. I breathed in the icy air, hoping it would take away the hot palpitations. Lucas chuckled. He was now lying on his side, propped on an elbow like someone in a painting.

"What are you laughing at?" I asked.

"Your heart is racing. I can hear it."

"Do you hear everything?"

"Pretty much." He grinned.

Great. "What did your dad do to become immortal?"

"You can't just sit still for a second, can you?"

"And you can't just answer a simple question, can you?"

He shook his head, chuckling under his breath. "The Aztecs believed that all gods were honored by human sacrifice. But being married to my mother, a goddess, my father knew that not all gods wanted human sacrifice. So after they met, he lived his entire life never performing that sort of ritual. After Tajin we moved to Yucatan, where he dedicated Tulum as a place where no human sacrifice would ever be made. It was extremely uncommon for an Aztec to commit to a bloodless life, but the Celestials cherished him for it and saw it as worthy."

"And Tita?"

Lucas sat up, facing me, but playing with the laces of his shoes again. "Tita *had* to turn immortal. If she died, Xavier's curse would be lifted."

I looked away, embracing the beauty of Lucas's snowy fortress. I listened to the song of the birds and stared across the frozen pond. The whiteness around us was pure and calming, but my mind unwillingly turned to what lurked in Xibalba.

"What lives in the Underworld?" I had seen more of the undead than I wished, but I needed to know what we were up against.

"Aztecs who died in battle against the Spaniards, the ones who were the most compelled, the die-hards, we call them. And the Mayans who had no sense of sin, the murderers and thieves who escaped punishment because of the community's lack of moral order. Because their behavior disturbed the balance of good, they were damned to the Underworld. And lastly, the wicked warriors, kings, and priests; the Xibalban gods hand-select their executioners from those ranks."

Lucas looked away, dipped his finger in the snow, and twirled it in circles. "The executioners were created for one purpose," he said, "and that is to capture the gods' sacrifices. In all my life, the executioners have never returned to the Underworld empty-handed."

His low tone made my eyes fog up with fear for my fate, but his hand moved suddenly to my knee.

"Don't worry. Things will be different this time," he said encouragingly. He looked at his watch. "We better get you home soon. It isn't safe for us to be out when it's dark."

"Aren't you worried about Solstice at all?" I asked, now twirling my hair obsessively.

"Are you?"

"Extremely."

My finger snagged in a knot. The tingle came on impact as his fingers touched mine. He moved my fingers away and untangled the snarl with speed and accuracy. I was disappointed when he backed away and stood seconds later. I needed him now.

"It isn't Solstice I'm worried about. It's closing the portal." The fear in his eyes this time transmitted painful electric arcs to my body.

"How come?"

"I have power over the creatures of the dead, but I cannot control what happens once the portal is closed. Technically, we will be committing an act of treason. That's what scares me."

The chemicals surging in my body mixed badly, producing intense nausea.

"What if we went to the Celestials for help and told them about the prophecy?"

He shook his head softly. "I've already thought of this. They wouldn't believe it. They think witches are weak, and the prophecy comes from one. It's too much of a risk. If they knew a human controlled the fate of all, I bet on my life that they'd give you over in a heartbeat."

My stomach dropped. He heard that too, except he didn't smile. He dropped to his knees.

"Zara, listen to me. Look around you," he said, and I glanced at the shimmering snow behind him. "Remember it. Let this be your out. When you feel your mind being tampered with, when you are in a place you don't want to be, I want you to think of this place. Can you do that for me?"

Suddenly his sapphire eyes were only inches from mine, fearless and determined. The icicles that hung from the church reflected in them like solid light. His brooding features seemed fairer here, almost angelic. I felt my lip quivering at this new, delicate perfection, far more appealing than winter's charms. It was then, staring into the depths of his sympathetic soul, that I knew *he* was my utopia, my way out of battle—I no longer felt trapped, no longer felt like his prisoner. In some strange way, we were bound together.

My bond with Lucas was never about taking my freedom away. It was a bond of honor, and I trusted with my life that he would protect me because he honored me too. But how could he be so unselfish while I was so ungrateful?

"I'll try," I said, staring back with a newfound respect.

I knew that he understood my luminous moment. His now-humble eyes tightened as he smiled. "That's all I need you to do."

Chapter Eighteen

Solstice

The clouds were gray the next day as Lucas and I drove to his house. My thoughts were on the letter in my bag: I had written a message to Mae, not knowing if I'd see her again, and I just needed to mail it. When we arrived at the Castillos' house, though, I broke out of my reverie. Gabriella was standing on a snow-layered boulder near the woods, bow in hand, her left arm extended forward and her right elbow bent by her ear. There was a tiny movement followed by a *boom*, and she reached for another arrow, tilting her head to aim into the woods again.

A loud ringing broke the silence. I couldn't help but watch the siren in the woods as I rooted through my bag for the phone. Her head snapped toward us at the second ring. Embarrassed, I finally thumbed the button and lifted it up.

"Yes?" I answered, unable to contain my annoyance.

"So, Mexico?" Max said.

"You coming?"

"Don't know yet. I have finals."

"That's what Mom said."

He was silent as I stared at the floor, sensing Gabrielle's curious gaze from outside.

"Did you need something? I'm sort of busy," I grumbled.

"Do I have to have a reason to talk to my little sis?"

"Max, what do you want?"

"I want to know what you're doing with that boy. What has he done to wrap you around his finger?"

"You don't know what you're talking about." I turned my back to Lucas's smirk, but just ended up facing Gabriella on the other side of the window. I had nowhere to look but out the windshield, toward the foggy lake.

Max's offended laugh startled me. "Mom told me how she listens to you cry at night."

My next breath was stolen from me. The clever smile across the car that I had grown to love vanished. The fact that he now knew the truth horrified me. I couldn't break away from his shocked gaze as guilt turned me to stone.

"So I *am* right," Max heckled on the other end. "And when was the last time you thought about applications for another college? Jett says you don't talk about it anymore, and that's all you used to talk about."

I was suddenly depressed. Instead of racing as it usually did in Lucas's car, my heart had slowed to a near halt.

"I'm working on that," I muttered.

"With him?"

"No. I'm doing it on my own, when I have free time, *without* him," I blurted without thinking.

Lucas's door slammed. He joined Gabriella at the hood of the car and unleashed an anguished yell I felt responsible for.

"Look, I've got to go," I said, watching as Gabriella defended herself against Lucas's sudden temper.

"I'm watching out for you, sis."

"Tell Casey hi."

Guilt flooded the car the moment I hung up. I had lied to Lucas about my misery by keeping it from him. But it wasn't that, the disgrace written all over me. For the first time since I'd met him, I had spoken of an independent future as if he didn't exist.

"Why didn't you tell me she was crying?" I heard Lucas say to Gabriella.

She replied in quick Spanish as I eased out of the car. When Lucas didn't acknowledge me, shame wrinkled me like a raisin. I wanted to disappear.

"Max and Casey would love you if they had a chance to know you," I said, hoping to make up for the lie.

He turned a wall of sarcasm to me. "Let's hope they can make the trip to Mexico, then."

"Would the executioners go after them if they don't get me?" I asked, my heart seizing anew.

Gabriela shrugged. "It's possible."

"What?"

Lucas exhaled in a rush. "Relax. They don't have a choice. One of us will drive to Reno and take care of it."

Although that was good news, I stormed to his car, grabbed my stuff, and headed inside. I beat him through the door, but he whisked past me to block the basement stairs.

"Get out of my way," I ordered rudely.

"Make me."

My blood boiled when he planted his feet and grinned selfishly.

"If I am such an inconvenience to you, why go through all this trouble to save me?" I argued.

He laughed, oddly loud. "If *I* am such an inconvenience to *you*, why ask me if I am coming back to Tahoe after we close the portal?"

"You are such a jerk!"

"And you are a confused, stubborn woman!" His voice echoed throughout the house. "Why didn't you tell me that you were so unhappy?"

Dylan materialized out of the basement. "What's going on?"

Dela

"Stubborn? Me? No, no, no. That's all you!" I stabbed a scornful finger at him.

"Because I am trying to protect *both* of us!" he shouted, a slight accent emerging from his unbelief. "Admit it, you can't stand relinquishing your independence to be saved. If it weren't for my *stubbornness*, you wouldn't trust me, and we both would be worse off!"

"I am done here." I threw my arms up and flipped around, heading straight for the garage.

"Oh, oh, oh," he chortled. "Don't let me deter your happiness, Your Majesty. Excuse me for caring."

Gabriella and Dylan were already waiting by her winter car, a sparkling pale-gold Escalade, but Lucas had not joined them. Gabriella walked delicately to me.

"I'm sorry, but I cannot be around him for another minute," I sniffed.

She took my bag and opened the passenger door without question. I slid in and slouched, laying my forehead on the cool dash. Gabriella and Dylan exchanged a few words, kissed quickly, and the next thing I saw was Niya and Malik running alongside the car until we passed the gates.

"Want to talk?" Gabriella asked once her house was out of view—or, rather, once Lucas's ears were out of range.

"Why is he such a jerk sometimes?"

She cackled. "Lucas isn't a jerk. He's stupid, but far from a jerk. He's too smart for his own good."

I covered my mouth as a hiccupping laugh tried to escape my throat. She gave me a knowing look.

"Stupid?" I asked.

"He takes what he feels in his heart and puts it all in his head. He isn't much better at home either. He's uptight around us too. I don't like it. He's never been this way." She looked at me. "I'm sorry, but I would be lying if I said it wasn't you that makes him this way."

The guilt sank into me like a heavy chain I couldn't lift. "He did admit yesterday that I made him crazy."

She laughed. "He's created his own hell with his professional book-smart thinking, hasn't he?"

"Just how book smart is he?"

"Would two masters, four bachelors, and degrees in medicine and law count?"

My breath stumbled out in small gasps. "Did he ever practice anything?"

"Not once."

"Why?"

She gripped the wheel gently with her delicate hand. "Because he couldn't focus. His life revolved around finding you."

I slid my hands between my knees and shivered, feeling more selfish than ever. "Do you think this is permanent?"

"I don't know. He's too worried he could ruin everything if he involves himself with you."

"And I'm not?"

Her eyes narrowed at me. "Good point."

Gabriella pulled onto my street long before dusk. The snow that had piled over my wagon was gone, and two snowmen had appeared on my neighbors' lawn. I was glad my car was useful for something.

"Anyway, Dylan and I think it's a good idea if you two take some time off from each other. I can take you to school until we get out for winter break."

"Thank you, Gabriella."

Her smile was comforting. "*De nada*."

Dark clouds covered the valley the next morning when Gabriella and Tita showed up promptly at seven. Gabriella was dressed appropriately today, with black boots over shrink-wrap pants and a long sweater woven with gold thread. I looked twice at my last-year's clothes: a white sweater and jeans so thin there were holes at the knees.

At lunch, I told Tita I needed a break and sat with my friends. It was nice sitting with humans. Their conversations were normal, nothing to do with blood or power, or about how different I was. I felt my life coming back until Ashley began asking strange questions.

"So Zara, is it true that Lucas imports his shampoo?" she asked.

"What?"

"Well, he does have the best hair in school—sorry, Hayden."

Hayden reached for his hair, a hamburger in his other hand, and humphed. Tana leaned in enthusiastically. Her hair was curly and stiff with way too much hairspray.

"I heard he imports it from Brazil and that he pays a hundred dollars a pop," she said.

"What? No, you're wrong. Who would do that? That's ridiculous," I remarked.

I glanced at where they waited on the other side of the cafeteria. Gabriella was trying to contain a laugh, while Lucas looked upset.

"He's crushing on you like mad," Tommy noted from the far side of the table.

A cough erupted from the back of my throat. I chugged a big gulp of juice and cleared my throat.

"No, he isn't," I said, but blushed with mortification when I noticed Lucas's mouth crack and form soft dimples in his cheeks. I looked away.

"Zara, what is the deal with their tattoos?" Jett asked before shoving a handful of fries into his mouth. I'd forgotten that eating with boys was sometimes like feeding time at the circus.

"What do you mean, 'what is the deal'?"

"What do they mean?" he clarified.

"I don't know, Jett. That's a good question. Why don't you ask them yourself?"

My response shut him up for the moment, but then he asked, "Is something wrong with your car?"

"No."

"Then why are you riding to school with Enrique every day?"

I pursed my lips, bothered by the name-calling.

"You seem to be awfully quiet for someone who spends a lot of time with them," Tommy said.

The sip I had just swallowed got stuck as my throat contracted. It inched its way down with painful slowness. Afterward, when I could breathe again, I stood up.

"See you guys later," I said.

Jett looked confused. "Where you going?"

"For a walk."

Tita had already turned toward me.

"It's a blizzard out there," Jett stated, bewildered.

"Well then, nothing will change, will it?"

I pulled my coat on, gathered my stuff, and walked outside. I hadn't expected this storm from such a calm morning. Strong wind pushed me toward the outside tables. I heard a whisper and spun to follow it, but the whizzing flakes created an opaque wall.

Something grabbed my left arm, and I screamed.

"Zara!" Tita's voice was almost mute in the storm, and I could barely see her through the tangled flurries. "Come inside!"

She escorted me inside to an empty hall, where Lucas leaned against the wall with his arms crossed. He looked so dashing, all in black with his bright blue sneakers, and a part of me was mad that I was excited to talk to him again.

"I let you go for one minute, and see what happens? I'm sorry, but I cannot grant your wish. You are stuck with me until this is all over. You're coming home with me after class."

"Whatever." I started walking in the opposite direction.

"Where are you going?" he called.

"Back to class. I still have two more hours of school."

A gust of wind blew the damp hair off my shoulders. Lucas suddenly appeared in front of me, so close that I could smell his imported shampoo. There was spice in it. I took another deep breath to identify it as he leaned in with a smirk.

"It's the ginger," he said with lazy eyes. "And no, I don't import my shampoo from Brazil. You forget that I can hear you."

"Actually, I did *not* forget." I rolled my eyes and pushed past him. He stopped in front of me again with another gust of wind, leaning in closer this time.

"You are coming with me right now," he ordered.

"What's going on?" Jett remarked.

Lucas and I glanced at him, the snowflakes waging war behind his back as he approached. I stepped sideways.

"Nothing, Jett. Go away," I said.

Jett stopped at Lucas's side and looked up with a territorial look. "Leave Zara alone."

Lucas raised his eyebrows with disbelief when I grabbed Jett's arm quickly. "Jett, just go. Please."

He shrugged my hand away and got in Lucas's face. "*Comprende*, Fernando?"

"Jett, stop!"

Lucas tucked his fingers into fists. "If you ever touch Zara again, I will hurt you."

They were ridiculous. Blue versus green. It was a Jedi battle waiting to happen, both fighting over the same *possession*—though I was certain Jett would lose, and fairly quickly. Jett finally stepped away, preserving the remainder of his dignity, and turned to me with a bewildered expression. "I'm looking out for you, Zara. Be careful." Then he turned back into the slushy wind and disappeared.

"We're leaving. Now," Lucas insisted.

My knees suddenly went weak. "How?"

He perked up, almost laughing. "I can carry you, or you can

walk," he joked.

I groped for words as I followed him outside to the parking lot, where he shielded me from the storm with his jacket. It was toasty inside the car, but I observed that the storm gave us privacy as well. I couldn't see past his speckled windshield.

"I'm sorry," he said as he cranked the heat to the highest setting. "I never should have reacted the way I did. And I'm sorry I ever made you cry."

His eyes were swelling, but he chuckled ironically, tilting his head back as he looked up at the padded ceiling while his Adam's apple moved slowly downward. He reached for his dark hair and tugged. "Know what's funny? You wish to be rid of me, and I wish to be with you."

"Lucas, I don't . . ."

He turned to me in our bubble. "My family admitted to me last night how much you cried. All those nights—" He choked. The lump in his throat stilled. He turned to the whiteout outside.

"Lucas, it's not what you think. I wasn't crying because I want to be rid of you. I cried because I wanted you to act on how you felt."

"I can't."

His anguished face was unbearable, and it was my turn to look away, ashamed to be putting him through this torture. "I know."

"I have always been able to do whatever I've set myself to do, except with you. You are the hardest thing I've ever done."

"Do I take that as cruel irony or flattery?"

He smiled a little and then fell silent, lifting his hand to touch my hair gently. The warm tingle made me lean into him. "You are the only person I would do this for."

"I know," I repeated in a whisper.

Then his hand cupped my cheek softly, and I grabbed his wrist for strength. "What do you want me to do?"

"Never leave me," I said.

"I promise."

The car was a furnace, forcing me to move away from his warm touch. As I was turning down the heat his phone rang, if only for half a beat before he answered it. A moment passed, and he became distraught. His fingers combed distractingly through his dewy hair.

"What is it?" I asked.

"It's Andrés. He says to go home. If the executioners came while we were driving in these conditions, we wouldn't be fast enough."

A minute later Lucas was shifting gears and driving away. "Are your parents home?"

"They are both at the shop."

"Then I will wait with you until Valentina can come for the night watch."

He looked at his watch as he wheeled onto our barely visible driveway a few minutes later. "She should be here soon."

"Why do you call your parents by their first names?" I asked.

"I've spent enough time away from them that it became natural."

A loud boom of thunder overhead made me jerk. Lucas slowly rolled his eyes to the sky.

"The Milky Way's dark rift is aligning with the sun. There's only two weeks left until Solstice. If the weather stays like this, you will come straight home after class," he said.

I nodded as the pushing wind whistled inside the car.

"Have you had more problems with blacking out?" he asked.

"No."

"Good." He sat up and looked behind him. "She's pulling into the neighborhood."

I followed his eyes to the back windows but could only see the inside of his clean car. The wall of whiteness outside blocked my view of the street. I grabbed my bag and shuffled my hand through the junk in search of the house key. "So I'll see you tomorrow?"

His smile was a wide beam spread from cheek to cheek. "*Claro.*"

"What does that mean?" I asked, opening the door.

"Of course."

"Oh, right." I grinned, though it felt funny, and then hurriedly closed the door.

Inside, I went straight to the window of my room and looked out. Valentina's red Mercedes was at the curb across the street, polka-dotted by the storm's swelling bluster. I grabbed my phone to send Lucas a text.

For what it's worth, I wish it were you outside my window tonight.

I'm here, no matter where my body is.

Oh . . .

Does that bother you? I can switch with Valentina if it helps you feel better.

Not bothered, I'm just working through some things. It's just that . . .

Just what?

Never mind, have a good night.

Now you've got me thinking real hard, not possible to rest . . .

I turned for the bathroom and cleaned my makeup off. I hadn't planned to reply, but my phone beeped again.

Don't be shy . . .I need to know . . .

It's embarrassing.

I'm coming over.

NO!! I'll tell . . .

Time passed as I waited for the courage to say how I now felt about him. It scared me that he didn't scare me anymore. It scared me how *in* I was. I rolled onto my back and stretched, smiling as the embarrassment got the best of me. I pictured him distracting himself while he waited for me. There wouldn't be any rug left if he kept picking at it like he had when I was there. Another beep sounded from the edge of the bed.

Really?? Is it really that bad?

We need to work on your patience.

You're killing me.

I'm not into you for your body. I mean, I like your body, but I like your brain too, as stupid as it is sometimes . . . oh gosh, can't believe I just said that. This is so bad, isn't it? What I'm trying to say is . . . I feel calm when you're near. And you never judge me for something that I feel might upset you. Sorry, I know this sounds stupid.

I know exactly what you mean. I feel the same. Only difference . . . I'm infatuated with your brain . . . you're perfect, Zara Moss.

So truce?

the 52nd

Si, muñeca. Truce.

I set the phone down and rolled over. I wanted to know what things he'd done that I wouldn't judge him for. I knew we were an unlikely pair, but pieces of me thrived on our togetherness, our witty remarks, and our flirty texts. I felt I had a pretty good idea of who Lucas was, but—not now, but sooner rather than later—he'd have to tell me everything about himself. That wall needed to be broken down.

As the gale weeks passed, training stopped, winter break came, and I spent every waking hour at home with Lucas. I didn't understand it, but I felt dingy. It was a sort of darkness that webbed within, making the bright wintry weather seem dreary. Dylan saw it as a blessing because it seemed to have replaced my blackouts, but I didn't feel myself.

I knew I really wasn't right when I woke up on December twenty-first, the day before Solstice, ran to the toilet first thing, and heaved. Nothing came out, but I was pale in the mirror, and I felt dehydrated. My lips were chapped. I rubbed my arms and went back to my room, where the air felt stagnant and cold. I shivered again and thought about packing for Mexico, but instead I put my phone on silent and fell back asleep.

It was dark outside when I woke, and a rainbow of colors from the Christmas lights on the roof lit my room. I heard Mom return from the mall, and though I curled into a tighter ball on my bed, there came a knock on my door.

"Zara, Lucas is downstairs," she called.

I checked my cell on the pillow. There were eight missed calls from him.

"Coming," I moaned.

Mom was waiting at my door. "You look horrible. What happened to you?"

"Nothing did. I just woke up."

"Well, you look it."

I ignored her and made my shaky way downstairs, wrapping my sweater around my waist. Lucas was sitting in the high-back chair in the living room but stood as I approached.

He gave me a funny look. "Are you okay?"

"Why does everybody keep asking me that?"

He took a step closer. "Have you packed?"

"Not exactly."

I could tell he was waiting for Mom to leave. He leaned in and whispered, "Andrés will be out front tonight. I just needed to see how you were doing."

"I feel funny," I responded.

I stared at his blue shoes while the roiling in my stomach surged.

"Nausea?"

I crossed my arms over my queasy belly. "I feel like I've been poisoned."

He lifted my chin gently. "Just try and get some rest tonight."

"You should too," I said.

He chuckled. "That's not going to happen."

When Mom moved to the family room and gave us some privacy, I started panicking. "I'm confused about tomorrow. How can we leave for Mexico if the executioners haven't come yet?"

"They will come. Trust me."

"But . . ."

"Zara. Enough. Let it go. Have faith, please, because this is completely out of your control," he pleaded.

I looked down, unsure if I should say it, but sure enough to speak. "I'm not worried about me. I'm worried about you and your family. If things get badly . . ."

"Never."

"Lucas, you have to think clearly here."

He grabbed my shoulders and squeezed gently. "I'm not sure I'm the one not thinking clearly. Listen to yourself . . . leave you . . . let you go?"

My stomach tightened. I bent over it and winced. "Yes, I want you to promise me you'll let me go if any of you are at risk of dying."

"We don't die."

"You know what I mean." I snapped.

He lifted my chin again to meet my gaze. A soft tickle formed where our skin met. His soft eyes understood, comforting me enough to relax my muscles and stand straight.

"You're going to be okay," he whispered. "We have taken extra measures to make sure you are protected."

"Like what?"

He looked at his watch and took a step toward the door. "I have to go. I will come get you when it is time."

"When?" My voice quivered as I followed him.

"Whenever the executioners decide to come." He shrugged carelessly and pivoted to the door. "But pack, please."

I shook my head again, scared that he was leaving.

"I will see you soon." There was a silent pause, and then he slanted his head down to kiss my cheek and slid outside before I could recover.

Packing was impossible. When I realized I had debated on which pair of shorts to bring for ten minutes, I gave up and slid into the chilled bed. What would it matter if I wasn't alive? Underneath the peacock-colored flannel, I prayed for the slightest bit of sleep, but it was impossible on my deathbed.

At midnight the fear subsided, and I finally fell into unconsciousness. In my dream, there were no visions of chestnuts roasting or sugarplums dancing. There was a bitter blackness that consumed me until I found myself staring at a face I'd only seen once before: the handsome, dark-haired man with the chiseled face from my blackouts. The one who brought the dagger down into those girls' chests. He seemed to be looking at me as his mouth creased in an evil grin. *You're mine*, he mouthed as my body swayed back and forth.

"Zara! Zara wake up!" a voice whispered in the dark.

"Zara, you have to wake up!" It whispered again as my body shook violently.

When the blackness lightened to the gray darkness of my room, I awoke, groggy and disappointed to see two thirty on my clock. I rolled onto my side to go back to sleep, but the shaking started again and rolled me back over. My eyes focused slowly in the dark until I saw Lucas's face. It was obscured by the black hood pulled over his head, but his eyes glistened in the glare of light through the open window.

"Zara . . . it's time," he whispered impatiently. "You have to get up; we don't have much time."

"Already? It's not even morning yet," I mumbled, trying to roll back over, but his warm fingers held me firmly.

"Yes. Now."

"Fine," I groaned.

My sweater and pants sailed at my face as I plodded out of bed. Lucas's back was already turned so that I could change. As I stumbled in the dark, missing each pant leg, Lucas obsessively checked the watch on his wrist.

"I'm ready," I said, tugging my sweater down.

Within the space of a breath, the window was thrust open noiselessly and he sat on the sill, silently beckoning me to come. As white flurries flew inside, I walked to the ledge nervously and looked down at the twilit snow beneath. Knots formed in my stomach, and I shook my head. I hated heights.

"Don't you trust me?" Lucas now looked concerned.

"Yes."

I looked once more at the drop, shaking in terror, and he motioned me over to sit on his lap. "Then come here and hold on."

As I slowly sat, his arms snapped around me, and he jumped without warning. My stomach dropped instantly as I fought the urge to scream. When my mouth flew open anyway, his hand clasped tightly over it. We landed softly in the powdery snow, and he carried me to his car without a word and set me down on the heated seat.

"You okay?" he asked. I hadn't even seen him open his door, but the headlights were already on, and we were speeding toward Fallen Leaf Lake.

"I'm fine." I shivered.

My hand collided with his as I reached for the heater vent. It was he who backed away, though, smiling.

"What are my parents going to think when I'm not in my bed in the morning?" I felt like I was about to hyperventilate.

"You'll be back in bed before they even get up."

His voice was calm, but he looked at his watch again and accelerated onto the icy two-lane freeway. I was beginning to worry about speeding over black ice when a smoky black corpse appeared at my window.

"Lucas!" I screeched.

I leaned into Lucas just as the bony hand reached through the window, shattering the glass into thousands of tiny shards. Lucas reached over, clenched the deadly hand, and squeezed. There was a crunching sound, then a high-pitched screech. The demon's mouth, which was inches from mine, gaped long and hollow as it shrieked. I slapped hands over my ears as Lucas released the dead creature, which shot away into the night.

The car fishtailed as Lucas swerved away from another executioner. It flew at my window, but the Rover surged as Lucas gained control and turned sharply on the exit. The engine revved loudly as another wave of executioners came. I knew their bones, ropy like veins, but this time I clearly saw the dark silver bands that adorned their legs and arms as they followed us into the dense trees at the hidden turnoff.

The road was untouched by the moonlight, a black, tree-lined tunnel lit only by the beam of headlights. Lucas barreled over the potholes as the executioners swarmed around us. But then I could see the black scrolls of the gate ahead, glimmering like gunmetal in the moon's silver light—still closed.

"Lucas, gates!" I screamed.

"ANDRÉS!" Lucas yelled as the gates stood, unmoving.

The gates moved, but slowly. The opening didn't look wide enough for our car, and the passing black trees weren't slowing. I screamed when Lucas floored it and we barreled through the gates, centimeters away from impact.

On the other side, I panted and watched as Niya and Malik chased executioners through the snow at our side. Within seconds the mansion was before us. It was pitch black except for a trail of light to the open garage. As we pulled in, our headlights caught an executioner just as a sharp-tipped stick halted in its heart, and its black dust billowed around the car. Then the executioners wailed as one, some flying away as others evaporated into dust.

Within seconds the way was clear, a glowing pathway behind the garage snaking down to the lake's moonlit shore. I could vaguely see Gabriella and Dylan there, but then the awful whispers buzzed like bees in a hive, and I knew they were angry. My heart pounded once as Lucas cut the engine, and then he was helping me out as Andrés and Valentina ran toward us from the woods, dressed in black.

"Where's Tita?" Lucas asked. I sensed his heart racing, driving short puffs of air from his mouth.

"*Aqui!*" Tita hustled out of the house toward us. A folded pile of thick, white fabric blazed against her black clothing. "Zara, put this on and don't take it off until I say. It will shield you from the executioners, but the moment you take it off, you won't be protected."

I nodded and grabbed the soft fabric with trembling fingers. It was heavy, woven with a thick, velvety pile and plush feathers. When I pushed my arms through the long sleeves, only the tiniest portion of my fingertips poked out. The feathers on the shoulders tickled my chin, but right away Lucas was in front of me, securing it around my neck with a satin sash. When he was done, he grabbed my hand and took a step toward the lake.

Abruptly, shrieks split the night. I dropped his hand to reach for my ears in agony. Lucas threw his hands over mine, shouting urgently at me as our noses touched. But I couldn't hear him. He pointed to the demons and held up all ten fingers. I still didn't understand, but he squeezed my hand and began running, tugging me across the gravel toward the black lake.

My body stumbled within his iron grip. My bones rattled in the heavy cloak as I tried to match his pace over the gravel—he was clearly moving slowly for me. But when the shadows of the woods approached, Lucas threw an arm around my waist and lifted slightly before speeding up to his inhuman pace. My toes danced over the loose dirt as my eyes blurred in the cold wind.

Gabriella and Dylan opened safe passage for us as we crossed the dark expanse. Black camouflaged their bodies too, but the quiver's glimmer just behind Gabriella's shoulder caught my eye. It was filled with exotic, feather-fletched arrows. Dylan held a long, ridged stick with a steel-colored tip, a sort of spear, I supposed. But when he threw it, another appeared in his hand. Lucas sped toward them as Gabriella fired arrow after arrow and Dylan speared the executioners, reducing their numbers when the weapons struck their hearts.

As we approached, they stopped and hopped onto the dock, but more black shadows swooped into range and circled us.

"Dylan!" Lucas yelled, his arm tightening around my waist.

My feet dangled in the air as he carried me closer to the water. "Behind you!"

Gabriella spun and shot and faced us again before I could blink, black dust glittering behind her.

"Hurry!" she ordered as another wave of shadows appeared. She shot another shadow with laser precision and reached for another arrow.

Lucas stopped at the boat as she reloaded. Silver flurries drifted over the lake as I stared; no ropes bound its cleat to the dock.

"You're going in here," Lucas said quickly, jutting his chin at the forward deck.

"What?" I fought to catch my breath now that my lungs were free. I tugged at the sash around my neck as if it would help. "Why can't I stay with you?"

Another shattering shriek pierced my ears as more dust filled the air overhead. There was a murderous roar just beyond that, and more black specks followed. The battle raged all around us, growing louder with each breath. My head spun with trying to follow it.

"Zara!" Lucas shouted. I looked back, scared. The muscles in his forehead pinched together with distress. "Valentina can protect you over the water better than I can protect you on the land. And remember, the executioners can't get within ten feet of you with that cloak on."

I shuddered as I thought about what he was about to do. Gabriella squeezed my shoulder sympathetically, then ran into the darkness. I watched Dylan disappear too, feeling sicker the farther they moved from me.

"I'll be struck by lightning," I stuttered.

Lucas squared his tall body in front of me and held my shoulders. "Valentina controls the lightning; it doesn't control her."

My fingertips prickled with fear as my shoulders tingled at his touch. "Where will you be?"

"Each of us will be around the lake at different spots. We'll try to keep them off the lake as much as we can." He spoke quickly, watching the spot Gabriella and Dylan had just left.

Then he grabbed the loose fabric behind my neck and lifted it over my head. As the hood dropped over my forehead, I lifted my head to see his face. He cupped a hand on my left cheek as I placed my hand on the crease of his elbow. He watched me for the slightest second amid the commotion, his face a mask of pain.

"We'll bring you back to us when it's safe," he said.

He leaned in and kissed the other cheek. I closed my eyes as he lingered, inhaling my scent. I wished the chaos would vanish, but all too quickly he backed away.

"Lucas!" Dylan roared from the trees.

The marching chant was growing stronger. Lucas lifted me into the boat and leaped away. The deck jerked under my feet. I grabbed the railing for stability and saw that the water below was rippling—the boat was moving slowly into the black lake. I looked back up, panicking when I saw Lucas vanish into the dark forest. My body tensed with such brittle force that the rush of icy air was more than I could handle. And then the first cold tear ran down my cheek. I was alone.

My breathing grew shallower as the boat stopped in the center of the lake. The cloak kept me dry, but it didn't keep the noise out, and I shivered relentlessly before it.

"Tita!" Valentina's urgent voice echoed from the trees.

"Dylan, to the right!" Lucas yelled somewhere.

I watched the rumbling trees and heard the screams and shrieks. Stiffness crept over me as I waited, feeling weak, expecting a black form to appear over the water at any moment. I squinted through the moon's pale light, searching for anything through the dark trees. Somewhere to my right, a familiar aqua glow faded in and out as it weaved through the trees. Then another appeared, moving up and down as it sped through the darkness.

Suddenly, across the dark waters, Lucas appeared on the snowy lakeshore. His arm glowed dimly under his black jacket, but he watched me steadily.

"Lucas, MOVE!" Andrés screamed deep in the black forest.

My fingers trembled as they touched my frozen lips. Lucas hesitated as he stared at me, unwilling to leave, but then disappeared back into the woods when an executioner appeared there, only the water between us. The black glare of the distorted human form locked down my gaze.

"Lucas," I whispered to myself, imagining him as my anchor as I felt a darkness growing inside.

I prepared myself for the freezing invasion of my mind, but Lucas flew from behind, roped his arms around the creature, and crashed to the ground. Then he sprinted back into the trees, dragging the black form across the ground with him. I followed their trail through the snow and Lucas's light in the trees until I could no longer see either in the thick brush.

Another executioner passed the shore a moment later. It didn't get far—a long spear struck its back. As the spear fell into the water, another executioner flew toward me from the right, but in the time I took to gasp, Gabriella's arrow destroyed it. My body trembled when I realized, peeking past the cloak's rim, that the horizon was graying. Dawn was coming.

I dropped my chin again, lifting my eyes barely high enough to scan the woods, worried for the Castillos. Turquoise lights darted through the charcoal trees like fireflies as a swarm of executioners flew overhead. I pinched my eyes shut, hoping the shadows couldn't get close enough to test Tita's bewitching powers. But I noticed something different in their voices, the tone—it was gratifying, and instantly a strange sensation popped through me. The curiosity that had tempted me in the past exploded into a desire to go with these demons.

"No!" My voice was a feeble whisper, powerless against my treacherous heart.

I planted my feet on the deck as I resisted the urge. I reached for memories of Lucas at our utopia, but the seductive voices messed with my thoughts. *I should go. I must go. I belong with them.*

Then one strong voice rose above the hundreds of whispers. It soothed my raging fear with indecipherable but ravishing Spanish. The dormant darkness I had felt for the past weeks now forced me to raise my head and look, curious and sickened. I did, and then I held my breath.

Xavier stood alone on the shoreline with a vengeful grin. His hair was the color of sand against the snowy background, and he looked weak, but I feared for the turquoise lights moving throughout the trees. They weren't getting any closer to him. A handful of executioners appeared by his side.

"Valentina, now!" Lucas's voice rang out, so weary and desperate, but so far away. "They broke my line!"

A sudden bright light came from above, and I threw my palms over my eyes to shield them from the bolts that pierced each shadow. When the darkness returned, Xavier was alone, surrounded by glistening dust. But more shadows came from the trees. I counted, bile rising as they flooded in. Six. Eleven. Twenty. My breathing faltered as the black forms began to inch their way over the water. Then the sky showered arrows, and the remaining executioners fled angrily back to pursue Gabriella into the trees.

"Dylan!" Gabriella screamed. A faint blue light flew through the trees with great speed.

I quailed as Xavier turned a pleased, evil grin on me. I didn't understand what he was doing until I felt a chamber in my heart open. It forced out all logic and all thoughts of Lucas. My eyes widened. My fear washed away before it, and I felt inclined—willing, even—to go in peace with these beautiful creatures of the dead. I belonged with them. It was a lovely sensation.

My gaze narrowed on the pale god in desirous contemplation. My last few memories of Lucas had nearly faded when a faint pricking jarred my mind. I focused harder on Xavier, my eyes twitching from the burn of staring so long.

"Zara! Quit looking at him!" Dylan shouted.

His call was so powerful it rippled over my skin, and hatred replaced my dazed trance. Fear drove my focus to my feet, although it was a struggle to ignore the black-speckled shoreline.

I fought to keep my head down, watching my short, foggy breaths as I waited for the fighting to stop, wondering whether anyone would be hurt. Or worse. Suddenly a flash of light illuminated my feet. As it brightened, I thought it might hit the boat, but it disappeared faster than it came.

"Dylan, move!" Gabriella roared. "Malik, follow him!"

I looked up in time to catch sight of Dylan chasing his pale brother into the woods.

Right then executioners formed a wedge and zoomed over the lake. Before I could scream, knifelike bolts shot through them and dragged them down. I shielded my eyes with my forearm and squinted through the afterglow. Rays splashed down into the water, piercing each form as though they were black cotton balls. Anchored on tethers of light, their bodies bobbed for a moment, and then one demon burst into tiny rays of light. A millisecond later another dematerialized, then another. They popped like popcorn until the sky filled with their essence.

But still one weaved through the dust, and the next seconds passed like hours until it stopped ten feet from me. The demon's hazy figure bounced against Tita's invisible boundary. The viny ligaments of his brow furrowed with anger as he looked at me. I held my breath and watched him, trembling, terrified that Valentina's powers wouldn't be strong enough to keep him from me. Abruptly its contorted anger changed into a lively smile, and a rush of interest ran up my spine. I couldn't help but stare harder into the eyes of the beautiful dead king. A tarnished silver crown graced his brow above large sockets deeply set in a face shaped with innocence, and I felt pity for this hollow creature as he beckoned me to come.

As I breathed his smoke into my lungs and took a shaking step closer, the noise around me muted. He extended a bony hand stitched with petrified ligaments to me. I pondered this and took another step across the deck, lifting my hand to his.

I was no more than two feet from his touch when a man's scream made small ripples in the water.

"Zara, no!" it yelled again, a nuisance jarring my reverie.

The fabric draped over my head kept me from seeing this creature in full. I slowly removed it and stepped closer to the peculiar king floating above the water. I felt clearer when he grinned, pleased to no longer be suffocating with fear and insecurity. I smiled.

Then, as my foot moved closer, brightness blinded me. I fell into a crouch, my face against my knees, my fingers jammed over my ears in pain as a shriek rang out.

"Lucas!" I screamed, but it was inaudible over the high-pitched peal.

Finally it stopped. I stood, a bit wobbly despite the calm that had come upon the lake. The skeleton king was gone, his dusty remnants floating away in a beam of yellow sunlight that had just peeked over the trees. Then a biting wind stroked my face, and the boat began its return to the house.

"Lucas," I gasped, searching for him in the circling trees.

When he appeared, his hair blew wildly in every direction, and his shoulders jerked up and down as he panted. The dawn's light picked out figures emerging from the trees at different places and gathering at the dock, but the warmth of the sun couldn't stop my shivering. The boat was only feet away when I whimpered.

"Lucas!" I cried again, reaching for him as he jumped into the boat.

His hands on my cheeks, he frantically searched my face for the slightest scratch. There was dirt on his. A moment later, his brows released the worry they held. Then he grabbed my shoulders and frowned.

"Zara, what were you doing?" he asked.

"What was I doing?" I repeated, confused.

He stared at me incredulously, as if we spoke in different languages. "Why were you taking your hood off?"

"I . . . I . . ." I stuttered, realizing with horror that I had no memory of doing so.

He swooped me up and carried me to the end of the dock, where his family stood in a semicircle. As Lucas removed the cloak, I looked anxiously to my protectors. Dirt clung to Dylan's clothes, and pine needles stuck out of his hair. There was a hole in Gabriella's left sleeve, and her prized hair was tangled in knots. Niya and Malik lay on their bellies, tongues lolling as they panted. Dried blood ran down Tita's nose and Valentina's cheek, while Andrés had a fresh gash across his forehead that appeared to be resealing itself.

Valentina stepped forward. "Are you okay?"

I stumbled, more from fear of what I felt than what I saw. The desire I had warned Lucas about had nearly taken over, and now I was confused about how I felt safe with them too. I hadn't expected that. I hardly noticed that Lucas had nuzzled close to me. His body was trembling.

Andrés looked at his watch. "Lucas, please take Zara home. You will need to move quickly to make it before her parents wake up."

"We'll see you in a few hours at the airport," Valentina said, gently rubbing my arm.

I lifted my weak head from Lucas's warm chest. "No, wait.

What happened?"

"The executioners are on their way back to the Underworld. And Xavier . . ." Andrés sounded unsure.

"That was too close," Dylan added.

"He's getting stronger. I can feel it," I blurted.

Their heads snapped to me, the pressure of royal eyes making me timid.

"What do you mean?" Lucas was first to ask.

I swallowed before I could speak. "It isn't just the blacking out. It's the connection. It's controlling me in a way I can't resist."

Andrés moved. "Tita, is there any way Xavier might gain power without Zara?"

"No."

He pulled a set of keys from his pocket. "Lucas, take Zara home in my car."

When Lucas nodded, there was a sudden pressure against my back, pushing me toward the car.

"Wait, I want to stay. What's going to happen?" I protested.

"We wait for Xavier to return to the Underworld so that we can trap him down there," Lucas answered, pressing his hand again against my resisting back.

And so the plan began, slowly, secretly. My shivering was relentless, even with the heater blasting inside the black Mercedes-Benz. Lucas was entering the freeway by the time the warmth heated through my bones. It was a perfect, cloudless morning, but I couldn't seem to breathe normally.

"Are you sure you're okay?" Lucas eyed me as he pulled up to my sleeping house.

I looked up to my room on the second story. "Am I safe?"

He followed my gaze and smiled slightly. "You are, yes."

"So the executioners are out of time? They can't come after me anymore?"

"Yes. But if we are breaking the treaty, I wouldn't be surprised if they do too."

"What!?"

"Calm down. This is why you are coming with us to Mexico. We will protect you until everything is back to normal."

I rested my head on the seat and stared out the tinted window as a new problem abruptly formed. "So, how do you propose I get back in my room without anyone seeing?"

His arrogant chuckle was comforting. "I would think you trusted me more."

"I do trust you," I admitted, though it didn't sound very convincing.

He hopped out, half snickering and half shaking his head, muttering something in Spanish. He stopped on the driveway under my window and waited. I stayed in the car, looking from him to the window and then to the front door, which I desperately wanted to use.

"To get up there, you have to come to me," he joked.

"How are you so sure we won't be seen?" I asked, moving slowly over the slippery driveway.

He sauntered forward, pulled me into his arms, and jumped. My eyes clamped shut as I tugged at his shirt for support, and then it was over. The air was suddenly warm. I opened the eye closest to the window first and looked around my room. Lucas put me down and took a step back as he ran his hand through his tangled hair.

"Thank you," I mouthed quietly. The clock read six o'clock, but I couldn't be sure my parents were still sleeping.

All of a sudden, his face seemed strained.

"What's wrong?" I asked.

"We're alone, in your room," he stated, deep in thought.

The rush of the Solstice battle had left me too exhausted to deal with his problems. *Not after what I just went through.* Frustrated, I plopped down on the unmade bed and looked up at the ceiling. He stood there like a statue until I rolled my head over to him.

"Are you going to do something about it?" I stabbed sarcastically.

His eyes finally blinked as he moved to the side of the bed and looked down. He was so close I could see his chest rise when he breathed in. My cheeks suddenly felt much warmer. I had again underestimated the power he had over me. I braced myself for the collision of his body against mine—I nearly imagined it, wanting it—but all he did was sigh.

"You don't know what you're asking of me. You don't know me," he said.

"Because you won't let me."

He paused a good three breaths, his eyes locked on mine. "I envy you . . ."

"For what?"

"You live in the moment, no matter the consequence."

"You should try it sometime," I said, stretching my arms above my head.

Lucas took another big breath. This time his shirt pulled tightly over his chest, and the roundness of his pecs peered through. "It's impossible. I fear the consequence too much."

"I have a friend who's allergic to sugar. Literally. His throat starts to itch when he eats too many sweets. Does that mean he never eats candy? No. In fact, he eats it until his stomach hurts and he can't take any more."

"Sounds like an idiot."

"Sounds like someone who's living life. He chooses to be gratified now and deal with the consequences later."

Lucas shook his head and laughed mockingly. "If only my consequence was an upset stomach."

"What does it matter what the consequences are? What's wrong is wrong; the consequences don't change it to a lesser degree.

If you're going to choose your actions based on consequences, you don't know who you are. If you're going to do something because you want to, no matter what the consequences, then I reckon you know who you are and what you want."

"I've been alive for more than twenty generations' worth of your ancestors, and you think I don't know what I want? And who ever said you were wrong? What if I thought you were right?"

I gulped. "If I was *wrong* for you, what are the consequences if I say 'yes, you don't know what you want'?" It was rude, but it was the truth, and I needed to pronounce it slowly and clearly. "Y-e-s. You don't know what you want, whether I'm wrong or right for you."

The glare of his eyes hardened, and his Adam's apple moved slowly downward, and then he took a step back. "You'd better get some rest; we've got a long trip coming," he said, expressionless.

I propped myself up on my elbows. "But—"

"We're done talking about you and me. I don't care what the stupid prophecy says. I care about you, and me—with you—is a cause with too many consequences."

"Like what?"

"First, I could hurt you."

I rolled my eyes, remembering all the times a boy had broken up with me. "I'm stronger than you think."

"I'm not talking about me breaking up with you; I'm talking physically. If you haven't noticed, I'm much stronger than you. I can hurt you . . . badly."

"Oh . . ."

"I haven't been with a human since I've changed, so I really don't know how hard . . . okay, I'm not talking about this anymore."

I threw my hands in the air. "You started it."

"And another reason, of course, is that I don't age." He stepped sideways, pulling at his hair, then rested his fists atop his skull in the mess. The crooks of his arms blocked portions of his face, but I could see enough of the pain creasing his face. "It makes me sick."

"That I'll get ugly and wrinkly?" My heart nearly stopped. In one swift step he was at my side, his hands reaching for mine, but then he stuffed them in his pockets instead.

"Hell no," he said. He sounded upset that I would even suggest it. My heart continued to pump at its normal pace. "It makes me sick that *I* could never grow old and wrinkly. Nobody should be immortal. It's unnatural. Couples belong together in all their forms, and they should change together too. I could never give that to you."

"And?"

"And what?"

"What else? What else is stopping you from doing what you really want?"

He glanced at the corner of my room. "You don't want to know."

"Try me."

We heard footsteps a few doors down and fell silent, waiting to see if they would approach. When they didn't, Lucas took a step toward the window.

"It would be wise to rest before the flight," he whispered.

"But I thought the flight wasn't that long."

"It's not. It's the other part that's going to be long. All this time we've talked about the Underworld, but there is a whole other world you've yet to learn about."

"Which world is that?"

His gentle lips crinkled upward. "Mine."

I imagined he heard the galumph in my heart and thus gave me a moment to breathe before he said, seriously, "I'll be here at two thirty to pick you up."

"You're leaving me alone?" I started to panic.

"Dylan and Gabriella are tracking them. And I shouldn't be here in your room, alone."

I raised my eyebrows, waiting for more excuses as he lingered, but none came. He looked around the room, resisting, his fists balled in his pockets. It should have been me feeling embarrassed, the way my room looked like a pigsty, but I didn't care. I stared him down. *Just do it,* I thought.

"I need to clean myself up," he finally coughed, now looking outright uncomfortable. Avoiding eye contact, he hurriedly crossed to the windowsill. "I'll see you soon."

He escaped out the window before I could speak another word.

Chapter Nineteen

Playa de Castillo

I shut the window and drew the drapes, suddenly drowsy now that my body had thawed in the heat of the house. There were clusters of clothes and shoes on the floor that belonged in my suitcase, but I could rest for a while. Lucas wouldn't be here for six more hours.

The alarm woke me at two o'clock. I wiped drool off my cheek and went to the bathroom to splash cold water over my face, hoping it would ease the pounding in my head. I was running a brush through my hair robotically when I heard familiar cackling downstairs. I flew down the steps and stopped at the bottom, clutching the railing.

"You're home," I said.

The twins turned with mouths full of Pop Tarts.

"Case and I got done earlier than we thought, thanks to our new professor, who let us off the hook," Max said cockishly.

"What professor? What hook?"

"Whoa there, sis. We can't tell you *all* our college secrets. And besides, what kind of question is that?"

I shook my head at the idiot. "It's no secret, you moron."

"Nice to see you too," Casey added. He sounded annoyed.

I realized that they didn't remember. It was Dylan who had made them forget. I left them and went back to my room. I flipped on the TV, paranoid about anyone noticing last night's peculiar stormy weather. But it soon became background noise as I threw anything that might be of use in a hot climate into my suitcase.

"Mom, hurry please. Lucas will be here soon," I hollered as I tossed in a pair of gladiator sandals.

I frantically smoothed out the wrinkles in the bedspread and then ravaged it again to find anything left behind. I had picked up a gray tank when a word struck me like lightning. I dropped the shirt and spun to the TV.

"Government officials are leaning toward the conclusion that this was a freak storm. However, given the unusual size of the electromagnetic field that accompanied the storm, NOAA scientists will be running tests and observing over the next two weeks," the weatherman said.

I sighed and flipped the TV off. I picked the shirt up again and moved it to the suitcase.

"Forgetting something?"

I about-faced, and my stomach dropped at the sight of him. Lucas was leaning back in my desk chair, his feet rested atop my homework, dangling my bikini top on one finger. The twigs were gone from his hair, and his face had been freshly shaven, revealing the smoothness of his ageless skin. His grin was fluid this morning, the flirty kind that made my breath skid and eyes flutter. I snatched the green polka-dot bikini away from him.

"How'd you get in here?" I whispered worriedly as I stuffed the suit into the outside pocket of the suitcase.

"You really should lock your window."

When I realized he wasn't going to leave, anxiety took over. "The storm is on the news right now."

"I know."

"You're not worried that anyone saw something?" Just saying it let the panic loose, and my breathing quickened.

He raised his eyebrows. "Are you?"

"Yes!"

Lucas stood. "No one saw anything, so you can stop worrying about it. I'll wait for you downstairs."

He kissed me on the cheek and then vanished out the window. Half a second later, the bells on the front door jingled as he entered.

"Mom, Dad, we have to go right now. Remember, the airport's in Reno!" I yelled.

I pulled my phone off my nightstand and began flipping through it as I reached for the suitcase on the bed, but my hand swung through empty space and I stumbled against the mattress. *Lucas!*

Downstairs, the barefaced prince sat on the living room couch next to Max. Casey faced them, leaning against the wall. There was an awkward silence when I entered, as if I'd interrupted a conversation about myself. The twins glanced at me, and I realized suddenly just how much they despised him.

"I was just telling Lucas that if anything happens to you while you're gone, he's going to have us to come home to," Max said.

Lucas held back a faint smile. I gave him a scornful look.

Casey stepped away from the wall. "Zara, just because you're going to be in Mexico hobnobbing doesn't mean you won't have a curfew," he announced flagrantly.

"Dad didn't tell you?" I asked, confused.

"Tell us what?" they both said.

"Boys, stop heckling your sister," Dad said. He wrestled a heavy suitcase down the stairs and set it near his feet. "I would have told you earlier, but you didn't exactly come *home* last night. The Castillos have been so kind as to invite you to their home for Christmas. Now, go get your suitcases, we leave for the airport in five. "

Max and Casey shot Dad a surprised look, then glanced at each other in utter shock. Then their annoying cackles filled the room.

"See, Case, this is how we roll!" Max said, and they chortled as they disappeared to their rooms.

I imagined them like this the entire trip and cringed. *As long as they're safe,* I reminded myself.

Once Dad was back upstairs, Lucas effortlessly lifted his giant suitcase in one hand. It swayed gently back and forth, as if it was full of feathers, as he carried it to the door. I followed him outside, where the silvery air spun with bitterly cold sweetness. I shivered, wondering if I'd ever be back at all. When I glanced back to the one thing keeping me safe, I realized how odd it was that he wore shorts and flip-flops and never shivered. I checked for goose bumps, but his skin was smooth as polished stone.

"Seriously?" I said, shivering even in the sheepskin lining of my bomber jacket.

"What?"

"Could you be any more obvious? Shorts in the winter?"

"We're going to the beach. And besides, I've been doing this a lot longer than you have."

We passed the sidewalk bend and approached a new black Escalade parked on the driveway. I stopped, but Lucas kept walking.

"Whose car is this?" I gasped.

He popped the hatch and leaned back so that it wouldn't clip him as it opened. "Mine."

"Since when?"

"Today."

"You bought a car just to take us to the airport?" I asked, perplexed.

He laughed. "No, I bought a new car because my window got crushed," he reminded me.

"Most normal people would have just bought a new window."

He chucked Dad's suitcase into the back and smiled. "You're probably right, but I don't place myself in that category."

I was silent when he tossed the keys at me. "I'm going to get the rest of the suitcases."

the 52nd

The car-lot sticker was still attached to the front window. I peeled it off, bunched it into a ball, and buried it underneath my seat. *So I can see better,* I told myself, *in case anything dead tries to fly at me again.* Just as the seat warmed, Max and Casey walked out empty-handed. Lucas must have insisted on carrying their suitcases. The twins were still enthusing about their fortunate turn of events as they slid into the seat behind me. Max wrapped his arm around my chair.

"Zara, isn't this going to be so fun?"

"Plenty," I moaned, turning to watch the front door.

The snow fell heavily as Lucas walked out with two suitcases in each hand, my parents behind him. Lucas loaded the car as Mom and Dad climbed into the open seats and shivered. When Lucas got in, he just wiped his wet hands on his jean shorts and ran them through his hair to pull it back up, no sign of a shiver.

Halfway there, I turned around to Dad. There was slight discomfort on his face as Lucas revved the engine that had only intensified as we barreled through the fresh snow. I turned back around to look anywhere but at his fright. It only reminded me of the fear I carried within, and the real reason why we were going on this trip.

Minutes later Lucas pulled into the valet stand. I didn't even know airports had valet parking. The uniformed man at the curb called Lucas by name as another opened my door. Lucas gave him a thick wad of folded bills and moved to my side. He grabbed my hand and pulled me closer, then gave orders to the other valets who had appeared out of nowhere.

"My family is waiting inside," Lucas announced three dollies later.

There were festive songs playing in the decorated terminal, a careful attempt at merriment, but on the ground it was anxious chaos as travelers rushed to their gates. I panicked, picturing an executioner swooping through the crush. Lucas's fingers tightened around mine almost before the thought had formed, as if he was reading my emotions, and then he led us through the masses.

Heads turned from all directions toward Lucas. I thought it was just Lucas's ridiculous beach attire, but then I spotted Andrés and the others, and I realized that all eyes were pulled toward the royal immortals. Together, they were alluring.

Max and Casey didn't blink when Lucas greeted Gabriella with a kiss on the cheek.

"Max, Casey, this is my sister Gabriella," he said.

Gabriella smiled as she leaned in and kissed their cheekbones. Her tight shirt exposed a lot of cleavage, but the button-up shirt skimming over it made her look tasteful. I imagined a piece of stone guffawing. That's how the twins looked. *Ridiculous.*

"Nice to meet you, boys. This is my husband, Dylan," she said, tugging slightly on Dylan's arm.

The twins seemed reluctant to look at Dylan. I could see Lucas laughing silently out of the corner of my eye as Dylan stepped forward in his fedora and shook their hands.

"Nice to meet you. I've heard a lot about you," he said.

For the first time in my life, the twins were speechless.

"I have a twin too," Dylan interjected, searching for something to break the awkward silence. "He's not as cool as you, though."

Max and Casey's paralysis finally broke into shaking laughter.

"He's okay sometimes," Max said with a shrug at his brother.

I sat in the aisle next to Lucas for all three hours of our first flight, eating bag after bag of pretzels out of nerves.

"Would you like me to buy you a meal?" Lucas asked.

"No way, plane meals are disgusting."

"Have you ever *had* a plane meal?"

"As a matter of fact I have. Once. I can't do it again," I said, putting pressure on my upset stomach.

"Very well."

Each time the attendant offered us another bag of pretzels,

Lucas graciously accepted and handed his over to me right away. My appetite returned in full force by the time we reached our layover in Houston, and my stomach was making all sorts of noises.

"Eat something now," Lucas said as we exited the plane. "They won't offer any meals on our next flight since it's only two hours."

He looked around at a few places in the terminal and then finally pointed to a restaurant with a display of different cheeses. "There. They have great mac and cheese."

"You like mac and cheese?" *Finally, something we can agree on.*

"Who doesn't like cheese?" he asked.

I smiled. "Sounds perfect."

By the time we arrived in Merida at midnight and got through customs, my starving state had returned. I had heard about street tacos in Mexico, and I wished we could stop and try some, but Andrés and Valentina insisted we wait to eat at their house, a place off the beach twenty minutes away.

The airport there was just as small as ours, but when I walked off the plane into the air-conditioned room, I felt a smudge of unfamiliar humidity. When I caught my reflection in the windows we passed along a wall, I realized that my hair had already gone all Medusa. Lucas looked past my frizzy hair and met my eyes in the glass, unable to contain a sort of anticipation. Then his hand rubbed the small of my back. I smiled, but wondered what it meant as we moved to the baggage claim.

Two men dressed in short-sleeved, collared blue shirts piled our luggage onto small trolley carts and followed us outside. They were short and had to sway from side to side to see around the piles of luggage. As we passed through the automated doors, the thickness of the warm night air clogged my lungs, and I grabbed my throat in despair. I felt suddenly sticky underneath my coat. I slumped it off and swung it over my arm.

"Are you okay?" Lucas asked.

"I'm fine," I said. I inhaled again and found the air wet but breathable. I didn't like it.

We walked past the taxi line and stopped at the curb, where five short chauffeurs stood under a dim streetlamp, holding papers bearing our names. Behind them were long white sedans that looked like they belonged on an English manor, not on the beach. I had already connected rich gods to expensive, foreign cars, but Max and Casey flipped out.

"No way!" Casey screamed.

"Maybach Landaulets?" Max asked giddily.

"What's that?" I asked.

They laughed at me and turned to Lucas, who looked outright guilty.

"What?" I asked again.

"They have suicide doors," Max added.

"What?"

Before I could object, Andrés turned to my parents.

"Valentina and I will take the first car. Mitch and Lori, you take the next. Max and Casey, you have your own car, as do Lucas and Zara. Dylan and Gabriella, you will follow," he arranged firmly.

"That is very nice of you, but we can take a cab. It's more practical," Dad said bravely when no one spoke up.

"Mr. Moss, you are my guest, and it is my pleasure to welcome you as I would my own family. If you took a cab, I would be offended. Now, not another word, please. I believe your daughter is starving."

Dad shot me a puzzled look. I shrugged innocently as my stomach grumbled. Dad finally nodded, and as Andrés and Valentina entered their car, I leaned against Dad and whispered into his ear.

"What bothers you more? The fact that he's rich or that he doesn't have gray hair?" I realized as I said it that I'd never asked Lucas how they really were so rich.

Dad reached for his salt-and-pepper hair. "I don't have *that* much gray hair, do I?"

"Get in the car, Mitch," Mom said as she stepped inside.

I glanced at my car. Lucas held a hand out to the open door. "After you."

The first thing I noticed was the bucket seat I slid into. Lucas was already getting in on the other side as I slid back and got comfortable. Then I noticed the oversized sunroof, open to reveal the stars. And then the space, and how my legs could stretch all the way out with room to spare. And the stark white color of the leather, the rugs, and the doors. I wondered then, since it was so spotless, whether they had just bought these cars as well. Lucas, who had been watching me all the while, chuckled softly.

"These are on loan to us from our dear friends in Germany," he said, answering my train of thought as the car moved.

"How do you read my mind?"

"I don't; I've just gotten really good at predicting what people are thinking, especially you."

"I see. Well then, what am I going to say next?"

He laced his fingers together and laid them on his flat stomach.

"You are going to ask how we pay for all of this," he said.

He confounded me, but then the window open to the driver's compartment caught my eye.

"No, wait, now you're going to ask why I speak so freely in the driver's presence," he added.

I blushed as the driver looked at us in the rearview mirror.

"Raul is a dear family friend."

Immediately the wrong questions flooded my mind. *Who is Raul? How does he know the Castillo family? Does he know about their secret? Does he know why we're here?* I shrank into the seat, scared that I knew so little about this new world, completely in over my head.

"Raul is an Alux," he said. I vaguely remembered hearing the word once before, in the garage at Fallen Leaf. He spoke before I could ask my obvious question. "You will learn more about them in time."

It's been time, I thought angrily, but I was also very tired and very hungry.

"So, where does all your money come from?" I settled for asking as I watched the black streets pass.

He threw a pressed smile at Raul and sighed. "Our Aluxes," he said. Then he chuckled lightly and glanced at Raul. "And so my answer comes to you once again," he said. Raul smiled but said nothing.

"What does that mean? Are they not human?" I whispered.

"Aluxes are Mayan, but not human. The Celestials assigned them to serve and protect us after the transformation. They remain invisible until it is time to serve. Niya and Malik have their beef with them every now and then. They both tend to get a bit protective of us." He winked.

"I wouldn't know the feeling," I joked back.

Lucas laughed.

"Do they have any powers?" I asked as we passed dim streetlights.

"They will use their powers to protect us only when my family and I are in imminent danger, and only against those who mean us harm."

"What can they do?"

"What the Mayans were good at: fighting. They probably seem short to you, but size is deceiving. They. Can. Fight. Some of the best fights I've ever had. After the transformation, well, I guess you can say we all had a big throwdown to see what everyone's strengths were."

"Do they launder money too?" I asked.

Lucas and Raul laughed together. I felt young and dumb.

"No, *muñeca,*" Lucas said, recovering. "They take work all

around the world. Their income goes into a pool. We have a few offshore bank accounts, which is what we use to pay for everything. It would be easier to compel people and just take from them, but we like to think we still have humanity left in us after all. So we pay for our material things just as any normal person would."

"Oh."

He remained patiently silent, expecting more questions.

"Where are Tita, Niya, and Malik?" Dim lights turned to small outdoor restaurants with flashy signs in all colors, and taco kiosks on every street corner. I was surprised at the number of customers they had at this late hour.

"They're coming tomorrow."

"How do Niya and Malik travel? Were they on the plane in a crate, with the dogs and cats?"

Lucas let out a loud laugh. "No, babe, we have a private plane, so Niya and Malik can roam freely. Tita volunteered to stay behind so that they didn't have to fly alone. They will arrive tomorrow night."

"Oh." I shut up then, trying to control the jittery nerves in my gut, and realized he had just called me *babe*.

"How are you doing with everything?" he asked a minute later as I rested my head against the window.

"I try not to think about it."

Soon the city lights were behind us, and the tropical trees were black silhouettes against the stars. The Milky Way swirled above us, a golden glow bursting with burning stars. Lucas shifted and angled his knees closer to mine.

"Since I got mad at you for withholding information from me, I feel I can't be a hypocrite and do the same," he said dutifully.

"Okay." My stomach cramped suddenly.

"The Celestials would come after anyone responsible for killing another Celestial. If they come after us, they will find that we have saved a sacrifice as well as killed one of their own. They like their peace, and if anyone meddles with it, the consequences . . . would not be favorable."

"Why are you telling me this?" I felt the blood rush from my head and the poisonous nausea come back. "Who said anything about killing a Celestial?"

"Xavier may not return to the Underworld when it is time to close the portal. And if that is the case, he must die."

"You can't." It came out before I realized what I was saying, but I knew I was right by the way my body pounded.

"We don't have a choice. He's here to harm you!"

"What if you're wrong?"

Lucas raised his voice through gritted teeth, and his striking features were dark with disbelief. "I am doing this to protect you."

"I know, and I am grateful, but it doesn't make sense. Think about it. It's too easy. I don't know how, but since . . . what happened this morning, I feel it in my bones that something very bad would happen if Xavier died."

"Of course you do. You're connected to him," Lucas sniffed sourly.

"No, Lucas. That's not it."

Lucas sat at the edge of his seat and drew his heels in.

"Xavier knows I swore an oath to the Celestials that I would never break this rule. This gives me leverage, Zara. He would never suspect it."

"You can't!"

"Xavier's plan, Zara, is to kill you on an altar in *this* world. He's not even going to bring you to the Underworld!" he said, disgust clear in his tone. "You dying here will bring his spirit out of Xibalba and back to life. He wants to kill you soon—any day now. I'm sorry, Zara, but my first priority is keeping you safe. We can worry about the Celestials later."

Tears swelled in my eyes. He looked away with grief and sat still. Finally, as the car slowed, he cast a tight smile in my direction.

"We're here."

It was pitch black outside when Raul turned onto a sandy road. The car's headlights revealed a waist-high gate in a wall of high bushes. Raul followed the caravan's taillights through its open doors. The road was slightly bumpy and dimly lit by flaming torches encased in glass atop modern-looking pillars every ten feet. At the end of the road stood a tall, bright house. Short servants stood waiting at the steps to the front door, between more pillars of fire.

"Welcome to my home, Zara," Lucas said as Raul stopped at the steps.

A dark-haired man in a black collared shirt opened my door. He wore a jade-colored ribbon tied in a bow just under his neck, leaving the ends hanging down his chest. I took his hand nervously and stepped out into the awful wall of humidity.

Then I looked up, and up, and up. The house rose three stories high above a large central terrace. Floodlights beamed up each thick tropical tree lining the perimeter of the house. As the cool, salty breeze blew against my face, I recognized the sound of ocean waves crashing against the shore.

"Lucas, your home . . ." I said.

"Lucas, hey Lucas!" Max and Casey called as they ran over to us. Lucas turned toward them.

"Hey Lucas, I just wanted to let you know—" Max began, but Casey jabbed him in the ribs. "Okay, we *both* wanted to let you know that this is awesome. Maybe we can go get some drinks later and talk?"

"Talk about our sister, of course," Casey added, trying to regain control over his excitement.

Lucas chuckled. "Sure. I would like that." Then he slapped each of their shoulders and slyly pushed them toward the door. "Come inside, I will show you where your rooms are."

"Wait, rooms? We have our own rooms?" Casey asked.

Dela

As the twins ascended the stairs in a near run, snorting like pigs, Lucas stepped back and reached for my hand. I jerked away in confusion, asking myself what his gestures meant.

"It's only my hand," he said, but his eyes were different. They were open and free, and I could see the truth in the depths of them. *No more secrets,* I thought.

I smiled and fitted my hand into his slowly. The tingling fire was fierce at first, but then it calmed to a cool touch as he grasped it more firmly. It was a simple tickle when we reached the top of the stairs.

Another servant waited inside the foyer, a short woman wearing a modern-day Puebla dress with a top of black ruffled lace draping across her chest and off-shoulder sleeves, above a sheath fitted tightly from her bust to her knees. A jade-colored feather extension dangled next to her right ear. She was holding a silver platter of ice-cold beverages.

I was beyond parched, but I recognized none of the offerings. I grabbed the first one that looked refreshing, a Coke-type bottle with a picture of an apple on it. Cold condensation wet my fingertips and dripped on the floor as I lifted it.

"Thank you," I said.

She looked up at me and smiled wordlessly.

"*Gracias,* Marifer," Lucas said from behind me, choosing a fluted glass filled with clear liquid.

We passed a spiral staircase and stepped into a museum-sized room open to the balcony walkways of each floor above it. I froze when I saw a tall Christmas tree lit with soft white lights in the middle. Some twinkled on and off beneath elaborate decorations in shades of white, cream, and jade. There were glass balls, seashells, glittering sprays, and snowflakes. Not a single branch remained bare.

"Do you approve?" Lucas whispered in one ear.

"How did you know?" I stared at it—it was another of Lucas's recent gestures, proof he was changing, softening, *weakening.* I turned to him and saw the warm smile on his face.

"How could I not? I would have to be an idiot not to notice how your face lights up at everything Christmas."

"This is beautiful, Valentina," Mom said in awe.

Andrés spoke from the other side of the tree. "Lucas, would you please show the boys and Zara where their rooms are? Your mother and I will show Mr. and Mrs. Moss their rooms. We will join you in the dining room in fifteen minutes for dinner."

I was wondering about the second set of stairs behind him when Mom shot her *Our rules still apply* glance at me. I understood clearly. No messing around, and no boys in my room. It didn't bother me. I was used to her believing we were a couple. It was an easy story to explain the amount of time we spent with each other, but the stare was still uncomfortable. *What does she think I'm going to do?*

Valentina quickly ushered her up the stairs. Short servants followed them with the luggage.

Lucas took me up the spiral stairs. Thick, fresh evergreen garlands draped over the railing. It smelled like home. One flight up, we reached two rooms side by side that faced the ocean.

"Max this is your room," Lucas said, pointing to the left door. Max disappeared inside as Lucas pointed to the right. "Casey, this is yours."

Casey shook Lucas's hand hard, overexcitement making his arm look like spaghetti.

"Thanks so much, man. I'll see you at dinner." Casey practically leaped inside and shut the door behind him. I could hear them laughing and talking to each other through the walls. *I'm betting these rooms are a major upgrade over their apartment.*

Lucas subtly tugged my hand, and we ascended the spiral stairs to the third floor. The two rooms on this floor were larger, separated by a vaulted great room. When we entered the door on the right, a summery breeze hit my face.

Dela

"This is your room," Lucas said.

The ceiling was exceptionally high, but it had to be to fit the four-poster bed at my right. My reflection moved in the mirror of the vanity next to the bed. I looked away quickly, frightened by my hair. French doors across the white marble floor had been left open to the balcony beyond, allowing warm, salty air to sweep through the room. I could hear the waves below.

I gulped. "Where is your room?" I asked, glancing at the sand-colored linen on the king-sized square of goodness and squelching a sudden, irrational thought that we'd be sharing it.

Lucas chuckled lightly, walked to the balcony, and pointed left. "Right there."

Relief washed over me. I followed him outside and stared across a gap at another long balcony. The distance seemed miniscule. I gulped again, knowing it couldn't keep him away.

"Close enough to keep an eye on you. That's all," he added with longing eyes, predicting my human thoughts.

"Your home is beautiful."

Beautiful didn't seem like the right word to describe this mansion. *Fit for a king* was more like it. He stiffened uncomfortably and cleared his throat.

"I'll let you get comfortable. When you are ready, I'll be waiting for you outside your door."

When he shut the door behind him, I hurriedly unpacked my belongings into the huge closet and dresser and moved to the bathroom. Its size was ridiculous. It reminded me of a honeymoon suite on TV. The same white-and-gray marble covered every horizontal surface, and turquoise crystals hung from a chandelier above, creating endless illusions in the mirrored walls. A beautiful Aztec mural of glass tile embellished the doorless walk-in shower, and the toilet had a nicely decorated room of its own that smelled like gardenia. Black feathers had been embroidered on the small jade towels that sat next to the sink. I looked in the mirror.

Clearly, the humidity had gotten the best of me. I changed into a loose dress, but it was pointless: it stuck to me in a few strides. I tried taming my wavy frizz with some hair product Bri had lent me, but I quickly accepted the fact that my hair wasn't cut out for this kind of weather, and I braided it before I got more upset.

When I stepped out of my room, Lucas was leaning against the banister, looking at the top of the Christmas tree, which twinkled just a few feet from him. When he turned to me, there was a light in his eyes that matched his new smile, and the chambers of my heart swelled.

He led me to the first floor, following the rich aroma of chili and beans. My stomach grumbled when we entered the kitchen. Marifer and a short man were standing at the stove. Every now and then, Marifer threw ingredients into a large pot, and the man stirred it, releasing that wonderful smell. She smiled at us as we crossed the kitchen and passed through another door.

We arrived in a formal dining room. Three of the walls were floor-to-ceiling windows. The light spilling through them revealed palm trees just outside, and I wondered what view lay out there in the dark. A large, rustic chandelier, mostly iron but with some crystal, hung above a large table set for sixteen. Our families were already seated at the far end of the table when we arrived.

Andrés stood, holding a crystal goblet. "Welcome to our home. We are happy you have chosen to share the holidays with us. Valentina and I couldn't be happier. Now, it's been a long day of traveling, and there is plenty of food, so please, eat up."

I sighed, exhausted, and pushed Xavier to the back of my mind, pretending he didn't exist. Lucas smiled—it was different again, tender, maybe. Not as stiff or restrained as it was in Tahoe. Hungry, even. I wondered what he was thinking as I took a bite from the salsa-covered plate now in front of me. New flavors burst inside my mouth, and my thoughts stopped, aware only of the explosion in my mouth. I took in another forkful. It was splendid. Each bite was full of spices, and it filled my stomach to the maximum capacity as pleasurably as possible.

When my plate was clean and my stomach so full it hurt, I set down my fork. Everyone else seemed to be engaged in quiet small talk. I stood up.

"Excuse me, everyone. I'm about to fall asleep at the table. If you don't mind, I think I'll go to bed now."

My parents said good night, Max and Casey ignored me as they devoured an inappropriate amount of food, and the Castillos smiled. I could feel Lucas's eyes following me as I left the room, and I imagined I felt them even as I closed the door of my borrowed room.

CHAPTER TWENTY

MULAC

To my mind, an overnight stay at a king's estate, built on a beach in the Caribbean, should be exquisite: from the moment you nestle your cheek against that satiny pillow, to the dream about the prince behind your soft eyelids, to the sound of ocean waves as you wake up. You feel more beautiful each day than the day before, alive and renewed, ready to conquer the world, all because you slept on luxurious sheets in a cordially majestic house.

My night was none of these. Try devilish.

The humidity nearly suffocated me in my sleep, for one thing. As I fought against its invisible moistness, I tossed and turned for a good hour, frustrated that sweat drenched my pajamas and my body stuck to the sheets. Soon I realized I would not win the fight, and I stripped down to my underwear. When I finally did fall asleep, a young woman with creamy skin and braided black hair came to me in a gust of blackness.

Her voice was muffled at first, but it grew louder until her faint words echoed.

Please don't kill my son. It would be treason. The Celestials would find you. You must stop Mulac, she pleaded.

Mulac?

Lucas? You mean Lucas? I tried to say, but I was mute. My voice didn't exist in the dark, dingy space. However, the woman smiled gravely and nodded.

Please don't kill my son, she repeated.

Who's your son?

In your tongue, you know him as Xavier.

Her hands reached out to touch me, but I backed away.

Why? I asked.

She looked to the abyss at her side abruptly, and then her dark eyes flicked back to me. *I am out of time. You must stop Mulac. I have seen what will happen if Xavier dies. It would put you in a more dangerous place.*

What do you mean?

Xavier isn't the threat. I am out of time. Please, don't kill my son. Let me deal with him.

She vanished, and I lunged into consciousness, sweating and heaving for air. When the thickness subsided and it was easier to get breath to my lungs, I eased back down, pulling the silk sheets up to my chin as if they might protect me. I stared at the dark wall in discomfort until my eyes got heavy.

It was sunny when I woke. I rubbed my eyes and walked unsteadily to the chaise on the balcony. The wild blue horizon went on for eternities. Lucas stepped out of his room, his sapphire shirt waving gently as he hopped over the gap between our balconies.

I closed my eyes and rubbed my temples. My throat was scratchy. "I'm so tired, I . . ."

"I know," he cut me off. "I was checking on you last night."

I looked up at him, ignoring the spontaneous twittering in my gut, and replayed my sleepless night.

"When?"

"Three times. The first, you were tossing and turning, cursing at the humidity. The second, you were covering your head with a pillow. The third time, you were stripped down to . . . well . . ."

He raised his eyebrows and looked down at my boy shorts and

barely-there tank top. I looked up, embarrassed.

"No need to explain. I will have Marifer bring you something better to sleep in for tonight," he said.

"Thank you."

It was peaceful this warm morning. We stared across the limitless December sea together while I gnawed at my tongue, trying to figure out how to tell Lucas about my dream. I knew his mind was already made up. Xavier would be dead soon. I wanted him dead too. But somehow I knew that wasn't what needed to happen.

"The red tide is coming in," Lucas said.

I stayed silent. My knees shook as I attempted to count the number of hours I'd slept in the past forty-eight.

"We have a couple of days, and then it will be time," Lucas said.

I picked at my nails. Lucas's hands suddenly wrapped around mine and squeezed mildly.

"What's wrong?" he asked.

"Xavier's mother came to me last night," I choked out.

The change in his expression concerned me. The fine lines were harsher.

"In a . . . in a . . . in my dream."

His unearthly features froze as his eyes dissected me. "How are you feeling? You pretty much haven't slept in two days."

"Don't worry about me. Just listen."

He sat next to me. "I'm listening. But I should warn you that whatever you tell me will not change my mind."

"How did you know what I was going to say?"

"Why else would Xavier's mother come to you, save for her poor, bastard son? She wants you to stop me, doesn't she?"

"Lucas, she said that Xavier isn't the threat. Doesn't that mean anything?"

He stared away from me because that's what he did when he didn't want me to see his emotions, but I still saw his jaw tighten.

"She said that she has seen what would happen if we kill him. She said that I would be in a more dangerous place," I finished.

"Of course she did."

"Look, I believe you, and I know that you are trying to protect me. But," I looked at my hands in shame, "I believe her more."

He rose tall, and his chest ballooned out as he breathed in deeply.

"Get dressed; pack a swimsuit. I will wait for you outside your door," he said. Without another word, he hopped back over to his room and disappeared inside.

I could hardly remember when I'd showered last, so I let Lucas go without argument. I sniffed my hair and gagged. I dragged my feet to the shower and let the spray from the large showerhead soothe my hot skin. When I stepped out, my skin remained warm and wet. After three attempts to towel dry I surrendered. I controlled my frizzy waves with wax, smacked lip-gloss on, and slipped cutoff shorts and an old T-shirt over my bikini.

Lucas was waiting as promised, leaning casually on one arm against the wall. He straightened as I came to him. His intense stare and closed grin proved he was thinking that I looked nice. He didn't need to say it. I just knew. And I also knew that he was still thinking about Xavier's mom.

He led me down the other set of stairs to the second floor. In the daylight the place seemed larger, the central ceiling vaulting higher over the Christmas tree—even the ocean beyond the glass wall seemed bigger. I marveled at the hieroglyphic murals of antique metal that adorned the walls, wondering as we passed what each one meant, who each one was.

The door to Gabriella and Dylan's room, which was directly below Lucas's room, was open. Lucas barged in.

"Her *way* is getting stronger," he said, sounding stressed as he threw his hands in the air.

Gabriella and Dylan were playing a card game on the king-sized bed. The fluff of the duvet hid the cards.

"My what?" I asked.

"Your way. It's an alter ego. How a god can contact you in your dream," Dylan responded without looking up, still in his game.

"You can thank Lucas for that. He's your *wayob*," Gabriella added. Her smoldering eyes were glinting brown gems in her mermaid's face. She ignored Lucas's disapproving scowl as she set her cards down and rose to her feet.

"My what?"

"Your spiritual companion," she added lightly as she walked to her dresser.

Lucas paced, distraught. "Xquic came to her. Begged Zara to change my mind about Xavier."

"Change your mind about what?" Dylan huffed.

"What do you think?" Lucas snapped.

Dylan looked bewildered. "Why?"

"Zara, I have something for you," Gabriella said.

She handed me a small turquoise box wrapped with soft, white satin ribbon. Under the ribbon, embossed letters read *Tiffany's*.

"Gabriella, I can't take this." I held the box back out toward her.

"Why?"

"It's too much."

"You haven't even seen it." Gabriella looked to Lucas like I was crazy for not wanting jewelry.

"Zara, if you don't open that, Gabriella will make me force it on you," Lucas commented. He strolled past me, one hand on a hip, the other rubbing the stubble on his chin.

I opened the box obediently and pulled out stone—lots of stone. Jade, turquoise, and smoky topaz stones, each angled differently, concocting a long bracelet rimmed with gold. It was heavier than any bracelet I'd ever worn.

Gabriella's soft hands tugged it from my rough fingers and

wrapped it around my wrist three times. I noticed the same bracelet on her wrist. It looked better on copper skin. When she finished, she stepped back and put a hand to her cheek proudly. Her fingernails were painted a pearly color.

"It fits perfectly," she said, satisfied. "I told you, Dylan, she has tiny wrists just like me."

Dylan came over and examined the evidence, then chuckled. "Zara, I have never met anyone with wrists as small as Gabriella's. Congratulations." He pivoted to Lucas. "Enough of the drama talk—when are you guys heading out?"

Lucas shifted his feet and looked at me awkwardly as he cleared his throat.

"Right after breakfast. We have to tell her parents first," he said stiffly.

"Tell my parents what?" I asked.

"Oh, parents." Dylan snorted. "Right, well, don't screw this one up, Lucas. Humans can be relentless."

"Thanks for the encouragement," Lucas grunted.

It was like they were speaking a different language.

"Is this a date?" I asked incredulously.

"What are you guys doing?" Gabriella added in her melodious voice.

Lucas's eyes inched to mine uneasily. Dylan laughed harder. It didn't bother me to be laughed at like this. I was used to it with Max and Casey. But I couldn't take my eyes off Lucas, as guilty as he was. Why'd he have to make life so difficult? He wanted me, and I knew it.

"What are you laughing at?" Gabriella asked Dylan. "Once upon a time you *used* to do that for me."

As I blinked, a burst of air blew past me. Gabriella was now pinned to the bed beneath Dylan's hands and knees.

"So Paris doesn't count? What does a god have to do for you?"

Dylan asked—playing offended, but his voice was cheery.

"Oh, sorry babe." Gabriella kissed him and then gracefully escaped through his arms like it was a dance. She shrugged innocently as she walked back to the door. "I forgot."

"See, man. You do something nice for them, and they just keep wanting more," Dylan said with a wink at his lovely wife.

A short servant I hadn't seen before, wearing a white dress shirt and jade tie, entered with a soft knock. "*Desayuno, señor.*"

Lucas answered politely in Spanish and then said to me, "Breakfast is ready."

Breakfast was served on a patio behind the house, half a story above the beach. The salty air rose up and kissed my skin. My parents, Max, and Casey were already waiting at a table decorated with fresh red and pink flowers. There were matching napkins and placemats splashed with bright primary colors. The glasses were the thick, bubbly green of recycled material, and the plates were traditional-looking stoneware with colorful hand-painted designs on them.

Valentina and Andrés rose and bestowed gentle salutatory kisses on our cheeks.

"*Buenas dias,*" they said.

My parents observed from their seats. Dylan smirked when he noticed the twins gawking at Gabriella.

"Zara, how did you sleep last night?" Valentina asked as the small, dark-haired Aluxes brought in large platters.

The plate uncovered before me bore assorted tropical fruits, including some sort of white fruit with tiny black seeds.

"It was hard for me to get used to the humidity," I replied, watching wearily as another plate arrived. It looked like tortilla chips smothered in red sauce with melted white cheese and onion slices on top. Tortilla chips for breakfast was a first for me.

"Chilaquiles are my favorite dish," Lucas assured me.

Max and Casey were already chewing on the strange combination as I picked up a forkful of soggy chips and took a bite. It was the most exuberant red sauce I'd ever tasted. Lucas smiled, pleased, as I took a more enthusiastic bite.

"Mr. and Mrs. Moss, would you mind if I took Zara out on a tour?" Lucas asked.

"Will you be home for dinner?" Valentina asked.

"No, I already have dinner arrangements for us."

"You're not going to Chichen-ee—er, whatever you call that place?" Dad wondered. "That place is far from here, isn't it?"

"No, sir, that would definitely be too far. Local areas," Lucas replied.

Andrés tilted his head. "Be careful."

Max and Casey watched us closely, and I silently blamed Jett. They were probably reporting everything to him. I couldn't help but feel bad for him, stuck with just his mom on Christmas, in a town where he had no friends. Then I reminded myself I was the one to feel sorry for. My life was in danger. I narrowed my eyes at Max and Casey.

"What are you guys going to do today?" I asked.

They looked from the beach to the pool, back to the beach, and then to each other.

"Absolutely nothing," Casey said blissfully.

"Maybe we can see if we can rent Sea-Doos," Max reckoned.

Dylan knuckled Max on the arm. "I'll take you guys out, man."

"Really, you want to go? We figured you probably get sick of doing that sort of thing since you come here all the time," Max said.

"No, it never gets old for me. Don't worry about renting, we have some in the garage downstairs."

"Are you sure, man?" Casey asked, practically already off his chair.

"Yeah, bro." Dylan grinned and stood.

"*Portate, mi amor,*" Gabriella said through clenched teeth, making it seem like a warning.

Dylan kissed her, a certain eagerness suddenly taking over, then looked to my brothers. "Meet me in the garage when you are ready."

After I devoured breakfast, I followed Lucas down the wooden stairs to the beach and over the sand to a shaded path between tall, mature palm trees. Shrubs and exotic flowers grew thickly around the trees' bases, creating the illusion of a green wall.

"What did Gabriella say to Dylan?" I asked, trying to keep up.

"Dylan is a show-off. She told him to behave."

"Won't his tattoo glow in the water?" My calves burned as we finally stepped onto a paved driveway.

"It only glows in waters of another land, as a reminder of where we come from."

My eyes flickered from Lucas, who kept walking, to the four wide double doors before us. When opened, they revealed a garage the size of my entire house. Inside were three fancy sports cars, Sea-Doos, and a large, shiny boat. Dylan was bending over the Sea-Doos, checking the engines.

"So, which one is yours?" I asked, observing the rainbow of metals.

"That one." Lucas pointed to a French blue convertible with the famous Jaguar logo and the letters *XKR-S* on the back. It looked dangerous.

"And those other two?" They were convertibles as well. I made a clever distinction: yellow car, black car.

"That one is Dylan's." He pointed to the black one and then glanced at the smaller, yellow convertible. "And that one is Gabriella's."

I read the brand on the back. "His-and-hers Porsches?"

"Anniversary gifts to one another a couple years ago."

Nice. "Where is your parents' car?"

"In the other garage."

Of course you have another garage. If we ended up together, I wondered, *what color of car would I have?* Suddenly there was noise and loud laughter.

"No way! Is that a Porsche 959?" Casey ran to the shiny yellow convertible and gently petted the waxy metal.

"Casey, look at this Jag!" Max seemed glued to Lucas's car, but he wrenched his gaze away from it for a moment and then gaped. "Oh, man. Are you serious? A Spyder? Dylan, bro, which car is yours?"

"The Spyder," Dylan replied with a devious smile, wiping his hands on a dirty rag as he joined them.

"What does your father-in-law drive?" Max wondered.

"A Maybach Exelero."

They turned as one, searching.

"It's in the other garage," Dylan said.

The spinning stopped, mouths gaped, and Max and Casey giggled like little girls. Lucas and I slid into the beige leather seats of his car.

"You can take a spin in my car later if you want," Dylan was saying.

"Seriously?"

"Sure, no problem. It's not like you're going to crash it," he joked.

Casey stiffened.

Dylan pounded him on the shoulder—maybe a little too hard; Casey grabbed his shoulder and rubbed it. "I'm just kidding, Case."

Max came around the boat as Lucas started the engine. "Lucas, I just wanted to tell you that earlier, we were only looking out for our sister, okay? Brotherly love, you understand, right?"

Lucas nodded. "Fully. If anyone ever did anything to Gabriella, I would kill him." Max didn't move until Lucas forced a deliberate fake chuckle.

"Yeah man, right," Max replied shakily. "So look, just take care of our sister. Okay?"

"All right, man," Lucas said.

The tires squealed as Lucas sped down the driveway and then drifted silently over the long, narrow stretch of packed sand. I kept my head back, letting the cool wind on my skin revive me. After Lucas passed the gate, which daylight revealed to be flanked by lush flowering trees, he turned right onto paved highway. Minutes later, I saw a flock of flamingos, uninterested in us, wading in a small pond.

Lucas sped to our destination, and I watched the thick green jungle and white sand, holding my hair back, for what seemed like hours. I began to feel the sunshine soaking through my skin, tinting it with pink. We approached a small town and started passing other cars, which moved like snails as we passed them. I looked at the speedometer.

"Holy crow! You're going one sixty!" I shouted.

"It's kilometers per hour, not miles. So really, I'm only going a hundred." His shirt flapped in the abrasive wind as he grinned. "I *was* going one thirty."

"If you don't want me to die of a heart attack, could you please slow down?"

The airflow grew softer.

"Better?" he asked. The needle now pointed to 140.

"Barely," I groaned.

The sparse traffic increased with knots of taxis and buses, and a green sign flashed reflective letters that spelled *Tulum 5 km.*

"Tulum?"

He slowed significantly, and a smoldering heat descended upon me. The sound of rattling bus engines replaced the barreling wind.

"I'm going to tell you about my transformation," he said. He sounded strangely meek.

I sat, stunned, as he turned off the road, paid a small fee at a white hut, and fell in behind a line of cars waiting to park. Finally, the last car ahead of us turned into a parking spot, but he carefully inched the car through the crowd, toward the entrance to the site. Barricades prevented cars from moving beyond the parking lot.

"Lucas, I think we need to park with the others," I suggested.

He leaned out the window over his bent arm and whistled. Two dark-skinned workers with *Tulum* written across their shirts emerged from the shade of the souvenir shop and moved one barricade to the right. We passed without a word; they moved it back and returned to the shop.

"Aluxes," Lucas commented, seeing my bewilderment.

He drove at nearly the same speed as the sweaty pedestrians, waiting patiently for them to clear the grainy road, usually after a few moments of gawking at him. The shaded path rose slowly, walled in by wild trees. As the leaves thinned and the sun penetrated the canopy, he pulled off to the side and parked in a shady spot.

He was there as I crouched up from the low seat, reaching for my hand tenderly. My heart stuttered as his thumb pressed firmly over mine. I glanced up, awed by the change, how he was before Solstice and how he was now. Black sunglasses concealed his emotions, but he swallowed hard as he watched me, perhaps wanting to say more, maybe even what was on his mind.

"This way," he said, calm, though I was certain he was ready to burst.

I let him lead me through a small stone archway into a roofless, narrow hall, brushing past the unavoidable tourists. Then I saw it on the edge of the cliff, across a field of summery grass: an ancient temple, nearly perfect despite the damage inflicted by time. A flat-roofed room with three doorways sat atop the steep steps.

But Lucas drew me in the opposite direction, passing other classic stone structures less well preserved than the temple. He slowed at the easternmost edge of the cliff, where a makeshift fence of brown rope suggested we should stop. Behind it was a smaller platform reached by a short flight of stone steps.

We slid under the rope, and I followed him up the uneven stone stairs to a single room with a narrow door in each wall. We hunched over to enter, then wedged close together in the opening of the door facing the ocean. I took my sandals off and sat down, dangling my feet over the edge. Sun poured over us as we stared across the endless green expanse of paradise.

"This is the only place in Mexico where you can watch the sunrise from the same room every single morning, no matter the sun's position," Lucas said.

"It's amazing."

"I use to come here every morning to watch the sun, and sometimes Venus, when it was there."

"What is this place?"

"This was our watchtower. We burned fires here to direct the men out at sea."

"Did you ever have to go out to sea with your father, trading?"

"I wasn't allowed. It was *too dangerous*." He sneered a bit at the old hurt. Then he looked serious, picked up a broken piece of rock, and threw it over the cliff. "Not that I was weak. But many men who traveled by sea never came back because of the pirates and storms. I couldn't risk having our people find out I was only half-human. So I came to the watchtower to dream of other places and survive my boredom." A sad, ironic chuckle fluttered out of his mouth. "And now I get to see the world, just as I dreamed—only it's not what I thought it would be."

"Nothing is ever really what you expect."

I didn't mean anything by my thoughtless proclamation—habit, I guess—but he looked at me seriously. "You are how I imagined."

I chuckled even as my heart beat a good few paces more quickly. "Good one."

"You saved Jett. That takes courage."

I sighed doubtfully. He pulled his citla out of his pocket and began spinning it between his fingers.

"I remember my last night here as if it was yesterday," he said. He gazed away from me once more, emotion stilling as he stared beyond the horizon.

"My parents received word from a messenger that Cortez, who had already seized Tenochtitlan, was going to come after the cities in the south. At that time, we weren't Watchers yet, but we knew we were going to be, and we were trying to find a replacement for my father. We knew that we couldn't live among our people for many years without aging, but we didn't want to abandon them. We were trying to do it as inconspicuously as possible, but when soldiers started invading the south, the Celestials ordered an immediate evacuation of Tulum. My parents had no choice but to do what any other rulers who cared for their people would have done: we abandoned the city before we could be slaughtered.

"We evacuated at night because the passageways were not safe during the day. There were too many soldiers waiting. The children cried as their mothers pulled them from their beds in the middle of the night. Tita and Gabriella led the women and children out of the city to the east, where they could hide in the thick jungle, while Dylan and I took up arms with my father's warriors to secure the main roads in the north. We were ambushed: an army of Spanish soldiers was waiting for us. When they realized that only the men were fighting them, some of the soldiers went after the women and children. We fought and killed many of the white men that ambushed us, but our warriors dropped like flies. Dylan and I knew that if we stayed, our human father risked death, and that if we remained untouched, it would reveal our identity. Neither option would have been . . . acceptable . . . to the Celestials. We had no choice but to flee and pray the survivors would be okay."

I looked away from the turquoise glare to see the prince in pain.

His eyes brimmed over as he choked up. "We abandoned our people, Zara."

I didn't move. I envisioned women and children crying, forced to flee into the wild jungle before heartless hunters. This glimpse of Lucas, bound up with emotion and regret, was somehow frightening. He wiped a tear with the back of his hand.

I touched his back lightly, uncertain of what to do. "I'm so sorry."

He cleared his throat and sniffed as he straightened up. "Don't be. I got even after the transformation."

The sun reflected off his face as he hiked his knees to his chest. He looked peaceful again, but I also felt a sorrow there, brimming with hate and rage that went much deeper than I imagined. I felt bad for him.

"When the transformation nears the end," he began suddenly, "every human feeling, whether good or bad, burns from your insides out: greed, rage, jealousy, love, faith, hope, hatred. All those feelings become so intense that you are your own worst enemy. My father, Gabriella, and Tita were able to control it quickly. But for me . . . it turned me to an unreasonable monster.

"The hatred and the greed created a thirst for revenge that I didn't know how to control. It nearly destroyed me. I blamed Cortez and Xibalba for making me become a Watcher. With the massacre fresh in my mind, I hunted down each soldier who was there the night we evacuated. The ones who killed the children I hunted first.

"But it wasn't enough. I wanted redemption. My father ordered me to leave Cortez alone. *He's nothing,* he would say, *let it go—justice will find him.* But I couldn't do it. I couldn't let it go. I blamed Cortez for making me this way, and I couldn't let him get away with everything that he'd done. So I decided to leave my family."

"Where did you go?"

"I went after justice, to Cuernavaca, where Cortez had just built his prized mansion to prove to the natives that he held all the power.

I studied him, trying to figure out how a man could do such things. I watched him in the day with his wife and in the night with other women. I hated that lowlife, his conviction that he was invincible. I had his life in my hands; one swift movement and he'd be dead. I was ready to do it one night. I came close. I was in his bedchamber, waiting for him to return. But as I waited, and as much as I wanted his life, something inside me had changed. I realized it wasn't my job to worry about him. I needed to be with my family, to worry about the balance of the Cosmos. I knew that eventually, as my father had said, justice would find him."

I sat motionless beneath the image of all that bloodshed in Lucas's lifetime. Lucas noticed and cupped my hands with his. I shifted my gaze away, confounded by his history, and by ours. How long had I wanted his touch on me—and now, after learning this, I shivered for a new reason. His bare hands, hands that killed, were touching mine. But his skin was soft and his fingers gentle, not the kind that murdered people. I looked toward him again, shaky.

"That was a long time ago. I have learned to control my feelings," he said softly.

I nodded, waiting a moment until I could force a swallow down. "When did you go back to your family?"

"As soon as I realized I was out of control. They helped me learn to control my feelings. It was easier for a while, until I had to witness the taking of the first fifty-two victims. That was hard for me, but then I saw how hard Gabriella took it, and I supposed that my time away helped me be stronger as a Watcher."

"How long did it take for you to get back to normal?"

"A few months."

Moments passed silently before he smiled. "There's one more thing I want you to know: I'm not the jealous type—well, never was until I changed. Throughout my entire existence, I've never had anyone to be jealous over. But any time I saw you with Jett, I felt a new emotion stirring. I'm sorry if back in Tahoe I ever seemed possessive of you. I felt that you were *my* girl, not Jett's. He hadn't been waiting for you for three hundred years like I had, so somehow . . . all that time, I legitimately believed that you belonged to me. Then, when I realized that was insane—that you would never *belong* to me—I acted like a jerk. And I am sorry, truly."

Belong? My stomach fluttered, kind of liking his twisted confession. I waited for it to settle, staring at his dark lashes, wondering how he saw us now.

"I accept your apology. But why would I never belong to you? You never asked." Not that it would matter, even though I secretly desired him.

He turned toward me, gripping my hands with more pressure. "I want you to know, Zara, that even though I made my commitment to the Celestials, my allegiance is with you now. You are my life. If anybody, or any soul, ever laid a finger on you, I would go to hell and back to tear them apart."

I loved hearing it, but I suddenly shivered as if Xavier's mother's ghost was watching, hoping I could do her bidding.

"Lucas," I began softly.

"That includes Xavier," he added sternly, and then he stood.

I was disappointed with myself for not speaking up. I stretched my legs and followed him outside, already thinking of when I would ask him next. He pointed across the land to the south side of the cliff.

"My room was just over there," he said.

"And what was that?" I pointed to the large castle in the center.

"Where the transformation took place, and where we meet with the Council when we find out who is going to be sacrificed. It was there that I first heard your name."

I touched his arm lightly. "Can we go there?"

"If you wish."

As we moved across the public plateau toward the castle, the tourists bustled like ants in the scorching sun, snapping pictures of each landmark from every angle imaginable.

"Does it bother you that all these people are here?" I asked after bumping into a child.

"Not anymore."

He stopped at the castle steps and looked up briefly, then glanced at me.

"We have to be quick before security comes," he cautioned.

I looked up the stairs of rotting stone, then down at the thin line of rope blocking them off. Lucas hopped over and held out his hand. I squeezed it painfully hard as I crossed the line, trying not to fall as we took the first few steps. When we reached the top, Lucas's breathing was slow and even. He smiled at my human exhaustion as I panted.

"Were these stairs ever hard for you to climb?" I gasped out.

"I've never been fully human," he reminded me.

We hid ourselves in the shaded room and sat down in a corner against the wall. It was dewy and cold here, and awkwardly quiet. Lucas opened his mouth, but seemed hesitant to speak.

"You don't have to share anything with me you don't want to," I said.

He pulled my hand over to his leg and patted the back of it gently, a human gesture. It was nice. It made me picture us back in Tahoe after all this, at college, giving each other affection as humans do. It made me forget who he was, who *I* was, and there was only . . . *us*. It felt right.

"When we came back here for the transformation," he began slowly, "the city had been empty for a while. There were no torches, no children, no noise. It was a dark space, a new ghost town. We waited all night for the Celestials to come. I sat right here for hours, torn up inside after what had just happened. Then, right before sunrise, the Council appeared. They spoke only of what we were to do as Watchers, and then they marked us with a sacred paint called Maya blue."

Lucas intently rubbed the black drawing on his arm. His head dropped back against the wall as he stared at the door and into its emanating light.

"When they finished, they left us alone, and our tattoos began to appear. First they were faint lines, unfinished. Then, as the sun peeked over the horizon, the lines connected and began burning with a bright blue flame. And then it began."

"What did?"

"The transformation. Nothing changed for Mother and Dylan because they were already immortal. The only change for them was the markings, which appeared without trouble. But Father, Gabriella, Tita, and I fell to the ground with the pain of it. It felt like every atom in my body was exploding. Dylan tried to comfort Gabriella, but there was nothing he could do. I could hear Gabriella and my father screaming, as I was, begging and pleading for it to stop. My mother tried to be with me, but my father needed her most. He fell into a coma for three days. We all thought he was going to die, but the sun rose on the third day and he woke up, changed. He was strong and fast and godlike."

Minutes passed before I realized I hadn't moved at all. My dry eyes burned from not blinking, picturing Lucas and the others screaming with unbearable pain in this very room. I should have been repelled, but a tiny portion of guilt trickled in, and my heart ached with remorse.

"How long did the transformation take?" I asked.

"I recovered first, only because I was the strongest. I was well by the next morning, Gabriella and Tita by the second night, and my father on that third day. Watching Dylan as Gabriella transformed—it was the only time in five hundred years that I've ever seen fear on his face. He thought she wasn't going to make it."

I cringed, thinking of the beautiful Aztec princess helpless on the floor in agonizing pain. A thought popped into my head, and I looked at Lucas anew. This beloved—and hated—gift of immortality that he possessed was going to be our biggest challenge if we'd ever get to be together. I cringed again, thinking of *me* squirming on the floor in pain. I would never want to do it, but I would, if it meant I could spend eternity with Lucas.

"Does your dad remember anything about it?"

"He says he can vividly remember the tattoo appearing, like fire etching a mark on his skin. After that, he doesn't remember much. He blacked out pretty early on."

"What do you remember?"

"Everything."

Lucas clung to my hand more tightly as he stretched his legs. The tingling sensation had dulled, and our pressing hands had become a furnace, but he hung on.

"Like what my dad said: fire singeing your skin, trying to get to your core. When the tattoo was complete, a new level of pain started. Every fiber inside your body ripped apart and rebuilt into your new self. I wished death would come for me," he said.

"I can't imagine." *Me becoming immortal is out of the question. I would die . . . I know I would . . . I'm weak . . . and then what good would that do for anyone?* A rush of hopelessness washed through me.

"You will never have to." Then he kissed the back of my hand, confident, and said as he stood, "Come, enough of the pity."

Chapter Twenty-One

Escapade

As we left Tulum, Lucas insisted on opening my door. For another careless moment, I wondered if we were taking the next step in our relationship, but then I forced myself to stop thinking about us—as if there would ever be an *us*. It was impossible, and stupid. Lucas was immortal and beautiful and a prince; he had very specific laws to obey and a plethora of gods watching him. I didn't belong in any of that.

I held my loose strands of hair so that they wouldn't fly up in the convertible's breeze. After miles of flat, thick jungle, we approached an unmarked road hidden in that green wall. Lucas slowed and turned into an overgrown labyrinth, weaving bumpily in and out until he stopped at a small gap in the trees spilling over with white sand.

He hopped out and walked to the opening, motioning cheerfully for me to join him.

"Where are we going?" I asked as I followed him through the primeval jungle.

"We're nearly there."

I heard water when he stopped. Behind him was a hidden stream bordered with moss-covered rocks and waxy plants that hung over its rippling water.

Lucas slipped off his shoes. "Time to change."

"What are we doing?" My eyes moved from the stream to Lucas, who was now pulling off his shirt. His physique was enthralling: slender for my idea of a stereotypical god, but his stomach had major ripples of hardness and was extremely pleasing to watch. Suddenly aware of my unsubtle stare, I looked up.

"You'll see," Lucas said with a grin.

I stripped to my bikini and let my hair out of its unwinding braid. I was timid as I neared him, a fool to think that he could ever find me seductive. But as I set my clothes next to his on a dry boulder, trying hard to conceal my emotions, he turned. His eyes, full of intentions too great for a human, numbed me. I watched him nervously, my feet pricked by the jungle floor, as I invented my own reasons for his actions.

Before I could come up with anything solid, he broke his stare and stepped into the stream. I smiled, uncertain, then went in after him. The bath-warm water went up to my ankles. He held my hand as he guided me down the stream to a sinkhole.

"We're going in there," Lucas said.

I edged up behind him and glanced down over his shoulder. The sparkling stream of water fell into a small, emerald-green pond below and went tranquil. White sand ringed the miniature cove, which opened into a cave across from our perch. It was beautiful.

Suddenly he backed up close against me and bent down, grabbing my knees and hoisting me onto his back. Startled, I dug my fingernails into his skin at first, but then unglued them and settled my arms around his shoulders.

He cocked his head to the side. "Hang on."

I tucked my chin into his shoulder, and he jumped. It was a thrill, like the drop of a rollercoaster, but the moment I thought to scream it was over, and my feet slid gently down to touch the warm sand. I looked up and saw icicle-shaped stone formations suspended beneath the ledge from which we had just jumped. Underneath, earthy spikes rose up to meet them, slowly reaching for some distant future reunion. *Stalactites and stalagmites,* I thought absently, not sure which was which. *I used to know . . .*

Lucas jumped into the crystalline pond and swam into the cave. I saw colorful fish speeding away from his powerful strokes, his tattoo black and dull. He stopped and treaded water, looking at me.

"What are you doing?" I hissed, planting my feet stubbornly on the sand.

"Zara, I had you bring your swimsuit for a reason. Are you coming, or am I going to have to come out and get you?"

I huffed and put my feet in the water. I took baby steps over the slimy stone, but then there was a quick splash as I was dunked in the deep end.

He chuckled when I came up for air, hair straggling over my face. I ducked my head back in the water, swept my hair back, and reemerged to find him there, embracing my body. His strong kicks kept me afloat so that I could swing my arms around his neck, making me all the more aware of our bare skin touching.

"Take a deep breath and hang on," he warned. "I'm going to count to three."

"Wait, what?"

"One," he smiled.

"Wait, what are you doing?" I asked, my unthinking hands pressing his slippery skin closer to me.

"Two."

"Lucas, no!" My legs wrapped around him, my thighs squeezing tightly.

"Three!"

I breathed in deeply, and we sank. It felt normal at first to be underwater as he pulled me slowly through the semishaded waters. I unwound my legs and drifted, letting Lucas guide me. As the sun shone through the water in diagonal streaks, Lucas pointed to a school of colorful fish. One brushed against my foot . . . and suddenly a whirlwind whisked us into the dark emptiness beyond the rocks. I jerked away, but Lucas's grip was too strong, and the sudden current pulled us, twisting, into a tunnel.

I clenched my eyes tightly and focused on saving precious oxygen, but the pull stopped ten seconds later, and Lucas pushed me up into open air. I panted hard as my head spun, glimpsing another cave around me, lit by sunlight sneaking through a hole above us. When I had my bearings, I swam after Lucas toward an island of sand. We settled on it, Lucas looking all Zen, legs sprawled, and me still recovering from the trip. I looked up to see more stone icicles over our heads.

"Do you remember which is which?" I asked. "Stalactites are . . . growing down, right?"

"Yes, stalactites are the ones on the ceiling. They formed thousands of years ago when the acid in the rain dissolved the limestone and created cenotes, which is what we're in right now."

"This place is incredible." I combed through my damp hair with my fingers. "Do you come here a lot?"

My movement seemed to distract him. Instead of looking away or backing away—as he usually did—he watched, a lazy smile lifting his cheeks. Did he . . . was I . . . *sexy* to him?

"Not too often. It's sort of dingy in here," he finally said.

The water was pure crystal. I looked through bluish green straight to the floor below.

"I don't think it's dingy," I replied. "If I were a pirate, I'd bury my treasure here."

His deep laugh swirled around me. "You, Ms. Claustrophobia?"

"Maybe you don't know me as well as you think," I alleged, just as my stomach growled. It had to be getting close to dinnertime, but I ignored it.

He looked up. "I'm going to take you to get some of my favorite tacos in the city."

My stomach sighed graciously. "When I was a little girl, I begged Mom to make me tacos every night for dinner. She did, but by the third night she put her foot down. So the next few years after that, Mom made tacos for me every Tuesday."

His belly rippled with a silent laugh. "Taco Tuesday. How come I didn't know that about you?"

"Probably because hearing about you was more interesting."

He frowned. "No, it's not. I want you to share all those things with me. I want to know everything about you."

"You do?"

Lucas shifted toward me. "Of course, why wouldn't I?"

I wiggled my butt in the sand and made myself more comfortable. "Shoot. Ask me something."

He grinned foxily at the challenge and sat up. "Favorite pastime."

"Snowboarding. Duh." I giggled.

He snickered. "Yeah, I guess I already knew that, though I would have pegged you for a reader. Favorite movie?"

"*Empire Records.*"

"Seriously?"

"Yeah, why not? I'm obsessed with music *and* Liv Tyler."

"I always thought you were a proper club sport lady: tennis, golf, equestrian."

"Like I have enough time or money for a horse."

"Well, you did say that horses were your favorite animals."

"That doesn't mean that I have to give my whole life to them."

Lucas looked away briefly, pondering his index finger as he swerved it through the sand. "Where do you *really* want to go to college?"

I supposed I had expected this conversation to come up since our hash-out at Fallen Leaf. At least I was somewhat prepared this time—and secretly dreaming he'd follow me wherever I chose to go, like in a fairytale. *And the prince and princess lived happily ever after.* It sounded dreamy, but very unlikely. Not because Lucas wasn't into me—*he sees me differently now, I can tell, there's potential*—but because in fairytales, princesses don't grow old and wrinkly while their princes stay young and timeless. I sighed. *I'm not even a princess.*

"I always imagined that I would end up somewhere back east. Maybe Maine or New Hampshire," I shared reservedly.

He frowned a slanted smirk, swaying his head side to side as he thought. His finger continued to scribble.

"Is that not good?" I wondered.

"No, Harvard and Dartmouth are always good choices." He eyed the grains on his fingers, not really into the conversation. It made me uncomfortable, wondering if he was thinking about how I would financially accomplish this.

"Gabriella told me about your degrees." His hands didn't move as he looked up. *Must have cost a fortune.* "Why didn't you ever practice?"

He swiped his palms together to brush the sand away and scuffed his feet on the bar of sand as he leaned back. "None of that matters. I gave up my life five hundred years ago when I became a Watcher."

"Don't be silly. Everybody, including you, has the power to write their own future, no matter what's happened in the past."

"My future was taken from me, Zara, including my posterity," he said bitterly. "So I don't really see the need to excel any more than I already have."

"Oh . . . I didn't know that. I'm sorry." *One more "consequence" in the bucket.* My heart sank.

He sighed, crossed his legs, and grabbed his ankles as he slouched. "No, I'm sorry. None of this is your problem."

He seemed distracted. I couldn't help but think it was about what they needed to do to save me. The sand seemed like a good distraction, so I dangled my own finger in it.

"Lucas, we need to talk about Xavier," I started.

He stared at me now with calculation, like Agent 007. There was no fear in his eyes, only precision and calm as he spun his citla between his fingertips. "Zara, if you found out there was a hit on me and you had the ability to stop it, what would you do?"

I stared at him, imagining that I'd probably try to take the diplomatic way out. I believed everybody had good in their hearts.

He looked at his star as it spun and continued. "Would you try to speak to the hit man and convince him to leave me alone, or would you just kill him?"

I shook my head because he was wrong. "It's not the same, Lucas."

"It's very much the same. You can't help the unwilling, Zara."

As I rubbed a rusty chill from my arms, my stomach rumbled again and he hopped up. He started for the water.

"We better get you some tacos," he said.

"This conversation isn't over," I replied stubbornly as I waded in.

He chortled mildly before we dove.

By the time we reached the car I was full-on starving. The trees' shadows edged the road until we turned onto the small highway and drove west into the lowering sun.

Late-afternoon traffic on Main Street in Merida crowded into the heart of the city. Brightly lit restaurants lined the streets, small storefronts with plastic tables and chairs set outside. As we approached the city center, the wide avenue dropped us into a maze of narrow one-way streets packed with old cement buildings caged in by cement walls.

When we finally reached the center, a spacious square fringed with bushes and sidewalks and local tourist businesses, we passed an enormous cathedral. It was maybe hundreds of years old, with European details fashioned into its bone-colored stone. I wondered if Lucas was here when the people who took his lands built it. I couldn't imagine him helping them. I pictured him watching from the shadows, upset.

Lucas rounded the corner into an alley, where he stopped beside a small podium and a black carpet that extended into the building. An usher with buzzed, coarse hair and a black suit welcomed Lucas by name and opened my door. He dipped his head in a courteous nod before raising his arms.

"Come, your table is ready," he said in heavily accented English.

We followed him into a small hallway. Iron sconces appeared at even intervals on the dungeon-like walls, flickering in the darkness until we reached an elevator. An usher with slicked-back hair waited inside to direct the ancient moving box to a higher floor.

"*Hola*, Guillermo," Lucas said.

The valet left us as the elevator operator smiled and slid the iron doors shut. "*Hola, señor.*"

We stood silently, watching the floors pass just beyond the cage. Lucas smelled like he had just taken a shower, which only made me more aware of how I must smell. *Sweat and dirt and fish water, yuck!* Thankfully, when the elevator stopped, the air flooded with the smell of fresh tortillas.

Beyond was a dark floor lit by neon and cheap candles on the tables. We followed Guillermo into the cantina, past customers already enjoying their dinners, through double glass-paned doors, and onto a balcony that overlooked a square courtyard. Swags of red flowers and white fairy lights dressed every inch of its ceiling and walls. Ours was the only table here.

Mariachis on the street below played trumpets and guitars, catchy tunes that floated up to us. I watched Lucas incredulously, his foreign world spinning around me, as he pulled out my chair. Again, his glance never moved from me. He watched me with something more than the possessiveness I'd felt in Tahoe. He looked at me with longing; he looked at me with caring. The sideburns he'd had this morning were gone, blended with the shadow on his dark, prickly chin. *I've never dated anyone that looked this old.* I didn't mind at all—he was just the kind of guy I'd pictured being with ten years from now—I felt young. *Celebrities do it all the time, right? And according to everyone we know, he's only five years older than me, so yeah, it could work.* I pretended to adjust my chair to let my nerves calm down.

"This is my family's favorite place to eat when we are in town," he said as a short waiter approached.

Lucas spoke to him in Spanish; the waiter nodded and walked to the double doors, where he delivered instructions to a pair of waiters. The two nodded and disappeared inside the restaurant while the headwaiter returned to us. He pressed his palms together, a white towel hanging over one forearm. "What would the *señorita* like to drink?"

"Just some water would be fine," I said politely.

Lucas nodded to him, and then he too disappeared.

"I ordered all my favorites. I hope you don't mind. No offense taken if you don't like it."

Stray voices had joined the fiesta band downstairs. They were loud and cheerful and knew every word, like a street version of karaoke.

"So, how long have you been coming to this place?" I asked, laughing at the people below.

Lucas rested his elbows on the table and pressed his fingers together. "Since it opened in the fifties."

I looked away and pretended to be engrossed in the eclectic decorations. Large floor candelabras and the scattered fairy lights produced a romantic ambiance, and the red flowers were fresh, full of life on their vine. It was very romantic.

"Do you always sit out here?" I asked, picturing him here with other women.

Lucas leaned back and rested an ankle on his other knee. "No one sits on the balcony except me or a member of my family."

"Ever?"

He grinned. "Ever."

I set the glass on the table gently, feeling that immense pressure as he watched me.

"We bought this place so it could be ours indefinitely," Lucas added, sipping his Coke.

I leaned in and whispered, "Don't they suspect something, like your nonaging face?"

His hair fell forward as he leaned in with a dimply smile and copied my whisper. "No."

Then he swiped his hand through his hair and laughed.

"What is so funny?" I asked.

"You are. Worried about the disclosure of my identity."

"Well, how do you do it? How is it that these people have been working here for years and you return, looking the same?"

"For starters, it helps to have friends that you can trust. Those two waiters over there?" Lucas jutted his chin at the two men standing by the door.

I looked over my shoulder. "I see them."

"They are new; they've never seen me before. The owner of this place is a good friend of the family. Whenever we have plans to come here, we call him in advance, and he arranges for waiters unfamiliar with us. But the headwaiter, he is the only one allowed on this balcony. He takes our orders and then directs the other waiters."

"How can you be so sure to trust them?"

"Because the owner and headwaiter are Aluxes."

I paused, confused on the timing thing.

"When it is time for *them* to get older," Lucas said, casually taking another sip of his Coke, "a new Alux will take over as owner or headwaiter."

"Seems to me these Aluxes are convenient for a lot more than your protection."

"You could say that."

"Must be nice. I spent two summers working at Lucky Pin, and I barely have enough to get me through one year at an Ivy League college, assuming my parents will pay for my tuition."

Lucas folded his arms over the table and leaned in. "You're amazing."

"What?" I asked. I swallowed a sip of warm water. *What is with the no ice?*

"Why do I get the impression that you will do whatever you set your mind to do, even when the odds are against you?"

"Because it's true. I can't let my fear hold me back. I'll take out loans if I have to." I laughed, messing with the slight condensation on my glass. "Maybe my fear of regret outweighs all other fears. So there, I *am* afraid of something."

He threw his hands in the air. "Finally!"

When our laughs died down, I fidgeted with my fork and thought out loud. "But seriously, someday . . ."

"Someday what?"

"I'm going to be able to do things for myself. I won't need anyone paying my way or teaching me the way the world works. I'm going to be *powerful*, I just know it."

His body was attentive, though he leaned his head on one hand as he swirled his fork through the runny sour cream on his plate.

"Did I offend you?" I asked.

"Of course not, *muñeca*." He paused, put his fork down, and glanced up to me. "What else is on your someday list?"

"My *someday* list?"

"You know, an imaginary list of things you want to accomplish in your life." Then his voice changed to mimic a teenage girl. "Someday I'm going to have a house on the beach with two horses, and a boat, and four kids, and a fat dog named Pepe . . ." He chuckled and straightened up. "Come on, Zara," he said, his raspy voice deeper again. "What's on your someday list? Are money and power the only things on your list? Because if they are, you're very well off: you will accomplish both. And without my help, I can assure you. But there must be other things that you want out of life."

I pondered a moment, watching him closely for the slightest flinch. This had to be tough for him, to hear of all the things he would never have. But he didn't move at all as he watched me intently. "Someday," I began slowly, careful not to overdo it, "I'm going to be married. And someday we'll have children, though I have no idea how many. I guess I'll just have to see how well the first one goes."

Lucas laughed.

"And someday," I continued, "we'll travel to Scotland, or France, I don't know, somewhere in Europe. And someday, I'll take my kids to the lake and teach them how to swim, and someday . . . I'll ride an elephant. There, how's that list? Is it any good?"

He picked up his water glass, set his lips gently against the rim, and took a sip. He grinned as he set it down, looking pleased. "It's very good."

I threw a chip in my mouth. "What about you, what's your someday?" I mumbled around it.

His smile broadened as if he was going to laugh, but he didn't, and then he leaned in and took a deep breath. "This is my someday."

My heart spun fast. "Oh . . . as in dinner . . . or finishing the sacrifices . . . or . . . or me . . . ?"

He answered with a wide grin. As I opened my mouth to speak, though, the Alux headwaiter brought in platters full of food. Lucas took another drink, keeping his lips from lifting any higher than they already were. There was rice and beans; a mouthwatering tray of fresh fruit; tacos; a soup with thin, short noodles; and something involving seafood.

"What is that?" I asked, glancing at the red glass full of shrimp in sauce. I tried not to make a face, but I feared I didn't fool Lucas when he chuckled softly.

"A seafood cocktail called ceviche. It's very popular here in the south." Lucas pointed to a darker, red meat. "And those are tacos *al pastor*, my favorite."

He picked up a tiny corn tortilla and piled it with cheese, cilantro, and lime. I mimicked him. The savory meat mixed with the citrus and fresh herb was just the right thing to satisfy my stomach's complaints.

"This is the best taco I've ever tasted," I said, breathing through my nostrils with my mouth full of food.

He chuckled, unsurprised. "I knew you'd like it." I felt his eyes on me as I helped myself to probably too much food for a girl my size. "Zara?"

"Yeah?"

"I can pay for your college."

Before I choked, I quickly finished chewing and swallowed my food with a big gulp of water. "What?"

"Let me do it. I want to, and I have plenty of money. Don't let your parents carry that burden."

"Lucas, I can't, that's like asking you to buy me a house."

"Well . . . maybe that too, someday . . . but for now, let's figure out your schooling. I think education is very important, and I find it extremely attractive that you are so eager to go."

"Lucas, I . . ." I leaned over the table, our faces a foot away from each other. "We don't even know if I'll still be alive."

He didn't respond, though his lips pinched, and his eyes glazed over without even a single blink. "Very well, I won't bring this back up."

Sometime between eating the rice and the soup, the mariachis stopped and the balcony became peaceful. Even though I felt Lucas observing me, thinking about what I'd said, I ate until my stomach felt like it was going to pop the button on my shorts. When I finished, I fell back in the chair, rubbing my stomach.

"I can't eat any more, I'm stuffed," I said.

"Would you like dessert?"

"I'm afraid I'll explode if I try to eat one more thing."

Lucas called in the headwaiter, who asked him something softly in Spanish. Lucas shook his head, and the Alux bowed and left, the other two waiters trailing behind him.

"How many Aluxes are there?" I asked.

"We have twenty; eight of them live here in Merida or with us in Progresso, and the rest are spread throughout the world."

"What do they do for work? Don't they have to move around to go unnoticed?"

"The world is too big and too arrogant to notice us under their noses. Our Aluxes move around, yes, but they keep their professions, which range from school professors to zoologists to heart surgeons."

"That's crazy."

Lucas snickered. "It's normal for me."

I leaned back and stretched. I hadn't realized how tired I was until the food settled in.

"There's one more thing to do before the day is over, but only if you're up for it," Lucas said, noticing my yawn.

"You're going to have to take me home at some point, before my dad comes looking for you," I said.

"Well then, it's just my luck."

"Why?"

"Because we have to go home first to change."

It only took ten minutes to get back to the beach palace. When we walked in from the garage, there wasn't a person in sight. Lucas offered to accompany me to my room, and we hiked the three flights of stairs side by side.

"I guess you don't need to worry about your dad. He must be out with Andrés and Valentina still," Lucas said.

As we reached my bedroom door, a daze of complete exhaustion descended on me.

Lucas briefly glanced at his watch. "Would you rather stay home?"

"No, I'm okay. Really."

"How much time do you need to get ready?"

I reached for the sand-infested, salt-infused strands I used to call hair. "Thirty minutes. Is that okay?"

"Sure. See you in thirty. And wear something nice."

"Nice?"

"Beach nice," he clarified, kissing my cheek and leaving for his room.

I turned the shower on first, letting the water heat up while I picked out my outfit. I chose a black blouse with a white blazer and a gray, high-waisted, ruffled skirt. I didn't realize how cold I had gotten until the hot water hit between my shoulder blades, and I allowed myself one more minute under the scalding water. Then a quick towel dry, a few dabs of product to subdue my wavy hair, and some makeup basics. Before I left, I slipped on Gabriella's jade bracelet, which went nicely with the gray, and layered it with a couple of other bracelets I'd brought from home.

The hall was empty when I swung the door open. The windows and doors were open, letting in the calming crash of the waves as I made my way to Lucas's room. I knocked.

"Lucas?" I called when he didn't answer.

I headed downstairs, rubbing my arms against the ghostly chill.

I entered the kitchen and saw Lucas on the patio outside. The glow from inside lit one side of his face, showing his lips moving as he spoke to someone hidden by the curtain panels. As I stepped closer, he did a double take and ran inside to meet me.

"You look gorgeous," he said, resting a hand on my waist as

he gave me the customary cheek kiss. "Are you ready to go? Your brothers, Dylan, and Gabriella are all waiting for us."

"Yes." He looked as delicious as he smelled. I never knew that a cardigan could look so good on a man over shorts and a T-shirt.

"*Hola*, Zara."

I peeked past Lucas's shoulders to see Tita entering the house with Niya and Malik. She gave me a small hug.

"How are you?" I asked into her shoulder. "When did you arrive?" I petted the mellow jaguars' heads as if it came naturally.

"Just now. How do you like Mexico?" she asked.

"It's good. Lucas said we had some time before, you know, so he took me out. Showed me Tulum and the restaurant in Merida."

"So how are you feeling? Lucas told me about your dream."

I threw a condemning glance at Lucas. "Did he tell you what Xavier's mom asked of me?"

"He did."

"And?"

"We were just discussing that, but since you two are going out, we'll reconvene later tonight."

Lucas added, "When you are asleep."

"We'll see," I replied.

Ten minutes later, just off the deserted main drag, Lucas pulled into a small parking lot covered with more sand. Dusk was a rainbow of colors, the queen palms rising as black figures against its rosiness. The sign over the building, which looked like a miniature Colosseum, said *Luz*.

"Luz?" I asked as the music raging inside vibrated the ground beneath me.

We bypassed the long line behind red swags of rope and went straight to the fat bouncer, who noticed Lucas, jerked his chin up, and moved the plush barrier for us to pass.

"Lucas, I'm not twenty-one," I said anxiously. As Lucas opened the door, the musky bar air brushed my skin.

He squeezed my hesitant hand harder and pulled me through the short hallway. Once the room had opened into a large domed space, he tilted his head toward me.

"You only have to be eighteen to come here," he announced over the music.

Behind the bar was a huge tank full of bright tropical fish. The dance floor in the center of the room was packed with sweaty people. The ground underneath their feet lit up with changing colors. A face I'd seen on magazine covers was on the stage across the room, performing a song I'd heard in English.

Lucas gave a subtle wave to the performer, then pointed up and to the right. "There's Dylan."

My body tensed, and I started to think that entering the mass of people wasn't a good idea. His thumb instantly circled the back of my hand, gripping it even harder as he did, and we headed into the crowd.

The club was laid out on different levels. To get to Dylan, we had to step down onto a lower level, cut a path that curved to the right around the dance floor, then ascend a few steps. A black rope at the top blocked off a private area, and Lucas unhooked it without pausing. The space up here was large and nearly vacant. Max and Casey sat on one of the twenty boxy lounge chairs talking to Dylan, who made swooshing motions with his hands. Gabriella sat on a low, modern-style table, and the leg that she had crossed over the other bounced out of boredom.

"*Hola*, Zara." She smiled, looking relieved, as she rose to kiss my cheek. She looked stunning in a short yellow dress and pink lipstick. A bracelet matching mine dangled with others along her arm.

She smiled approvingly as Lucas fastened his arm around my side. The boys looked up from Dylan and toward us with contagious laughs.

Dela

"Zara, you should have seen Dylan, he was sick!" Max cackled, grabbing his stomach from laughing too hard.

Dylan's face went devout behind his glass. *Great, Max and Casey have met their long-lost triplet, and Dylan has gained lost brothers.* It was a perfect reunion, though it made me feel guilty about Xavier.

"*Vamos, amor,*" Gabriella moaned, tugging Dylan off the chair.

Dylan smiled at the twins and shrugged his shoulders submissively, though he followed her without complaint. She swayed her hips like a duck as they glided off to the dance floor. Max and Casey stared at the incapacitated Dylan in awe.

Lucas threw his sweater on the table next to the boys and looked to me. "You too!"

"What?"

He grabbed my hand and yanked me off in the same direction.

"What are you doing?" I asked, tugging in the other direction, even though I couldn't overpower him. I didn't want to be next to Gabriella as she danced. I imagined her, graceful and seductive, her movement and body flawless—as it should be when you dance. After Lucas had dragged me ten feet closer to the dance floor, I gave up resisting. Gabriella and Dylan were already in the zone by the time we joined them. I looked away, feeling shy. *How am I going to top that? Every move is like a Tony Award–winning bit of choreography.*

"Don't think," Lucas said before I could protest that I shouldn't dance.

I was worried about the bodies bumping into us, but he angled himself in front of me as if they didn't exist. My body pulsed as he decreased the space between us, watching me intently as he did, and rested his hands on my hips and moved them in rhythm. As his body moved slowly with mine, and he looked down, engulfed in our movement, I surrendered. I put my arms around his neck and stepped closer. Soon our bodies rocked in sync, our hips swaying together. Our skin grew sweaty with close contact, but Lucas only pressed himself harder against me.

Songs later, when my legs grew tired, Lucas broke the space between us.

"Let's take a break." He smiled, fanning out his shirt, which was stuck to his chest. I shook my head and realized that I was out of breath.

Max and Casey were standing at the rope at the top of the stairs, pointing to girls below and whispering.

"I wish I spoke Spanish," I heard Casey say.

Max threw a hand to his chest. "Bro, all you say is, ¿Señorita baile?" His pronunciation was embarrassing, but worse was the motion of two stick figures he made with his fingers.

Casey nodded like some stoned hipster. "Zara, hands down, this is the best Christmas ever."

"Good," I replied, amazed that I was getting along with my brothers.

"Where did you take our sis today, bro?" Max asked.

"To one of the homes I grew up in."

"That's it?" Casey replied, sounding kind of shocked.

"Pretty much."

Max and Casey looked away as if we were boring and continued where they left off.

"Max, Case, we're leaving," Dylan said from behind us. "We'll catch you at home, Lucas."

Casey nodded, looking disappointed.

"Don't worry, the ladies will be here tomorrow too," Dylan promised.

Outside, the cool night breeze graced my skin as Lucas tugged me toward the black tree line with a secret grin.

"This way," he whispered.

I caught his excitement, and we ran into the forest, plunging into the shadows until the parking lot was out of view. The branches brushed along my arms and behind my back, but I was focused on Lucas, who watched me back. My heart picked up its pace again as he slid his arms around my waist and pulled me into him.

"This is more like it," he whispered.

I stared back, sensing a wall inside him crumbling further as he leaned his head against mine.

"This is my someday," I finally said in the silence.

He responded with a closed, velvety smile that made my head spin and my toes tingle. As he tilted his head toward me, I inched closer and prepared. I puckered my lips just as his briskly touched mine, but then they turned to stone. He pushed himself away from me, his eyes large with shock. I stared at him, confused, but then I heard it too: the loud beat of a drum.

I covered my ears as it grew even louder and yelled, "What is that?"

His skin suddenly looked pale in the darkness. "We must go."

I backed away in confusion.

"NOW!" he yelled.

We rushed to the car and bolted for home, my hands still fumbling for my seatbelt.

"What's going on?" I asked.

"The executioners are declaring war. They will be here by morning," Lucas said through tight lips.

"But I thought you said they couldn't come back after Solstice."

He swerved onto the small gateway road, the boxy palace ahead a beacon in the dark. "I said they wouldn't come after Solstice, not that they *couldn't*. They are breaking the laws now too."

Lucas swerved toward the light. The fluorescent whiteness made the garage seem like a surgical theater. The Castillos were standing together next to the boat Dylan had taken out earlier, the jaguars at their feet.

"Did you hear it, their drums of war?" Valentina asked nervously as we pulled in.

"Yeah." Lucas met me on the other side of the car, looking distracted.

The ghostly drumbeat pounded in our heads again.

"What *is* that?" I asked irritably.

"It's Xibalba," Tita answered in a daze. She turned a deathlike gaze on me, her eyes void of expression. "They're coming for you."

"Tita, *silencio por favor,*" Andrés interrupted. "Zara, honey, I need you to stay in the house with your family until we return. The Aluxes will be here to guard you, but you cannot leave the house," he stressed. "You will tell your family that we had last-minute family business, and that we will be back in a couple of days at the most."

"A couple of days?" I shrieked.

"Tita will put a spell on the house to protect you, but no one will be allowed to enter or leave. It will be safe," he added in a reassuring tone, though his body betrayed his unease.

"I don't like this," I said.

"Yeah, me either," Gabriella said.

"Aren't you forgetting about one little detail . . . like the prophecy?" I didn't mean to raise my voice. I took a deep breath and calmed myself. "The Milky Way's dark rift, what about that? Isn't that just another means to another portal? So if you close this one, the Underworld will still have another way of getting out, only then you would have a Celestial coming after you for killing a god!"

"We've run out of options. It's the only shot we have right now at guaranteeing your safety," Lucas said. His face was tight with frustration as he pulled his fingers through his hair.

"He's right, Zara. Please, go inside and be with your family," Andrés said.

"No, I will *not* just listen. You listen to me!"

I waited for their shocked faces to smooth, but when they didn't, I continued. "Xavier's mother came to me for a reason. She was scared, and very cautious, like she was being watched. She risked coming because it was important. There has to be another way to deal with Xavier."

"Like what?" Lucas said. He looked scared, like someone was about to come and rob him of his rightful property. I had to remind myself that *I* was the possession he was worried about.

"What if Dylan called for her and asked her to join you? Have her go with you to where the portal is located. Promise Xavier that you will break the curse if he promises to disappear forever. I mean, that's what he wants, isn't it? His freedom?"

There were a few disconcerted nods.

"From there, she takes Xavier away, if *and only if* he promises to stay out of your way, never cross your paths. You know, that sort of thing." I ran out of things to say.

"That can't work," Tita clarified. "The spell I put on him is called a curse because it cannot be revoked."

"Unless they have Zara," Dylan mused.

Lucas glared at him. "Out of the question."

"It's too dangerous," Valentina added.

"We can't trust Xavier. I'm sorry." Andrés turned to his family. "We leave at dawn's first light."

I glared back at all of them, expecting Lucas to speak up. But he stood with his family on this one, not even man enough to look me in the eye. The pressure in my head suddenly made my face throb. I fled without another word through the kitchen, past my family in the great room, and into my room.

I belly flopped on the bed and pushed my face into the pillow to muffle my sobs. But when I rolled to one side, my cheeks wet with tears, Lucas was standing by the dresser. I looked away and sniffed.

"What do you want from me, Zara?" he said. "The executioners are on their way, right now. We have to block them before they come with an army to kidnap you and deliver you to Mictlan."

"Aren't you worried about the Milky Way being another way for them to come?" I asked, shocked that he wasn't freaking out.

"Not really, no."

"And you're sure you can seal the portal for good?"

He sighed and added an encouraging, "Yes."

I moved to the edge of the bed and wedged my hands between my knees.

He moved in front of me noiselessly, his face full of remorse. "Look, if roles were reversed, I would feel the same way as you do right now: angry and betrayed. But you need to understand how important it is that you stay in this house. You don't know how much you mean to me." He paused. "What happened with your connection and Xavier at Fallen Leaf was too dangerous, and Xavier would do anything to get you now. I don't know how I could protect you from an army." His voice trembled as he looked at me.

I picked at my fingernails and, with hesitation, dismissed my own judgment. "I will stay here."

He watched me closely. "I will come back for you, I promise."

I fell back and stared up at the ceiling. My instincts still screamed against every grain of this plan, but I had to trust him now. "How do you even kill Xavier? He's a god."

The whites of Lucas's eyes widened, and I could see the risk they were willing to take in his fearful face. "We remove his heart and burn it on an altar."

I waited a moment as the pieces of their plan came together. I rolled my head sideways to look at him. "So you're going to lock me in the house?"

"It's the only way I know how to protect you. We are trying to keep everything as normal as possible so your family doesn't suspect anything."

I shot up with a brilliant idea, the last piece of hope I had. "I have a better plan. How about we contact the Celestials?"

"What?" He shook his head as if I were crazy. "We can't."

"Tell them everything, let them make the decision. You don't have to do this!" I cried.

He looked torn as he nodded slowly. "I do."

I looked down, partially frustrated, partially fighting the pounding in my head. It killed me that everything was out of my control. Because of me, the Castillos were willing to risk exposing their identity. Because of me, Lucas was willing to put his life on the line. Because of me, my family was in the most danger they would ever face, and they didn't even know it.

His feet moved into the patch of floor I was staring at, so close that our knees touched. He tilted my chin upward, and the dim lamp highlighted his features as he raised his eyebrows.

"We're not over. I am coming back for you," he confirmed, the deep promise splitting the air between us.

He held on to me, and I could almost feel him still questioning his desire to act on how he felt. I wanted him to do it, get it over with, because I knew with every fiber of my being that my first time would be with him.

"What are you waiting for?" I whispered, pushing away just enough to look him squarely in the eyes. I wished I had the courage to do it myself, but I didn't.

His passion was there, in all its drowning intensity, but he looked conflicted. "I'm holding on to anything I can as a reason not to do this."

In that moment, his closeness consumed me—I had never wanted him more. I could think of many reasons why he *should*. Then, before I could reach for him, he swallowed, kissed my cheek, and vanished, the curtains on the French doors flapping with his passage.

I stayed on the bed. As much as it ate at me inside, I would not go to him tonight. If he wanted me, he would come. I left the doors open, already feeling somehow trapped, and went to the bathroom to get ready for bed. There was the nightgown that Lucas had promised me, fine white cotton soft as silk, folded by the sink. It slid cool and smooth over my skin. As I brushed my teeth, imagining never seeing Lucas again, I choked.

He promised me. He promised he will return.

CHAPTER TWENTY-TWO

Eternal Engagement

Midnight approached, and I still couldn't sleep, no matter how exhausted I was. My body pounded for Lucas. As I rested on my back, imagining Lucas resting on the other side of the house, a dark figure appeared between the French doors. The sheer drapes blew lightly around Lucas's black silhouette, shirtless and barefoot. A smile grew on my face as the hunger flashed in his eye. I sat up as he stepped inside.

He didn't speak. Instead, the prince came silently, passing the foot of the bed with fiery purpose. I reached for the silk sheet and weakly pulled it over my chest as he turned the corner of the bed. His determination was a shield, and now I saw weakness when he stopped at my side.

"Are you nervous?" he asked softly.

I nodded robotically.

He studied me for a moment, my face, my body, before setting a knee on the bed. I slid to the center, trembling. He crawled over to me and knelt at my side. Then he took my hand and placed it on his bare chest. It was sticky in the humidity, but I felt his heart pumping underneath, beating as fast as mine.

He cupped a hand behind my neck and lowered me to my back, leaning over me.

"I've no more reasons. Somewhere over the past few months, I've fallen for every piece of you . . . your body, your soul, your mind," he said.

I panicked. I'd always considered myself good looking, but I never dreamed someone like Lucas would want me. He belonged with someone just as exotic as himself, just as timeless, just as royal. That wasn't me. I looked away, ashamed.

"I don't deserve you," I rushed out.

He pushed my chin up with a finger, forcing my eyes to meet his. "It is I who doesn't deserve you. But I want you. I choose you, Zara, consequences and all."

"Lucas, I'm scared," I said quickly. I knew that once we did this, my heart would belong to him forever. "Aren't you?"

He rolled onto his side and swept a loose hair past my ear. His thumb brushed my lips and made me tremble inside.

"*This* is my someday," he whispered.

When I didn't budge, frozen by his words, he moved. "Hold still, *muñeca*," he warned softly, lowering his head.

I stared, expressionless, afraid of what was coming, but then a fiery passion overwhelmed my fear.

He rolled again and pressed his bare skin to mine. He trailed slow, lingering kisses down my neck and across my jaw to the rim of my lips. Then he gently cupped my cheeks with both hands and paused, staring deeply into my eyes. Second-guessing, perhaps? But suddenly, his lips met mine unerringly in the darkness.

A golden burst rose behind my closed eyelids like fireworks. The unfamiliar rush of emotion made every atom in my body explode. I knew he felt it too, because he backed away with a startled expression. But then he grinned with pleasure and leaned in again. I was ready this time as he pulled me to his starving lips.

I clenched my fingers in his hair and brought him closer. I wanted to feel the entirety of him. He slipped one hand under the front of my nightgown and touched my inner thigh. My body throbbed as he kissed me harder. I moaned—he was squeezing me too hard, but I didn't want him to stop. The foreignness of his touch set fire to my body, a hotness I'd never experienced, and I wanted more. But he let go and rose to his knees. His hands swept mine up quickly, locking them over my head as he nibbled my ear.

My toes clung to the sheets as he cinched my waist and pulled me toward him, kissing all over my body. I grunted with pleasure as time slipped away. When he released my wrists to draw me closer, I cupped my hands carefully around his neck to pull him back up against me, wanting more of his poison. His lips found mine again, that golden energy derailing my intent again. Lucas parted my lips this time, intertwining his tongue with mine, and I panted, trying to take as much of him as I could.

I gasped when he unlocked our lips and eased us back down to the bed. He pushed my nightgown up above my navel and began licking slowly around it. Then he hooked a finger in my panties and drew them down slightly, licking. A ripple of shivers racked me.

He looked up with fiery eyes, his hot breath inches from my body. It made me pulse even harder for him.

"I'm trying so hard to be good," he whispered, before licking above the lacy hem again.

The throbbing grew out of control as he scooted back. He slouched over and spread my knees slightly, but then he stopped.

"What?" I panted, nearly exploding with expectation.

He studied my blazing face, then closed my legs, pulled the nightgown down, and lay down on his side next to me.

"I love you," he whispered unexpectedly.

He draped a hand over my body and brushed fingers over my arm.

Coming to my senses, I smiled bashfully and whispered back what I'd always known. "I love you too."

I knew it wasn't normal. I would marry him in a heartbeat—elope, even. But I was still on fire, pulsing, and I wondered why he had stopped.

"There's no need to rush this. I want you, but later. When we are both ready for it," he said.

"Are you afraid that you'll hurt me?"

He laughed loudly. "Not exactly."

"Well then, what is it?" I hoped I sounded less nervous to him than I did to myself.

His lips brushed my ear as he whispered, "My parents can hear everything we are doing right now."

I sat up in shock, covering myself with the sheets as if it would help. Lucas chuckled softly and fluffed the pillows. He held his arm out, and I leaned into him, embarrassed.

I tried to think of something else, something that didn't have anything to do with his parents' supernatural abilities, or his sultry abs, or me being the start of an apocalypse. I tried to think of something safe.

As I twisted the edge of the blanket, resting my head on Lucas's arm, a term I learned in high school chemistry came to mind. *Covalent bonding.* A simple term for when a chemical bond between atoms shared electrons. But I remembered that this bond was strongest when atoms shared similar electronegativities. That was Lucas and I. We were made up of different atoms—different cultures, different classes—but electronegativity formed that unseen connection between us, and I felt it every time we touched. *Our relationship can work. I know it.*

Lucas stood. "Come outside with me."

I reached for my shorts in the dark, but he held his hand up.

"No. We aren't going far."

I followed him to the balcony, where my nightgown flowed in the breeze. Lucas picked me up and stepped onto the ledge. I hung on tight as he jumped to the sand below and carried me toward the shore. As we got closer, I saw something shining in the water. Lucas put me down, and I walked to the shoreline, curious. A bright aqua glimmer came and went, twinkling in different spots like pixie dust, giving the waves a constant sparkling glow. I looked both ways down the shore. The water shimmered along the coast as far as I could see.

"Why does the water glow? Is it bewitched?"

He looked to the black waters that sparkled so brightly. "No witch involved. It's a bioluminescent organism that comes in with the red tide. When the waves crash, it sets them off."

"Bri would love this place."

Without a word, he knelt down and placed a hand in the water, catching one of the glowing specks on his fingertip. It was as tiny as a grain of sand. He took my arm, pressed the glowing seed to my skin, and began to draw. The small grain disintegrated as he moved, leaving a trail of glimmering, glowing light behind. When he finished, a heart shone on my arm in the same bright aqua as his tattoo. It was imperfect—dewy drops leaked down from the heart like dripping blood—but to me, it was flawless.

"You are *mi princesa,* and I promise that I will spend the rest of my life making you happy," he said, brushing windblown hair out of my eyes.

His endearment didn't surprise me, but the eyes that rose to mine—that I knew even with my eyes closed—still did.

"Do I scare you?" he asked.

"No. I—" I couldn't find the words I wanted. "I never imagined my life would end like this."

"End?"

"A fairytale."

"Hmm." He smiled and gave me a small kiss. "A sick fairytale, if you ask me."

"Twisted," I agreed, and then he pulled me into him.

The soft sand crunched between my toes as the waves washed

our legs. A cool gust of wind swooped up my gown, but Lucas was quick to hold it down with one hand, the other pressed against the hollow of my back. The kiss felt new. It was a fresh passion that fired every nerve in my body and left a warmth that settled into my heart.

All too soon, Lucas backed away, his wet lips glimmering in the moonlight. He brushed my cheeks softly and tilted his forehead to mine. He was a beautiful creature in the dark. I couldn't stop my heart from beating harmony, a soft percussive moan of wanting, craving, and needing everything Lucas.

"You taste good," he said.

I reached for his cheeks, but his hands clasped my wrists and pulled them down.

"Don't, please. I need a break," he pleaded, embarrassment coloring his request. I didn't get it.

"A human break or an immortal break?"

"A man break." He chuckled.

I backed away. "Oh . . ."

He reached for my hand as I began to step away and pulled me close. "Best to not go too far. It isn't safe."

I played with my hair as I blushed. "Right."

He held his arms out. "May I?"

I let him pick me up and carry me back to the room. The heart on my arm had faded, and I already wanted it back as he set me on the bed. I sat up, feeling a little clammy.

"I need a moment," I said, heading for the bathroom.

When I returned, Lucas was resting on the bed with one arm behind his head, the other outstretched for me. I curled into him and inhaled his immortal aura. I yawned. Sleep was my new enemy.

"You must rest," he said.

"Not yet." I burrowed my face into his arm.

I fought the urge to fall asleep for as long as I could. I told Lucas stories of past Christmases with my family, including one where my brothers told me that there was no Santa Claus and I cried for two days. Lucas laughed at my innocence. He asked and I answered for hours. He tried not to laugh, but there were some stories he couldn't resist.

"I'm glad I can amuse you," I yawned again.

"I've never had any of those experiences. And I thought my life was odd," he teased.

I pinched Lucas, partly because he deserved it for laughing, and partly to make sure he was still by my side. I yawned again, a deep one that reached inside, and a sullen blackness consumed me. I awoke on a cold slab in a still, quiet room. Torches burned in each corner of the small, square space. I tried to sit up, but thick leather straps tugged my wrists and ankles back.

"Lucas?" I called, frantically looking from side to side as thunder crashed outside.

Footsteps tapped toward me on the stone, and then an eerie laugh echoed around me.

"Lucas's precious virgin," the voice said, its owner staying to the shadows where I couldn't see his face.

"Who are you? Where's Lucas?" I asked, trying to wiggle free.

"Lucas is looking for you." The man taunted, sounding pleased with himself. He loosed a triumphant guffaw. "My plan worked perfectly."

"Where am I?"

"You don't know?" The man clicked his tongue. *Shame on me*, it said. "It's your own sacrifice ceremony."

The skinny figure walked into the light of the torch, revealing a slightly concave face. Xavier.

I forced myself up, heart shredding through my chest, but nothing held me back this time. My hair stuck to my face as I looked around, the pounding in my head unbearable. I was back at the beach house, in my bed, alone, the sun seeping through the closed patio doors. I rubbed my forehead. It was too vivid to be just a dream. It was different from a blackout. I sat still for a moment, pondering as my body pulsed, and then I realized what I had guessed all along.

"Oh no, oh no," I muttered, freaking out as I scooted to the edge of the bed.

My connection isn't with Xavier. It's with Mictlan. That's why I felt a connection to that executioner at Solstice—because it belonged to Mictlan. That's why I felt it was a bad idea to kill Xavier. He'd be a casualty, a useless, messy death that would cause more problems than we'd know what to do with. That's what Xquic meant, He's not the threat.

My hand flew to my mouth, covering its growing gape. "Mictlan knows," I said, petrified.

Your own sacrifice ceremony. Xavier's words rang in my mind. Mictlan wouldn't have done it like that. He'd have all of Xibalba watch, or he'd just have me. As what? His slave? His lover? I shivered. I had to warn Lucas about Xavier. He wasn't working with Mictlan. I needed to be there, to tell him he didn't have to kill Xavier. To let his mother deal with it.

I ran to Lucas's room and knocked urgently. He didn't answer. I ran to Gabriella's room and knocked harder, but she didn't answer either.

"Gabriella, Dylan!" I called, pounding my fist on their door.

Still nothing. I rubbed my head as the drumming grew louder. I ran to Andrés and Valentina's room, pounding and pounding until my knuckles were raw.

"Tita!" I yelled into the still-sleeping house. No one answered.

I ran to the kitchen, hoping to find Marifer, but she wasn't in the kitchen. Another short Alux with a big head stood at the stove, cooking something that smelled wonderful. He was a foot shorter than me, but underneath his uniform, I could tell that he was strong.

I rushed over to him. "Hey you, what is your name?"

He looked at me as if he didn't understand and kept stirring the black contents of the pot. I stared at him relentlessly, but he didn't change. *Great—language barrier.* I threw my hands in the air in disbelief and walked away.

"My name is Nicolás," he called with a thick accent.

I spun and rushed back to him on the verge of hysteria. "You speak English?"

"*Un poco,*" he said, watching the pot as he stirred.

"Nicolás, where is Lucas? Where is Gabriella?"

He looked up from the heat and stared at me. I tried to retrieve a quick Spanish lesson from memory, but I just kicked myself for not paying better attention in class.

"*Donde es . . .*" No, that wasn't it.

"They are gone, *señora,*" he said.

My eyes zoomed to him. "Where is Marifer?"

"Wow, Zara, nice pajamas." Max walked in, yawning.

"Nicolás!" I pressed, but he was watching Max now.

I tapped my hand on the counter when Nicolás looked away silently and stirred the pot again. I was positive he knew what I needed to know, and I was determined to crack him, even if Max was here now.

"Merry Christmas Eve to you too," Max added with a stretch as he walked toward the balcony doors.

That seemed to get Nicolás on his toes. He moved away from the stove and stepped toward Max. "Señor, the weather is supposed to be worsening this morning, so we will be dining inside today. Mr. and Mrs. Castillo had last-minute business to attend to. They will be back shortly."

I tapped my foot and crossed my arms, waiting for him to give me something. His eyes avoided me as they swiftly returned to the pot.

"Nicolás, I really want to tell you about my dream." I opened my eyes wide, hoping he'd catch on.

"Hah, your dream! Why would he want to know about that?"

Max sat at the bar. "Sorry about that, man, my sister thinks we all want to be bored with her dreams."

Nicolás only had one face and one speed for stirring. I watched him incredulously.

"You know what, you're right. Since Nicolás doesn't want to hear about it, and you do, I will tell you all about it." I watched Nicolás as I sat next to Max. He twitched a little, enough for me to think he was paying attention.

"No, Zara, I really don't want to hear about it," Max said, bugged.

I ignored Max and watched Nicolás. "It was really weird."

"Zara, he doesn't want to hear it," Max whispered in my ear.

"So anyway, in my dream I woke up on a large stone, sort of like an altar, and I was tied down," I said loudly, emphasizing the last part.

Nicolás finally looked up.

"I was alone, and then I heard a voice, a laugh, so to speak. This man would not show his face in the light. He was mad, saying something about my sacrifice ceremony. And then at the very end, he stepped into the light, and guess who he looked like?" I asked, turning theatrically to Max.

Max glanced at me funnily. "Who?"

"Dylan."

Nicolás took the pot off the stove and spooned the hot contents onto a plate, which he handed to Max before leaning against the counter with as much nonchalance as an Alux could manage.

"Tell me, *señorita,* what did this man say? Where were you in your dream?"

Max chuckled and then choked on his bite. "You care?"

I leaned in to Nicolás. "Tell me where everyone is."

Nicolás stood there, face blank.

Max set his fork down and looked at us suspiciously. "Am I

missing something?"

"Shut up, Max." I stood in front of Nicolás and looked down at him. "Nicolás, this is important. You know where everyone is, don't you? I think something is going to happen that shouldn't, and you need to help me warn them."

A flash of lightning washed his brown face, and thunder rumbled the sky. I flipped around to view the backyard. Dark purple storm clouds rolled in so quickly that the sunshine was extinguished in moments. The churning clouds pulsed horror.

Nicolás looked toward it. "It has begun. You have to stay here now, Zara. It is my duty to keep you inside this house."

"Wow, man, what are you talking about? Your duty?" Max was on his feet now with his *I don't like what you've said* look on Nicolás.

"Stay out of this, Max," I hollered. I pointed to the black, cottony sky. "Valentina is doing this, isn't she?"

I couldn't control my anger or my fear, and tears started to run down my cheek.

"Nicolás, don't you see? If Xavier goes, things will get worse. Much worse. We need to warn them."

"No," Nicolás said, walking back to the kitchen.

Max touched my back lightly. "Zara, I think you need to go back to bed. Maybe you're getting sick."

I shrugged him off. "I'm fine, Max. Nicolás has information that he isn't telling me."

Max raised his voice. "No you're not, look at you. You are a wreck! I think you overdid it yesterday. Too much sun maybe."

The booming and the flashes of light outside grew more intense. I rushed to Nicolás and cuffed his forearm, afraid I was running out of time.

"Please, Nicolás, please. Help me escape. We've got to help them," I pleaded.

"What do you mean, Zara? Help you *escape*?" Max grabbed my

arms and tugged me upstairs.

I kicked and shoved, trying to get away from him. "Let go of me, jerk!"

"Zara, you've lost it. Seriously, let's go!" he yelled as I clawed at him.

"Nicolás! Nicolás! You're making a big mistake!" I screamed as Max forced me to my room.

Nicolás watched with no emotion as Max wrestled me around the corner. As his big flat head disappeared, I thought about how much I hated that Alux, and that if anything went wrong, I was going to blame him.

Once we reached my prison of silk and crystal, I jerked my arm away and ran inside, trying to slam the door behind me. The door jammed. I looked down at Max's foot and then up. His index finger pressed to his lips.

"Shh." He pointed downstairs toward the kitchen.

I opened the door, puzzled, and Max slipped in and closed it softly behind him. He grabbed a pen and paper from the dresser and handed it to me.

What is wrong? he mouthed. Then he pointed to the paper, motioning me to write.

It was too dangerous to tell Max the truth. I swore to Lucas that I wouldn't tell a soul, but I couldn't have predicted this. I have to get out of this house, and Max might be the only one who could help.

I scribbled as fast as I could, holding the pen so tightly my palm hurt.

We are trapped in this house, I wrote.

What? he mouthed, looking shocked. That simple response carried so many emotions on his stupid face, but the only one that mattered was belief. I let myself grieve for the shortest second. *Max: my heckling brother, my accomplice.*

I need you to help me get out of here, I scribbled.

Why? Where is Lucas?

I looked away bitterly as the rain pounded against my doors. The waves were now powerful enough to slap the idle boats against the small dock.

No time to explain. Will you help me? I wrote anxiously.

What is your plan? Max grinned, clearly thrilled at the thought of danger, not doubting the weirdness for a second. It worried me that he didn't know the deadly potential in all of this.

"Why are we trapped in this house? What's going on?" Max finally said aloud, and when he did, the answer dawned on me.

I bolted off the bed and ran to the darkened doors. I hadn't actually tried to *leave* the house. Lucas just said that they were going to put a spell on it, but I had never officially tried to leave. I pressed my face against the glass and stared past the dripping streaks of water. Xavier was standing on the sand below with a bloodthirsty grin.

I fell back and landed hard on my butt on the floor.

"What the . . .? Zara, stop being ridiculous, and tell me what's going on." Max demanded.

As he lifted me off the floor, his face shifted to panic. It scared me.

"You are whiter than white, and your skin is all sweaty. I really think you are getting sick. You're not having woman problems, are you?" He sounded grossed out.

"Seriously?"

"Because if I need to get you a cotton cigar, I won't do it!"

"MAX!"

Without another protest, he helped me to the bed. As he eased me down, I felt imaginary spiders rushing over my limbs, prickling like a shot of novocaine at the dentist. It stung coldly a few more seconds, and then I lost all sensation in my feet and my hands. But the stinging sensation didn't stop. It moved upward and inward toward my torso.

I turned to Max in panic. "Hurry, I think you need to go get

Nicolás, like RIGHT NOW! Something is happening!"

Max looked scared, but he zoomed out of the room without another word. I listened to his footsteps until they faded down the stairs, and then I waited, alone and numb, as the storm pushed against my door. I tested my leg, trying to lift it, but it wouldn't respond to the orders my mind issued. I was paralyzed.

Moments felt like hours as I stared at my lifeless body in the mirror above the dresser. And then suddenly I realized it was too quiet.

I could barely move my lips. "Max?"

Tears clogged my eyes when that murky laugh pricked my ears. *He can't get in, he can't get in*, I repeated to myself.

I doubted Tita's spell when, out of the corner of my eye, I watched dark shadows creep onto the balcony. In their smoky form, they squeezed under the doors and into my room, passing in front of the mirror and surrounding my bed. I clenched my eyes tightly like a child, pretending the shadows weren't there. But the smell of death was right under my nose, and it made me nauseous.

And then a cold hand wrapped around my wrist. My eyes flung open as my heart ricocheted inside my chest cavity, and I saw the ring of dark, hovering executioners. Their bodies were more skeletons than smoke, some wearing ancient crowns on their heads and others with metal cuffs interlaced with their bones. The invisible, freezing grip increased its pressure on my small wrist. As it squeezed, immobility burned like a disease throughout my body.

"Max!" I screamed, but my voice was a burst of fumes, inaudible, and then the room spun and went black.

CHAPTER TWENTY-THREE

Pyramid of Niches

My head ached in the back, feeling dented, like a bruise on an apple. My sight flickered as my eyes adjusted. I felt a cool smoothness around my forehead. It weighed me down as I heaved upward and then banged loudly as my held fell back in defeat. I wiggled sideways, but my arms and legs were caught fast and clanged loudly each time I moved. Straining my gaze downward, I saw that underneath bracelets of dull gold metal, leather straps cinched my wrists; I felt them on my ankles as well.

Hairs suddenly rose along my skin at the faint touch of a musky coldness. *I don't remember Xibalba being this cold.* I burrowed my chin into my chest and looked down the bare landscape of my body. A red brazier pressed an itchy tightness against my chest, while, frighteningly, my southern region was protected only by a small piece of red fabric draped loosely around my waist.

I closed my eyes, feeling sick, pressuring myself to wake up with a pinch. As I did, a low rumble rolled outside, and I jerked, bringing the room into a clearer focus. This was not Xibalba. The temple room there was open to the outside, and new. The walls in this dingy space were deteriorated, speckled with hollowness in places where the wall had crumbled from age. I thrashed, trying to squirm off the raised altar to which I now knew I was bound for my own sacrifice.

The 52nd

My eyes shifted to the dark door at an abrupt sound just as my wrist was nearly loose.

"Help!" I screamed as his laugh began.

My skin shredded as I twisted my wrist hurriedly, but the echo reached me, and Xavier's lanky figure walked out of the dark. He stepped into the flicker, and as it shadowed the contours of his face, I saw for the briefest moment a resemblance to Dylan. Then he grinned cruelly, and I shuddered.

He took two steps toward me. "Stupid girl. Or should I say, stupid boyfriend? He left you all alone with no protection. Maybe now he'll learn not to trust a witch."

"How did I get here?" I asked dizzily as the pounding in my head persisted.

Xavier stopped by my side and stared at me like some basket case before his eyes shifted down my body.

"You are a pretty one," he said, running a long fingernail up from my navel toward my breasts.

I wormed away as his fingernail continued upward. The sharpness poked my chest as he leaned into my ear. "Lucas failed to figure out one slightly important detail: I'm not here for Mictlan. I'm here of my own accord."

His breath was the stench of rotten milk. I turned my head away and gagged. He straightened up with a snicker that sharpened the angle of his cheekbones. "But you already know that, don't you?"

I jerked my chest away from his finger when he poked it harder. He laughed.

"I was surprised he left you in the hands of a witch," Xavier continued, his accent heavier than Dylan's. "I mean, if I was going to leave my girlfriend when a god was after me, I would at least have all my bases covered. Tita isn't, what do humans say, the sharpest tool in the shed?"

With a gloating grin, he drew the dagger cinched in his torn waistband and wiped the blade carefully.

"Has it been that long that they forgot the cardinal rule? Here's something you couldn't know, little human. Witches have no power over a god's body if his spirit and body are not one. That wench may have cursed my soul to Xibalba, but fortunately for me, she doesn't have control of my body right now. And"—he let out a psychotic bellow and smiled crookedly—"it looks like the Cosmos favors me this year after all."

He circled the altar, studying me. "You've made quite a big mess with the gods now, haven't you? Mictlan is borderline loony. You see, he has it in his mind that you belong to him." A deep cackle swayed him off balance. "As if you belong to him," he crooned again, softly. I shied away from the blade each time he carelessly jerked it toward me. "And the Celestials . . . if only they could know the real reason for Lucas's disobedience to their stupid little arrangement. Too bad you won't be here to see what happens to your precious little prince. With your death, I will be made whole again. He will try to avenge you, but I will be long gone. But the Celestials will find out that your lover boy's family skipped out on their sacred deal, not because they killed a god or tried to save a sacrifice, but because Mictlan will go to them in anger once this is all over. Do you think the Celestials will tolerate such behavior? They will smite the royal family in an attempt to salvage peace, but it won't work. Mictlan has a temper."

He drew himself close to me, but tilted his head slightly to look behind me. Then he froze, his dead eyes distant. "And he will declare war against the Celestials. A war that neither your world nor the Celestials would have a hope of surviving."

I have to get out of here now!

I thrashed again against my bindings until my muscles were weak and shaking and I tasted blood. I sucked my lip and got a new taste of metal. I'd bitten into my lip. I whimpered as I desperately summoned all my anger.

"And what of you?" I shouted. "Will you remain a coward forever and run? Because last I checked, you were a Celestial too. Mictlan will come after you."

His laugh was short. He seemed preoccupied, the way he wiped his blade again.

"My pretty girl, so foolish. It's such a shame your connection was always with Mictlan. I could have made you great."

When he finished, he lowered his dagger to his side, but I cringed as he rubbed a strand of my hair between the fingers of his other hand.

"How do you know about my connection?" I asked.

"Don't you know who I am? I've been living with Mictlan for almost five hundred years in that cursed world of his. Why else do you think he sent me to the Middleworld? I came here to retrieve you for him, since the executioners weren't getting the job done. But I fooled him. I'm not going to give you up—I never was. I need you to break my curse." He paused, and sarcasm tinged his flat smile. "He's really upset right now. I wouldn't want to mess with him."

His crazed laugh echoed again. The bones underneath his thinned skin made weird angles in his torso as he paced around the altar. "I'm the legendary Hero Twin, a master of trickery. Nobody can fool me, not even Mictlan. My stupid, outwitted father was a Celestial, and my mother a Xibalban goddess, which makes me the only worthy heir to both worlds. I *will* take back what's mine."

"Your mother lives with the humans now. You will destroy her if you do this. Go with her and leave us be. You don't have to do this," I urged. "I can get Lucas to break the curse if you promise to just leave us alone."

Xavier's face was stone. "My mother means as much to me as I mean to her—nothing. And Lucas, that pathetic crossbreed, damning me to Mictlan's world. He's as good as dead when I'm through with you."

"You're wrong about your mother. She came to me begging for your life."

He stopped pacing. He leaned forward so quickly hair fell over his eyes. "You fool! She doesn't care for me. And who are the Celestials to judge? I think it's time for a change around here."

At once, familiar yells sounded on the other side of the wall. I froze, listening, but a boom of thunder deafened me and shook the walls. Stone shards pattered down around us. Xavier looked up into it, but I squinted hard to block the debris from my eyes as a chilly finger poked one side of my brain. *No! This can't be happening right now!*

The shouts grew closer, and another tremor vibrated my bones. This time Xavier looked toward the door. He turned and headed for it. *Good, leave.* Abruptly he stopped, looked at me over his shoulder, then sprinted toward the noise.

"Come on," I muttered, trying to wiggle my hands free. I couldn't see him anymore. I had to hurry. The skin on my wrist split, and I froze with the agony of it. My heart paced, waiting for Xavier to return as I stared at the orange flicker of the light. *This is it. I'm going to die.*

But the icy throbbing expanded.

I pictured Lucas in my mind, fighting the mental assault that grew as the pain in my wrists worsened. It hurt so bad. It dulled my concentration until I could focus only on the stone altar, cool against my cheek. *Fight, Zara, fight. Dark hair, dimples, blue eyes, blue sneakers, perfect lips* . . . a zing of frost nailed my right side, bringing in swirling images of the place to which I never wanted to return. *Lucas's musky voice, the prickles of his chin, the*—OW!

I blinked hard once and saw a circle of people staring at me when they opened. I blinked again, hoping it wasn't real, but when my eyes reopened, the people were still there. I was on my feet in the center of Xibalba by the pyramid. The town encircled me, packed tight next to the pile of burning flesh. The charred bones nearly touched my naked feet, and I was still wearing the red sacrificial loincloth. *Oh no.*

Abruptly the silent crowd split, and the man with long black hair, the one who carried out the sacrifices in the pyramid, came forward.

Mictlan.

He wore a heavy robe that dragged as he walked and a large headdress with sprays of feathers. War paint streaked down from his eyes like black tears. When he grinned, my heart pulsed. It was creepy, the way I was frightened and fascinated all at once. He stretched out his arms as he approached.

"Stay away," I warned, crouching lower, ready to pick up a bone and use it as a weapon if need be.

He stopped to study me as I shoved back the hair that fell into my face.

The earth suddenly shook and screams carried on the wind, jarring us both from our shared stare. I looked back to Mictlan frantically, but he hadn't moved an inch. I glanced up the pyramid. The temple up top was empty, and the blood on the steps was dark burgundy. It had been dry for days. Then Lucas's scream surrounded us. Mictlan's hair blew back slightly as it passed through us.

"You . . . me . . .," he said. His accent was so thick I could barely understand him.

"LUCAS," I screamed. "HELP ME!"

Mictlan cocked his head. "Zara?"

"Do not say my name." My legs had quivered as I stepped back onto a lump. I heard a crunch and looked down. Gray fragments spread beneath my feet. I winced. *Was that a hand?*

Zara! Wake up, this isn't real.

I breathed deeply, though I didn't want to. It stunk like sewer and burnt hair. And then I remembered my utopia with eyes wide open. I watched Mictlan without a blink as my mind raced home: *a soft pillow against my cheek, the rose on the windowsill, the smell of coconut and ginger when Lucas's hair got wet.*

Out of nowhere my vision flickered. *It's working.*

I let my thoughts wander faster than I could control: *the snowfall, the flirting, the soft tickle when our skin touched—*

Mictlan jabbed a finger at me and yelled. At his word, four undead men charged me, their bones visible beneath their skin. I turned and fled.

Sharp bones sliced my feet as I cut across the charnel pile and ran toward the edge of the city. *Lucas's lips, their smoothness, the dimple in his smile,* I thought, crying as it produced another flicker in my vision. *His arrogant laugh that I hated for so long, his wild hair, and his hands running through it in frustration.*

I saw a clay room too tiny for a living space and ran toward it. As I got closer I saw wooden bars instead of a door. It was a prison. I stopped to catch my breath and looked inside. It was empty, but across the room on the dirt floor was a plastic pink necklace. It had belonged to a sacrifice. I cried out, throwing my hands to my mouth, and an abrupt coolness touched my back. I turned.

Mictlan and his men had me cornered. I pushed my back into the wooden bars. The raw bark scratched me.

"Zara, come," Mictlan said. He held his hand out for me.

When I stared back into his eyes, the tightness in my heart unwound and I fell into his grace. *Go with him.*

Slowly, my hands eased off the wood. I lifted one hand, but something told me to stop. I retracted my hand and looked at him, confused, as blue eyes came back to me.

"I am not yours," I whispered.

Mictlan gave one more nod, pleading for me to go with him.

"I am not yours," I said louder.

Mictlan retracted his waiting hand and watched me for a moment. When he didn't move, I screamed with all my strength. "I am not yours! I am not yours!"

I didn't see what Mictlan did because my vision flickered steadily, more blackness than light. When I focused again, executioners were coming for me.

"I CHOOSE LUCAS! I CHOOSE LUCAS!!" It was my last chance, my desperate plea, but it meant more to me than any sensation I felt. My body burned, and my chest swelled with knowledge. I could hear them coming for me, but I continued to scream blindly. "I CHOOSE LUCAS. I CHOOSE LUCAS. I CHOOSE LUCAS!"

"How did you get out of the bands?"

My eyes jolted open. I was back in the musky room, and Xavier was too. I clung to the altar for support, shaking away the rising burn in my body.

"I . . . uh . . ."

I was on the verge of puking, but I glowered at him with a new energy.

"The witch who sent your soul to the Underworld will kill you today if you don't take my offer," I snarled.

"Enough!" he screamed. "I am tired of waiting."

He blew out the torch nearest him and slowly walked to the next one. As he circled the room, I sprinted to the dark door that promised nothing, but he was there in a flash, cackling as he blocked my way. I ran to the opposite wall and groped in the darkness, hoping the room had other doors, like the other temples I'd seen. But the wall was solid stone, and I turned to my laughing killer with horror as he strolled back to the altar.

"I promise this will only hurt for a minute. Now, come to me, child." He flicked a finger, and my feet carried me toward him, unresisting.

I glanced up at the decayed teeth that colored the puppeteer's savage grin and gasped. "No."

Dela

"Good girl."

I could see the dark space of the door behind him. Xavier held a small twisted dagger in one hand and a clay bowl in the other as my feet stopped me well within his grasp. Suddenly a spark of neon aqua blazed in the blackness behind him. It was on the move, growing bigger, coming toward us.

I dragged my eyes back to Xavier, who snatched my wrist with icy fingers and made a small, slow incision with the knife. I screamed as pain far greater than the cut itself racked my body and he squeezed my wrist, forcing the gushing blood into the bowl. When it covered the bottom of the bowl, he stopped, satisfied. I clamped my hand around my wound, but warm thickness still oozed between my fingers as he slit and squeezed his own wrist. Blackish blood drizzled out of his wrist and into the bowl, slowing to a trickle on its own. He held up the bowl.

"Drink this," he ordered.

"No. Don't, please. I can't," I begged weakly.

"DRINK IT!"

My traitor body moved on its own again. I brought the rim to my lips, and hot blood touched my tongue. I pulled it away, gagging. Xavier yanked my head back and forced my mouth open, pouring the thick blood into my half-closed mouth. I choked as the sour, metallic contents flowed like lava down my throat. Xavier released me after the last drop and I fell to the floor, coughing. I struggled against his compulsion, my stomach trying to retch the horrible mixture up, and my throat closed against it.

I looked up at a loud thud, my stomach muscles still pulsing to get the foreign contents out, and caught sight of Xavier's body slamming into the wall across the room with another dull crunch. Lucas was suddenly at my side, swooping me up and out of the room before I could convince my arms to hold on to him.

Lucas's tattoo tinted our faces blue in the swallowing blackness of the hallway. I felt wet blood soaking the collar of his shirt and tried to press the wound more tightly against his back. Lucas had turned a corner when I heard the executioners' whispers.

"Lucas!" I warned as their voices got louder.

"Shh." He held me more closely to him as he sped into the darkness.

I was wondering how he could see in the dark when a barely visible executioner tackled Lucas from behind. I slipped from Lucas's hands and crashed against the wall with a crunch. The unknown band on my head clattered to the floor, and warm fluid dripped down my temple. I tried to get up, but my battered body refused.

I looked toward the blue glow that was Lucas, head throbbing. He was already standing, struggling to break free from the fleshy dead that clung to him like leeches. He looked up for me, but when he found me, a look of absolute fear changed his face. It frightened me.

"No!" he screamed, reaching for me, but a cold, thin grip cinched my ankle and pulled. I skidded back, stomach scraping the rock, hands scrambling for purchase as the cold grip dragged me into darkness.

"LUCAS!" I watched him, nails clawing against stone, until the glow of his tattoo was no longer visible.

I felt my body leave the ground and sail through ebony air to land like a ragdoll on damp stone. I winced at an excruciating pop in my right shoulder. I tried to push myself upright, legs kicked off to the side, but I fell to my side. My right collarbone ached, and the throbbing in my head was uncontrollable as Mictlan tried to get back in. The gash on my wrist stung as I listened to my short breaths and decided that this was a different room than the first. Its suffocating stillness felt smaller.

Then Xavier lit a wick and stepped over me, tiny flame in one hand and the dagger in the other. He set the candle in a wall niche above what I realized was another stone altar.

"First, the virgin must drink the blood. Next, the heart of the virgin," he chanted, and then he raised the dagger high and recited a phrase in another language.

"No," I cried, dizzy. "Don't do this, please."

His chanting continued, and some invisible force lifted me again and slammed me down onto the stone altar. Something cracked in my back, followed by withering pain, and I couldn't seem to catch my breath. My right collarbone was pulsing, screaming at me. I followed his dark figure around the room with fuzzy eyesight and black stars circling around.

"No, Xavier," I panted, choking on the blood curdling behind my throat.

At a jerk of his chin, my arms swept agonizingly up over my head, and he held them with one hand as his other brought the rust-colored blade down. It pierced my chest like a thousand burning blades. I screamed as the blade ate through my flesh. But as the burning ate deeper into my chest, an explosion jerked his hands away. My hands suddenly freed, I saw Xavier thrown against the wall beside the altar and pinned there by some unseen mass. The blood-tipped dagger fell to the floor.

"Tita!" he roared, flailing against the invisible force.

As he struggled to reach me, I tried to stand but just collapsed at the foot of the altar. The rushing wind felt warm on my chest, and I knew I was colder than I should be. Then Lucas was at my side, one arm behind my neck while the other brushed blood-sticky hair away from my chest. I gasped raggedly and watched him as he inspected the wound, afraid I was already slipping away. Without a glance at the pinned god, Lucas cradled me gently and fled.

He turned into a hall where gray light slanted in through tiny square windows. I looked through them. Dark clouds hovered low outside, creating a misty haze that foamed through the windows and dewed our skin. As he passed another niche, an arctic chill slithered around my wounded wrist and tugged. I screamed as the freezing tourniquet seemed to peel the flesh off my wrist and pulled my arm straight. Lucas raced into a hall too narrow for him to twist me away, and the hand dug harder into my torn skin.

"Dylan!" he roared over my screams, windows blurring to wisps as he ran with inhuman speed.

Rock exploded through the outer wall, firing shards like bullets around us. My ears rang with Xavier's angry screams, and the cold hand released me.

We were climbing now, Lucas's knees bashing into my throbbing back, and then we emerged atop the pyramid. The saturated air was warm on my freezing skin, which helped take the edge off the cold invading my core, but it was impossible to see anything in the thick clouds around us.

Lucas arrowed toward the edge of the roof, and I screamed, "Lucas, no!"

But he leaped. My stomach dropped as we arced away from the pyramid's point and then plummeted toward the inky waves of executioners surging below. Miraculously we hit grass, not grasping skeletal hands, and my heartbeat spiked as Lucas clenched me more tightly and we fled the infestation down a green-carpeted street.

The storm swirled angrily around the grass-covered stone buildings. I burrowed my face into his chest, legs hanging limply to the side, as lightning stabbed through the pursuing executioners. Suddenly Malik was running at our side in the tempest. Still the executioners gained ground, and as a shield of light blinded me, I felt Lucas's chest warm and wet with my blood. I dropped my head against him, feeling the last energy drain from me.

"Lucas, I'm so cold," I quavered.

"We're almost there, baby."

Just then heavy raindrops hit my skin, stinging in my open cuts like saltwater. I bit my lip and cringed, but ahead of us, in an open field roiling with gray smoke, I saw three blurry aqua lights glowing.

"Lucas, you've got something that belongs to me," came Xavier's raging voice from behind us.

I lifted my head to look over Lucas's shoulder. Xavier descended the ancient temple stairs slowly, hands outstretched, as if he expected Lucas to turn around and deliver me to him. Lucas held to his course, his family almost within reach, but there was a new coldness in my body that felt like icicles prickling through my numb limbs.

"Lucas, my connection isn't with Xavier. It's with Mictlan," I said feebly.

The calm pace of his heart, so close to my ear, picked up. "What?"

"Spare Xavier. He doesn't matter," I forced out with one precious breath, wondering if I'd have another chance to tell him.

The smoky field was an overgrown arena where moss-covered stairs ascended the perimeter like bleachers. The aqua glow resolved into Andrés, Valentina, and Gabriella, battling executioners in a whirl of gray dust. *Are Dylan and Tita hurt? Where are they?* It was hard to focus as dull cold invaded my brain.

Valentina was rushing toward us. "Is she hurt?" I heard her gasp as her eyes darted to my chest.

"Mom!" Gabriella shouted.

I swiveled my head to where dark creatures swarmed the green grass of the court. Gabriella was yards away, drawing another lethal arrow. She nocked it, aimed, and shot. Black dust exploded, and she reloaded as even more executioners advanced. Valentina looked murderous as she slammed her hands down. I closed my eyes, feeling the burn of bolts striking through every shadowed knot of sinew and bone that surrounded us. When the light turned gray again, I opened my eyes.

Andrés rose from the ground, shaking off the dust of the attackers that had pinned him down. "*Gracias, mi amor.*"

"Where's Tita?" Gabriella asked urgently as she joined us in the middle of the field.

"Right here," Tita called, running in from the direction Lucas and I had just come. Niya trailed her. "Xavier's on our tail."

"Zara's connection isn't with Xavier," Lucas cried.

"What?" Andrés asked in shock.

Valentina breathed deeply and touched Andrés's arm lightly. "*Amor*, let us call on Xquic then, *por favor*. Let us try."

Andrés glanced at Tita, questioning. "Is it possible?"

She nodded fervently. "It must be done quickly, though. Andrés, call on Xquic. Lucas, Dylan, and I will handle Xavier when she arrives. Valentina and Gabriella, you two keep us clear and wait for my word. As soon as I say so, you must seal the portal quickly or it won't work."

Andrés nodded and dashed into the fog.

Lucas lowered me to the ground. I tried to cling harder, my frail fingers digging into his skin, but a sudden riff of pressure made my hands jerk to my chest.

"Lucas, no. Don't leave me!" I whimpered, clasping my hands more tightly over my heart against the burning rain.

Thunder rolled through the clouds as Valentina prepared her defenses with a blank face. Niya and Malik pulled lips back to bare sharp teeth and roared, then bounded into the approaching front of executioners. Tita ran behind them, while Dylan raced around to catch them from behind. He struck with unbelievable speed, engaging one monster even as he yanked the heart from another's chest.

Lucas knelt by my side and gently swiped the hair out of my face. Then he looked up, and my eyes shifted to Xavier's pale figure walking down the broken street. Lucas stood with a vengeful snort.

"I have to finish this. You'll be fine with Mother," he reassured me, angling himself to stand between Xavier and me.

I reached up for him, but Lucas had already picked up a boulder.

With impossible speed, he threw it at Xavier. The impact pushed Xavier back twenty feet. Lucas had another already in hand.

"Good one, bro!" Dylan yelled from the court's green steps, hoisting another boulder. He aimed it at Xavier and threw without hesitation. I winced at the crunching sound of Xavier's body driven into the ground. Even if I wanted him to stay clear of us, the sound of shattering bone was too much.

Tita appeared at Lucas's side. "Push him back to the pyramid!"

But Xavier had cracked a stone off a ruin near his feet and barreled it at Lucas. Lucas caught it, barely protecting me from the blow, and chucked it right back with fresh-stoked anger. Xavier dodged, and it only nicked his shoulder, but he staggered forward as Dylan landed a slab on his back. Lucas and Dylan showered stone after stone upon him. I watched, aching, as he struggled to his feet and retreated, the other two in pursuit. Tita followed them, keeping the platoon of executioners off their backs.

As the distance between us grew, the horde of executioners grew denser, now a black wall around us. I squirmed as Valentina and Gabriella dealt death through the downpour. Niya and Malik were visible only as flashes of black in the field of smoky warriors. As Lucas, Dylan, and Xavier battled closer to the pyramid, increasingly clouded by fog, I grew doubtful. *I'm not losing Lucas over Xavier.*

"Gabriella," I wheezed, my vision weaker still in the falling sheets of water. "The arrows . . . shoot . . . Xavier."

"They won't work on him," she shouted back as she nocked and drew in one graceful motion and shot another attacker. "He's stronger now."

I glanced back at Lucas, afraid for his life. Then a gust of wind warmed me. I could see Andrés back in our circle, accompanying a woman with light caramel skin and black braided hair. When she turned to me, I held my breath. She was beautiful.

"This is her," Andrés said.

The 52nd

Xavier's mother came to me in a burst of wind, splattering raindrops against my face. She knelt by my side, indifferent to the rain, and looked into my face with piercing eyes.

"Do you know who I am?"

I forced a stiff nod of my head.

Her hand touched the soaking wound in my chest softly. Deep red greased her fingertips. She held it to her nose and sniffed. "Xavier grows stronger."

She stood and looked toward the battle in the distance. "I go now with them. Take the sacrifice; get her safe."

I did not expect the drumbeat that burst into my ears as Xavier made a move for me, coming through the storm like an unstoppable train. As I shrieked, Lucas intercepted and tackled him to the wet sod. There was a sudden ringing in my ears as Xquic rushed to them.

"Come with me, son," Xquic said.

A look of terror crossed Xavier's face, and he broke away and fled back toward the pyramid.

"The portal! Don't let him go through," Tita yelled in alarm, and Dylan, Tita, and Xquic vanished in pursuit.

The warm raindrops suddenly didn't sting, but instead made my eyelids heavy. My body relaxed into the numbness. It was a relief when my hand slid off my chest, to no longer have to hold it there, and I closed my eyes. Whiteness filled my head, and I wanted to float into it, away from the pain. Still, each time I inched closer to it, my body shook relentlessly and the agony returned.

"She's losing too much blood. Lucas, you have to take her now!" I heard Andrés demand, so far away, so faint. Fingers put pressure around my heart. I screamed in pain. "If you don't, she won't make it."

"Zara!" I felt Lucas's warmth by my side instantly. "No, no, no, no, no! You're going to be okay, I promise." He paused, his voice strained. "What about Xavier?"

"Dylan, Tita, and Xquic can take care of him," Andrés reasoned.

Dela

When Lucas paused again, I thought maybe I could slip back to the place of cloudy comfort, but his arms scooped down and pressed me firmly into him. I struggled to catch a breath as he took a step, squeezing my arms tightly against my throbbing ribs.

"Okay, cover me. We will see you back at the house," he said.

Then, as the rain seeped into my lips, into my eyes slit open enough to see the blur of passing trees, Lucas escaped with me into the dense jungle.

Lucas

CHAPTER TWENTY-FOUR

Anew

Rubble clattered loudly in my ears as I carried Zara southwest along the coast. I found the freeway and ran alongside its edge, keeping to the cover of the overgrown forest. The leaves brushed me like feathers as I sprinted. At my speed, it was impossible to avoid being hit. But I hunched my back and wrapped my arms more secure around Zara so that her skin wouldn't be clawed.

Zara was whimpering when a loud explosion came from Tajin, different than the clunking of stone on flesh. I glanced over my shoulder and looked up. Black smoke furled upward above the tree lines. *It's done. The portal is gone.* I spun around and ran harder.

I reached Tabasco an hour later and headed straight through a biosphere reserve, landing somewhere in the middle by the Grijalva River. Zara was losing consciousness and needed medical assistance, but without Dylan I couldn't chance anybody seeing us. I stayed away from the river, where locals and tourists would be boating, and moved deeper into the jungle. It was more swampland here. I slowed down when the mangroves grew dark and thick, and their tangled surface roots and dense thickets threatened to trip me.

Zara hadn't moved for the last twenty minutes. I knew her body was cooling fast by the deepening of her purple lips, but then a startling coolness zinged my skin. *Why am I feeling temperature?* When I heard wheezing coming from the gash in her chest, I stopped below a tree—my feet sinking in the sucking mud—and laid Zara across its knotty roots.

My stomach was still cool from her touch. My body tingled, wanting to test the tickle that urged me to have her. I shook my body, trying to free myself from this vulnerability. I wanted to reach for my citla, but my hand was covered with her blood . . . blood that never bothered me, until now. It was *Zara's* blood, and it ticked me off that my vulnerability had caused this. The vulnerability she wanted, that I'd finally wanted, and now I was losing her.

I checked the slashed flesh that poured her blood in a steady flow out of her chest and down her painted stomach. It was all over, swirls of red and white over her bare skin, worse now that my body had pressed against hers, smearing it in places it shouldn't be. My failing, and now my blue shirt was drenched black, stiff with both dried fluids, and the hairs on my arms had crusted crimson with her blood. But worse, the blood was bubbling. *Dammit, air is escaping.* A sign that either her lung was punctured or air was filling her pleural space. And I knew, if I didn't address the cut now, either her lung would collapse, or she would drown in her own blood.

Just as I stood to see what I could use, knowing the swamp was full of medicinal plants used when I was a boy, Zara coughed, and a spew of blood forced its way out and spattered my face. Then her throat gurgled as she struggled for air. I fell by her side and propped her head up. She exhaled, and more blood bubbled. *She was right. She's going to be so angry that I didn't listen.*

Her breathing was shallower. *I'm not going to lose you.* I needed to cover the gaping hole in her chest to close the air off, and my shirt wouldn't do. It would only cling to the blood and seal the incision, not leave any space for blood to escape. I needed a solid, waxy leaf, firm enough to hold its own against the raging blood flow. I gave the plants around me a hurried review. I was looking for a green plant with a ridged leaf. The shamans used it as a poultice to treat infections when wounded warriors returned from battle—if I remembered correctly. And I hoped that I did, because there were a lot of poisonous plants in these parts.

I spotted a plant some good paces away. I brought Zara with me, balancing her on one arm and plucking a few leaves, enough to cover the entire cut. As her inconsistent breaths graced my chest, I realized that I wanted to be wrong about a lot of things and have Zara point them all out. She'd stab her tiny finger at me and scorn me until her face turned blue, and I would smile back, squeeze her waist, and pull her close to me. I'd kiss her hard and not let her slip away, because I never wanted anyone but her to call my name.

I'd like very much to be vulnerable to her forever, but that day isn't today.

My keen ears listened for lurking predators in the swamp, particularly the crocodiles that infested these waters, as I set Zara down. When her back was flat against the ground, I noticed a bump over her right clavicle. At first I thought her collarbone was dislocated, but when her body jerked upward as she flinched from pain, it stayed behind and sagged, and a large bump had started to swell over the break. I raised her right arm slowly, cautiously, and a sharp point rose underneath the bump. I grunted, frustrated. *Her collarbone is broken.*

I examined the damage quickly. Blood vessels good, swelling minimal. This injury could wait.

Already running out of time, I needed to find a sappy tree. A quick scramble up the tree next to Zara revealed a grove of copal trees a half a mile away. I hopped down just as Zara choked for air. I propped her up into my arms—still and pale as if she were dead already—and sprinted through the trees.

On my way there, I spotted a small plant that bloomed pink flowers. *Antiseptic! Perfect to mix with the sap.* I snatched a few leaves and mulled them as best I could with one hand as I continued for the trees. The copal grove was packed tightly, so dense that not a sliver of sun broke through its umbrella of leaves and branches. I set Zara down and put my handful of pulverized leaves in my pocket, ready to dig underneath their trunks for fossilized sap, but the bark was blistered in bubbles of white resin. I scraped my fingers deep into the grain and scooped one off, then three more, until my hand was full and sticking together, and then rushed to Zara.

I pulled the uncrushed leaves from my pocket and laid them over her wound, quieting the sucking sound, and kneaded the sap and the ground herbs from my other pocket together between my fingers a few times before working it over the leaves' edges to bond them to her skin. Scent rose off the sap as it warmed—Mayans had burned copal as incense for centuries, to worship, to heal, to mourn the dead . . . I adhered the leaf all the way around and left a small hole on the bottom for the air to pass and the blood to leak out. I couldn't be sure if she needed a tube until I got home and had clean hands, and could really see how bad the bleeding was. I cradled Zara in my arms again, careful with her collarbone, and turned toward home.

My feet sank deep as I stood, and each step in the swampy mud took extra strength. Eventually I stopped treading on ground and leaped from root to root. It was easier to avoid the crocodiles that way, and for Zara, less rough. The jungle path was slower but more direct. Thirty minutes later, I reached a small gas station in Campeche with bathrooms at the back of the building.

Perfect, no one will see us.

My arms were slick with blood and clammy sweat. I propped Zara underneath the shade of a tree and rushed to the bathroom. I rinsed off only what I needed to have a better grip on her, dried my hands on my legs since there was no paper, and pulled my phone out of my back pocket and dialed Nicolás.

"Nico," I commanded when he picked up. "I'm coming with

Zara in twenty-five minutes. Move her family to the living room. They can't see her how she is . . . and probably not me, either . . . and she needs spare clothes . . . and I need my medical bag at her bedside." I was about to hang up, but added, "Wait, I need blood. I don't know what her blood type is. Tell the Aluxes to get it and have it waiting in the room."

I hung up and walked back to Zara. She looked like a paper doll: pale, ripped, fragile. I fought back tears, picked up her limp body, and resumed our journey. When I reached the beach, I picked up speed on the packed sand, racing until I saw Nicolás and Marifer waiting right outside the house. I stopped and fell to my knees. Zara's breath was weaker, and I had to lean my ear to her heart to hear it. Marifer rushed over and peeled the tangled, crusted hair off her chest. I could see again the leaf moving gently up and down as she breathed. The flow was much less now. It shocked me—I didn't expect the bleeding to stop at all, not if the wound was deep beyond repair. *He didn't sever an artery; there's a chance.* I shot back up and whisked her to the back door.

Nicolás abruptly raised his hand. "*No! Otra puerto, señor.*"

I rushed to the garage door instead, turning to Nicolás as he followed me. "Is her family not in the living room?"

"They are playing cards with Raul and Eugenio. But it is not them, it is Señor Max. He won't stop watching the back door."

I stopped briefly and glanced up to the doors that opened onto the balcony. Max was there, watching me through the glass. I froze and squeezed Zara a little more tightly into me. When Max didn't look down at her, I took another step, but he flashed away and the doors suddenly bounced as he tried to tug them open. The curse wouldn't lift until Tita got back; we'd have to deal with him inside.

My jaw tensed with irritation as I continued to move. "Keep him away from Zara's room for as long as possible. Marifer, come with me."

Dela

Marifer and I shot through the garage, up the stairs, and into Zara's bedroom before the garage door quietly shut. The room had everything we needed. A small cooler I assumed held the blood was sitting on the floor by the bed, next to my black leather medical bag. And there was a fresh nightgown on the nightstand.

"Marifer," I called, laying Zara across the sheets. Her head rolled to the side and her arms fell off her chest, unnaturally relaxed. I froze, and then the faintest beat of her heart echoed in my ears and I broke. "Watch her."

I rushed to the bathroom, scrubbed my arms and hands until the water ran clean, and ran back to the room. "Get a warm, damp towel and clean off the blood and paint around the wound," I ordered, grabbing my leather bag. I pulled out a pair of gloves and threw it to her and then put on a pair myself. As Marifer left for the bathroom, I used forceps to pick off the hardened clumps of sap across her breast. I imagined it would be painful for Zara, so I lifted it slowly, but she was unresponsive and I moved faster. I shut out all outside noise and listened only for her weak heartbeat. When the leaves were mostly loose, I held them in place with one hand while the other removed the smaller, stickier parts that I had missed.

Marifer returned and worked around my hands, slowly wiping the mixed layers of dried blood and white paint from Zara's chest. When she stepped away for a clean cloth, I carefully lifted the leaves off. Marifer grabbed them from me and put them in the trash. With both hands, I placed my first two fingers on either side of the gash and spread her skin apart slightly. I leaned in closer for a better look. The cut had gone through cartilage, but it didn't puncture her lung, and the bleeding was minimal now. *She'll need the bandage until the cartilage can heal and block the air from entering.*

Marifer returned and started cleaning another layer of blood. Moments later it was gone, and there was only a long slash across her left breast. I handed Marifer a sterile sponge and bottle of Betadine from my kit.

"Use this to clean around the wound," I said. "We'll stitch her when you're done."

As Marifer wiped gently around the wound, I reached for Zara's wrist. Then a loud shout erupted downstairs. Marifer looked at me.

"Quick, don't stop," I urged.

I looked back to Zara's wrist. It worried me again that I could feel the coolness of her skin underneath my fingers. I gulped. Her skin was ghostly white, enough to see her blue veins underneath. My stomach pulsed at the sight of Xavier's fingerprints bruised around the slit flesh. I wiped the area clean, rubbing around it with Betadine, wondering how she didn't die from this alone. The cut was not across, it was lengthwise, straight through half her artery. I pulled out a needle and thread and sewed the wound shut.

"Do not lie to me," Max yelled. He was still downstairs, but it was getting heated down there, and I knew he'd come looking for Zara soon.

"Marifer!" I yelled. She was staring at the door. "Look at me."

She glared back with wide eyes.

"We . . ."

The next sound jolted me. The low beat I was always listening for had stopped. Terrified, I looked back to Zara. Her face was slack. I panicked for half a second before I screamed, "Her heart stopped! Marifer, prep the blood IV!"

Careful of her clavicle, I crossed one hand over the other and started compressions on Zara's sternum. Her collarbone jutted at odd angles, her body jerked unnaturally, and blood sprayed out of her wound with each push. It caught me in the mouth as I counted in my head.

Marifer moved in and stabbed the syringe into Zara's inner elbow as I pumped her chest, harder—more consistently—expelling the air trapped in her pleural space all at once. There was a crack deep within her bones that made me cringe, but I didn't stop. "Prime the saline port!" *One, two, three.* "Then flush it and connect it to the IV, and crank it up to one hundred milliliters." *Come on, Zara. Come on!* I plugged Zara's nose and pushed air into her mouth.

Marifer carried out my orders as I thrust my hands down again. Somewhere between pumps her heart moved.

"Did you hear that!?" I gasped. "Come back to me, Zara."

Another soft beat graced my ears as Marifer connected the blood. Zara's torso flinched. Marifer and I froze, wondering if it was either of us.

"Wasn't me," I said. Zara's eyelids were closed, but her body convulsed again, and a shrieking scream erupted from her lips.

She wasn't awake, let alone able to feel the pain, but her body flopped on the bed like a fish out of water, clutching her right side below her sternum. And then I saw it: her rib. It was broken. A light swelling formed over it. I shuddered. *I* did this. It was only CPR, but I did this. I broke her. I had to—she was dead.

"Give me another IV," I demanded. Wetness glazed my eyes as she screamed again.

Marifer handed me a needle. "Hold her arm down," I said, directing the needle into a vein on Zara's free wrist.

"Morphine," I ordered next, holding my hand out. "Hurry, before she knocks out the blood line." Marifer handed me a small vial. I injected it into Zara's thrashing body, and we both stood back and waited. Her body went limp for half a second before the convulsions restarted.

"Ah!" I cried, frustrated.

I pulled out the line and started over. Another vial of morphine, and nothing. Her body was shaking uncontrollably, and her jaw was locking. I pulled the line and poked her two more times. Finally, after the last vial of a smaller dosage of morphine, her body steadied, though her legs remained restless. A small whimper hummed out of her mouth.

Zara was definitely in pain—that much I knew. But any more morphine would kill her, again. What mattered was that her heartbeat was coming back, steady, stronger.

"Fifteen minutes until I check vitals and any signs of a reaction," I said, wiping blood off my face.

I glanced at the silk sheets. It was like someone had poured a bucket of blood on Zara, and it splashed like spray paint around her. I looked back up to Zara's purpled chest. *How long have I wanted to see her naked, and this is what I get?* Battered, bruised, a small trail of blood oozing out of the uncovered wound? It made my stomach turn. I reached for the needle again and began sewing the chest cut.

At last I tied the knot at the end and looked to Marifer. "Get the others in here and take care of this mess. But watch her right clavicle when you clean her up, I'm afraid it's broken, and her rib below—I just broke that too. I'm going to shower. I'll be back to check her vitals."

I should have known better than to go out the door. I should have hopped over the balcony. I'd thought I had taken enough precautions. And yet Max was coming straight at me when I opened the door, Nicolás at his heels.

"Lucas!" Max yelled.

I froze, my eyes wide with guilt. I forced myself not to check the amount of blood on my clothes. Luckily it had drowned out most the white paint. Max had stopped cold seeing it, and then his vengeful eyes locked on me.

"What have you done with my sister?!" he shouted.

I angled my head enough to see Marifer and other Aluxes cleaning like busy little ants. Half of the bed was changed; the other half was waiting for Zara, who was sprawled on it with her drip while the ladies gave her a sponge bath worthy of the best hospital. Someone even had her hair swirling in a bucket while another shampooed her hair. I glanced back to Max.

"Zara is fine, Max," I said. "I called a doctor. He'll be here soon."

"Whose blood is that on you?" he snarled.

"A little of both." *Think, Lucas, think.* "I went for a jog this morning, and on my way back, I saw Zara stuck in a rip tide. She must have decided to swim alone. I swam out and got her. It was rough out there. We both got scraped up pretty bad. Marifer is with her now, getting her cleaned up. She's going to be okay, I promise." *He can't go in; he'll see the transfusion line.* I stepped closer to Max, blocking his view, and judged his face. He didn't flinch, so I started closing it slowly behind me. "They're going to be undressing her now." I looked down at myself. "And I need to get cleaned up too. Meet me here in fifteen minutes, and she'll be ready for visitors."

"Visitors?" he spat. "I'm her brother. I ain't no visitor. Zara! ZARA!" He stepped toward the door, but I blocked him.

"She can't hear you, Max."

"How come?"

Lie, Lucas. "She's a little out of it. She keeps repeating the same thing over and over." My hand tightened on the knob, ready to slam it in his face should he move one more step, but maybe . . . I moved clear of the door and raised my hands, defenseless. "But help yourself then . . . if you're the kind of person who likes to see his sister naked."

He sidestepped to me. "What did you just say?"

I took a chance by stepping farther from him and closer to my door. "Fifteen minutes," I bargained, and then I darted for my room.

He stomped to the wall, leaned against it, and sat down. "You're not wet," he hollered at my back. I stopped midway through my door.

"What?"

"You said you saved her in the ocean. The only drop of wetness your clothes have is with blood. I know you're lying."

I broke my shock with a laugh. I glared at him with months of suppressed revulsion. *It was me, Max, who saved your sister from something so horrifying you'd piss your pants if you could only see. It was me, Max, who saved her from having her living heart ripped out of her chest.* "Your sister is safer now than she has been the last three months."

He looked as if he didn't care—or didn't believe me. He kept bumping the back of his head against the wall as if he were bored. It was weird. Then he laughed cynically. I didn't like it. "Zara will tell me the truth."

I shook my head. "I suppose she will."

When I returned in fresh clothes, Max wasn't there anymore; Zara's door was wide open. I ran inside it. Max was standing by Zara, who was tucked underneath sparkling clean sheets with no sign of an IV. Max was still, though his eyes flicked incessantly back and forth from Marifer to Zara.

Zara's eyes were still closed and she looked peaceful, but there was a startling paleness about her. She needed to have more blood. Max had to leave.

"See, Max," I said as he turned to me. "Zara is okay."

"Why is she asleep? Did you knock her out with some drugs or something?"

I ignored him momentarily, even when his nostrils flared. He was such an idiot. "Marifer, please go tell the Mosses that Zara got hurt and that she is up here . . . and safe." I turned to Max to satisfy him for now. "Marifer must have given her painkillers. She's a nurse; she always has that sort of stuff lying around."

"How come you're not hurt?" Max asked suspiciously as Marifer left.

"Because *I* know how to swim in a tide."

He looked out the windows down to the beach. The corners of his mouth drooped into a frown. "That is not anything like what you're describing."

Zara's stomach started convulsing as if she were going to cough. I was worried it'd be blood. "Despite how you feel about me, Zara knows I would never do anything to hurt her. What I am telling you is the truth." I glanced at my clock. Vital time. I snagged Lupe, the Alux cleaning the bathroom, and asked her in our native tongue to perform the check. Me doing it would be too suspicious—as far as Max knew, I was only an undergrad. Max watched Lupe grab the clipboard on the nightstand and assess Zara's blood pressure and heart rate.

"What's she doing?"

"Checking her vitals."

"Is everyone a nurse around here?"

"They went to school together."

"I don't like—"

"Look! If you're going to be in here, could you please not talk? You're not helping the situation."

Max ground his teeth and stormed out the door. I shot up and dragged the medical equipment from the closet back to Zara. I uncovered her arm underneath the sheet, plugged in the tubes, and started the drip. Afterwards I pictured what other things could have gone wrong as I watched her chest rise with its low pulse. *You were dead,* muñeca, *and still you are here with me, still fighting.*

The fight in her made me realize that Zara was made for me, and I loved her more for not leaving me.

I left the beautiful thought and tried calling Andrés.

"Lupe, has anyone been in contact with my family?" I asked as my cell beeped out of service. I flipped the TV on and turned to the news. It was exploding with coverage of Tajin. *Huitzilihuitl will definitely hear about this.* Fear hollowed my core—*Huitzilihuitl will pay us a visit soon.*

"They arrive in five minutes."

"Thank you, Lupe." I sat next to Zara on the edge of the bed, lifted up the sheets and blankets, and peeked underneath. Her belly was covered again by a short satin nightgown. A gauzy bandage over the cut showed under the shoulder strap. It was turning pink in the center.

"*Todo bien,*" Lupe said.

I held Zara's hand. "*Gracias.*"

The images on the channel were disturbing to the locals but heart pleasing to me. I stared at the damage my family did until they returned home. The Pyramid of the Niches was collapsed and burning, the surrounding buildings were tattered, the stones we'd torn out of them littered throughout the park, but the Tlatchi courts where the executioners had swarmed us were deserted.

Zara's door swung open.

"Lucas!" Valentina rushed over and threw her arms around me as I stood.

"Mama."

"Zara?" Gabriella asked, walking in with Dylan and Andrés.

My eyes swelled. I put my hand in my pocket and spun my citla. "She will be okay once the transfusion is done."

"Why isn't she awake?"

"Because she is in a coma. She will wake up when she is ready."

"How long can that be?"

I shook my head. "I don't know." I spun around to Father. "Are we safe? Is Zara safe?"

"Xavier went with his mother, and the portal is demolished," he said. He turned to the television. "We should expect a visit from Huitzilihuitl."

Chairs scraped across the floor downstairs, and the muffled sounds loudened into clear sentences. Zara's family moved toward us in a panic.

"Esteban, we need you," I called. The Alux appeared next to me in a second, wearing black slacks and a polo shirt.

"Everyone come with me downstairs. We'll sneak out the back and wait outside for Huitzilihuitl to show up," Andrés directed.

"Esteban, come downstairs and go through the front door like a normal doctor would. Lucas, stay here with Zara. Her parents are going to want answers—which you have already, I presume?"

I shrugged. "I saved Zara from a riptide."

Dylan laughed and pointed his fingers outside. "From those baby waves? Seriously, you couldn't think of anything better?"

"I didn't have time, Dylan. Max was waiting for me when I got home."

"Dylan, shh. It will work," Valentina said. The noises were moving up the first flight of stairs. "Let's move."

As they hurried out, I checked the transfusion. Zara had taken nearly the entire bag. Color was returning in her cheeks. I unhooked the blood bag and stored it in the cooler, which had been hidden in the bathroom shower. *I'll give her more later tonight.*

I ran over and sat next to Zara on the bed just as her family walked in. Her mom gasped and ran over.

"Zara!" she cried.

"I was jogging, and I saw her in the ocean by herself. I could see she couldn't get out, so I ran in there and got her," I lied.

"Why would she go out in a storm alone?" Mitch asked. *Storm? Good, my story should work out.*

"I don't know." I lowered my head. "I'm so sorry. This is my fault. I shouldn't have left her on her own."

Mitch placed a hand on my shoulder. "You did fine, son."

I could hear Max behind me, his heart rate picking up. "Dad, you believe him?"

"Why wouldn't I?"

I peeked over at Max behind my shoulder. His face was red with anger. Casey stood next to him, confusion arching his eyebrows. "What's wrong with you, Max?" he asked.

Max glared at me two whole seconds before he huffed and stormed out of the room again.

"Did I do something wrong?" I asked.

"No, no, honey," Mrs. Moss said, sitting on the other side of the bed. Her eyes never left Zara. "Does Zara need to go to the hospital?"

Just then the doorbell rang. A minute later Esteban walked in, and I felt the stress in the room dissipating.

"This is Doctor Esteban," I said. "He's an old friend who works in the ER in Merida. I called him to come over and take a look at Zara."

"Oh, thank you," Mrs. Moss said, moving over so Esteban could do his "job."

Esteban did a few assessments, checked her vitals, and asked me questions in Spanish. He turned to her parents and explained in English, "Zara is in a coma, but she will most likely be out of it in a few days. I wouldn't recommend moving her, as long as you have a nurse watching her around the clock and giving me updated vital stats. She has some cuts and bruises, and her collarbone is broken. Unfortunately, for those kinds of breaks, there really is nothing I can do. The break isn't bad enough to need surgery, so she just needs to keep her arm in a sling for eight weeks. She will need to rest quietly while she heals, and I will send some painkillers for when she wakes up."

He did his job with comforting them, but he lied. We didn't know *when* Zara would wake up. And he didn't comfort me. *I* was the one who broke her bone.

The Mosses were asking more questions, and I was looking at the new bump on her chest, half covered by the sheets, when my ears caught the sound of Tez and Huitzilihuitl's arrival. It was dulled by distance, maybe a quarter mile away on the beach. I looked around for Marifer, and she appeared as if from thin air by the long dresser behind the Mosses.

"Mr. and Mrs. Moss, you've met Marifer." I lifted my chin to point her out. "She is an RN. She will look after Zara so that she can rest here in our home." I pulled the sheets up to Zara's neck and patted the side lightly, and then I stood.

"I will give you some time alone," I said. Marifer and Esteban silently asked what I wanted them to do. I switched to their Mayan language to tell them, "Don't let the sheets come down. Don't let them see her wounds." Marifer bowed her chin and stood against the bed with the Mosses while Esteban busied himself with Zara's bandaged wrist, conveniently keeping her family at a distance.

Huitzilihuitl and Tez were standing with my family and Tita in a circle by the water, out of view of the house.

I nodded. "Huitzilihuitl. Tez."

"Lucas." They nodded.

I glanced back to my family, glad to see they looked well and not as damaged as I expected. One look at the others, though, made me exhausted. Huitzilihuitl, stained and reeking of oil again, and Tez, slick and clean, with tired yet very sharp eyes, made me wish for a new life. I didn't want a laborious life. I wanted a free life. Free to love, free to speak, free to feel—a life with purpose. I wanted to sit on a country porch and play guitar as children ran around, to watch the sunset with Zara, counting each, knowing they were numbered in our short lives, savoring each one more than the last. I would not have *that* life, not with my invisible bonds, but I could give myself to Zara—serve her—for one human lifespan and still feel freer, more alive, than I ever would in the rest of my eternity. I felt anew because I *chose* Zara. And I supposed I always had.

"It has been explained to me that Xavier is out," Huitzilihuitl said, shifting his gaze to Andrés.

"Yes. He won't be a problem anymore."

Perhaps I spoke as if this were a light topic. Huitzilihuitl's face burst with anger at my undermining comment. I looked to the ground.

"Where is the sacrifice?" he asked.

My throat tightened. I glanced at Andrés to make sure it was okay to speak freely. He nodded. "Inside, being watched over by her family and two Aluxes," I answered carefully.

He folded his large arms across his chest. "Do the humans know our secrets?"

"No."

"Explain . . . spare no details."

I recounted everything, from Tita's vision to all that had happened in the past year. The pad of his wide thumb rubbed his chin as he listened. When I finished, he looked to my family and then to Tita.

"Now I will explain something to you. I don't trust witches; I *hate* witches. And now I don't trust you." My body tensed, and Tita froze. I watched the muscles around her eyes deepen with sadness. "But I have been told that Xibalba has been experiencing certain tremors. They grow weaker." He studied me a moment. "I believe it is because of you, and this . . ."

"Zara," I said.

A low grumble escaped his mouth. ". . . this girl, with you, starts these tremors. I do *not* believe in prophecies that come from witches, but I believe in fate. Everyone will get what they deserve. Mictlan got what he deserved, and we will too. We broke a binding agreement. We stole from Mictlan. There will be a price to pay."

"Why? Why do we have to pay the price for someone else's wrong?"

"Someone else's wrong? You stole from him! You lied to ME!"

"Don't hurt her," I pleaded.

"*Silencio,* Lucas! We are not thieves; we pay for what we take."

"Don't give her to him, I beg you!"

"I've made my law . . ."

"*Your* law? Isn't this supposed to be *our* law? You don't represent the others; you represent yourself!" I shouted.

"Lucas! Watch your tongue," Valentina snapped.

I fell to my knees. The sand was powder, damp with my tears. "Huitzilihuitl, do not make this mistake. Give me a chance to show you."

"Lucas," he spat, his face disgusted. "I am *not* giving her up. You are keeping her."

"What?"

"Why would I give up a possession that can make Xibalba tremble?"

I sniffed. "Then what do you mean, 'price to pay'?"

"The portal is closed, and I cannot reopen it. The sacrifices will no longer take place. The *price*, Lucas, will be the price of breaking our agreement."

"What will that be?"

"A wrath of revenge." A sickening calmness controlled him. He rubbed one hand over the other in slow motion.

"How? They have no way of getting to us. The Milky Way has passed."

"They do not now. But they will, I assure you."

Tez's footprints in the sand flooded as he stepped deeper into our circle. "Lucas, the Council agreed to let you keep the girl, contingent upon you further exploring your connection and reporting to us. She will be our greatest weapon, and when they return, we will need her."

It was hard to hear Zara being called a *weapon*. Tez was on my side, but he didn't know the side effects of Zara's ability. I shuddered, remembering Zara collapsing before the mental assaults. The girl was just a girl, not a weapon.

"What if they come after she has already grown old and died? What then?" I wondered.

"You die first, then your family, then we come up with another arrangement before they bring war on us."

"One that doesn't involve people dying, please," Gabriella said.

"Gabriella," Dylan said. "After we've done this, they won't take anything but."

"What about bloodletting?" she asked, hopeful.

"No, babe."

An unexpected laugh choked my throat. "It wouldn't matter because we'd be dead." *More like murdered.*

Gabriella frowned and turned to me with a determination made of pure fear. "Lucas, you love that girl so hard your heart hurts." Her voice shook, and strands of hair flew over her face. She cinched it into a ponytail in one hand and brushed the strays away with the other. "Keep her. You hear me? Otherwise, I'll kill you myself."

I blinked at her, then switched my attention to Huitzilihuitl with a crazy notion. "Do I have permission to marry her, Huitzilihuitl?"

"You want to marry her?" He laughed. I gulped back a ball of pressure and let the joy of proposing root a new stress inside me. I had heard of men becoming sick with worry whether a woman would say yes. I was beginning to feel the same, only worse. If Zara said no, I'd face denial and possibly death. *But then again, if she says no, I'd rather be dead anyway.*

"Huit, look at Valentina and Andrés. Chac admires them, god and human together, and they have served us well thus far," Tez said, eying me carefully afterward. I understood now that he was here for damage control, in case Huitzilihuitl acted against us. I was glad he was here. "This girl is our weapon; she needs the proper care to grow, doesn't she?"

Huitzilihuitl whipped around. His mouth shrank like a fish's as his black eyebrows slanted in. "Mulac doesn't know anything about caring for a woman. And she isn't here so you can sleep with her. The *only* reason she is still here is because she is our weapon."

"I agree, she is special," I said. "But in order for Zara to *grow* as you wish, she must grow into a woman first . . . sexually too. When that time comes, it will be me who lies with her. No one else. I can help her. Let me try . . . and . . . I *will* take care of her."

"How do you know this?"

"Because I have felt it."

"And I have seen it," Tez added.

"The girl does no good to us alone. The connection must be bound," Tita abruptly said.

Huitzilihuitl looked away from her in contempt. "Why?"

I could tell his cruelty toward Tita was another slash at her self-worth, but she stood tall, her hair still spiked from battle. "Security."

"I will watch and make sure Lucas keeps his end of the deal," Andrés said as a wave splashed around his ankles. But this wasn't a *deal*; this was my decision. I loved Zara and wanted this.

Huitzilihuitl grunted and said, "*Don't* disappoint me." And then he vanished.

Dylan's laughter broke our silence. "This has got to be the biggest pressure any man has ever had to marry a woman. I do not envy you, brother."

I swallowed, nearly choking with shock that we had stopped the sacrifices, and Zara and I were still alive, and that it was actually *okay* to love each other and even marry. I stared off into the limitless turquoise water, unable to fathom it all. My shackles were gone. I could breathe. A torrent of gratitude suddenly made me quiver. I stretched my back and stood taller. Today would mark my last day in hell, and my first of utopia.

Zara

Chapter Twenty-Five

Meant but Never Said

I drifted into the expanding whiteness until I was back in Tahoe at the wintery pond. I walked along the edge slowly, watching white butterflies land on the silver lily pads. I saw a pair of bright blue eyes staring at me through the aspens.

I followed them, wondering why the observer looked so familiar. I stopped and circled the soft snow where they had appeared, searching for anything with a tint of blue.

"Zara," a voice said behind me.

I flipped around and he was there, taller than me, hair as dark as ebony. I knew this man. His name was on the tip of my tongue. He reached for me with smooth hands, and mine felt rough and callused against them.

"Zara," he whispered again. "Come back to me."

Then the dark angel bent his head and touched his lips to mine, sending a surge of electricity rippling through my body. I broke away and touched my poisoned lips, shocked.

"Come home," he said, anguished, and then he vanished.

Whiteness consumed me again, and I floated into nothingness. The poison of his kiss streamed downward and set my heart to aching. But I wanted more. I wanted more of his poison; I wanted him. *What is his name?* It irked me until one memory arose in my mind.

I glanced at my arm. The aqua heart glowed in the silver light. I stroked it, feeling his warm, gentle touch when he put it there. I closed my eyes, remembering. He and I walking along the beach at night, the fine sand squeezing in between our toes while the water glittered bright blue. Him bending down to touch the water, his finger glowing as he lifted it. Him scribbling on my arm, producing a heart that blazed aqua in the night. *Mi princesa*, he said.

Lucas!

My throat scratched as I struggled to say his name. A deep, catching breath brought in fresh air and the scent of laundry detergent. I cracked my eyes open and squinted down at myself. White satin pajamas robed my aching body. A fuzzy figure moved at my side. I squinted at it, trying to force my eyes to adjust to the bright light.

"She's awake," Lucas said. He turned. "Go get her parents."

I tried to identify the dark figures at his left, but they fled too quickly.

His warm hand quickly filled the space in mine. "I'm right here."

My head felt like it weighed a thousand pounds, and it pounded horrifically when I moved.

"Be still. You got beat up pretty bad," he said, brushing hair gently off my cheek.

"Is Xavier . . .?" I whispered.

Lucas nodded.

I choked down a cry. "And the portal?"

"Yes."

"And Xquic?"

"We were lucky that she persuaded Xavier to go. Dylan and Tita were close to destroying him."

"Are you safe from the Council?" I asked.

"As far as I know, yes."

the 52nd

An overwhelming sense of relief eased some of the pain, but then the image of Max running from my room brought the anxiety rushing back. "Max," I gasped. "He went to go get Nicolás for help."

My head itched. I raised my hand to scratch, but pain stabbed across my upper chest and my hand stopped short. I moaned.

Lucas softly pulled my hand away and laid it back on the bed. "You need time to heal. Those have to stay on there, and don't raise your arm. Your collarbone is broken . . . and a rib."

"What's that?" There were puncture wounds in my undamaged wrist.

He stroked the bruises gently before looking away. "Your parents will be here soon."

My heart skipped. *How can I think of a lie to cover this up?*

"It's okay," he said. "You drowned. The tide took you pretty hard. You got cut up when it thrashed you down into the reef."

"How did I get out?" I wondered, catching on to his raised eyebrow.

His troubled face broke into an endearing smile. "I saved you, of course. That's five now."

He sat gingerly on the edge of my bed as I secretly counted.

"What day is it?" I asked.

"Two days after Christmas."

I began to sob, imagining my poor brother. "What about Max? I disappeared from my bed, Lucas."

"When I showed up with you at the house, Nicolás warned me that Max was involved, with a little too much information," Lucas said. I didn't like his reprimanding tone.

"Sorry. Nicolás was ignoring me," I said defensively.

"On my orders."

"Yeah, well, your plan didn't exactly work as agreed, did it?"

There was a tickling sensation on the inside of my fingers, where Lucas had settled his hand again. There was grief in his eyes. "Zara, everything I did was to protect you. If I'd known that he could take you . . . this wouldn't have happened."

I gazed away, embarrassed to seem ungrateful but still angry, and realized just how much gauze covered my body beneath the silk. Lucas was already holding up a small mirror when I looked up. The first thing I noticed was the cloth wrapped tightly around my forehead and a scrape along my cheekbone. The wound left by Xavier's dagger over my left breast was bandaged and taped. Thick white gauze encircled my wrist, a slight pink tint marking the surface. The disturbing dark impression of fingers spread from beneath the dressing, and similar purple spots marked much of my body.

"You're lucky you didn't break your back," Lucas said, picking up a roll of gauze. He lifted my wrist and gently wrapped a fresh layer over the fingerprints. "We can't let anyone see this."

Everything throbbed. I wondered why I wasn't healing fast like before.

"What is wrong with my body?" I asked, shifting to a more comfortable position.

"You suffered a concussion, broke your collarbone, broke a rib. And . . ."

"And what?"

"You died, Zara. I had to resuscitate you," he said gravely. "We took blood from a local hospital and gave you a transfusion."

"Am I curable?" I asked, worry compounding when I breathed in deeply and felt a sharp pain in my ribs.

"You mean will you heal fast?" He shook his head apologetically.

I wanted to cry when I couldn't breathe in all the way. "Why not?"

"Did you drink Xavier's blood?" he asked.

"He made me."

"Xavier was trying to rid himself of the curse, but it bonded you two."

I gasped sharply, then gasped again as pain shrieked through my torso. "What?"

"Only for the time being. But Dylan's power will only work on humans."

"What are you saying? That I'm not human anymore?"

There was light laughter suddenly. "You will always be human, but you have a god's blood inside you. Until your blood runs clear, your body won't allow Dylan to change it."

"Will morphine work, at least?"

He looked toward the puncture wounds over the veins on my wrist. "We've already tried two days' worth of doses. It didn't take—that's why we took the IV out."

I slouched with despair.

"So what did you tell Max when you got home?"

He fixed his gaze on me and interlaced our fingers before speaking. "When I got home, Max wasn't exactly talkative. He saw me outside holding you, and saw all the blood on my clothes. He knew something was up, but I only told him that I saved you from a tide. Your parents didn't see anything until you were already cleaned up and in bed. I told them the same, that you tried to go for a swim in the middle of a rainstorm, and that I had to get you out of it. Max still hasn't said anything to anyone, but I know he is spooked. You scared him pretty bad. I mean, I would be too, if my sister was telling me to run for help and then disappeared to who knows where, only to return wounded and unconscious in the hands of a stranger."

His tone held subtle sympathy for Max. My nose scrunched at my hideous behavior. He was right, and considering how awful I looked and felt now, I could only imagine how Max felt when Lucas brought me in, bloody and mostly dead. "Has he seen me yet?"

"He came as soon as I got home with you."

I suddenly remembered that I'd left the temple naked, except for that awful loincloth. "Was I decent? I mean, was I still in . . ."

Lucas sighed, flashing a tender smile, and kissed the bandage on my wrist. "No."

My body warmed as I flushed in embarrassment. "How did I get into these clothes?"

Lucas chuckled quietly. "I wish I could say it was me, but unfortunately it wasn't. Marifer changed you so that your family wouldn't see you like that. I may be bad, but I am still a gentleman."

As I snickered with him, my heart swelled with gratitude for Marifer.

"Max is torn over everything," Lucas said. "He believed you earlier—that something was wrong—so he doesn't believe that you were trying to go for a swim in the storm. He's your brother, Zara. I don't want to ruin your relationship with him, and we didn't want to . . . intervene with him unless you want us to. If you need Dylan to help, he will, but I thought you wouldn't want that. We are leaving Max up to you, to tell him what you think is necessary. Just know that nothing good can come from him knowing even the slightest bit of truth."

"I know."

Right then I decided to lie to protect him. I had a funny feeling in my stomach. I knew he'd be hard to persuade, but I had to try. I couldn't have his mind tampered with.

Lucas's face suddenly went bland, and he stood abruptly and turned his back to me. My eyes wandered to the door, where my family waited.

"Come in," I said hoarsely.

My eyes watered when Max entered. His shaggy hair looked greasy, sticking out from his baseball cap. His face had been wrung dry of expression, leaving only confusion as he stood back against the wall, watching me as if I were a ghost. A large lump in my throat prevented me from talking. *This is going to be harder than I thought.*

Mom sat at my side. "How are you feeling, hon?"

"I've been better."

"You are so lucky Lucas came home when he did. We probably would have never found you," she griped, attempting cheer. Her eyes were sunken with exhaustion.

"I know, Mom. I'm so sorry." Max shook his head in the back, calling me on my lie. I flicked my guilty eyes away.

"I'm just happy you're okay," Mom said, wrapping her arms around my neck.

I screamed as pain racked me from my collarbone down to my ribs. She rocketed up and covered her mouth.

"I'm so sorry," she cried into cupped hands.

Dad patted her slouched shoulders, then took the bunched seat at my side, kissing the bandage on my forehead as he did. "Merry Christmas, honey."

"Merry Christmas, Dad."

He looked happier than the others. "I can't wait to show you all the pictures we took."

"Me too."

It was nice to smile back. It was the one thing that didn't hurt.

"I'm sorry you had to miss out on so much," he said.

"Dad, it's okay. Really. It's entirely my fault. I was just being stupid."

"Maybe. You're lucky Lucas got you out," he said, getting off the bed.

Casey moved into his spot. It was disgraceful how he scanned me head to toe with a sly, disgusted smirk. "How you feeling, sis?"

"What do you think?"

There were wrinkles on his forehead when he smiled. "No offense, but Jett is going to hear about this one. This definitely wasn't your smartest moment."

"I know, I figured." I sighed.

Max moved up behind Casey, glaring accusations at me, but then he shook his head and ran out the door.

I froze, wanting to get up and run after him, but I couldn't even wiggle my toes. Lucas chased after him, and I began to tear up.

"We should probably let Zara rest," Andrés said quickly, noticing the water gathering in my eyes. "Marifer will keep an eye on her while we get some food into the rest of us. Zara will be fine. Please, let's go get you all some dinner."

Mom wiggled out of Dad's embrace and kissed me softly on my uncut cheek. "Get some rest," she said. "I'll check back on you soon."

When the last of them had left, Andrés bent over and applied a gentle kiss over Mom's. "I'm glad you are okay."

"Thank you, Andrés," I sniffled.

Valentina followed with the same light kiss, but she left her hands delicately on my skin. "I knew you were tough, but it's important that you get your rest now."

But I knew that I couldn't rest until I knew one thing. "Where did Xavier and Xquic go?"

"To Peru, for now." She paused, reading the fear in my eyes. "They will not come after you. I swear to it. Now rest, my child."

As Valentina left with Andrés, Gabriella moved to my side with happy tears. Dylan stood next to her with his arms crossed.

"Zara, you made it," she said.

"Barely."

Dylan's emerald eyes were kind and inviting as he stepped closer, the complete opposite of Xavier's harsh coldness. "What did Xavier say to you, Zara?"

"Tita's spell didn't keep him out because his body and soul were separate."

Dylan dropped into the chair against the wall in full concentration, resting his chin on a balled fist and tapping his foot. "He was stronger than I thought, that little bastard."

Then he stood, directed a torrent of Spanish at Gabriella, and headed out the door.

"Dylan," I called to his back.

He stopped short of the door and turned.

"I'm sorry about your brother."

There was a distracted glaze over his nod, and then he left.

I looked around for pain pills, hoping they'd work better than the useless morphine. As I spotted a small orange bottle on the dresser, Gabriella grabbed it and passed me three.

"It won't do much, but it should take the edge off," she said, handing me a cup of water.

"Thanks."

She sat at the edge of the bed, her large brown eyes watching me too closely as I swallowed.

"What?" I asked.

"Just wondering what you will choose to do next."

"What do you mean?"

She shoved her feet forward, suddenly antsy, then chuckled silently to herself and looked up. "You haven't just stolen Lucas's heart. We all love you. We don't want to lose you."

I scratched my reeling head, wondering whether the pills could have kicked in that fast.

"Oh, I, uh . . ." I remembered drowsily Lucas saying his family could hear us in the bedroom. I snickered with equal parts embarrassment and curiosity. "Did you hear us the other night?"

She stood with a grin, pulled the loose sheets up over my satin-and-gauze-wrapped body, and tucked them softly underneath. "There's nothing wrong with love, especially when Lucas was broken for so long." She walked to the arch of the door and, holding the jamb, glanced back. "You've given him a reason to be fixed."

I lay still as the words sank in.

"Good night, Zara," she said, and then left me alone.

Once her words faded from my restless mind, I dozed and

slipped into a deep sleep. When I woke, Lucas was lying next to me on the bed. It was dark and the house was quiet. As I tried to make myself more comfortable, his lips suddenly pressed to mine, sending gentle sparks throughout my body.

"Good morning, sleepyhead," he whispered softly.

I rubbed my eyes and yawned. "How long have you been here?"

"I came right after you fell asleep."

I tried to look for a clock, but my injuries restricted my movement. "What time is it?"

"Three in the morning."

"How long have I been out for?"

"Twelve hours. How are you feeling?"

My bloodied bandages had been changed, glowing whiter in the dark, and I was in clean pajamas. I eyed Lucas with a curious accusation.

He pointed to his chest and laughed as he shook his head. "It wasn't me."

"Do you want to?" Something about knowing he could have taken advantage of me built an unnerving excitement.

He messed with his hair, an arrogant grin spreading across his face that stretched his dimple beautifully. "Trust me, I tried, but Marifer wasn't having it."

"Well then, I will have to remember to thank her for that." Then I remembered the ridiculous wrapping and sticky misery of the pyramid. "What *was* on me in the pyramid?"

His porcelain teeth flashed in the dark. "When the people of my time offered virgins as sacrifices, they painted them white and dressed them in red. The two together to symbolize what was then and what is now. The white symbolized their purity and the red represented the act they were about to perform, giving themselves—their lives—to death."

I gulped against the hard pit of nausea that wanted to spread throughout me. "And what was on my head?"

"A feather crown," he said.

"Feathers? It didn't feel like feathers at all. That thing was so heavy."

"And gold," he added with a chuckle. "You've seen mine. Try lifting it sometime."

"No, thank you."

His fingers gently brushed the surface of my arm, easing away my disgust, and I sighed with pleasure. The rest of the night we laughed over the hideous wardrobe faux pas we'd had as children. We argued about whose clothes were more awful, though it was hard to compare the nineteen nineties to the fifteenth century. Lucas finally caved when I pointed out that he practically grew up naked, and then we agreed that the nineties were not kind to either of us.

Soon light seeped over the horizon, pouring a beautiful orange light into the room. The house was still quiet. Only the ocean waves were audible when Lucas left my bed and bent down over me with his arms outstretched.

"What are you doing?" I said, as he tucked me lightly into him. I winced at first, but then his outer arm moved enough to not press so tightly and his steps didn't jar me.

"We're watching the sunrise," he answered, and he carried me down the stairs.

"Lucas, my parents are going to see."

He hushed me. "They are asleep. Stop talking, or they'll wake up."

I shut my mouth as he passed the kitchen. The double glass doors had been left wide open, letting the fresh breeze blow inside. I smelled sweet water as Lucas trekked across the sand toward the sea. A copse of palms and bushes gave us privacy, and we were far enough away that my family, at least, wouldn't be able to hear us from the house. Lucas set me down carefully under the curve of a palm.

Dela

The black ocean was lightening as rays peeked over the edge of the water. I couldn't take my eyes off the colors blooming in the sky.

"This is my favorite place to watch the sunrise," Lucas said, resting his elbows on his knees.

"It's so pretty."

Lucas turned to me. "Max won't talk to me. Other than to say it's all my fault."

"But that's stupid," I said, distress coloring my voice.

"Is it?"

"Yes."

"Zara, none of this would have happened if I had just listened to you." He choked and barely clamped down his rising emotions. "I almost lost you."

"I'm okay now, and Max can't ignore me forever. I'm his sister!" I declared.

Lucas looked away again to the horizon. "Zara, he's a guy. You need to give him time."

"Maybe you're right," I muttered.

"I know I'm right. I speak guy."

"Oh, is that a new language you invented?"

"Nah. It's always been around. Only guys would understand it, though."

When I didn't answer, Lucas turned to me with a serious expression. And as the sun rose in the distance, he cupped my cheeks carefully and kissed me with every reason in the universe. There was no more fear in his lips, and the kisses left words on my heart, as if setting his love in stone.

Our lips popped when he broke away.

"Whatever it takes to keep you, I will do. Just tell me what to do. Whatever I meant but never said when I first met you, I'm saying it now. I will wait for you forever and serve you in all your remaining days. Choose where you want to live, and I will follow. I am yours.

I'll rub your feet every night for the rest of your life if you want, and you have my blessing on whatever it is you desire. I'll build a mansion for you, or an army—" he promised, sounding nearly scared.

I cut him short when I cupped his scruff gently and smiled, honored. "How about college?"

"It's yours . . . but I'm paying your way."

"I'm sure we can work something out."

He looked happily away into the sunrise and sighed. "I had to make sure you saw this at least once before we go home."

"We're going home?"

"Yes. You need to be at home in your own bed, where your mom can take care of you. As much as I would love to be crazy and run off together, we need to act like a normal couple would. And it's critical that you act your age." He kissed my forehead and sniffed. "But I don't want you to. I want to be the old couple already. I want to surprise you with trips to Paris and new cars."

"Is that what you think is normal for people my age?"

"My perception, yes. I've only had Gabriella and Dylan as an example."

I laughed. "Okay, *that* is not normal. Normal people struggle with finances, health, and even their own love for one another."

He frowned. "But I don't want you to have any of that."

I leaned as far back into his shoulder as I could without hurting. "You'll be surprised. Having trials makes the good times even better."

He kissed the top of my head, leaving his face buried in my hair. "I'm so in love with you." Each time he breathed out, it warmed my head. I didn't want it to go away ever, but he lifted his head and looked toward the ocean. "You may have to show me how to be normal, then."

"Gladly."

We sat in each other's embrace, watching the waves on the shore in the most comfortable silence I'd ever felt. If this was how Lucas's money was spent—luxurious homes where I could feel the sand between my toes—then I wanted a part of it.

"When are we leaving?" I wondered, feeling the breeze cool my sun-kissed cheeks.

"This afternoon."

I closed my eyes and breathed in deeply, never wanting to forget this place.

As Lucas packed my suitcase, Aluxes checked on me every thirty minutes. I was reading a magazine when Marifer came in, and even though it hurt, I gave her a weak one-armed hug, hoping it was a universal language for *thank you*. I was pretty confident she understood when she squeezed me back gently. We exchanged a few short words in broken English and Spanish and ended up laughing at each other for our silly attempts.

Max kept quiet, though, and I was really starting to worry. He'd always been the type to let problems fester inside until he blew up. Things were not okay between us, and I knew that as we boarded the plane. It didn't help that Lucas was pushing my wheelchair. But Max would have to talk to me sooner or later, so I decided to blindside him as soon as we got home.

CHAPTER TWENTY-SIX

A New Year

Snow was piled high at the front of the house, leaving Lucas no option but to carry me across the unplowed expanse. It was ridiculous; I could walk. But I played along as he set me down at the bottom of the stairs.

"Thanks so much, Lucas, for all your help. Please drive home safe," Mom said.

He bowed his head. "I will, Mrs. Moss."

"Come by the shop sometime if you get a chance. I would love to show you our pictures," Dad said.

"Thank you. I would love that." He glanced up the stairs, making my heart skip a beat. "Get some rest. I will call you later."

"Drive safe," I said.

As he pulled out into the icy night, I wobbled into my room, realizing I hadn't turned on my cell phone. There were ten missed calls, mostly from Bri. I was surprised to see one from Jett, who sounded upset in his voicemail.

I dialed him first. I only had a few minutes before Lucas would come back to check on me.

"Hello?" Jett answered, half asleep.

I glanced at the clock. It was two in the morning in New York.

"Oh, sorry. I didn't realize how late it was. I'll call you

tomorrow."

"No, no." Jett yawned. "I've been waiting for you to call me. How are you?"

"I'm okay. Did you talk to Max?" His alarmed voice message made me suspicious. I pictured him scratching his mussed hair, his eyes puffy, wrinkly lines dented down the side of his face, and bad breath, all of which were, well, human.

"He's really upset about something, but he won't tell me anything. What happened?"

"I don't know why he's so upset still," I lied. "I got caught in the tide and got pretty cut up on a reef, but I'm okay now."

"That's it? He made it seem like something more." I could hear his sheets sliding as he rolled over.

"How was Christmas with your mom?"

"It wasn't too bad. I'll be home for New Year's though. Want to hang out? I heard the slopes got tons of snow."

"I don't think I'm in any condition to do much boarding, so I will probably be doing something with Lucas. Maybe we could all do something together?"

"Yeah, okay. Sure." He didn't sound thrilled. "Well, I uh . . ." He yawned again. "I will get something planned and then let you know."

"All right." I yawned too.

"I'll call you when I get back in town."

I hung up the phone and looked at the clock, surprised that Lucas hadn't returned yet. I decided to call Bri. She picked up the phone on the first ring.

"You are so getting it from me," she answered.

"Bri, hey. Sorry. It's been crazy."

"I know. I want to hear it all. And don't you dare leave out any details. It's the least you can do for not calling me once while you were there."

"Well, what do you want to know?" My body had started to

ache. I wasn't sure I had a chatty conversation in me.

"First, did you do it?" She could barely breathe as she waited for my response.

"Bri, gross. No!"

"What do you mean gross? You have the hottest boyfriend in Tahoe."

"It's not like that, Bri . . ." I said, remembering our unnatural lack of privacy.

A freezing draft came from the window. The window was already shut and Lucas was lying on his side next to me when I turned. He tickled my arm with his fingers, and talking normally became a difficult task.

"Well, what is this thing I heard about you breaking your collarbone? Is it true?" she asked.

I couldn't help but to look down and sigh. "Yes."

I heard muffled screams on the other end.

"Bri, calm down. It's not that bad."

"How could you not tell me something this big? What happened?"

"I got caught in a riptide, Lucas saved me, yadda yadda . . ."

I pulled the phone from my ear as more screams shrieked through. "Lucas saved you? That is so romantic!"

That was too easy.

"I know, right? He's way cute." I wrinkled my nose at him.

"So what did you guys do preaccidento?"

I yawned again and lay down carefully in Lucas's arms. He nuzzled his nose into the hollow of my neck and stroked his tongue along the skin. I shivered, leaned away out of his reach, and replied in a higher pitch. "Not much. Beach mainly."

"So not fair. I bet you've got the nicest tan. Anyway, we've got to plan New Year's, but we can talk about it tomorrow. Tommy's beeping in, 'night, chica."

Dela

I had just turned to Lucas when a knock rattled my door. I looked at Lucas, but he had already vanished. There was a small indentation on the blankets where he'd been, still warm.

Max poked his head past the door. "Can I come in?"

"Sure."

Max sat where Lucas had been and stared at his hands. I twisted my hair nervously in the awkward silence between us.

"Max, I . . ." I began.

"No, stop, Zara. I don't want to hear your lies anymore. What the hell happened?"

My hair started knotting around itself. "I don't know, exactly," I stuttered.

"What do you mean you don't know? It's simple. You tell me to run for help because you weren't feeling good. I mean, I've never seen you that white in my life. I come back and you're missing. Not gone, but *missing*, Zara. Where did you go? How did you really get those cuts?"

"What do you think happened?" I said, more loudly than I'd intended.

"Honestly, I haven't got a clue. Why don't you start by telling me how you got those bruises on your wrist." He pointed to Xavier's fingerprints, slipping out underneath the gauze. "Did Lucas do that to you?"

"No, Lucas did not do this to me," I answered firmly as I pulled the loosened bandage over the prints.

"Lucas isn't good for you. I want you to stay away from him."

"Is this what you came to tell me?"

"No. I came to find out the truth, but you won't tell me. So I'm saying that I want you to stay away from Lucas."

"The truth is I got stuck in a tide. Why can't you just accept that like everyone else?"

Max stood, his face a new shade of red. "I know that you are lying. I was in the kitchen, getting Nicolás. You would have gone through the kitchen to get out to the ocean—there's a privacy wall that makes it impossible to go around from the front. And guess what, you didn't go out the back!" He was nearly screaming, his hands slicing the air.

"Just go away, now!"

He paused with a pathetic half chuckle.

"Way to go, Zara. Is that what you think of me? That I am stupid enough to believe your lame story? You're in a heap of trouble if you think you can go around lying to us. I won't say anything, but it's only a matter of time until Mom and Dad find out you're lying to them." He walked to the door. "Whatever it is you're trying to do, good luck." Then he left, and I felt more wrecked than ever.

I tried to lie down, but my collarbone wouldn't let me get comfortable. I shifted around, frustrated, knowing that Max was right. How long could I keep on lying to my family? Bitter air wisped my skin as Lucas came in again. He dropped his jacket on the chair and smoothly wrapped his firm arms around me.

"Zara," he whispered after a minute of silence. "Your brother is right. We can't keep pretending that nothing happened."

I felt sick. "I just wasn't ready for him to know the truth."

He looked away. "Me either."

As I looked around, trying to let the adrenaline simmer off, I noticed the messy list of college applications I'd left on the desk. I imagined the pressure on our budding relationship as the realities of college life flooded in—not to mention everything after. I felt weak. "How will it ever work, us going to college together?"

"I've been thinking of putting my doctorate to good use. I could practice wherever you decide to go."

"Really?"

He shrugged. "It's seems practical enough. Remember, I'm paying your way. We need a reason for me to be rich."

"Right, because you'd be a ridiculously young doctor with no student debt. Makes sense," I joked, scooting down to rest on his tattooed arm.

"I'm kidding."

"My parents know I can't pay for it on my own. They'd have to know where I got the rest of my money, and you a doctor straight out of high school? Highly impractical."

"Nah, you'd just win a really good private scholarship. Your parents wouldn't even have to know that I was working. As far as anyone we know was aware, I'd be a freshman at college with you."

I stretched. "It could work."

Lucas pulled the sheets over my arms and played with my hair. The mixture of his warm body and the flannel covers warmed me to the core. I yawned again, gave up fighting it any longer, and shut my eyes.

"Zara?" His voice chimed softly around my ear.

"Hmm?"

"I want to take you to the New Year's party." The kiss on the side of my head was gentle. "We can go out with your friends if you want. I know you miss them."

His lips grazed underneath my chin. Then they moved to the other side of my neck, setting off a good throbbing in my body as his breath caressed my skin. "I can take you out to dinner, and then we can go to the Lodge to watch the fireworks."

He lifted a strand of hair and sniffed. "I wonder if you taste how you smell."

My body was on fire, and it was difficult to breathe as he teased. All I could think about was my blood rushing south. "Lucas . . ."

He rose onto his knees and brushed his lips across my bandaged chest. His breath was warm as his fingers pulled the dressing back slightly and kissed the skin beneath it. My breathing slowed as he lingered there, studying the wound, infatuated with my body.

"I can't take your virginity," he finally said with an anguished edge. His fingers took their time grazing across my collarbone to the other side, where he swept my hair behind my shoulder and kissed my neck.

"I love you, Zara," he whispered. "For always. We have a lifetime to make love. There's no need to rush."

"I love you too, Lucas. But don't you want to just play around?"

"This isn't right," he said. "You're not well, and when I have you, I need you whole."

"Whole?"

He chuckled. "I tend to get a little rough in the bedroom. So I need you healed, and . . ." he lifted up my left hand and pinched my ring finger, sliding his fingers up and down softly. "I need your hand."

"Hand?"

"I need you to be mine. All mine."

"Oh . . ." *Marriage*. That word I used casually to talk about my reason for keeping my virginity. I felt guilty for forgetting, but it was impossible to think straight with Lucas so close. "How . . ."

"Is that a yes?"

"Was that a proposal?"

His brows lowered over his perfectly blue eyes. "No, I suppose not."

"What about . . ."

"Kids?"

"Gosh, no." My eyes fluttered, my cheeks heated. "Didn't you say you couldn't have kids?"

"Does that matter?"

"Well, no, but what about . . ."

"Phew! My heart nearly stopped; oh wait, it doesn't matter. I can't die." He began chuckling. It was funny and sweet, him living in only this moment—but what about . . .

"Lucas!"

"What?" The smile dropped from his lovely cheer.

"What about our age . . . in the future?"

He stared blankly as I struggled to lie down again. He shifted on his back and lifted his arm up. "Come here, *muñeca*."

I rested my head in the crook of his arm. Lucas had unlimited funds. There had to be a fertility doctor who would look at him. *Though I suppose there probably hasn't been research done on immortals' fertility.*

"You know I've thought a lot about this," he said. "And the answer always comes back to me the same. The gray hair leaves me no choice . . .I'm going to marry you anyway."

"Ha! You might want to look at pictures of my grandmas before you make up your mind. I'm not sure my family ages well."

"Say yes, Zara."

I nuzzled my cheek along his arm and breathed in his musk. "You smell good."

"Why are you tormenting me?"

I laughed. "Why are you tormenting yourself?"

"What do you mean?"

"Why would you want to be with me when I'm old and wrinkly?" I yawned. "Come on, it's ridiculous."

"Because I have no choice. Being *without* you torments me. I'd rather be tormented with you than without you. I love your beauty and all, but I love your guts more—the things I love most about you don't age. *You* are my someday, and I will wait as long as it takes to get you."

My heart pumped with a happiness that I couldn't contain. "I guess you leave me no choice then."

"Is that a yes?"

I grinned. "Maybe."

His chest rose and he let out a long breath. "I'll take it."

"Good night, Lucas," I said, and without a chance to even

protest, I fell asleep.

When I woke, Lucas had set recovery terms. No more late nights. We both knew we played with fire in my room, where somebody could hear us. I might have disagreed, but it didn't matter, I didn't have the energy to change his mind. Over the next few days we filled out applications to colleges out east, played card games (though it was nearly impossible for me to hold cards with both hands), and watched TV until eleven every night. I complained, but I had to admit that I felt much better for it.

Later in the week, Dad insisted we stop at his shop to see the pictures from Mexico before going to the New Year's dance.

Lucas knocked on the front door promptly at ten in the morning. Max, who had kept his distance from us, watched intently, waiting for Lucas to make one wrong move—or to find something different about him. I could see in Lucas's eyes the urge to help me as I maneuvered slowly down the stairs, but he restrained himself and crammed his hands deeper into his pockets.

"Gabriella and Dylan are in the car. She's quite fond of your dad and insisted that she see the pictures too," Lucas said.

I didn't mind. I hadn't seen her for days.

"*Hola*, Zara. You look much better since I last saw you," Gabriella said as Lucas helped me into the car.

We passed a snowplow along the highway, trying to keep up with the accumulation of new fluff. As we turned onto a less thoroughly plowed, cobbled road, the lake's vignette of white and black opened before us. Snow covered the gray rocks peeking above the water and the teetering trees that leaned over them. The old cobblestone house sat just at the water's rocky edge. Smoke puffed from the chimney as Lucas pulled in, the shop's open sign blinking brightly in the gloom.

Lucas looked calculatingly at the ice glazing the cement. "I'm carrying you to the door."

"No. I can do it." I said, struggling to lever my door far enough out to stay open.

"Don't be ridiculous." His door closed soundlessly, and mine was open in the second it took me to spread my fingers. "I'm helping you whether you like it or not. Did you see all the ice?"

He scooped me up and skimmed over the sleekness. I leaned into his ear. "I'm getting a good idea of what it will be like when I'm old and incapable, and you young and strong."

"You're not changing my mind," he said, setting me down at the door just as Dad opened it.

"Hey, come in the back. And close that door tight—it likes to creep open in the winter," he said.

We followed Dad to the back room, where he edited all his work. It was a tight workspace, cramped with camera equipment and storage, but there was one computer at its center, miraculously uncluttered.

He sat down at it and shook the mouse.

The first picture was of him and Mom on a pier. Then hundreds of tropical landscapes and exotic things popped up.

"This one is my favorite," he said. It was the twins and Dylan, standing on the beach with sandals in their hands.

"Yes, I like that one too," Dylan said, smiling as he leaned toward the screen for a better look.

"Those are all so beautiful, Mr. Moss," Gabriella said.

"When I get them printed, I am going to give one to your parents as a thank-you gift."

"They would love that," she said.

Dad swiveled his chair around and slapped his hands on his knees. "So, what are you kids up to for New Year's?"

"We're going to the Lodge to watch the fireworks," Lucas said.

Dad looked at Lucas and then threw a funny look at me. "The dance? How?"

"I won't be doing much dancing," I confirmed. "And I doubt I'll last long. But I want to see everyone."

We followed Dad back to the front room. He walked behind the cashier's desk and put on his glasses.

"Well, you kids have fun," he said, looking down at his receipts.

"I will bring her home right after the fireworks, Mr. Moss," Lucas said.

As Dylan and Gabriella strolled around the room, looking at the portraits on the walls, I leaned on Lucas as we headed to the front door.

Inside the car, I put my free hand in front of the vent and hoarded all the heat, figuring the other passengers wouldn't mind. If I wasn't here, the heater probably wouldn't be on.

Gabriella leaned forward and grabbed my headrest. "So, Zara, for tonight, would you want to come over and get ready with me?"

I checked my watch. "What time?"

"Well, now."

"Zara needs to eat lunch," Lucas reminded her.

She rolled her eyes and slouched back in her seat. "Oh okay, fine. After lunch then."

"Do you think we could stop by my house so I can pick up my clothes?" I asked.

"You don't need to worry about that. I already have it taken care of," she said. I imagined her playing with her long hair, twirling it around her finger with a victorious grin.

After a salad and shake at a café, we pulled into their garage. I remembered I'd promised to call Bri an hour before. I dialed her at once, hoping she wasn't upset.

She sounded drowsy when she answered. "What time is it?"

"One."

"Oh, man, I dozed off. We still good for tonight?" she asked.

"Everyone is meeting at eight inside the Lodge."

"Where are you?"

I looked around at the gods, Gabriella busying herself with product and the boys idly watching sports. I wondered if sports grew duller the longer you lived. I spoke softly into the phone. "I am at Lucas's. I'm just going to get ready here. I will meet you there."

"Seriously? Is Gabriella helping you?"

"If you saw me, you'd know that I need the help."

She laughed. "That may be true. But I will be damned if she can tame your hair. Tell her I said good luck."

"You're such a good friend," I remarked sourly and then hung up.

Gabriella shooed the boys out of the room, shut the door on their protesting faces, and turned to me gleefully. Her and Dylan's room overlooked the infinite expanse of low clouds over the lake. Two dresses sprawled across the bed, one gold and the other black. The gold was a short, sequined cocktail dress, the black a long, flowing sweetheart dress.

"Yours is the long one, of course, so we can cover up those bruises," she said.

I nodded in agreement and sat on a cushiony ottoman in her cream-colored bathroom.

Makeup in colors I hadn't imagined spread over the countertop. Gabriella seemed to have a process down, a nice, painless routine. I thought of Mom and her brutal pageant tricks, and I teared up just remembering. Gabriella's hands were careful, and she never jerked my head once as she brushed my hair. She hummed a song to herself. As she did something in the back, I glanced over at the black dress on the bed.

"How much was that dress?" I asked.

"Don't worry about it." She pulled my head back to face her.

She hummed the same song what seemed like ten more times, and then she backed away. Her delicate face looked pleased.

"Now, let me help you into your dress," she said, grabbing the expensive fabric off her bed. "Oh, you will need this too. Don't worry, it's your size."

She handed me a strapless bra with a pink-and-black tag still attached. As I gingerly stretched my shirt upward, it caught somewhere in the back of my head.

"Oh, for goodness's sake, you are a wreck, Zara." Gabriella lifted it over my head and then waited as I unbuttoned my pants slowly.

"Don't be shy, Zara," she said, tapping her foot.

"I'm not, my pants are . . . hard . . . to . . . get . . . off." I tugged at them with my good arm.

In a swift movement, my pants were around my ankles, the dress was slipped on and zipped, and Gabriella was flipping around the floor-length mirror.

I looked like I belonged in ancient Greece. Gabriella had smudged metallic copper around my brown eyes, and whatever she'd done to my hair, it somehow looked longer. Half of it fell down my back in tight waves while the other half was pulled loosely back. The embellished belt under my bust accentuated my waist, leaving the rest of the fabric to flow loosely to the floor. I couldn't look away.

"You look gorgeous," Gabriella said, handing me a pair of flats with attached anklets of gold and stones. "Put these on."

I slipped into them obediently as she opened her door. "Now, here comes the test."

Lucas was leaning against the wall, wearing a sleek black suit with a thin blue tie. His hair was parted to the side and combed back. He looked like he was getting ready to hit the set of a telenovela. I stood tall and confident, feeling deserving of him, until his blue eyes struck me and I wavered. He raised an eyebrow.

"You look incredible," he said.

"Thank you," Gabriella responded, curtseying. Then she shut her door and left us alone in the hall. We walked to the front door and waited.

"Wow," he said again.

"You clean up nice too," I added cordially, though I was steaming underneath my clothes, sensing our connection intensely in this moment.

He moved his hands to my hips slyly. "You sure you want to go out tonight? We could just stay here if you wanted. Play a little game of striptease."

"Really?" I asked.

He chuckled. "No. That would definitely not be good."

"You play with me too hard. Don't underestimate me," I teased, tugging lightly on his tie.

He played along and drew closer. "I'm begging you, stop."

I waited until I could feel the warmth of his breath on my forehead. "No."

Out of nowhere, his hands were around my waist, and he was pulling me toward him until my chest pressed hard against his. Then he lowered his head to my ear. "I want to teach you a lesson so bad," he whispered in a low, husky voice. It had summoning powers, and all I wanted to do in that moment was run upstairs with him to his bedroom.

We separated reluctantly, realizing that Dylan and Gabriella had appeared. The short gold dress glimmered over her body, and she held a matching clutch in one hand. Dylan went out first and pulled the car up to the front. We hopped in, and then Gabriella handed me a coat.

"Thanks," I said, shivering as I draped it across my lap.

After dinner, when we pulled up to the Lodge, I saw Jett waiting in the doorway, standing next to an easel with his full name on it in large black type. He wore a vest over a suit shirt and tie, his cuffs rolled. He looked nice, and my heart paced anxiously. He hadn't seen me since I'd been back, and though I stressed over what he'd think of my unforgiving injuries, I yearned to see him. In fact, I missed him.

The 52nd

"Will you be okay?" Lucas asked, squeezing my hand as Jett turned to look at us.

"Yeah. My friends haven't seen me since I left."

Lucas glanced at my fingers, which were fidgeting with my long hair, and then he nodded to Dylan and Gabriella. At his signal, they exited the car and glided down the red rug. I felt overdressed when I saw how many stares they drew.

"Listen, forget about them," Lucas said, putting a hand on my shaking knee.

"I guess I am the most nervous about what Jett will think," I admitted.

He glanced past me and out the window toward Jett. "You have to face him eventually."

"Aren't you worried about what other people are going to think about us, about *you*, when they see me like this? They'll think you hurt me."

He looked back, nearly appalled. "No."

I slumped on my good arm, hard enough to hurt my collarbone, and sat right back up.

"Relax. We're supposed to be having a good time, remember?"

I shook my head and repeated in my mind, *I can't hide forever.*

"I can't hide forever," I reaffirmed out loud. I put a hand on the handle and paused. "You coming?"

Lucas nodded and moved at a normal human pace to open my door. As he did, I could feel Jett's glare.

We walked in beneath a rainbow of false pretenses, and I felt Lucas's muscles tighten when we approached Jett. He glowered at Jett as he gave me a one-armed hug. I knew it was only protective, but Jett didn't. He angled his shoulder away from Lucas when he glanced back at me.

"Hi," I said nervously. Jett took a long look at the dress over my body, like maybe I didn't belong in it.

"Can I talk to you for a minute, alone?" Jett asked.

Lucas's eyes widened. I settled my hand softly on his arm.

"Go find Gabriella and Dylan. I will be there in a minute."

Lucas scowled at Jett as a warning not to do anything stupid, but then he kissed my cheek softly and whispered in my ear, "Of course, *princesa.*"

I had chills as he straightened up and adjusted his suit stiffly. He spoke again, looking at me, but we all knew it was meant for Jett. "If you're not back in ten minutes, I'm coming to look for you."

"I'll be fine. Jett will help me," I said. "Right, Jett?"

Jett pinched his lips tightly, but then grinned. "Of course."

After Lucas left, we walked to the back balcony that balanced on stilts over the steep slope. The moon was reflected perfectly in the still lake.

"Zara, are you okay?" Jett asked.

My skin rippled with chills from the freezing air. I rubbed my limp arm, trying to produce heat. "I'm fine. Why?"

"Because you come back from your trip beat up, and the guy who did this to you won't leave your side. He is possessive. Actually, I think he's crazy," Jett said, shaking his head.

"Lucas didn't do this to me," I blurted, but then I paused, thinking. "Wait, did Max tell you that Lucas did this to me?"

He shrugged. "Maybe."

"Max doesn't know what he's talking about—" I said, raising my finger.

"Look," he interrupted. "You know that I don't like this guy. But if he is the one you want to be with, I want you to be happy." Then he looked at his feet, and I felt the sadness swallowing his baby face. "I won't stand between you two."

My mouth snapped shut, my finger falling away from him. "Really?"

He recovered and abruptly trapped my hands in his. They were just as cold as mine, and I noticed his mortal nose pinking in the biting air. "But it doesn't mean that I don't care about you, because I do. More than you know."

I looked down, ashamed. "I am happy with Lucas. He wouldn't hurt me."

Unexpectedly, his finger lifted my chin and forced me to stare into his chocolate eyes. "Neither would I."

I knew that was true, and that we could maybe be happy together someday. But that was before Lucas, before gods and Aluxes and demons trying to kill me. Jett couldn't protect me from that—if they ever came again.

I shied away from his expression, resisting the swelling in my eyes. "I know you wouldn't." *I never asked for this.* A few months ago I didn't need anybody in my life, nothing except college. I wanted no reciprocation. *Now, I've fallen into an impossible relationship just as my best bud decides to pour out his heart to me.* "But I chose Lucas, Jett. I always have. Just like you will always be one of my greatest friends."

He breathed out a deep, piercing sigh and looked away. "That's all I wanted to say. I needed to get it off my chest."

"I'm glad you told me this." When he shivered and put his hands in his pockets, I recalled the poster in the front with his name on it. "Are you singing tonight?"

"Yeah. Will you be here to hear it?"

I poked his arm playfully. "Are you kidding?"

"Good," he smiled. His bottom lip trembled as he shivered again. "Let's get inside. It's freezing out here."

The convention hall had been transformed into a spectacular ballroom. The round tables circling the dance floor were decorated with candles and feathers and shiny silver ornaments. Swaths of fabric draped from the ceiling. Above the stage on one end of the hall, a large screen played the news channel, showing the east coast crowds at Times Square just moments after the ball dropped. They were hollering, "Happy New Year!" and sharing wild kisses.

Lucas, Gabriella, and Dylan were standing around a table with Bri, Ashley, and Tana. As the girls' gazes snapped to us, it was hard to say whether they approved of the makeover or disapproved of my injuries. My nerves frayed. They wore cocktail dresses, probably something they'd picked up on sale at the local department store, with cheaper fabric and uneven seams. For a moment I wished I was dressed like them: plainer, less attention-grabbing. And then Gabriella glanced at me, proud of her work, and I felt grateful.

Lucas fixed his gaze on Jett as we neared.

"Thanks, Lucas, for letting me borrow her for a few minutes," Jett said.

Everyone stared at Jett, shocked at his civil statement, and doubly so when Lucas stretched his hand out. Jett looked down, confused as I, and then shook it.

"Thanks for not making me come looking for her," Lucas replied coolly, though I felt the truth behind it.

Jett shot me a cracked smile and turned to Lucas. "I would never hurt her."

When they broke their stare, Jett turned his back to Lucas and closed the space between us.

"I've got to go backstage. See you around?" he asked.

"Sure." I nodded.

"You were right, Gabriella," Bri started as Jett walked toward the stage. "It doesn't look like her."

Ashley touched my hair. "Gabriella, you've got to show me how you did this."

"Extensions," Gabriella said.

I knew it.

Someone tapped the microphone, and we turned toward the stage as New York City faded off the screen.

"Welcome to the Lodge's fifth annual New Year's Ball," a lean man with mousy hair said. "The countdown to the new year draws near, and I know you're all anxious, but first we have a special program for you. Our first guest this evening is a very talented young man who was recently invited by Gold Label Records to tour this summer. I wouldn't be surprised if the label picks him up afterward. We were thrilled when he agreed to sing for us tonight. So, ladies and gentlemen, please put your hands together for our very own Jett Christensen!"

The crowd rose to its feet, clapping as the lights dimmed, and Jett's dark figure walked to the center of the stage. He sat down on a barstool and propped one leg up as he adjusted his shoulder strap. Then he strummed his guitar once, and a spotlight beamed down on him. My ears rang as girls shrieked and ran to the stage. I rolled my eyes, though I maybe felt slightly jealous of their swooning nonsense, in which case I was grateful Lucas couldn't see my face.

Jett paused, waiting for the screaming to stop, and when it didn't, he casually waved his hand.

"I just wanted to thank you all for being here tonight. I love singing, and I appreciate your support. This first song I'm going to sing I wrote for a girl who has been my best friend for many years. But I made a mistake, a big one. And if I could take it back, I would."

He looked in my direction, though he probably couldn't see me in the spotlight's glare, and a lump congealed in my throat. A few woos rose from the crowd, and he chuckled to himself. They shushed as he pulled the microphone closer.

"I'd like to give some words of advice to you men out there, which I can, 'cause you know, I'm speaking from experience. Don't waste any time telling the woman you love how you feel, because before you know it, some other man might say it first and take her away from you."

No he didn't. I stiffened, mortified, and then checked Lucas, who was statue still.

Jett held his hand up to the awwing crowd and shook his head, looking pleased. "Yes, I know. I lost." He shrugged his shoulders. "She fell in love with someone else because I was stupid and immature." He strummed a chord on his guitar and leaned into the microphone again. "But I learned something, and that is that I will *never* make that mistake again."

More awws filled the room. It made me want to shrivel up and die.

"So she is here tonight," he announced through the mic.

Heads turned in every direction, trying to find her . . . trying to find me. I forgot to breathe until Lucas slid his arm around my waist, easing the immense pressure in my throat and releasing the breath caught behind it.

Jett found me in the crowd and whispered into the microphone, "And I am dedicating this song to her."

From the corner of my eye, I noticed Bri staring, admiring what Jett had just done. *That is so sweet,* she mouthed. I nodded in agreement and leaned happily into my prince, feeling his warm body pressed next to mine.

Why did it have to be the most perfect song? Jett hit every note true, even when he went into falsetto. He sang it with soul, with visible emotion. In that moment, I felt what he did, I really did. But how could I choose between an immortal who'd been waiting hundreds of years for me and a human boy pouring out his heart to me? What more could any human do than be as completely vulnerable and honest as he was right now?

Jett sang a few more songs, some faster, upbeat ones, with keyboard, drums, and other instruments backing him up. In the middle of one of his songs, a boy came out with a microphone in hand and sang in unison with Jett. Bri screamed. I wondered why her eyes were popping out, but then I recognized him. He was the lead singer of one of her favorite rock bands, known for his great dark hair and sexy voice.

Jett looked happy on the stage. It was a good direction for him. He was meant to be in the spotlight, but that truth made me anxious. I couldn't bear to not see him after this. If this really happened for him, he would travel and meet new people. I was proud of how far Jett had come with his career, but I didn't like the feeling of him leaving me forever.

Lucas was trying to read my blank expression.

"What is wrong?" he asked.

"Just thinking about next year."

"What about it?"

"Well, look at Jett. I think it's kind of obvious that he is going to move to Los Angeles and make it big."

"So?"

"So, we have been friends for so long. It just makes me sad that we are growing up. Life isn't the same anymore."

"That may be true. But growing up is a good thing, Zara."

The guilt came as I felt his envy of my ability to age. "I know, you're right. It's just hard saying good-bye to people."

"Good-bye to people, or good-bye to Jett?" Lucas wondered.

My mind weighed heavier, imagining all the people Lucas had said good-bye to, and now I could be one of them. I'd cause him more pain. This was a sick game we played, but I couldn't *not* play; I loved him too much. I paused to clear the thought, eventually letting the truth settle in, and then answered hesitantly, "The former."

Lucas didn't answer. We both stood still, watching silently as Jett wrapped up on stage. When a new performer took over, Lucas moved.

"Want to go outside?" he asked. I nodded quietly.

He helped me to the balcony where Jett and I had talked earlier. Lucas handed me his jacket because I'd forgotten mine in the car.

"Thanks," I said, sliding into the lined jacket, which smelled like warm, fresh coconut.

"Can I ask you something?" he said.

"Anything."

I was wary about what he would say, and I watched him carefully as I felt my nose changing colors. It hurt to breathe in the sharp pinch of coldness. His nose, of course, stayed the same color. He stepped closer nervously, his shirt brushing against my dress and the bandages beneath it.

"I *need* to ask you this," he said, his chin almost touching my forehead as he looked down.

"What?" I asked, suddenly weakened by his proximity.

His eyes didn't waver from mine. "Do you love Jett?"

"Why . . ." I shook my head, feeling almost upset. "Why would you ask that?"

"You're incredible." Lucas smiled, though it was crooked.

"Why?"

"Because you are more powerful than you know," he said, his face unchanging now.

I looked back blankly.

"You have both Jett and I locked inside a cage. Each of us wanting your love, right?"

"Well, *you* have it," I assured him.

"That may be, but what about Jett? Someone locked in a cage will do only one thing: try to get out."

I wasn't following, so I just looked at Lucas.

His feet shuffled through the grainy snow, but then his calmness evaporated and he burst out, "You can't keep Jett locked up if you are planning to be with me, or anyone else for that matter. It isn't fair. If you care for him, you will let him go. Let him move on and be happy."

His bluntness stunned me at first, and then its unvarnished principle stung my core. It was the truth. I couldn't hold on to Jett and move on with Lucas. It was like trying to live in summer and winter at the same time. It was impossible. One had to go.

"I know!" I lowered my head and fussed with the buttons of his shirt, the feeling of losing Jett still settling into my heart. "You're right," I whispered. "I let him go. I told him so earlier."

"I'm not trying to be right. I just want you to know how I feel." He wrapped his arms around me and squeezed gently. "It's unfortunate that you were Jett's worst mistake, because you were by far my best mistake."

I squeezed back and breathed in his tropical scent. "And I want you to know how I feel. I want *you* . . . I just hope we know what we're doing."

There was a clear expression of fear on his face before he pressed his forehead to mine. "I don't want to lose you."

"You're not," I said.

"No, I mean, I don't want to *lose* you."

The reality of our conversation went from sad to horrifying as he finally realized the time bomb that was our relationship. I shivered, picturing myself seventy years from now. I couldn't think of that now. He cinched my young self tightly, until I could feel his belt buckle pressed against my belly.

The music inside suddenly blared, shaking the double-paned windows. But it didn't break his fond stare as I grazed my fingertips along his cheek and then upward across his forehead, searching for anything like me—a wrinkle, a mole, a crease. But his face was perfectly polished, except for the short hairs shadowing his chin. My eyes fluttered as I tried to regain the breath he'd unintentionally stolen. *He will always be this beautiful.*

"I am not going to lose you," he said.

I twisted my fingers into his. "In time you may, but as long as I live, you will always have my heart."

Lucas joined our lips, a graze barely there before he straightened up. He led me inside to join the others as the last few minutes of the year drifted by in laughter, singing, and dancing, not caring how silly we looked in fancy clothes and cheap New Year's hats.

Then, as the clock counted down, we chanted as a group, "Ten, nine, eight . . ."

Lucas drew me into his arms and stilled, keeping me tucked into him as he smiled. "Happy New Year."

"Happy New Year," I responded.

And then I leaned in to kiss my prince.

Acknowledgments

In honor of finishing my first novel, I am putting on my headphones and pushing play on my playlist, Zama, one last time. After all, that's what THE 52ND was called for three years before deciding on the title. Zama—once the name of Tulum, meaning "City of Dawn" because it faced the sunrise—always had a place in my heart from the moment it was created. To this day, I occasionally use the name.

I want to publicly thank my wonderful husband, Rodney, who through the end has been here at my side—sending emails, making phone calls, and going on late night food runs—and thanks to my small nuggets; Luke, Mia, and Chloe. The sacrifices that my family made in order for me to complete this journey were incredible. It wasn't easy, and most times it felt like we were slugging through the trenches of mac 'n' cheese, cereal, frozen burritos, and Eggo Waffles.

Thank you to my Pubslush supporters who surprised me with their high donations: Alberto De La Paz (my funny, Latino dad), Daryl Carlson, Jamie Feller, Audrey Miller, and Ryanne Nigro. I still can't seem to comprehend the generosity, love, and interest that each of you have shown over the course of publishing.

Thank you my beloved beta readers. Without your opinions—and fearlessness to *tell* me those opinions—THE 52ND wouldn't be the same. Zara might have still been in high school, Lucas would have repeated the same shiz over and over, and their relationship would have been dull: Ashley Davidson; Kaymee Cottrell; Lindsey Bailey; Amber Stewart; Morgan Baldwin; Charlie Melvin; Erin Burton; Katie Gregory; Ashley Gaskell; and mi abuela, Bertha Szilady, aka "Grandma Titi" Titina.

Okay okay, Charlie deserves a little more. She helped me with my very first draft. That alone merits her a special spot in here, not to mention the *hours* she took reviewing and pointing out my mistakes. Love you, prima. Let's go to Cancun now . . . on me.

And my fabulous team: Kellie Hultgren, my power editor who gives harsh truths in the gentlest way possible . . . she says it how it is. Kellie had me working so hard my brain still hurts. Thanks to Jay Monroe for the design. Where did you come from, Jay?! The first draft he showed me was magic, no changes needed—it blew my mind. Amy Quale, my Wise Ink manager. Let's go to conception; thank you for being at the Writer's Digest Conference in LA. I know you traveled far to be there, but phew, THE 52ND and you were a pair meant to be.

And lastly, thank *you*, my readers. This story was never supposed to be for me. It was always meant for you.

About the Author

Dela is the debut author of THE 52ND saga. Before tracing the minds of Aztec gods with her writing, Dela worked as a paralegal and could be found snowboarding at Brianhead, Utah. She currently lives in Las Vegas with her husband, three kids, and two exceptionally fat Chihuahuas. Her website is www.delaauthor.com.